ASHES *and* ICE

ASHES
and
ICE

TRACIE PETERSON

BETHANYHOUSE
MINNEAPOLIS, MINNESOTA

Ashes and Ice
Copyright © 2001
Tracie Peterson

Cover design by Jenny Parker

Published by Bethany House Publishers
A Ministry of Bethany Fellowship International
11400 Hampshire Avenue South
Bloomington, Minnesota 55438
www.bethanyhouse.com

Printed in the United States of America by
Bethany Press International, Bloomington, Minnesota 55438

Library of Congress Cataloging-in-Publication Data

Peterson, Tracie.
   Ashes and ice / by Tracie Peterson.
      p. cm. — (Yukon quest ; 2)
   ISBN 0-7642-2379-8
   1. Married people—Fiction. 2. Alaska—Fiction. I. Title.
   PS3566.E7717 A9   2001
   813'.54—dc21   2001002507

BOOKS *by* TRACIE PETERSON

Controlling Interests
Entangled
Framed
The Long-Awaited Child
A Slender Thread
Tidings of Peace

WESTWARD CHRONICLES

A Shelter of Hope
Hidden in a Whisper
A Veiled Reflection

RIBBONS OF STEEL*

Distant Dreams
A Hope Beyond
A Promise for Tomorrow

RIBBONS WEST*

Westward the Dream
Separate Roads
Ties That Bind

SHANNON SAGA†

City of Angels

YUKON QUEST

Treasures of the North
Ashes and Ice

*with Judith Pella   †with James Scott Bell

TRACIE PETERSON is an award-winning speaker and writer who has authored over forty-five books, both historical and contemporary fiction. *City of Angels*, a recent collaboration with James Scott Bell, highlights the courtrooms of 1903 Los Angeles. Tracie and her family make their home in Montana.

Visit Tracie's Web site at: http://members.aol.com/tjpbooks

Part One

MARCH 1898

When thou passest through the waters,
I will be with thee; and through the rivers,
they shall not overflow thee; when thou
walkest through the fire, thou shalt not
be burned; neither shall the flame kindle
upon thee.

ISAIAH 43:2

⊣ CHAPTER ONE ⊢

"FIRE!"

From somewhere in the deepest recesses of Karen Pierce's slumbering mind, she heard the word, yet she failed to make sense of it. Licking her lips, she tasted the acrid smoke in the air and felt a burning sensation in her lungs.

Something didn't seem right, but in the world in which she found herself, Karen slipped deeper and deeper into darkness. With an indescribable weight pressing her down, she was helpless.

"Fire!"

It was that word again. A word that seemed to have some sort of importance—urgency. Karen struggled against the hold of sleep. There was something she needed to do. Something . . .

Then a scream pierced the night, and Karen felt a chill

rush through her body. The cry sounded like that of her young charge, Leah Barringer. Now realizing that some element of danger existed, Karen forced herself to awaken.

Groggy and barely able to comprehend the need, she teetered on the edge of her cot. Drawing a deep breath, she coughed and sputtered against the bitter smoke.

Fire!

Her heart raced. That word. That was the word she had tried to figure out—the word that made all too much sense now.

"Aunt Doris!" she called, choking on the thick air. Karen pulled on her robe and tried to feel her way through the darkness to the door. "Aunt Doris, wake up! There's a fire!"

Karen knew her elderly aunt slept not four feet away, but in the blackness, Karen could see nothing. With burning eyes and lungs that ached to draw a real breath, Karen pushed herself beyond her fear. Her hand brushed the door and finally the knob. Both were hot to the touch, but it didn't stop Karen from deciding to survey the situation beyond her room.

As soon as the door was open, an assault of more hot, smoky air bombarded her face. Flames engulfed the interior room, and panic immediately gripped her. Frozen in place momentarily, she thought she saw a figure moving through the fire. A big, broad-shouldered figure. Surely her mind played tricks on her.

"Karen! It's me—Adrik."

The voice was muffled, but nevertheless welcomed. "The children!" she called.

"I'll get them," he yelled above the crackling of the flames. "You have to get out of here. The whole store is on fire. Come on. Now!" His command alarmed her more than the sight of the fire. The urgency was clear.

"I have to get Aunt Doris."

Karen turned back to the room and saw her aunt straining to get up. "Aunt Doris, we have to hurry. The building is on fire." With the intensity of the smoke, Karen could barely make out the older woman's form.

Coughing, her aunt replied, "Hurry, child. Don't wait for me."

Karen took up the Bible by the stand at the door. It was all that she had left of her mother and father. Only a few months earlier her father had succumbed to illness himself while nursing and ministering to some of the sick Tlingit Indians. Adrik Ivankov, their trusted family friend, had set out to bring him back to her and Dyea for better care, but God had other ideas. Karen was heartbroken at the loss.

"Hurry, Aunt Doris," she begged again. "The flames are already blocking a good portion of the room. We will have to run through the fire in order to get to the door."

Doris bent over in a fit of coughing before recovering momentarily. "Wrap a blanket around you, child."

Karen nodded and struggled to breathe. She felt panic anew wash over her as she sensed her body was no longer reacting as it should. Her movements were labored, her thinking less clear. She pulled the blanket from the bed and covered her head and shoulders. It seemed like the process was taking hours instead of minutes.

"Here," she said, taking hold of her aunt's blanket. "Let me help." She secured the wrap, then kept a good hold on the blanket. "Come on. I'll lead the way."

Stepping into the interior room was akin to stepping into a furnace. The feeling of panic and desperation mounted. They had to get out now!

Flames licked at their blankets as Karen pulled Doris to

safety. She stepped out into the alleyway and gasped for fresh air only to find the smoke had permeated the air there as well.

Wracked with coughing, Karen collapsed to her knees and might have fainted but for the strong arms that lifted her and carried her to safety.

She fell back against Adrik's strong chest, desperate for air . . . questioning whether she would live or die.

"Aunt . . . Doris . . ." she gasped as Adrik lowered her to the ground. "Jacob . . . Leah?"

"I got the kids out. They're over there being tended to by the preacher," Adrik replied, pushing back Karen's unruly curls.

She looked up at him and saw the fear in his expression. "You saved us," she whispered, then fell into another fit of coughing.

Adrik gently grasped her about her arms with one hand while pounding her back with the other. "You're full of smoke," he said, as if she hadn't already figured it out.

Regaining control, Karen nodded. "Help me up, please."

He did as she asked, supporting her firmly against him. Karen's knees wobbled. "Where's Aunt Doris?" she questioned, looking up at the burning building. Several men were fighting to keep the flames under control. Panic began anew. "Where is she?"

Adrik looked around. "I never saw her."

Karen tried to head back to the building. "I helped her out. She was right here with me."

Adrik shook his head. "No, you were alone."

"I had hold of her . . . I . . ." Karen came back to the spot where she'd fallen. Doris's blanket lay on the frozen ground. "I had hold of her blanket."

Adrik saw where her gaze had fallen. The light from the

flames made it easy enough to read the expression of her rescuer as Adrik raised his eyes back to hers.

"She's still inside," Karen said, barely able to speak. She jerked away from Adrik as he reached out to take hold of her. "Aunt Doris!"

"You can't go back inside. The place is ready to collapse," Adrik stated firmly. He took hold of her and refused to let go.

She fought him with the last remnants of her strength, sobbing. "I have to try. I have to. She's probably just inside the door. I know she was with me as we crossed to the door."

She turned her pleading expression to him and saw him study her only a moment before letting go of her arm. "I'll go," he said.

Karen watched in stunned silence as he pushed back several men. He pulled a woolen scarf to his face and reentered the burning building. Karen felt her breathing quicken in the smoke-filled air. *Dear God, let him find her,* she pleaded in anguish.

It seemed like an eternity before Adrik returned to the alleyway door, a small, unmoving bundle in his arms.

"Thank God!" Karen cried, hurrying forward to pull Adrik to a less smoky area than he'd previously taken her. "Put her down here," she commanded. Kneeling, she waited for Adrik to do as she said.

"Karen, I . . ."

"Put her right here," Karen insisted. She patted the frozen ground and looked up to see that he understood.

Adrik lowered Doris's still frame to the ground, but instead of leaving her to Karen's care, he pulled Karen to her feet. "She's gone."

The words were given so matter-of-factly that Karen could only stare at Adrik for several moments. "What?"

"I'm sorry, Karen."

"No!" she exclaimed, pushing his six-foot-two-inch frame aside. "She's just . . . overcome."

She knelt down again and stroked Doris's hand. The heat coming off the body caused steam to rise in the icy air. Karen pushed back the old woman's tangled and singed hair and gently rubbed her cheeks. "Aunt Doris. Aunt Doris, please wake up."

The woman's silence left Karen numb inside. She couldn't be dead. She just couldn't be. Once again, Adrik pulled her away from Doris and brought her to her feet.

"She's in better hands now," Adrik whispered.

"No," Karen moaned. "No!" She looked into the bearded man's face and saw the confirmation of her worst fears. "No." She fell against him in tears. This couldn't be happening. God wouldn't take her away from them. He just wouldn't.

Adrik wrapped her in his arms and stroked her hair. His words came in soothing whispers. "She's with God, Karen. She's in a better place. No pain. No suffering."

"I want her with me. She's all I have left."

Even as she said the words, Karen knew the statement was far from true. She had siblings in the lower states and friends right here in Dyea. There were many people who cared about her, including the Barringer children. Their father had deserted them for the goldfields of the Yukon. He had left them to her care, and in doing so, the trio had learned to cling to each other through their shared difficulties. Karen mourned the loss of the father she'd come north to find, while they mourned the loss of the father they'd come north only to lose.

They needed her. And somehow, she had to stay strong for them.

Adrik's comforting touch made the horrors of the night

seem less overwhelming. She wasn't alone. Karen knew that now. Remembering her father's promise that God would always be there to comfort His children, she put her head on Adrik's chest and stared off blankly at the burning building.

Everything she owned, with the exception of her father's Bible, which now lay on the ground near Doris's lifeless body, was gone. Her clothes, her books, everything. She saw the flames reach high—appearing to go upward until they touched the night skies—cinders blending with the stars to offer pinpoints of light.

She was glad her friend Grace wasn't here to see the destruction. Their home had been attached to the back of the Colton Trading Post, the store owned by Grace's husband of three months, Peter Colton. How hard it would be to share the news of this loss, Karen thought. Peter had looked to this store as a means of salvation—at least financial salvation.

Adrik released his hold. "You can plan to stay in my tent tonight, and I'll go bed down with Joe."

"Karen! Karen, are you all right?" Leah cried out as she rushed into the older woman's arms. "Oh, Karen, we could have died."

"We're safe now," Karen reassured her, holding Leah close and stroking her hair. "Are you burned or hurt?"

"No, just scared," Leah said, lifting her tear-filled eyes. "I couldn't find Jacob. I thought he was dead."

Jacob joined them. "Where's Aunt Doris?" he asked.

Karen frowned and hugged both of the children close. "She didn't make it." Tears blurred her burning eyes.

"She's dead?" Leah asked in disbelief.

Karen nodded and looked to Jacob, who stood shaking his head. "How?" Jacob asked as if he didn't believe her.

Karen felt a rush of guilt. "I had a hold of her, but she

slipped away without me noticing. When I got outside, Aunt Doris wasn't with me. Adrik tried to save her, but it was too late."

Jacob turned away as Leah hugged Karen. "Will they be able to put the fire out?" she asked.

Jacob answered before Karen could speak. "It's gonna burn to the ground."

With this thought in mind, Karen gazed toward what she first thought was an illusion. But upon a second glance, she saw the man clearly and knew he was no illusion. Martin Paxton.

Paxton. The man who'd chased poor Grace all the way to Alaska in order to force her hand in marriage, their most embittered enemy, stood away from the gathered crowd. Leaning against the wall of another business, Paxton seemed to watch her with defined interest.

Karen straightened, stepping a few paces away from Adrik and the children. She barely heard his words suggesting she and the kids settle down for the night. Instead, she fixed her gaze on Paxton, knowing that he was aware that she was watching him. He tipped his hat to her as though they were attending a cotillion rather than observing a scene of devastation and death.

"He did this," she murmured.

"What?" Adrik questioned. "What are you talking about?" He reached out to touch her arm.

Karen broke away from his hold and started toward Paxton. "He set the fire. He killed my aunt!"

Adrik took hold of her arm and pulled her back. "You don't know what you're saying. You're just upset."

She looked at him, feeling a growing panic. "You don't understand. He's getting his revenge for what we did. We snuck Grace out right under his nose. He intended to marry her, but Peter Colton married her instead. He warned us. He threatened to destroy us, and now he has."

Adrik shook his head slowly. "No, he hasn't. Not yet. But if you go to him now, he will have won. Don't you see?"

Karen wanted to deny Adrik's words as meaningless, but they hit hard and the truth of them rang clear, even in her crumbling reality. "He did this," she whimpered, feeling the defeat of the moment wash over her. "He did this."

Adrik never disputed her declaration but instead pulled her back into his arms. "Now is not the time for you to face him with accusations. He would only laugh at you—deny it. Come. See to Leah and Jacob. The morning will give you other thoughts on how to deal with this."

Karen fell against him, her last remnants of strength ebbing in the flow of tears that fell. "He did this. It's all his fault."

—{ C H A P T E R   T W O }—

SAN FRANCISCO HELD a charm for Grace Colton that she
never would have thought possible. She'd always disliked the
confines of her childhood city, Chicago, and the thought of
another big city after enjoying the wilds of the Alaskan Territory had been less than welcoming to her heart. But San Francisco had surprised her. There was something rather Old
World about it. A kind of antiquated appeal that wove its spell
around the young woman.

Of course, it wasn't just the city. Grace was in love with
her new husband, and life seemed very good indeed. Peter
Colton had a way of weaving his own charm in Grace's heart,
and despite the mounting differences of opinion on religious
matters and household routines, Grace was content with her
new life. At least most of the time.

Tying a ribboned cameo around her neck, Grace smoothed

down the layered muslin gown and sighed. Life, overall, was quite wonderful. She tried not to let her heart be worried by the increasing number of arguments she and Peter were having. Surely all couples had their quibbles. Even Peter's mother said it was true, adding also that her son was of a very stubborn cut of cloth.

"A ship's captain has to be strong and determined," Mrs. Colton had told her. "It's only natural that a certain degree of stubbornness accompany those strengths."

Grace supposed it was true, but she nevertheless found it a darkening shadow of doubt on her otherwise happy life. Had Martin Paxton not forced her hand, she probably wouldn't have married Peter—though it wouldn't have been for a lack of love, for she'd fallen in love with the man almost from the first moment they'd met. Rather, she knew the harm in marrying someone who didn't see life the same way. The issue of being unequally yoked had been something she had talked about for years with her governess, Karen Pierce. Karen was a strong Christian, knowledgeable in Scriptures and their teachings. Karen had been the one to point out to Grace that the verse warning against unequal yoking pertained to every element of life. Be it business, friendship, or love, committing yourself to someone whose convictions differed from your own would inevitably spell trouble. There lacked a common ground upon which to make decisions.

Grace could see that problem now as she dealt with her new husband. She loved him faithfully, but his negative response to her love for God made Grace quite uneasy.

"But surely God hasn't brought me this far only to leave me now," she murmured.

Her faith bolstered her spirits. God had a plan in all of this, she was certain. He had watched over her since the first moment Martin Paxton had tried to force his way into her life. God wouldn't desert her now. No, Grace's marriage was intact for a purpose. She felt confident that she would bring Peter to God. She could change the way he thought about spiritual matters. She was sure of that. After all, Peter loved her, and he would want to see her happy. In time, he'd see the truth of it all.

Sitting down to her writing table, Grace outlined her morning to be spent in letter writing. She wanted to share many things with her dear friend Karen. While Karen would forever remain her most beloved friend, Grace was pleased to discover that Peter's sister, Miranda, was a very amiable companion. The two women had grown quite close during the three months they lived together under the same roof. It helped to fill the void created by Karen's absence.

Picking up a pen, Grace dated the top of her letter. *March 26, the year of our Lord 1898.* Then she paused. Instead of writing a greeting to her friend, Grace was compelled to turn her thoughts elsewhere. She had felt for some time that she'd left unfinished business in Alaska. Martin Paxton had been the reason she fled Chicago and also the reason she fled Alaska. Now she felt it was time to settle the matter once and for all. After all, her father-in-law had been longtime friends with Paxton. She knew her arrival into the family was putting a strain on that relationship, and she had no desire to perpetuate it further. Putting her pen to paper, she wrote a greeting.

> *Dear Mr. Paxton,*
> *The days of strife are behind us now. It is my hope that you have come to understand the importance of my choices and decision. It is also my hope that you would know I have chosen to forgive you the past.*

Grace stared at the words momentarily, searching her heart to ensure the truth behind them. Yes, she could forgive Martin Paxton. He might have been responsible for ruining her family financially. He might even be responsible for her father's sudden onset of bad health and death. But Grace longed only for God's peace to settle upon her life, and to do that, she knew there could be no remnants of hatred or bitterness. Karen had taught her this much. She continued,

> I know that by now you must realize the truth of my circumstance and marriage to Peter Colton. He is a dear man, as your friendship with his family must have made you aware. He is honorable and generous, trustworthy and truthful, and it is my prayer that our marriage will prove to be blessed by God.
>
> That brings me to another point upon which I cannot remain silent. Mr. Paxton, you clearly harbor many painful memories of my father. Your desire for justice and even revenge on behalf of your departed mother are understandable. I am sorry for the pain my father caused you, but you must remember that people are fallible. Only God is without mistake. You will never find what you are looking for until you make right the path between you and your Maker. God is willing to hear your confession. He desires that you would give up your ways of anger and rage. He desires that you would turn to Him for comfort and peace instead of manipulating others.

"Ah, here is my lovely wife," Peter Colton called as he entered the room.

Grace looked up to find her sandy-haired husband dressed in that same casual manner in which she'd first met him. A costume of billowing white shirt with sleeves rolled up and sides barely tucked into tailored navy trousers was set off by black knee boots and a jauntily tied neck scarf.

"Good morning, darling," she said, setting the pen aside.

He pulled her to her feet and into his arms. Nuzzling his lips against her neck, he murmured approvingly. "Fortune has smiled upon me."

"I found myself counting God's blessings this morning, as well," Grace replied just before Peter's lips captured her own in a deep, passionate kiss.

Grace felt her body warm under his touch, and a tingling sensation ran down her back as she thrilled to her husband's obvious interest. She had not known that physical love could be so wonderful. She'd imagined the nervous butterflies fluttering in her stomach every time she'd set eyes upon Peter to be love's physical calling card. The sight of this man, well before they were married, could take her breath and set her heart to racing. She had presumed this was what passion and romance were all about. She was happy to be wrong.

Yielding to her husband's embrace, Grace trembled as Peter pressed his fingers into her carefully styled hair. She cared not one whit if the coiffure fell in disarray to her waist. She could remain in Peter's arms forever.

As if reading her mind, Peter pulled away to say in a low, husky voice, "I know I have work to do, but I would much rather remain here with you."

She laughed. "Then stay. I've only a few letters to write, and those can easily be put off until later."

He kissed her one more time, then drew away. "I'll never get anything done with you in this house." His voice betrayed his pleasure. "So whom are you writing to?"

Grace's joy drained away and her thoughts turned sober as she wondered how she might avoid a confrontation. Peter hated Martin Paxton, and although Grace had spoken of forgiveness, Peter saw no need for such declarations.

"I . . . um . . ." She looked to the letter and then back to her husband, who was even now tucking his shirttails more securely into his pants. "I have several letters to write. I owe Karen one and then I wanted to send my mother another letter. I do hope she'll join us here, at least for a visit."

Peter nodded. "So whom are you writing to now? Your mother?" He stopped and looked at her as though the answer were quite important.

"Uh, no," Grace began. "It's not to Mother."

Peter noted her hesitancy and crossed to the writing table. "Then it must be to Karen." He lifted the sheet of paper before Grace could stop him. He scanned the letter quickly, then lowered it to give Grace a hard look of disapproval.

"What do you think you're doing?" he questioned. "You can't send this letter. I forbid it."

"Peter," she said softly. "Please try to understand."

His mood changed instantly. "I do not understand. You bandy about words like forgiveness and peace to a man who would have forced a life of misery upon you, had he his own way. A man who is no doubt responsible, by his own admission, for the destruction and devastation of the life you once knew—the people you loved."

"You needn't remind me," Grace said. "I am the one who dealt with him. I know him for what he is."

"Then why?" Peter asked in obvious disgust. "Why do you throw about your religious nonsense and correspond with such a man? Haven't you come to understand he cares nothing about your beliefs?"

"Neither do you," Grace said without thought. She immediately wished she could take back the words. "But I still have hope that you will come to accept the truth for what it is. I hope no less for Martin Paxton."

"Outrageous. How dare you compare me to him? I offered

you rescue—salvation. He offered only pain and suffering."

Grace gently took the letter from her husband's hand. "And I offer peace between all parties. Your parents are long-time friends with this powerful man. He holds a financial interest in your shipping line. I would hate to see your company or you hurt by his vengeful nature. Peter, please understand me—I write this for you as much as I write it for me."

"Do not think to do me any favors, madam." He always reverted to formalities when angry with her. "I ask no such agreement to be made. Paxton must pay the price for his underhanded and corrupt business practices. He has caused this family grief enough already, sneaking around behind my back, loaning my father money and making contracts against the business without my approval. If you think I will overlook such matters in whimsical phrases of forgiveness, then you are mistaken."

"Peter, it will serve no purpose but that of darker forces if you continue this hateful battle." She let the letter fall to the desk and now reached out to take hold of Peter's arm. "Please listen to me. Forgiving Mr. Paxton is the only way to put the past to rest. If he sees that you wish him no further harm, perhaps your father will not suffer any adverse effects regarding their partnership. I desire only that we have a wonderful life together—you and I. I only want security for your family. Don't you see? Can't you understand?"

"What I can't understand is a wife who would undermine her husband's authority," Peter replied in a hard, cool tone. "Why not give yourself over to reading that Bible you so love and see what it says about obedience to authority."

He stalked from the room without waiting for her reply. Grace heard the front door slam shut. Despair washed over

her, and she sunk to the chair and stared blankly at the piece
of paper that had started the entire feud.

"How can it be, Lord, that forgiveness should wage such
wars between us?"

—┤CHAPTER THREE├—

"LOOK," MIRANDA WHISPERED to Grace, "Mrs. Haggarty is back."

Grace took her seat in the church pew and smiled at her sister-in-law. "I'm so glad. I know she was worried about traveling all the way to Salt Lake City to see her daughter, but she looks no worse for the wear."

"Mother says travel is for the young. She's absolutely appalled by the number of older men and women who head north for the goldfields."

Grace didn't have a chance to reply as the Sunday services began. She, too, was amazed at the sensation of gold fever in the nation. The discovery of gold had pulled the country out of a terrible slump, and everyone wanted in on the find. Never mind issues of greed and those who died for something so fleeting. People were starved for prosperity, and they were sure they'd find it in the Yukon. Grace had to smile. The Yukon had brought her a treasure in Peter. He might have his faults, but she loved him dearly. She only wished that he'd accompany her to church—to be a part of what she believed. It was her heart's only desire.

As the service continued and they joined together to sing and pray, Grace felt a loneliness that bothered her nowhere else in the world. She knew it was silly. Worshiping with God's people should be the last place to feel such longing, but she couldn't help it. Without her husband at her side, Grace felt as though she were the talk and gossip of the other married women. After all, what man of good sense and respect for his Creator would absent himself so commonly from Sunday worship? She felt separated from the others—alone and awkward.

The situation had never bothered her when she'd been single. Attending church with Karen or her mother and father had seemed a perfectly acceptable thing to do. No one anticipated that she should be accompanied by anyone else. Why, she had even attended services on her own when her mother had been ill and Karen had been visiting relatives out of town. She had never given it a second thought. She had enjoyed the services every bit as much as when in their company.

But being a married woman changed everything. She no longer fit in the circles of the young, unmarried women and men. They were still free to mingle and flirt, within proper limits, of course. But Grace no longer belonged to their world. Sadly enough, she didn't feel that she belonged to the world of those who were married, either. A woman who attended church without her husband was often seen as a rather dangerous person. After all, she had knowledge and experiences that put her on equal footing with her married church sisters, but unlike them, she had no husband to keep her in line on Sunday morning. She was free to move about and speak to whomever she chose, and that made a great many people uncomfortable.

This had been especially true in the oversized Presbyterian church she'd first attended upon her arrival in San Francisco. Women her own age seemed to scorn her, while older married women saw her as some kind of unspeakable threat. Grace found she didn't fit in with the older widows, either. They were not of a mind to have a young married woman in their midst as they talked of death, childbirth, and their grandchildren. So everyone nodded politely when Grace appeared, then turned their backs on her and hurried away.

Before long, it even seemed to Grace that the sermons were directed to her. Comments were made from the pulpit about sinful women who sought their own way in the suffrage movement, in employment, and in seeking to follow their own course rather than that of their husbands. Maybe she was just extra sensitive to the topics, but they made her uncomfortable nevertheless.

After a while, Grace simply found it easier to keep to herself, and eventually she left the stuffy and selective congregation of Presbyterians and joined a small gathering in a newly founded church within walking distance of home. Grace had learned about the church during tea with one of her neighbors. It seemed the opinion of this gathering that people had gotten too wrapped up in man-made rules and regulations. The goal of the minister was to bring his small, but growing, flock back to some of the most basic biblical truths.

That suited Grace just fine. Her hunger for spiritual truths had only been compounded since her marriage. Peter had no desire to make Bible reading and prayer a focus for his life.

He'd chided Grace about things they could better spend their time doing together, and while she'd tried to take it all in stride, her heart was torn. Grace's one consolation was Peter's sister, Miranda.

Miranda's presence comforted Grace like no other. She seemed to understand Grace's loneliness and shared feelings of her own that closely matched those of her sister-in-law. Miranda had few friends and knew the same sense of isolation that Grace experienced. Miranda became more and more compelled to participate in Grace's daily schedule, and Grace, in turn, eagerly encouraged her presence. This became especially true of church attendance.

It also didn't hurt that there were several eligible bachelors in the congregation. Miranda had confided to Grace that she had begun to fear never finding an appropriate suitor, but now Grace saw her sister-in-law quite enthusiastic. After the service, a host of men descended upon the two women like flies to a picnic.

"Miss Colton," a handsome man with flaming red hair said, taking up Miranda's hand, "I wonder if I might speak to you alone."

Miranda looked to Grace as many of the other congregation members filed past them. "I'm sure that anything you have to say to me can be said in front of my sister-in-law."

The man blushed furiously, his face nearly matching the color of his hair. "It's just that . . . well . . . I wondered . . ."

"Old Corky is trying to ask you to share lunch with him," another of the men proclaimed. "But you can just tell him no, because I asked you first. Remember?"

Grace wanted to laugh out loud at the man's obvious devotion to her sister-in-law. Miranda, on the other hand, looked quite perplexed as she tried to recall the earlier invitation.

"Miss Colton has no time for either of you gentlemen," yet a third man announced. "I sent a written invitation inviting not only Miss Colton, but her sister-in-law, as well. It's what true gentlemen of society do if they desire the company of dinner guests." He hooked his fingers in his waistcoat pocket and leaned back on his heels looking quite self-satisfied.

Grace nodded. "It's true, gentlemen. Mr. Barker has indeed requested our presence by means of a formal invitation."

The other two men, though disappointed, realized they'd lost out. They gave a graceful bow and promised to send their invitations in tomorrow's post. Grace could only imagine the confusion that promised to give the Colton household.

Miranda looked up at the dark-haired Mr. Barker and smiled. "My sister-in-law has agreed to accompany us to lunch. It is with her encouragement that we accept your invitation."

"Marvelous," the man said, flashing brilliant white teeth. "I shall cherish your company."

———

The luncheon seemed to last forever. Perhaps, Grace thought, it was due to the monotonous self-promoting lecture given by Mr. Barker. Or perhaps it was due to the bland and unappealing food. Either way, when Grace and Miranda made their way up the steps to the Colton house, both breathed a sigh of relief. Pausing on the porch, they looked at each other and broke into fits of laughter.

"I thought that it would never end," Miranda confided. "What a conceited man."

Grace nodded, completely agreeing. "He seemed so very much in love with himself, I seriously doubt he could have shared love for anyone else."

"Not without deeply wounding his own feelings," Miranda added.

"I had so hoped you would enjoy your outing. With so many dashing young bachelors vying for your attention, it seems only fair to expect that one of them should be the right one."

Miranda's smile faded. "I know. I keep thinking that, as well. There have been others, men who Peter said were not worthy of me. He's been so good to try and look out for me."

"Peter is a good man. He cares very much for you, but you have to make choices based on what your heart tells you. Peter might well think Mr. Barker a perfect suitor. The man is a banker and holds a respected position in the community. Your brother would probably admire him greatly and think you amicably suited."

"I suppose that is true. Peter does sometimes make choices for me that I would just as soon not have made."

Grace could well understand that, her husband being a strongly opinionated man. "Well, no harm done. Mr. Barker seemed to understand quite well that you lacked interest in his need for adoration." Grace smiled and opened the front door to the house. "Perhaps we should try Corky next time, eh?"

Miranda laughed. "All that red hair. My word, but it fairly glows."

"And just think of the redheaded children you might find yourself mother to," Grace laughed, and Miranda flushed at the thought as she giggled.

Their laughter quickly faded, however. Grace stepped into

the house to find Peter awaiting their return. She had thought he was on his way to Seattle and hadn't expected to find him home.

"Peter!" Grace could see the anger in his eyes and hoped to calm him. "Why, if we'd known you were still in town, you could have joined us for lunch."

"Where have you been?"

"Grace agreed to accompany me to lunch with Mr. Barker," Miranda answered.

Peter's expression darkened as his eyes narrowed. "Who is Mr. Barker?"

"Oh, surely you remember him, Peter. He came to see Father on business about a month ago."

Grace pulled the shawl from her shoulders and untied her bonnet. "He attends our church and was quite smitten with your sister."

"Why wasn't I consulted on this, Miranda?"

Grace could see the look of contrition on Miranda's face. "I'm sorry, Peter. I presumed you were quite busy with the company. You and Father have both had so much to do in transporting goods and people to Alaska. It simply never entered my mind that you would want to hear about Mr. Barker's invitation."

"Besides," Grace interjected, "she's a grown woman and fully capable of making up her own mind when it comes to the company she desires to keep. She learned easily over melon slices and strawberries that Mr. Barker is far more interested in Mr. Barker than in anyone else." Grace flashed Miranda a smile before placing her bonnet and shawl aside.

When she turned back to her husband, she found him most furious. "I will speak to you later, Miranda. For now, I will have words with Grace on the matter. Come to our room, madam, and let us resume this discussion."

Grace followed Peter, knowing that he would lash out at her in his anger. How many times would this be the course of their discussions? He always flared up like a fire feasting hungrily on old wood. Then he would become calm and apologetic, almost childlike in his desire to please. Sometimes Grace thought she'd married two different men.

They entered their bedroom, and before Peter could close the door, Grace jumped in to speak. "Please hear me out before you take offense with me."

He turned to eye her, the rage held in tight restraint as he replied, "Very well."

Grace took a seat and began to pull off her gloves. "I did not purposefully set out this morning to cause you irritation or pain. I am sorry that I have apparently managed both. As Miranda stated, we realized your busyness and thought only to take care of the situation ourselves. Your mother found it acceptable, and in your father's absence, as well as your own, we believed this to be the only necessary authority on which to act."

"Are you finished?" he asked in a low guarded tone.

"No." Grace surprised them both with her answer. She threw her gloves aside and worked to keep her own anger in check. "I'm tired of your accusing tones and angry lectures. Don't think me to be so ill-witted that I believe for one moment this is about Miranda. Oh, certainly you wish to have control over her life, but we both know that this behavior of yours is fueled by my desire to help ease the tensions between our family and Mr. Paxton. So rather than chide me for accompanying your sister on her outing, why not simply deal with the real issue at hand?"

Peter's jaw tightened, and Grace could clearly see that her

words had struck a chord. He paced the room a moment before stopping directly in front of her. "You had no right to interfere. You are my wife, and as such you answer to me. My sister is unmarried and answers to our father, and in his absence she, too, answers to me. Do you understand?"

"I understand that you wish to control the lives of the people around you. I understand that you hold no respect for God or His authority over you, yet you demand that others allow you your rightful authority over them. Seems to me there are double standards in this."

Peter shook his head, his sandy brown hair falling onto his forehead. "I do not care what it seems like to you. Grace, there are certain rules of society and decorum that I expect you to honor. My father has expected no less from my mother and sister, and I expect no less from you."

"You knew before marrying me that I didn't agree with this philosophy of life," Grace replied. "You blamed it on Karen, but in truth, I was raised to believe women have the ability to reason for themselves."

"Perhaps that's why your father arranged a marriage for you with Mr. Paxton."

Grace frowned. "My father arranged that engagement based on Mr. Paxton's blackmail and nothing more. He wouldn't have forced me into such a relationship had there been another way. And you and I wouldn't be married now had I stayed behind to be the dominated little woman that you demand of me now."

"Perhaps that would have been for the best," Peter snapped.

Grace was silent a moment, the strength of his words a blow to her heart. "Yes, perhaps you're right." She bowed her head and wondered why it should be that this man she loved so dearly should hurt her so deeply.

For several moments neither one spoke, then Peter came to her and put his hand under her chin. Lifting her face, Grace knew he would see her tears and be remorseful. For just once, however, she wished he could see the pain prior to the delivery and stop before apologies were necessary.

"I didn't mean what I said."

This was always his way. His words were to be respected, honored, and obeyed—except when he qualified them in the aftermath of his anger with that simple, meaningless statement.

"I didn't mean to hurt you," he continued, his thumb gently stroking her cheek.

Grace didn't know what to say. She didn't feel like accepting his lame excuses, and yet she had no desire to continue fighting.

"Peter," she said, forcing her gaze to meet his, "words are powerful. They can maim and injure just like any weapon forged by man. They can also nurture and encourage. I can't help but believe that you know my heart—know how very much I love you. But at the same time, I find it very difficult to accept that you love me. Especially when you say the things you do."

Peter pulled her up and wrapped her in his arms. "Grace, there are just certain things I wish you'd leave well enough alone. I don't mind that you are intelligent and witty, but I do mind when your actions make me to look the fool."

Grace shook her head. "How did I do that?"

Peter dropped his hold. "I told Barker nearly a month ago that I didn't wish for him to court my sister. I knew the man was conceited and full of his own accomplishments. I knew Miranda would abhor him."

Grace felt foolish. She'd not considered that Peter might have already spoken to Barker about Miranda. "I'm sorry. I didn't realize."

"I know that, but had you simply bothered to check, I would have given you my reasons. Miranda knows that, and it grieves me that she should seek other counsel."

"But she's lonely and she desires to marry and have a family of her own," Grace replied. "You can't expect her to wait around forever."

"I don't expect that at all. I only ask that she wait until the right man comes along. I want to save her the pain of being married to someone for whom she is completely ill suited."

The words penetrated Grace's heart like no other. Tears came to her eyes and she turned away before asking, "Ill suited as we are?"

Peter turned her to face him. "Grace, we are not ill suited. We're perfect for one another. We love so many of the same things, and while you get a little spirited from time to time, I know we'll come to work through our differences."

"You mean that in time I'll come to do things your way and then you'll be happy," Grace said, reaching up to wipe tears from her eyes. "Peter, I'm not that kind of a woman. My faith is the foundation for my existence. It's not a Sunday occupation or a social matter; it is my very life. I won't give it up as you think I should. I'll go on desiring to forgive those who've wronged me."

"With exception to your husband," Peter said, letting go of her. "Forgiveness is something you offer everyone else, but not me."

"That's not true, Peter. I do forgive you. I know you don't understand my need for church or my desire for us to pray together and share God's Word. I can even admit to knowing that you don't mean many of the words you speak in anger, but Peter, those words still hurt. Even after I've forgiven you, my heart is still tender."

He frowned, as if understanding for the first time. "It wasn't my intent to hurt you, Grace. I sometimes speak without thinking."

"That is a danger we must all work to avoid. Words spoken in haste cannot be taken back. And while they may be forgiven, the memories will linger to warn the heart of future encounters."

"But I don't mean anything by it," Peter said in self-defense.

"Perhaps that is what makes it even worse," Grace replied. "If you mean nothing by those words, perhaps you mean nothing by other words. How can I believe what you say when a good portion of the time you tell me you didn't mean it?"

Peter shrugged. "I don't have an answer for you. I lose my temper and I speak out of line. I'm sorry. I'm used to dealing with people who respect me and don't question my advice."

Grace knew her next statement could either send them deeper into the argument or settle the matter more peaceably. She felt a weariness in her heart and chose the latter.

"I'm sorry, Peter. I didn't mean to make you feel that I held no respect for your advice. I will suggest to Miranda that she speak to you on all these matters. Now, if you will excuse me, I'm feeling rather tired. I think perhaps I'll rest a bit."

Peter smiled and looked as though he might suggest joining her when a light knock sounded at their door. Grace felt relieved as Peter turned to see who it was.

Miranda stood on the other side, her expression rather tentative. "Peter, Father needs to see you in the study."

He glanced back at Grace and then nodded to his sister.

"Grace was just going to rest for a bit. Perhaps you and I might talk a bit on our way downstairs."

They left the room with Peter closing the door behind him. Grace sunk onto the bed and felt such utter despair that she immediately burst into tears. She loved this man so very much, yet he had the power to hurt her like no one else. Not even Martin Paxton had caused her this much pain. But then, she hadn't loved Martin Paxton.

Burying her face in the bed pillows, Grace sobbed herself to sleep, hoping and praying that God would somehow show her what she was to do in order to live in peace with this man she so dearly loved.

⊣[CHAPTER FOUR]⊢

KAREN STOOD SHIVERING in the cold. Staring at the charred rubble that had once been a prosperous business, she wondered what she should do next.

"You were sure lucky to get out of there alive."

Karen turned to find Mrs. Neal, the proprietor of the Gold Nugget Hotel. "Hello, Roberta. Yes, I suppose we were lucky." Her words were not at all enthusiastic, but Karen felt the truth of their meaning. They had all survived, everyone but Aunt Doris. That loss was more than Karen cared to dwell on, and she tried to put on a brave front for the sake of the children.

"I came over when I saw you out here. Wanted to tell you that you and the kids could take up a room at my place. I've had a good number of fellows head off for the north. There's a nice big room on the back side of the second floor. There's only one bed, but your boy could sleep on the floor. It ain't buggy at all, so you wouldn't have to worry about that."

Karen smiled and gave the old woman a hug. She'd become acquainted with Mrs. Neal through the small community church where the old woman pounded out church hymns on a well-worn piano. Most everyone in the area knew Roberta Neal. The widow always lent her opinion and support, be it solicited or otherwise.

"Thank you, Roberta. That would be most helpful. We've stayed a few days in Mr. Ivankov's tent down by the Tlingit village, but I'm sure he'd like to have his property back. He's heading north to Sheep Camp, and I wouldn't want him to be delayed on our account."

"Well, you just move your things right on in this afternoon," Mrs. Neal replied.

Karen laughed. "Well, there really isn't much in the way of things to move. The clothes on our backs are pretty much the sum total."

Mrs. Neal nodded and headed off down the street. "There's no need to fret about that. The Ladies Church Society is collecting things for you even now. They'll be bringing items over to the hotel this afternoon. You just gather your young'uns and come."

Relief flooded her at the news, giving her the tiniest hope for the future. Karen had wondered what they would do. She'd considered trying to buy a place or have something built, but the cold weather was hardly the time to start new projects.

"We'll be there after lunch," she called out after the woman.

Turning her gaze back to the charred remainders of the Colton Trading Post, Karen wondered how best to get word to Peter. She knew he'd be back within a week or two to bring supplies. She supposed it could wait until then, since there was no guarantee the mail would reach him any sooner.

To say she was discouraged would be an understatement. Karen tried to sort through her tattered emotions and determine what was to be done. She turned away from the rubble and made her way to the small cemetery where her mother was buried. Despite the cold and the dark, heavy clouds overhead, Karen felt confident that this was the only place she would find any real peace.

A handful of other graves kept company with her mother's resting-place. Karen knelt beside the simple white marker, mindless of the frozen ground. She gently touched the letters that spelled out her mother's name and sighed.

"I came here to find you both," she murmured. "I knew I'd find you already gone, Mother, but I honestly expected to reunite with Father. How can it be that you are both gone from me now? Now, when I need you the most."

She almost laughed at how silly that seemed. She was thirty years old, almost thirty-one. Surely at this age a person no longer needed their mother and father. But Karen had no one else. Grace was gone and married, and all the time and effort she'd poured into that relationship was now a thing of the past. There were, of course, Jacob and Leah Barringer, but they belonged to Bill, and he had pledged to come back for them. Karen had no reason to believe it would be otherwise.

Then there was Doris. Her beloved aunt was now resting in the arms of Jesus, as the simplistic eulogy delivered by Pastor Clark had suggested. It had been Aunt Doris's wish to eventually settle in Seattle, so Karen had arranged for her body to be shipped there. Karen knew her sister Willamina would be happy to handle the arrangements.

"Poor Aunt Doris." Karen thought it so tragic that the once-vibrant spinster's life should end this way. She had given

Karen such hope, especially on days when things had gone particularly bad. She had always reminded Karen to keep her focus on things above and not things below. But now Karen felt lost, without a purpose.

"I miss her so much," Karen again spoke aloud. "I can't remember a time in my life when she wasn't my very favorite aunt. It seems strange that she will never again advise me or speak to me of her past experiences." She turned her gaze to the thick blanket of clouds and asked, "Why, God? Why has this happened? Why have you allowed Martin Paxton to destroy my life?"

And she was convinced that the blame rested solely with Paxton. There was no doubt in her mind. The fire, according to those who had examined the remains, had begun in the front of the shop, well away from lanterns and stoves that might have sparked a flame. To Karen's way of thinking, that pretty much signaled that someone had set the fire. Martin Paxton had sworn revenge on each of them, so it seemed an easy conclusion that he had arranged the disaster—perhaps even set the blaze himself.

"I thought I might find you here," Adrik Ivankov announced.

Karen got to her feet quickly and nodded. "I just needed a few moments alone. I was about to come find you."

"It's always nice when a pretty lady seeks your company." Adrik smiled, causing the edges of his mustache to turn upward. He'd shaved his beard the day after the fire, and Karen found him much more appealing without it. His smile broadened as if he could read her mind. "So what's your pleasure?"

Karen blushed and looked away momentarily while she collected her thoughts. "Well, I know you're anxious to get up to Sheep Camp, and I wanted to let you know that Mrs. Neal has offered us a room at the Gold Nugget. She said we could move in after lunch, so you will have your tent back."

"I'm glad that you'll be in warmer surroundings, but there was really no need to rush. I could have just as easily headed up north without those few things."

Karen met his dark eyes and felt his expression warm away the chill of the day. She found his looks most appealing. Even the scars on his neck and jaw only seemed to make him more intriguing. She'd often thought to ask him about the encounter that had left him a marked man, but just as quickly had tucked away such questions. She didn't want to presume upon an intimacy that he'd shared with her father and mother. They were acquaintances and he had saved her life, but surely there was nothing more—nothing deeper.

"You seem pretty lost in thought," Adrik said. "You want to talk about it?"

Karen shrugged and looked down at the grave. "I was just feeling a bit overwhelmed. I really miss them, Adrik. I was so sure I would come north to spend time helping Father. I mean, it seemed right and all the pieces fell into place. I thought I would learn to minister to the Tlingits at his side and that I would spend the rest of my days here. Then, too, I was confident that Aunt Doris would be alive for a long, long time. How is it that they can be so quickly taken from me? How is that fair? How does it speak of a compassionate God?"

"Your pa was fond of quoting Scripture and saying that the rain falls on the just and the unjust. Bad things happen. There's no doubt about it."

Karen shook her head, her vision blurring with tears. "I want them back. I want the past to be nothing more than a bad dream. I want to sit down to tea with my mother. I want to hear my father preach, just one more time." She looked up at Adrik, not caring that he would see her tears. "I need them and now they're gone." Her voice broke and she buried her face in her gloved hands.

She had known he would come to her, and in some ways she thought she had willed him there by her desperate need. Adrik wrapped her in the warm safety of his embrace. This was the second time in a matter of days that she'd cried in his arms.

"I know I'm a poor substitute," Adrik told her, "but I'd like to think that my friendship with your parents would spill over to a friendship with you." He paused for a moment, and Karen lifted her face to see his contemplative expression. "I miss them, too," he added softly.

"Oh, Adrik, I am sorry. I hadn't thought—"

He put his finger to her lips. "You weren't expected to. You have enough to contend with. I just wanted you to know that we can share this grief together. You needn't bear it alone."

He lowered his face to better see her. Karen grew aware of his nearness, almost as if she hadn't realized it before. With his mouth only inches away from her own, she found herself wondering what it would be like to be kissed by this broad-shouldered native her father had put so much trust in. The thought so startled her that she pushed away from him.

"I'm sorry. I didn't . . . mean to . . . break down." Her voice betrayed her confusion as she stepped back several paces.

"There's nothing wrong with having a good cry now and then," Adrik said, appearing for all the world as though he had been completely unaffected by their encounter. "I just want you to know that I care—that I'm here for you and the children if you need me. I'll be heading up to Sheep Camp tomorrow, but I'll be back for Easter Sunday. Maybe we can share a dinner and discuss the future."

Karen laughed. "The future. That's exactly what I can't seem to figure out. I doubt discussing it would lend any more clarity to it than I've already gathered."

"You'd be surprised. Sometimes it just takes a bit of conversation to help a person think a thing through. For instance, I know that right now you're pretty wrapped up in the bad things that have happened. I'm thinkin', however, if you were to sit down and start talking about all the blessings you still have, you'd find that a lot of things have slipped your mind."

Karen knew he was probably right. "I know I've been blessed. It's just that right now the pain is much more evident."

"Life isn't without its moments of sorrow and pain," Adrik reminded her, "but it's also not without its pleasantries and good. God has a plan in all of this. We might not know what it is, but He is sovereign and we must trust His way."

"I don't know about that," Karen said, stiffening. She was angry at God right now and far from ready to put her feelings aside. "I trusted God with everything, and now I'm like Job sitting in the ashes, with most everyone dead and everything stripped away."

"That's not true," Adrik said, refusing to leave the matter well enough alone. "You told me yourself that you have money in the bank. Money enough to start over. That's not having everything stripped away."

"All right, then. Everything that's important to me has been stripped away. Grace is gone. My mother, father, and aunt are dead. I've lost all my wordly possessions with exception to my father's Bible, and I'm left with the charge of two children who are suffering from their own losses. It doesn't seem an easy thing to me to say that God has a plan. Frankly, if this is His plan, then I'm not impressed. Innocent people are dead, while a murderer walks free to plot further revenge."

Adrik gazed at her a moment before saying, "I know you're angry."

She shook her head, the sorrow quickly being replaced by feelings of rage. "You don't know the half of it. Martin Paxton has been a thorn in my side for nearly a year. He tormented and abused Grace, and he's threatened all of us on numerous occasions. I want the man to pay for what he's done."

"You can't be sure he was responsible."

"Oh, can't I?" She shoved her gloved hands deep into her coat pockets. The cold was beginning to seep into her bones. "He was there. He the same as announced it with that smug smile of his."

"You still can't be sure. You can't go around accusing a prominent citizen of arson."

"Prominent! That's hardly the word for him."

"I've been around Skagway long enough to know that he's well respected."

"Feared, you mean."

"No, I meant respected. He's poured money into the community, and that's made folks think rather highly of him. He's involved in helping to finance the railroad out of Skagway and has invested hundreds of dollars into improving the harbor. People see that as a real boon to business. With that kind of background, I doubt seriously anyone is going to believe your accusations." He stepped toward her and took hold of her arms. "And, Karen, that's all you have. Accusations. What if you're wrong? What if you heap some form of revenge upon this man, only to learn that a passing drunk started the fire instead?"

Karen tried to pull away, but he held her fast. "Let me go.

You don't know what he's like. You don't know what he's capable of."

"Maybe not, but I do know that justice and revenge rest in God's hands and not our own." His voice took on a tone of reproach. "You know full well your father would tell you to turn the other cheek. He'd tell you to suffer your enemy with patience and God's peace."

"He might very well say that, but he isn't here," Karen said rather hatefully. "And by your own words, you are a poor substitute." She saw the way her statement hurt him. She wanted to apologize, but at the same time she wanted nothing more than to get away from him.

He let her go with a nod. "That I am."

It was Adrik who walked away rather than Karen. She felt frozen to the place where she stood, her anger and bitterness now feeding off her last reserves of energy. Why did he have to say those things? Why had he argued with her in the first place? She would never have said anything so meanspirited had he not provoked her.

The argument in her heart seemed very lame considering that she could see how deeply she'd wounded him.

"But he's wrong," she whispered, putting aside her shame. "He's so very wrong. He doesn't know Martin Paxton like I do. He doesn't know what the man is capable of."

Slowly she made her way back to the Tlingit village. They were a silent and steady people, these Tlingit. They dressed for the most part like any white person, but their endurance and patience were hardly attributes Karen found in her own people. The gold fever brought new throngs of cheechakos on a daily basis, and most of them were white and incapable of the hardships of living in the wilderness. The Tlingit seemed to take the swell of population in stride. They were often misused

51

and abused by the newcomers, but Karen saw an attitude in them that held them proud and straight. It was almost as if without words they were saying, "We were here before you came, and we will be here after you're gone."

Karen approached the tent she shared with Leah and Jacob and squared her shoulders. They would be happy to hear about the move, of that she was certain. Leah was afraid of the noises at night, and the cold left her shivering even when sandwiched between Karen and Jacob. Jacob wouldn't care either way, but he worried about Leah, and Karen knew he'd be pleased to see her comforted. She found his love for Leah almost enviable. He knew his responsibility to her—knew that they were alone in the world at this point—and yet they had each other. For all his problems and times of despair, Karen knew Jacob cared deeply for Leah's welfare.

The children were just finishing a lunch of stew and bread when she pushed back the flap and stepped inside.

"We saved you a bowl," Leah declared. She pulled back a dish towel to reveal the awaiting meal.

Karen's stomach rumbled and she only then realized how hungry she was. "Thank you. I appreciate it." She hurried out of her gloves and bonnet, then sat down on the ground between the brother and sister.

"I have good news," she said, taking up the offered bowl.

"Have you heard from Papa?" Leah questioned excitedly.

Karen felt sorry for the child and patted her head. "No, I'm sorry. It's not that kind of news. But it is good, nevertheless. Mrs. Neal has offered us a room at the Gold Nugget. She also said the ladies at the church were collecting clothes and household goods for us. It will be like Christmas to see what they manage to put together." Karen tried to make it all sound like great fun.

She ate a bit of the stew and added, "There's just one bed, so Leah and I will have to sleep together. We'll buy you a cot, Jacob, and we'll just have to honor each other's needs for privacy. I don't look for us to stay there long, so it shouldn't be too great a hardship."

"If we aren't stayin' long," Jacob began, "then where are we going?"

Karen shrugged and tore off a piece of bread that Leah offered. "I'm not sure. My first thought was to go back to the States, but I can't do that. I can't take you away when your father has promised to come back for you."

"Why don't we go north—go after him?" Jacob questioned.

"That is a thought. I suppose we have enough money put aside that we could buy supplies. We could probably even pay for packers to see us over the summit. After that, I'm not sure what awaits on the other side."

"I heard one old fellow say that the summit is the worst of it," Jacob said, his tone taking on a hint of excitement. "There's plenty of water travel after you get on the other side of the mountain. We could just float north to Dawson City and find Pa."

"Could we?" Leah asked, the hope sparkling in her eyes.

"I suppose it is something to consider," Karen replied. She ate thoughtfully for several moments, then added, "There really is nothing to keep us here now."

"I can ask around about packers," Jacob offered. "I'll bet Mr. Ivankov could tell us where we can get help."

"Mr. Ivankov might not be feeling too kindly toward me just now," Karen replied. "We had some rather heated words. We should probably stick to asking someone else."

Jacob shrugged. "That's all right. I know lots of folks I can talk to."

Karen nodded. "Good. Let's see to getting settled over to the Gold Nugget first, and then we'll discuss the matter in more detail. There's a lot of work involved. It's not just money or the supplies. There's a great deal of distance between here and Dawson and a great many people of less than sparkling character who stand between here and there. We'll have to think this through and do what's best to ensure our safety."

"And we have to pray, too," Leah chimed in.

Karen nodded, but felt no desire to encourage any further thought on the matter. She was angry at God, and talking to Him just now was the last thing she wanted to do.

—{ CHAPTER FIVE }—

PETER WAS UNPREPARED for the sight that awaited him at breakfast. His father sat at the head of the table as usual, but before him was an open Bible, and he was reading to the women who sat at either side of him.

"Psalm 112 says, 'Praise ye the Lord. Blessed is the man that feareth the Lord, that delighteth greatly in his commandments. His seed shall be mighty upon earth: the generation of the upright shall be blessed. Wealth and riches shall be in his house: and his righteousness endureth forever.'"

The verse set Peter on edge. He could remember a time when he was very young that his father had read the Bible to them at bedtime, but that habit had certainly passed by the wayside for more constructive, beneficial habits. Peter cleared his throat before his father could continue. "I didn't realize we were having church this morning."

Ephraim looked up and smiled at his son. "You're often gone before the morning meal. Grace convinced us of this marvelous routine." He smiled at his daughter-in-law, and Peter watched her flush nervously. She knew he wouldn't approve, and yet she'd once again gone behind his back to manipulate his family.

Peter took his chair beside Grace and refused to look at her when he spoke. "Grace has a great many strange ideas. I wouldn't give all of them credence."

"Peter, what an ungracious thing to say. Grace is a lovely young woman with a fine mind," Amelia Colton admonished. "She has brought a certain light and joy into this house. I hardly think it fair to accuse her of having strange ideas."

"I do not recall that this family ever wasted time over meals with Bible readings," Peter said as he reached out for a platter of sausages.

"Then perhaps we should have," Miranda countered.

Peter paused, holding the platter aloft, but turned his attention to his younger sister. "I would think you, above the others, would know exactly how faulty Grace's advice can be."

"You are just being thickheaded," Miranda snapped.

"And you are being insolent, a trait I know without a doubt you have learned from my wife."

"Enough!" Ephraim declared. "I'm ashamed of your words, Peter. Did I not raise you to have respect for the women in this family? For any woman?"

Peter dropped the platter on the table. He slammed his fist down hard, causing all the contents on the table to vibrate. He got to his feet, barely able to contain his anger. Nothing had gone right since he'd brought Grace home.

"Perhaps you would find the meal less unpleasant if I simply took myself away."

"Son, we would just as soon have you stay," Ephraim began, and Peter felt some small amount of control returning. But just as he considered retaking his seat, his father added, "However, if you insist on treating your sister and wife in a poor manner, then perhaps it is just as well you go."

Peter had never been dismissed from the family table. He'd been honored and his words heeded as grains of wisdom until now. He looked at Grace, whose head was bowed, her gaze fixed on an empty plate. This was her fault. He should have known it would happen. Why had he been so foolish as to listen to his heart?

He turned and left the room without bothering to add further comment. *I will not stand around and be insulted by my own family. Let them have their Bible studies and prayers.* He turned the handle on the front door, then remembered some important papers he needed. The delay only served to anger him more.

Taking the stairs two at a time, he allowed his anger to fuel his stride. The papers were in his locked desk near the window. Leaving the door open, he fumbled in his pocket for the key and had barely managed to open the desk when Grace entered the room.

"Peter, I would like to talk to you."

He straightened and momentarily forgot the papers. He met her intense brown eyes, saw the flush to her cheeks, and thought her the most beautiful woman in the world. Why did she have to be so cantankerous and opinionated?

"I have nothing to say."

She nodded and closed the door. "Perhaps not, but I have something I want to say to you."

"I do not wish to hear it. You've caused enough harm already. I can't believe you could so quickly turn my family against me. But that, of course, has always been the power of religious nonsense. I suppose when you found you could not convert me, you went after them with the same ardor and zeal. Well, you have my congratulations, Grace. You have managed a feat I would have thought them above falling for."

"Peter, this isn't a game."

He watched her fold her hands calmly as she leaned back against the door. "I have only the highest regard for your family. They have been gracious and kind. They have willingly taken me into their fold without question and without resentment. I thought you wanted me to get along with them. On the trip here from Skagway you encouraged me to befriend your sister, and I have done that. She is a pleasant woman who has a sharp mind for detail. She knows a great deal and has much to offer. I enjoy her company, and I believe she enjoys mine, as well."

Peter gritted his teeth and turned back to the desk. He opened the drawer and took out a thick fold of papers. Relocking the desk, he looked back to Grace and cocked his head to one side. "Is that all?"

"No," she replied softly. "Peter, I love you with all my heart. I'm sorry that I have offended you by sharing my faith with your family, but I'm not sorry for having shared my faith. I did not do so with the intention of bringing you harm or causing ill will against you."

"Well, for something you never intended to do, you've done it well."

"I don't wish for you to leave in anger. We've had too many angry words of late." She moved toward him, but Peter quickly held up his hand.

"Stay your distance, madam. I will not be cajoled from my mood."

"I had no idea to offer such a plan. I merely hoped to offer my sincerest apology and tell you that my motivation has always been love. I love you and I love your family. But I also love God, and the love He has shown me gives me cause to want to share it with others."

Peter shoved the papers into his coat pocket. "I'm afraid if you are unwilling to put an end to this religious nonsense, we will constantly be at odds. I have no desire to fall into a routine of the masses. My Maker needs no such confirmation from me. God knows who He is and what He plans. He will not be swayed by my prayers or reading of the Bible.

"In turn, I need no such lessons in religious matters from my wife." He paused and eyed her hard. He knew it was a look that could wilt even the heartiest of his sailors, but he didn't care. "What I need from you is obedience and respect. Without that, we cannot have a marriage."

"I agree," Grace said. "I do respect you, Peter. I admire your abilities and your knowledge. I am sorry that I've overstepped my place at times, but I will not give up my faith because it makes you uncomfortable."

"It doesn't make me uncomfortable, madam. It makes me furious. You put a fence between us, with God sitting squarely on the top rail. You use your religion as an excuse to defy me and make me look the fool in my father's eyes, and that I find most unforgivable."

She again moved toward him, but once more he put up his arm to stop her. "I have business to attend to."

"Business that is more important than our marriage?"

"Quite frankly, I wish I had never married you at all."

He hadn't meant to say the words; they had simply poured from his mouth in his rage. So many times before he had come to regret speaking in anger, but nothing compared to the regret he felt now as he watched Grace's expression fall and tears come to her eyes.

Guilt propelled him past her and out of the room. He couldn't stand to see the anguish on her face. He couldn't bear to know that he had so neatly broken her spirit with one fatal blow. But break her he had. He was certain of it. There was a defeat in her eyes that he knew would always haunt him.

He hadn't meant the words. But he couldn't take them back.

Grace crumbled to the floor. She felt her chest tighten, her lungs desperate for air. She wanted to scream, but there were no sounds to utter. There was nothing but the hideous, abominable pain in her heart.

I only did what I thought was right, Father. She struggled to focus on prayer rather than give in to her misery. *I thought if I shared your mercy and goodness that Peter and his family would see the void in their lives and come to you. And they have . . . all except for Peter.*

Her breathing gradually returned to normal, and with it she found her voice. "Oh, Father, what am I to do? I was faithful to you. I was faithful, and now I feel as though death would be kinder than life."

———

Peter didn't return anytime during the day, and by night when Grace prepared for bed, she was certain he was gone for good. Word came to them the next morning that *Merry Maid* had set off for Seattle, giving confirmation to Grace's fear of desertion.

"I can't believe he has behaved so badly," Amelia said, putting her arm around Grace. "It isn't like him to be so cruel."

"He's not fighting against Grace, Mother," Miranda stated. "He's fighting against God."

"Not a healthy stand to take," Ephraim said as they gathered around the breakfast table. "Grace, perhaps I will have a chance to speak to him. I'm to take *Summer Song* north in the morning. I know it would be best if you could meet face-to-face to work out your differences. Once Peter calms down, he'll realize his foolishness and wish to make amends."

Grace said nothing but started when Amelia threw out the next suggestion. "Why don't we all go north? Grace hasn't seen her friends in some time, and with Easter approaching rather quickly, she could share the season with them as well."

"That would be splendid," Miranda declared. "I would love to make the trip again. I think the adventure would be perfect for all of us."

"I appreciate what you're trying to do," Grace said quietly, "but Peter has no interest in seeing me or resolving this issue. He told me he was sorry we married, and it wouldn't surprise me in the least if he sought to remedy the matter."

"He wouldn't dare!" Amelia exclaimed. "A divorce would be a disgrace. No son of mine is going to use such an underhanded method of facing difficulties. Now I'm certain we must go north. Ephraim, you need to talk some sense into that boy before he does something foolish."

"I should have taken him in hand long ago," Ephraim admitted. "I suppose it was just so much easier to give him a free hand than to oppose him."

"We can't dwell on 'should haves,'" Amelia said softly. "We can only work in the here and now. Whether or not Peter feels he needs to see Grace and work this matter out in a reasonable manner, we know the truth of it."

Grace thought of how wonderful it would be to see Karen.

She longed to sit down and have a lengthy discussion with her friend. Only Karen would understand her pain and suffering. Karen's faith was so strong, and she would applaud Grace's efforts to keep God at the center of her life and to bring Him into the hearts of those around her. Karen might even give her an idea of how to help Peter.

"I would like very much to go north," she finally spoke.

"It's settled, then," Ephraim replied, taking up the Bible. "We will have our things taken down to the ship tonight and be ready to leave at dawn." He thumbed through the Psalms. "Ah, here is where we left off. Psalm 112, verse four. 'Unto the upright there ariseth light in the darkness: he is gracious, and full of compassion, and righteous.' "

Grace barely heard the words. Her heart was so full of sorrow and pain. She thought of her mother and wished silently that she could somehow materialize at the table. They had had so little time of closeness, but their letters over the last few months had given Grace such peace and happiness. If it was possible to make up the lost years, then that was truly what was happening.

" 'He shall not be afraid of evil tidings,' " Ephraim read, catching Grace's attention. " 'His heart is fixed, trusting in the Lord.' "

Oh, I desire that my heart be fixed on you, oh Lord, Grace prayed in the silence of her heart. *You know my heart is in pieces, Father. You know the pain I suffer. Please help me in this time of need, just as you have in all the others.*

⊣ CHAPTER SIX ⊢

"KAREN, *MERRY MAID* is in the harbor," Jacob announced. He came into their cramped quarters and threw his fur-lined hat onto the bed. "I saw the ship anchored there. You want me to go wait on the dock for the captain?"

Karen shook her head and put aside the mending she'd been doing for Mrs. Neal. "No, I'll go. I've just finished mending three blankets and twice as many sheets. I need some fresh air."

He frowned and reached for his cap again. "You know how crazy it gets down at the docks. Won't be very safe. I'd better go with you."

"No, I'll be fine. If you go, it will mean you missing lunch." Karen pulled on her coat and reached for her bonnet. "Leah is helping Mrs. Neal in the kitchen. They should have lunch just about ready, so why don't you get something to eat before you head back to work?"

Jacob nodded, but Karen didn't wait for him to comment further. She was out the door and headed down the steps before she finished tying her bonnet. The thought of telling Peter what had happened was something she both dreaded and looked forward to. Peter would understand her anger at Paxton, and he would know what to do. He wouldn't treat her as Adrik had, expecting more from her than she could give. The dread came in knowing Peter would be devastated at the destruction of his store. Business had been very good and the profits quite high. The fire would set him back significantly, and Karen knew that wouldn't be welcome news.

Hurrying down the oozing thaw that was the street, Karen nodded and waved to this one and that, all the time weaving in and out of the growing crowd of newcomers. Thousands of miners had poured into Dyea for the winter, and now as the weather warmed, people came out in droves. In fact, every week more and more people poured into Skagway and Dyea, and with the growing populace came all manner of evil and hardship.

In Dyea, there were now over forty saloons, most of them in tents, but nevertheless they distributed an abundance of libations. Positioned not far from the saloons and sometimes even within their confines were the brothels and "daughters of joy," as the prostitutes were often called. Karen cringed as she passed by several of these less fortunate women. These sallow-faced women generally called out their propositions to the crowd, but they held a mutual silence as Karen passed by. She could not aid their need or better their situation, and that made her useless to these women. Karen, uncertain of how to deal with the issues at hand, hurried by with her head bowed. As one who was not very well acquainted with emotional love, much less physical intimacies, the women, quite frankly, embarrassed Karen. And as one who was struggling with her beliefs, Karen couldn't even muster the interest to share her faith or suggest a better life for these lost sisters.

She wanted to be charitable and treat them with decency, for her mother had always said Jesus did the same for the prostitutes of His time. But now, with her heart so hardened, so hurt, Karen was unsure of how to respond to anyone.

Pushing through a crowd gathered around one of the many con men, Karen shook her head in amazement. How foolish they were. The eager newcomers were fresh and unspoiled by the harsh elements of the frozen north. They faced their futures with keen enthusiasm and great pride. They were going north to make a fortune in gold—their future promised nothing but prosperity.

The con man promised them prosperity, as well—the quick and easy variety. They all did. From the underhanded salesman who sold secondhand saws—so dull they couldn't slice through butter without getting caught up—to the man who played three-ball pick-any, sliding a peanut under one of three balls and letting people pay two bits a guess to find the peanut. They always lost. Always. And still they didn't learn. They lined up for their moment—their prosperity.

Some prosperity!

Karen laughed in a cynical manner and lifted her skirts as she crossed the muddy streets. The weather had been so very unpredictable, and warm winds had caused a bit of a thaw, leaving the streets almost impassable as the hard frozen ground gave way to muck and standing water. Such was the paradise she had come to.

Sandwiched between the mountains and the west branch and main stem of the Taiya River, Dyea offered as much civilization as it could. Folks had big plans for the town, and a harbor with proper docks stood at the top of the list. The docks were even now in a constant state of improvement thanks to the Dyea-Klondike Transportation Company, or the DKT. Jacob had helped work on the piers and told Karen they were rapidly becoming first rate. The town was bound for popularity and wealth.

Of course, Dyea's sister city, Skagway, already had a decent harbor and soon they would have a railroad, as well, thanks to some Englishman's ingenuity. Karen frowned, but not because of Skagway's vast improvements. Thoughts of Skagway only served to bring unpleasant contemplations of Martin Paxton. Karen had tried her best not to think of him at all, knowing that even speaking his name made her blood run cold and her temper run hot.

"Yahoo!" The cry of exuberance came from one of the gambling halls as Karen came ever closer to the harbor. Day or night you could always find someone drinking or playing any number of games. Mostly it was naïve newcomers, cheechakos, those poor undaunted souls who had no idea what they were in for.

Having suffered an Alaskan winter, Karen was now considered a sourdough. She was well respected by the other more permanent residents of Dyea, earning her right to be among them. The thought turned bitter in her heart, however. She hadn't come here to earn rights or achieve titles. She had come to find her father—to join him—maybe even help in his ministry. Instead, she had come too late. Her father was dead, and so too her dream of working with him.

Gunfire rang out, along with laughter, screams, and the unmistakable sounds of fighting. Karen glanced ahead, cautiously watching in case a body were to be thrown out into the streets from the Lazy Dog Saloon. She passed quickly and unscathed, nevertheless glancing over her shoulder just in case something or someone came at her from behind. It was certainly no town to raise children in, and because she was caring for Jacob and Leah, her thoughts ran constantly to their welfare. She had no idea what would be best for them. Ideally, their father should have made those decisions, but Bill Barringer had selfishly headed north, deserting his family to Karen's care. And while Karen could admit that the children were probably better off with her than climbing over the golden stairs of the Chilkoot Pass, she fretted that she would somehow make a mess of their lives.

I suppose if I allow myself to stay angry all the time, she mused, *I won't be much good to them at all.* But even as she recognized the truth in her thoughts, Karen pushed it aside to acknowledge her growing desire for revenge. Paxton couldn't be allowed to go unpunished. He had long taken things into his own hands, and it was time someone stopped him. Karen knew she didn't have the ability to stop him on her own. That was why she had to enlist Peter's help. Peter would understand and help her to see that justice was done. Justice or revenge.

The shallow waters that reached the shores of Dyea were not suited for ship traffic. In the early days, boats would harbor quite a distance from shore, then small launch boats or Tlingit canoes would bring their freight to dry land. The new docks and wharves were making the task much easier, but their length required a considerable haul to bring the goods into town. It had made more than one sea captain give up the idea of docking in Dyea. And it was for this reason that Skagway seemed much more likely to succeed. Karen didn't care either way. She didn't plan to stay forever in Dyea, nor move to Skagway. In fact, her life was so topsy-turvy at this point that she really had no idea where to head.

I don't belong anywhere, she thought. *I don't belong to any place or to any person.* The loneliness of this thought was more chilling than the breezy April air.

"Watch yar step there, missy," a gruff-looking stranger said as Karen scooted past him on the docks. "Them are slippery ways."

Karen could see for herself that the docks were wet, and she slowed her steps to heed the man's warning. "Can you tell me if Captain Colton of the ship *Merry Maid* has come ashore?"

The man pulled off his wool cap and scratched his filthy head. His expression suggested his intent consideration of her question. "I kint say that I've seen him."

She nodded. "Thank you. I'll just press on."

He grunted, pulled his cap back on, and went back to his work. Karen scanned the wharves looking for any sign of Peter. She knew he would be there, for he always came ashore ahead of his freight. Even now, she could see that *Merry Maid* was being unloaded.

Soon her efforts were rewarded. She spotted Peter as he pressed through a crowd of heavily laden men. People were everywhere and so were their goods. Stacks of possessions, caches for the trip north, were guarded warily by rosy-cheeked boys who had no idea of what the days to come would bring. Some strutted around the docks as if they'd already discovered gold. Others were so eager to continue their journey that they worked at an exhausting pace. Karen felt sorry for them. Few were dressed for the north. Their lightweight coats and boots were no match for the blizzards of the Chilkoot. When she worked the store, Karen had tried to convince those poor souls coming in for goods that they'd need to buy heavier coats and snow gear. Sometimes they'd listened, but more often they'd ignored her. She'd given up trying after a time, and unless someone asked her opinion, she'd sell them only what they asked for. They'd learn soon enough that this was only the beginning of a lengthy and possibly deadly journey. No sense in wearing herself out trying to convince them of things they would blindly ignore.

"Peter Colton!" Karen called as a sea of people threatened to send her back up the wharf and onto the sandy shore. She reached out, waving her arms.

"What are you doing here?" Peter questioned. He pushed through the crowd to take hold of her arm. "It's sheer madness out here. You know it's always like this when the ships come to dock."

"I know, but I had to talk to you before you attempted to deliver goods to the store."

"Attempted?" Peter asked, raising a brow. "What's this all about?"

"There's been a fire," Karen said, seeing no reason to play out the telling of her tale.

"The store?"

She nodded. "Burned to the ground. We lost everything."

Karen could see his confusion and shock. Putting her hand on his arm she added, "The Barringer children and I managed to escape, thanks to Adrik Ivankov. But Aunt Doris didn't make it. She succumbed before reaching the door. I thought she was right behind me—in fact, I thought I had hold of her arm. I had her blanket and nothing more."

This news brought Peter from his stunned reverie. He looked at her with such tenderness that Karen knew his sorrow was sincere. "Miss Pierce is dead? I'm so sorry. I truly liked your aunt."

"It's been hard to imagine life without her—to look toward the future—but it seems the days are passing, the sun still rises and sets, and the ships still dock, bringing us boat-loads of people."

Peter nodded. "There's no sign of it slowing down, either. I had to turn people away in Seattle." He glanced across the madness, then suggested they go somewhere else to talk.

"The Glacier Restaurant looks swamped with newcomers," Karen observed. "Why don't we head over to the Pacific Hotel? They're boasting chicken and dumplings for lunch. The *North Star* came in yesterday with crates of chickens and fresh eggs. They sold for incredible prices."

"I can well imagine," Peter replied. "The Pacific sounds acceptable, and quite frankly, I'm famished."

They wove their way through the excited crowd, saying nothing as if by some mutual agreement. Karen realized that once they were alone, she would have to explain her theory about Paxton. Adrik's words of warning came back to haunt her. What if Paxton were an innocent bystander? What if he were merely gloating at their misfortune? But that just couldn't be true.

The Pacific Hotel was nothing elaborate. Built nearly over-night from plank boards and sheer gumption, it could accom-modate at least three hundred guests. Of course, most of those would find little other than a place to spread their blanket, but it nevertheless got them in out of the elements.

Peter found a small table and pulled out the chair for Karen. Considering her words carefully, Karen decided to ig-nore her pang of conscience. Without delay she leaned for-ward and explained what was on her mind.

"I think Martin Paxton was responsible for the fire."

Peter stared at her blankly, and for a moment Karen

thought he hadn't heard her. "I said—" she began again.

"I heard what you said," he growled and slammed his cap down on the table. "What makes you think this?"

"It was after Adrik had helped us from the burning building," Karen said softly. "I was standing there crying, and I looked up and gazed across the alleyway. He was there."

"Paxton?"

Karen saw the look of disbelief on Peter's face. "Yes! It was Paxton. Not only was he there—after all, half the town had come by this time—but it was the manner in which he conducted himself. He stared at me smugly and then tipped his hat as if to say, 'How do you like my handiwork?' That was when I felt confident that he was responsible. After all, he lives in Skagway, not Dyea. Why would he even be here in the middle of the night unless it was for something underhanded?"

Peter studied the table in silence. He ignored the aproned matron who plunked down two steaming bowls of dumplings.

"What are you drinking?" she asked in a tone that suggested she had little time for dallying.

"Leave us alone!" Peter demanded. "And take this away."

"Well, if you're gonna sit in this restaurant, you're gonna have to pay."

Peter dug into his pocket and threw several coins onto the table. "There. Leave the food and take your money."

The woman smiled, displaying her lack of front teeth. "Sure now, luv. You just stake your claim here and let me know when you strike it rich." She laughed as if terribly amused with herself, then grabbed the coins, worth three times the price of the dumplings, and tucked them down her blouse.

Karen threw her an irritated glare, hoping the woman

would speed up her retreat, but her action only made the woman laugh all the more.

"Where is Paxton now?" Peter asked, ignoring the woman.

"I don't know. I presume back in Skagway. Peter, I know this may sound ridiculous. After all, I have no proof. But I feel confident that he's guilty. You don't know him like I do. You know him from your father's stories of Paxton as a boy. I know him from the torment he put upon Grace."

"Grace would have me forgive him," Peter said angrily. "As if that animal deserved anything but the end of a gun."

"Grace is only trying to be a good Christian," Karen said with a shrug. "But even good Christians have their limits. Martin Paxton is evil. Plain and simple. He has caused us more problems than I can even begin to name. I have no desire to let this go unpunished."

"What about the law? Did anyone see anything?"

"Apparently not. Adrik thinks a lantern was thrown through the front window, for we found a lantern in the debris."

"But no one heard that happen? No one heard the glass shatter?"

Karen thought of the noisy nights in the small town. Gold fever combined with cabin fever made for a brand of rowdiness that could only be called chaotic, at best. Windows were often broken, in spite of the cost to replace them. Wars were waged on a nightly basis between those who felt they'd been cheated out of something they'd brought to the shores of Alaska and those who sought to relieve them of their possessions.

"I'm afraid many folks might well have heard the glass break, but they would have given it no further thought. Arson is such an unthinkable act that I'm sure no one would ever have suspected such a thing."

"But such a thing happened and it destroyed my livelihood with it. Not to mention it took the life of your aunt." Peter's face contorted in rage. "This is what Grace cannot understand. Her religious notions matter very little to men like Paxton. She believes the world to be a place of love and second chances."

"In all truth, I believe that, too," Karen murmured softly. "At least I used to."

Peter stared at her for a moment. "It doesn't take much to open your eyes if you're willing to see things for what they are. I find that religion clouds a man's judgment of what's real and what's illusion."

"And what is real?" Karen questioned, feeling a desperate need to understand. "Just when I think I have a clear understanding of that, it somehow seems to elude me."

"What's real is the ugliness and evil of some men. They will stop at nothing." His voice lowered in a menacing manner, chilling Karen with the hatred that rang clear in his next statement. "Death is the only way to keep them from causing more harm."

Karen shivered. "What are you suggesting?"

"Retribution," Peter stated flatly. "I suggest we find Paxton and exact our revenge."

"But what if he isn't guilty?"

"He's guilty. If not of the fire, then of much else."

Karen saw a blatant hatred in Peter's eyes that gave her reason to fear. He was serious. He meant every word. He had no qualms about seeing Paxton dead. There was a part of her that found his words intriguing, but there was a greater part of her that cautioned her to forget the scheme, to return to her faith and let God deal with the sordid details of her life.

"I think we should move with caution and consideration," she finally managed to say. "Paxton is revered in Skagway. People believe he's quite beneficial to their community." She remembered Adrik's words as if he'd just spoken them. "We can't just rush in with accusations and no way to prove his guilt."

"I don't plan to rush in with accusations," Peter said, meeting her gaze.

Karen saw a coldness in his eyes that reminded her of Martin Paxton. The lifelessness of it frightened her. Perhaps she had said too much—encouraged too much.

"Peter, this is very serious. You must remember Grace."

"Grace doesn't care about me. She's driven a wedge between me and my family. Taking care of Martin Paxton will return respect to me—at least in the eyes of my family."

"But it may destroy Grace's trust, her feelings for you," Karen countered.

"Those feelings are already destroyed," Peter said, refusing to look away. "Grace cares only for her God and nothing for me."

"I find that hard to believe. She's loved you from almost the very first moment you met. I can't believe she would put those feelings aside simply because you have differences of opinion where religion is concerned."

"Well, believe it." He narrowed his eyes and his tone took on an accusing nature. "I suppose you will defend her now— take her side?"

Karen realized that in order to see Paxton punished for what he'd done, she'd have to align herself with Peter. But in order to do that, she would have to put aside her friendship with Grace.

But Grace wasn't here. No one was here. Karen was left alone to fight her battles.

I will not fail thee, nor forsake thee. The verse of Scripture seemed to speak from her soul, reminding her of God's constant faithfulness.

But if you truly cared, Karen thought, *you'd never have allowed us to suffer so much.* Her anger resurfaced as she thought of the fire and of her aunt's death. She wanted revenge. She needed revenge.

"Grace is wrong," Karen finally said. She felt torn, as if she'd just put an end to something very special, but now that the words were out of her mouth, she couldn't take them back. Worse still, she didn't want to.

—{ C H A P T E R   S E V E N }—

ADRIK IVANKOV FOUND himself the voice of reason in a vast sea of gold-hungry travelers. The only trouble was, no one wanted a voice of reason. Gold fever made men do things they'd never otherwise consider. Adrik had seen grown men climb the trail with broken limbs and raging fevers. He'd also seen them die far from the goal that had brought them so far.

For over a week, Adrik worked alongside his Tlingit friends to pack goods from the Scales up to the summit. The Scales were so named because it was there the packers re-weighed the goods they were packing and increased their fees in accordance with the steep climb to the top of the Chilkoot Trail. Adrik found the extra money he earned transporting goods a much surer guarantee than looking for gold in the ground. He had saved an impressive amount of money, even while sharing much that he had with his friends and Tlingit relatives.

Money wasn't everything. In fact, Adrik had rarely even considered the stuff over the last week. His thoughts were more easily assigned to a pretty woman living in Dyea. Karen Pierce was more than just a pretty woman to him, however. She was the daughter of a man he greatly respected—a man whose death he felt somewhat responsible for.

"We're quitting," Dyea Joe said, releasing the pack frame he used for carrying goods.

The announcement didn't surprise Adrik. For the last two days the sky had been devoid of clouds, and with the sun bearing down on them in its April splendor, a new problem had arisen. Adrik's sense of the situation was confirmed as he listened to his friends speak out.

"Snows are very dangerous," one Indian told him.

"There's gonna be slides," another muttered. "Ain't gonna stay up here. Goin' back down."

Adrik nodded. He knew as well as his friends did that the trails were threatened by avalanches. The warm temperatures were making the newer snows less stable.

"I've tried to explain the situation to our rather ignorant—perhaps shortsighted—employers," Adrik told the men, "but they don't care. The fever has them and gold is all they can think on. Safety means nothing."

"We won't pack their goods," Joe announced to his friend. "Money isn't worth a life."

"I agree," Adrik said in a tone of exasperation. "I don't blame you for sitting this out. I'm not risking my life, either. The next few days are going to prove the situation one way or another. Look, it's Saturday night. Why don't we put our lots together and feast. We'll let the cheechakos figure this one out for themselves."

Dyea Joe nodded and picked up his things. "There's gonna be big trouble if they keep climbing to the summit."

"Plenty big," another man joined in.

Adrik knew the risks. Already the weather was chainging. As was typical of the area, the changes came quickly and dramatically. Heavy clouds had moved across the sky to blot out the sun. He could only nod and lend his silence to signal his agreement. Adrik greatly admired their knowledge of the land and their seeming sixth sense for danger. He had worked hard to learn from them, to take their bits of wisdom and use them to better his own existence. Now, as he tried to share such wisdom with others, he was met with disbelief and total disregard.

No one cared that the threat of an avalanche was so great that the Tlingits not only refused to move goods up to the Scales, they were heading well out of the established gathering and down to Sheep Camp. Adrik was moving as well. He knew their advice to be sound, and he cherished his life too much to risk it in pride or greed. Sheep Camp sat in the narrow valley between impressive mountains. The canyon offered no real place of escape, as was evidenced in earlier floods of Sheep Camp. But if the snowslides came from the summit, almost three thousand feet above them, they'd most likely not cause problems that far down the trail. He hoped.

Gathering his tent and a few supplies, Adrik followed the small group down the trail. The going was tough because the snow had started up again and the wind blew bitterly against their faces. Adrik didn't mind the hard climbs and descents, but he generally refused to travel when the weather was difficult. The heavy clouds stole the light from their path, and as night came upon them, Adrik was more than ready to pitch his tent and take his rest. The lantern light from the Seattle and Golden Gate restaurants perked up his spirits. He didn't plan to pay the exorbitant price for a meal there, but the light meant civilization and the end of his journey.

As if they'd prearranged the setting, the Tlingits and Adrik worked to put the camp in order beside the Taiya River. Soon a blazing fire warded off the night's worries and the chill. Sheltered among the fir, pine, and aspen, the winds and snows seemed less threatening. Adrik ate heartily, grateful for the dried reindeer meat and beans offered to him by Dyea Joe. Canned peaches were passed around the camp, and Adrik lanced a half peach with his knife and stuffed it into his mouth. The juice was icy cold and trickled down his face into the stubble of a newly growing beard, but nothing had ever tasted better.

"Say, I've got some biscuits left over from morning," Adrik suddenly remembered. Unwrapping a bundle from his coat pocket he added, "They're soaked in bacon grease and ought to warm up nice." He skewered several of the hard biscuits on a branch and held them out over the fire. The grease began to melt and popped and sizzled on the flaming logs. The aroma filled the air with an anticipated promise of filling their bellies.

"How is your mother?" Adrik asked Dyea Joe. The two were distant relatives. Joe's mother was in fact second cousin to Adrik's now deceased grandmother, and their families had always been close.

"She is well. She does not like the fuss over gold." Dyea Joe's English bore witness to his forced attendance at mission schools.

"I doubt any Tlingit or First Nations people are going to find the rush very appealing," Adrik said, shaking his head.

"The cheechakos are ruining the land. They run right for the gold, never seeing how priceless the land itself is."

"You speak the truth." Dyea Joe's dark eyes seemed to glow in the light of the fire. "People often throw away the gold in their hands for the promise of the gold hidden from them."

"Amen."

Adrik pulled the browned biscuits from the fire and pushed them from the stick onto a pie tin. "Help yourself," he said, passing the tin to Joe.

The tin circulated around the fire, the biscuits being taken up quickly by the hungry Tlingit packers. Adrik took the last biscuit and leaned back on his elbow to enjoy the rest of his meal. Thoughts of tragedy and mishaps from the trail threatened to put a damper on his mood. Determined to raise his spirits, he pushed aside the threat of snowslides and instead thought of Karen Pierce.

But thinking of Karen caused Adrik to think of her losses, and again his thoughts turned bleak. First her mother had passed on long before Karen had come north. Then her father had died with only a narrow distance separating them. Her friend had married and moved away, and now Karen had lost her aunt and her livelihood, as well.

Adrik knew, however, that it was the death of her father that gave Karen the most sorrow. She had been so close to reuniting with him. She had felt called to come north—perhaps to even work at her father's side—and now she was robbed of both seeing him and working with him. And a deep loss it was. Not only for her, but for the people who had come to care so much for her father. Including Adrik.

Adrik held the highest regard for Wilmont Pierce. The man had been both a good friend and mentor. Adrik had guided Pierce on more than one occasion and had been instrumental in seeing that he was accepted among the Indian people. Wilmont had been different from other missionaries. He had come in love and kindness, seeking to meet the people where they were. He lived with them, ate with them, and studied their ways to better understand them. This gave the Tlingit respect for Pierce, and although many of the Tlingit were already baptized into Russian Orthodoxy, they embraced Wilmont's preaching. In time, Adrik had even seen a change in the hearts of many of the natives.

"Hello, camp!" came a decidedly British voice.

Adrik looked up to find a shivering man, hardly dressed warmly enough for the cold. "Come warm yourself by the fire, stranger."

"My gratitude, sir." The man hurried to the edge of the fire and held out his gloved hands. "The night came upon me unaware. I was sent back to bring hot food to our camp, but I'm afraid the restaurants are packed. There's scarcely room for even one more."

Adrik lifted the pot of coffee. "Would you like a cup?"

The man sat down on a thick log beside Adrik and nodded enthusiastically. "I would be very grateful. I'm not fond of American coffee, but at this point I'll take anything hot."

"Where you from, stranger?" Adrik asked, pouring coffee into a tin cup.

"London, England. I have family in the Canadian provinces. I was visiting there when all this news of gold came. We decided to give it a go. Make our fortunes. And you?"

Adrik thought him a very amicable sort and smiled. "I've lived in these parts all of my life." He handed the man the coffee and saw a smile of satisfaction as the stranger wrapped his fingers around the warmth of the cup.

"How marvelous." He drank for a moment, then added,

"I suppose you already have a gold mine?"

Adrik laughed. "No. I'd say my people found more gold in salmon fishing and furs."

Dyea Joe passed by in silence, dropped a small package beside Adrik, and entered the tent directly behind the stranger. This drew the man's attention immediately. "Are these your packers? We hired a few, but the cost was draining our funds and there are still tariffs to pay."

"No. They're actually distant family members. And good friends." Adrik picked up the pack and unwrapped several pieces of dried salmon. Joe was offering the stranger food for himself and his companions. "This is jerked salmon. Eat some yourself and take the rest back to your friends."

The man nodded and snatched the offering quickly, as if Adrik might change his mind. Eating as though starved, the man alternated between sips of coffee and mouthfuls of jerky. When it was gone, he fidgeted nervously with his mustache, his gloved fingers pulling off pieces of ice that had become encrusted above his lip. For several moments Adrik actually wondered if he'd somehow offended the man. He seemed strangely quiet after having been so lively moments ago.

The stranger took a deep, long drink, then turned to Adrik. "So you trust these Tlingits?"

"With my life," Adrik replied.

"Our packers told us to stay away from the Scales and the summit. Said the snow is unstable. What do you make of that?"

"I make it as the truth, mister. That's the reason we're camped here. The weather has been too varied. We had a fierce snowstorm a few days back, then an icy rain. Then it dumped another few feet of snow. After that it warmed up, melting things a bit. It makes the snow on the mountains unstable. Slides are guaranteed."

As if to emphasize Adrik's words, a rumbling could be heard in the distance. It didn't last long, but Adrik knew it was a slide. "You hear that? That's the sound of snow barreling down the mountain. You don't want to hear that sound and be in the path of it. There's nothing you can do to get out of its way."

The man stood, looking rather alarmed. "My family—my friends. They're up there now."

Adrik shook his head. "I can't tell you what to do, mister, but you'd do well to get them back down in this direction. It's only the second of April. There's plenty of time to get north. I wouldn't start back up until the Tlingits do likewise. They're pretty good about figuring these things out."

Another rumble sounded, and even though Adrik knew these small slides were probably not stealing away life in the night, he also knew they were precursors of things to come.

"Thank you for your hospitality. I must go." He handed Adrik the cup and tipped his hat. "You were most kind."

Adrik saw the panic in the man's eyes. He understood his fear and could only pray that it might keep the younger man from death's clutches. Healthy fear had a way of doing that. If a person listened to that quiet little voice, a nudging of the Holy Spirit, Adrik's mother used to say, then a person could often avoid a great deal of misery. Adrik had tested that theory and knew it to be true.

With a yawn, Adrik gazed upward to the dark mountainsides before settling in for the night. The ominous sense of death surrounded him, leaving him uneasy. He began a wordless prayer, pleading with God for the protection of those who were exposed to danger. He also asked God's blessings on

Karen Pierce before he crawled into the tent and fell almost instantly asleep.

Around two in the morning a commotion awoke Adrik. He soon realized that the alarm announcing an avalanche was being sounded in the small village. Uncertain where the trouble was, Adrik pulled on his boots and coat to go in search of the problem and offer whatever help he could. Taking a lantern and a shovel, he made his way up the trail in the bitter cold and wind. Along the way, he heard tales of everything from the Scales camp being destroyed to there being little or no damage. Ignoring these conflicting stories, he pressed on up the trail and finally met up with a group of men with shovels.

"We're digging out at least a dozen people," one man told Adrik. "There may be more, but we saw a couple of parties headed through this direction. One man said there were at least twelve."

Adrik shook his head and took up a shovel. "We might as well get to work," he said, eyeing the ominous mound of snow and debris.

Twenty people were eventually rescued. The workers laughed and slapped each other on the back while the injured were treated to warm beds and strong coffee. The mountain had failed to claim their lives and so the folks were generally celebratory, having defeated the slide.

Adrik, however, was more apprehensive. He studied the dark shadows of Long Hill and stared upward toward the summit. Snow swirled around him, gentle and harmless. It was hard to imagine that such a thing could be so deadly.

The next morning there was talk of how they'd escaped the perils of the mountain. How things would be easier now that the threat of avalanche had passed. Adrik reminded more than one person that the Tlingits were still not convinced of a safe passage, and since they'd been the ones to warn of the situation in the first place, perhaps they should be heeded now. But folks generally ignored his suggestion.

Then around nine-thirty the slides began again. Word came down from the Scales that they were shutting the operation down and evacuating the camp. Adrik breathed a sigh of relief. Perhaps now they would avoid real disaster.

Around ten o'clock a low rumbling came from Long Hill, signaling yet another slide. Adrik shook his head as word came back that three people had been buried in their tents. He thought of the young Englishman and wondered if he'd convinced his party to bed down in Sheep Camp for the night.

With the evacuation of the Scales came the tram workers. The tram had been set up to assist those gold rushers who had extra money to spend. The tram owners were making a bundle, much to the disappointment of the natives who had found packing for the stampeders to be small compensation for the white man stealing their trail. They didn't mind Adrik working the line, for he often gave generously to their people, but they resented the intrusion of men from the outside. So, with this thought well etched in their minds, the Tlingits had little comment when the tram workers were caught in yet a second avalanche and killed. After all, they had warned them.

Now people were staring warily up the mountain, watching and wondering. Because the wind had picked up as well as the snow, visibility was near zero. Adrik sensed the impending disaster, but knew he was helpless to stop it. Through a combination of God's grace and wisdom along with his knowledge of the land, he was standing safe and protected, while others would meet their death.

And then it happened. The roar echoed and vibrated

against the mountainsides. The very earth seemed to move as a wall of snow poured down from the mountains above. Would-be rescuers could only wonder and wait, having no idea how bad the situation might be. Had there been others on the trail? Had they met their match in this devastating play of nature?

Adrik felt certain there would be trouble. He loaded up what he could carry and grabbed his shovel. There was work to do.

Rumors ran rampant. Announcements of two hundred or more dead filtered down the trail. Gunshots were fired off to signal the need for help. The stampeders were more than generous with their offering. They came in droves, responding in a way indicative of the frozen north. You helped your brother in his need, because next time it could just as easily be you.

Adrik dug in and worked along a line where the trail had once been. Someone said that the remaining two hundred people on the Scales had been making their way down the mountain. One man claimed to have been at the end of the line holding on to a rope that simply seemed to disappear as the snows assaulted them from every side.

Bodies, some battered beyond recognition, were lined up and transported down the trail to Sheep Camp, where a makeshift morgue was set up in a donated tent. An emergency committee was appointed for the task of identifying and tagging each body for burial or shipping.

Adrik shook his head at the loss of life. They'd been warned, but greed had kept them fearlessly ensconced in the path of danger.

"Here's another one!" someone yelled.

Adrik looked up to find the Englishman from the night before. He sighed. The man was dead. Shaking his head, he went back to work only to unbury another body.

"I've got one, too," he called out.

People came to help him dig out the man who surprised them all by moving his lips and fluttering his eyes. When he opened them, he stared up at Adrik as if he were God himself.

"He—he—lp me," the man stammered. Blood streamed from his face, which was crusted from the ice and snow in his beard and mustache.

"We're doing the best we can for you, mister," Adrik told him. "Look, just lie still. You'll be taken to Sheep Camp where there's a doctor." Even saying it, however, Adrik knew the man would never make it. The left side of his face had been crushed.

The man closed his eyes, then opened them again. Adrik could see he was laboring to breathe—to live. With a power that seemed beyond the man, Adrik watched him struggle to reach his coat pocket. Realizing the man would not be settled, Adrik moved his hand aside and reached into the pocket with his own gloved hand. He pulled out the contents: a pouch of tobacco, a pipe, and a folded piece of paper.

"Letter," the man mumbled. "Children."

Adrik looked at the possessions, not understanding. "You have children at Sheep Camp?" he finally questioned.

"No," the man replied.

The workers were ready to move the man to a plank for transport down the trail. Adrik held his hand up. "Wait just a minute. He's trying to tell me something."

"He needs attention," one surly man replied.

"You think I don't know that?" Adrik snapped. Turning to the dying man, he said, "Look, friend, I don't know what you're trying to tell me."

The man looked up at Adrik with lifeless eyes. "Letter to

children." With that he closed his eyes and stopped breathing.

"He's gone," the surly man announced. "Take him to the morgue."

Adrik looked at the dead man and then to the letter in his hand. Stuffing the pouch and pipe into his own pocket, Adrik opened the letter.

1898, 2nd of April.
Jacob and Leah Barringer, in care of Miss Karen Pierce, lately of Dyea.

The very breath left his lungs, and Adrik found himself almost gasping for air. Was it possible? Was the dead man Bill Barringer? "Wait!" he called. "I might know who that fellow is."

The workers paused. "Friend of yours?"

"Not exactly." He stuffed the letter into his pocket. Taking a better look at the dead man, Adrik scratched his jaw. It could be Barringer. He'd only met him twice, though, and there had been so many other men just like him.

"I'll take him down." Adrik could only pray the man wasn't Barringer.

He grabbed the end of the plank from the man who held it. "You can borrow my shovel. Name's Adrik Ivankov. Nearly everybody in Sheep Camp knows me. You can leave my shovel at the Summit Meat Market. They know me real well."

The man said nothing. He seemed surprised by Adrik's rapid instructions. Adrik motioned to the man on the other end of the plank. "Let's go." He couldn't help but think that he would once again bear bad tidings to Karen Pierce. It wasn't a job he wanted, but obviously God had given it to him for a reason.

—| C H A P T E R   E I G H T |—

KAREN WIPED HER HANDS on her apron and looked out the kitchen window of the Gold Nugget's kitchen. Steam fogged the windows on the inside, while ice frosted them on the outside. It was useless to try and see out.

"Fretting ain't gonna bring them here any faster," Mrs. Neal chided. The older woman dumped a huge wooden bowl filled with bread dough on the floured counter top. "Workin' will keep your mind off the rumors. I'm sure that Mr. Ivankov and Mr. Barringer are just fine."

Karen pushed her hands into the dough and began to mechanically knead the mass. "I just want to know if the slide was as bad as people are saying. That last guy said over three hundred people are dead." She fell silent, an image of Adrik Ivankov coming to mind.

"Adrik might be up there," she murmured, trying hard not

to sound worried. "But I doubt Bill would be. After all, he left us before Christmas. He might have gotten held up by the weather, though."

"Now, then, the world is full of might be's," Mrs. Neal chided. "No sense frettin' until you know something for sure."

"I know you're right, but I can't help it. I've had nothing but trouble since coming north. I don't know that I can bear losing anyone else." Karen's voice broke as she pushed the dough aside. "I need a breath of air."

Wiping her hands on her apron, Karen turned and grabbed her shawl. "I'm going to check on Leah." She left the aromas of the Gold Nugget kitchen behind and stepped out into the yard behind the building where Leah Barringer was supposed to be splitting wood. Leah was nowhere in sight, however.

The wind whipped up the edges of the shawl, causing Karen to tighten her hold. Spring thaw wouldn't come for at least another month or two, and the elements were rising up just to make themselves known. Karen sighed, silently longing for warm weather. Looking down the alley to see if Leah might have gone visiting with one of the neighboring proprietors or their help, Karen found the place surprisingly deserted.

Karen felt her pulse quicken. Only the day before the fire, Leah had been the center of some much undesired attention. Drunken miners had thought her rather pretty and accosted her on her walk from church to the store. Karen and Jacob had been delayed at the church, helping to organize plans for Easter. When they came upon Leah, backed against a wall with smelly, dirty men on all sides of her, Jacob and Karen were livid. Karen could only hope they weren't repeating the scene.

Heading down the alley, Karen called to the girl. "Leah! Leah, where are you?"

She heard the girl crying before she spotted her hiding behind a stack of crates. "What's wrong?" Karen questioned, kneeling in the mud beside Leah. The cold muck seeped through her layers of skirt, petticoat, and woolen hose. "Are you hurt? Has someone bothered you?"

"No," Leah sobbed. "I'm just scared."

"What are you scared about?"

"Papa." The single word needed no further explanation.

Karen reached out and lovingly touched the girl's cold cheek. "I know you're worried about your father, but we haven't heard anything that would indicate he was in the avalanche. Besides, you know how rumors are. Things are seldom as bad as they seem."

"But I feel it here," Leah said, pointing to her heart. "I just know Papa's in trouble—that he's hurt."

"You can't know that," Karen said, trying her best to sound convincing. She wasn't about to tell the girl of her own concerns. "Don't borrow trouble. Besides, your papa should be well on his way north."

"Karen, is God mad at us?"

Taken aback, Karen cleared her throat nervously. "Why would you ask that?"

Leah looked up, her dark brown curls falling in ringlets to frame her face. Her blue eyes were huge, pleading with Karen for answers. "Mama used to say that sometimes bad things happened 'cause we didn't listen to God. 'Cause we had to have things our own way instead of His way. She said God sometimes let the bad things happen to get our attention 'cause we were ignoring Him. I'm thinking maybe God is mad and trying to get our attention."

Karen wasn't about to agree with Leah's conclusion. She wanted to keep her distance from God just now. It wasn't that she didn't want to maintain her childhood beliefs. And it wasn't that she was refuting His existence or supremacy, Karen told herself. She was just angry and nursing a grudge, and she couldn't do that and cozy up to God at the same time.

There was a part of her that already worried she'd somehow brought this disaster on them. God no doubt wanted her to see that He was still in charge—that He could further strip her of what was dear and precious. That He, as Leah put it, might be trying to get her attention.

"I know for a fact that God isn't mad at you, Leah," Karen said, feeling confident of that one thing. "Come on, let's get the wood inside, and we can go upstairs and clean up. You're no doubt soaked clear through. Mrs. Neal baked a fresh batch of cinnamon rolls, and I know she'd spare one for you."

Karen got to her feet and reached out to help pull Leah up. The last thing she wanted to do was get involved in a discussion about God.

"I'm thinking we'll both feel better when we get some official word on what's happened. In the meantime, we need to keep a positive heart."

"I know Papa loves God," Leah whispered. "I know he loves me and Jacob, too." She said it in such a way that Karen believed the girl was desperate for affirmation.

"I know he loves you, too," Karen replied, putting her arm around Leah's shoulders. "He loved you enough to protect you from the worst of the trip and wait until he could send for you in a comfortable fashion. He just wanted to keep you safe."

Leah looked up and smiled. "I'm glad you were here to stay with us. I love you, Karen. I wish I could have had a sister just like you."

Karen hugged her close. "I'm happy to be a sister to you

now, Leah. I'll always be here for you and Jacob."

"Just like God," Leah said, smiling.

"Yes, just like God," Karen said, the words turning bitter in her mouth.

The afternoon brought more news of the Palm Sunday avalanche. Karen cringed as packers and would-be miners flooded into the Gold Nugget Restaurant with stories of the tragedy.

"We dug out bodies all day," one man said between bites of Mrs. Neal's dumplings. "Never seen nothin' like it. Don't plan to see nothin' like it again. I'm headin' back to Texas. No gold is worth this."

Karen listened to the stories as she helped Mrs. Neal serve the various customers. She finally worked up her courage and asked one particularly knowledgeable man if he knew exactly how many people had died.

The man scratched his ragged-looking beard. "I heard it said at least seventy. At first they was afeared it might be a couple hundred. The folks at the Scales were mighty slow in comin' down that mountain. There was still a few hundred up there, and we figured 'em all to be goners. Happy to be proven wrong."

Karen nodded. Seventy dead was still a high number. "How soon will they know who all was involved?"

"They been identifying bodies since the slide. Should have some of the bodies back here by the end of the day. Heard tell they was gonna make a cemetery just northwest of Dyea. There's already some folks over there lighting big bonfires to warm up the ground enough to dig."

Karen left the man to his meal and went to wait on the

new group of men just coming into the dining hall.

"We've got a few places at that far table," she announced, not realizing until she came to the last man that she was staring into the face of Adrik Ivankov. "You're all right!" She surprised the entire group by throwing her arms around Adrik and breaking into tears. "I thought you might be dead."

She pulled away and found Adrik staring at her in dumbfounded silence. "Sorry," she whispered. "Guess that was rather uncalled-for. It's just with the rumors of the avalanche and all, I was starting to get overly worried."

Adrik said nothing but pulled her back toward the front door. "We've gotta talk. The news isn't good."

"But of course it's good. You weren't killed in the slide." Karen didn't want to hear anything more about the slide. She was afraid of what news Adrik might share.

"Maybe not, but others weren't as fortunate."

"I know," Karen said, nervously letting go of Adrik. "I just heard that some seventy people are dead. Is that true?"

"At least seventy. They're still not sure if they've found everyone."

"How awful. Were you in the middle of it?"

Adrik shook his head. "Not when the slides came. I'd been earning a bit of money with Dyea Joe and his family. We decided the snows weren't safe and moved back to Sheep Camp. We tried to convince other folks to move back with us, but they wouldn't hear it. Now they paid for their greed with their lives."

"I'm so glad you were sensible. We've been worried sick." She paused and looked down at the well-worn rag rug. "Look, I know I said some things—that I wasn't very hospitable . . ."

"Never mind. I knew the grief was making you say things you didn't mean." Adrik's expression softened from worry to sympathy. "Karen, there's something else you need to see."

"What?"

He reached into his pocket and pulled out a letter. "I was given this by a dying man."

Karen looked at him quizzically. "Why do I need to see this?"

"Just open it."

Karen shrank away as a strange foreboding gripped her. Fear crept up her spine and settled on her heart. Slowly she unfolded the paper and read. Glancing up to meet Adrik's eyes, Karen shook her head. "You said you took this from a dying man. Bill Barringer is dead?"

"I'm not sure," Adrik replied. "I was helping to dig out the victims of the slide and came upon a man who begged me to take this letter. He died shortly afterward. He was pretty banged up, his face crushed—probably he hit his head on rocks as the snow swept him down the mountain. I went with him to the morgue, but as you know, I only saw Bill a couple of times."

Karen felt her head begin to swim. Poor Leah. Poor Jacob. They were all alone now. Completely deserted and orphaned in the world. Adrik was speaking to her, but Karen couldn't hear the words. The only thing she heard was Leah's question, over and over in her head. *Is God mad at us?*

"Karen, why don't you sit down for a minute and rest?" Adrik took hold of her by the elbow and led her away from the front door and into Mrs. Neal's office.

"I can't believe this is happening. God must hate me." She let the letter fall to the floor. "I can't give them that. I can't take away their hope."

"You can't give them false hopes, either."

Karen shook her head. "You don't understand. If that man was Bill, then they're all alone."

"They still have you. You were just telling me before I left that you would stay with the kids no matter what."

"And I will," Karen replied firmly. "But it isn't the same and you know it." She looked deep into his eyes, feeling some small comfort from his closeness. "It just isn't the same."

"Yes, I know that. But I also know that having someone love and care for you, even someone who wasn't born to the task, is better than no one at all. Maybe it's even better." His words warmed her strangely. She felt drawn into his gaze as he continued to speak. "You love those kids even though you don't have to. No one would blame you if you ran in the opposite direction, but I know you won't."

Karen saw the sincerity of his words in his expression. He knelt beside her and handed her the letter. "You may be the only person left for them. You have to give them this and you have to be with them when they learn the truth."

"But we don't know for sure that it was Bill. People carry posts all the time for folks. Someone might have been coming down to one of the camps to pass the letter on."

"That could be true," Adrik said softly, "but then again, it might not be. You have to be ready for the worst."

"Seems like the worst is all I'm getting these days," Karen said, looking again at the letter. She raised her eyes to Adrik's. "This is a hateful land. Cruel and inhumane. My father must have been crazy to love it so."

Adrik shook his head and got back to his feet. "You'll learn in the by-and-by that land has no choice in the matter. It is what it is by God's design. People, however—now, people have a choice. *You* have a choice, Karen."

Karen deliberated long after Adrik left as to how she might break the news to Jacob and Leah. There was no easy way to tell them the truth. Then again, what was the truth? Had the dead man truly been Bill Barringer? Would it be cruel if she suggested he was dead, when their father might well be miles away in safety? Sitting in Mrs. Neal's tiny room, Karen longed to run as far away from Alaska as she could possibly go. Her heart urged her to pray, but in her weariness she rejected such comfort.

Nothing I do is going to change a thing. I can't bring the dead back to life, and I can't give those kids a reason to have hope any more than I can figure one out for myself.

She looked to the ceiling. "I suppose this is all my fault. Will you just keep stripping away the things I need? Will you take everyone—everything? Why not kill Martin Paxton instead of Bill Barringer?"

"Oh, here you are," Mrs. Neal announced as she entered the room. "I have a couple of folks who are looking for you."

Karen looked up and shook her head. "I don't feel like company right now. Who is it?"

"It's your friend Grace." Mrs. Neal smiled. "That ought to cheer you up."

Karen jumped to her feet. "Grace is here?"

"She sure is. Just outside by the front door. She's brought another gal with her. Pretty little thing with hair the color of brown sugar. Can't say I've ever seen her before, but I could be wrong."

"Could I talk to her here? I just got bad news about Bill Barringer."

"The kids' pa?"

Karen nodded. "Adrik thinks he died in the slide. He took a letter from a man, and it's addressed to Jacob and Leah. I need to tell the kids and give them this letter from their father, but I don't want to do it just yet."

Mrs. Neal, a softly rounded woman, put her arm around Karen's shoulder in motherly comfort. "You just stay right here and I'll get Grace. You'll need her now."

Karen knew the truth in that. She sorely missed Grace and her friendship. She wondered how Grace had found her here instead of at the burned-out remains of the store.

Mrs. Neal paused by the door. "I'll keep Leah busy, and if Jacob comes in from work, I'll see to him, as well."

"Thank you," Karen murmured, feeling a bit of peace return to her heart at the sight of her friend. It had been over three months since she'd last seen Grace. How marvelous that she should arrive at just this moment.

"Karen!" Grace called out, hurrying across the room. She wrapped her arms around Karen and hugged her tight. "Oh, I've just learned about the fire. How very awful for you. Are you all right?"

Karen pulled away. "How did you learn about it? Did Peter find you and tell you?"

Grace frowned. "I've not seen Peter since docking in Skagway. Miranda, Peter's sister, accompanied me here. Oh, goodness, Miranda!" Grace went back to the door and motioned for the woman. "Miranda, come meet my dear friend and mentor."

Karen easily recognized the resemblance between Peter and Miranda. Although Miranda's hair and eyes were darker, her chin and mouth were clearly the same. The woman smiled and extended a gloved hand. "I've heard so much about you, Miss Pierce. Grace speaks of you often."

Grace smiled. "The pleasures and joys of one's life deserve

special consideration. Karen has been both to me. Karen, this is Miranda Colton."

Karen shook the woman's hand. "Miss Colton."

"Please call me Miranda."

"Only if you call me Karen."

The woman laughed. "Oh, I shall, for I feel I already know you very well through Grace."

Karen seriously doubted that either Grace or Miranda knew her at this point. She felt only rage, anger, and now complete confusion. She would soon have to tell the Barringer children about their father and then decide what was to be done in order to see to their welfare.

Grace picked up the conversation. "We went first to the store only to find it gone. Whatever happened?"

"Paxton."

Grace raised her brows. "Martin Paxton?"

"The very same. He burned down the store and killed Aunt Doris."

"What? Doris has passed on?"

Karen saw the pain in Grace's expression. She touched her friend's arm to offer comfort. "Adrik Ivankov woke us. He saved the rest of us—the Barringer children. I thought Aunt Doris was with me, but I only had hold of her blanket. The smoke had overcome her and she collapsed. Adrik went in after her, but . . ." She paused, trying to keep her voice from breaking. Taking a deep breath, Karen changed the subject. "But what of you? How is it that you're here? Aren't you worried about Martin Paxton?"

"I don't think he'll bother me now. I'm married. He knows he's lost."

"He knows nothing," Karen said, walking back to the wooden chair. Angrily she plopped down, not even caring that she had done so in a most unladylike manner. "Martin Paxton is to blame for the fire. He's promised to make all of us pay. He managed part of that threat with the fire."

"But how do you know it was Mr. Paxton?" Grace asked in grave concern.

"I saw him at the fire. He was watching us as we came out of the building. He smiled at me, Grace. Smiled that smug, ridiculous smile."

"That doesn't mean he actually set the fire," Grace protested.

"I suppose you would just forgive him even if he stood there acknowledging the deed. Peter said that would be your attitude. He said you didn't understand that men like Paxton never change."

Grace stepped back and frowned. "Peter spoke against me?"

Karen saw Miranda take hold of Grace's arm. "Surely he wouldn't," Miranda stated.

"He didn't say it to speak against you, but merely to explain to me why you wouldn't be inclined to believe anything against Paxton."

"I know Mr. Paxton to be an evil man. You forget, I was the one who had to deal with him first," Grace said, anger tingeing her tone.

"I don't forget, but apparently you do. Peter said you wanted to send the man a letter of forgiveness. Why would you ever want to do that? You owe him nothing. He's the one who should apologize."

"But the Bible calls us to forgive our enemies and do good to those who wrong us," Grace protested. "You taught me that."

"I don't care. The man is evil and deserves to pay for what

he's done. The Bible is also full of examples where people were justly punished."

"That's true, and if Mr. Paxton started the fire, he should indeed pay," Grace replied. "But, Karen, what if you're wrong?"

"Do you have proof?" Miranda asked. "Proof that the authorities might recognize?"

"I know Paxton, and I know what he's capable of. It was the middle of the night, and he had no other reason to be here in Dyea. I feel no doubt whatsoever. He was responsible, and he must pay for what he's done."

"Just listen to you," Grace said, shaking her head. "You don't even sound like the Karen Pierce who taught me to trust God in matters of revenge."

Karen didn't take her upbraiding easily. She got to her feet, hands on her waist. "I'm not the same Karen Pierce. I've lost my mother, my father, and now Aunt Doris. I nearly lost my own life. Not only that, but I just got word that the Barringer children's father has most likely died in an avalanche. Please don't expect me to be the same woman. You went off to safety with Peter. Safety and love and comfort. You had no idea of Paxton's threats, and you have no idea how badly I want that man punished."

"But, Karen," Grace tried to reason, "it isn't our job to punish him. If you have proof, take the matter to the law. Better yet, take it to God. Vengeance belongs to Him."

"If I wait for God, it might never be taken care of." Grace's mouth dropped open in surprise, but still Karen wasn't moved. "I don't have much faith in what might be done to put an end to Martin Paxton's evil deeds."

"Sounds to me like you don't have much faith, period."

Karen looked hard at Grace. "I don't want to discuss my

faith or lack of it. I only want to see Paxton suffer as he's made others suffer. Peter understands me. Why can't you?"

Karen stormed from the room, knowing that she'd deeply wounded her friend. It hadn't been her intention. She had been happy to see Grace once again, but something in her gentle demeanor set Karen on edge. Something in her peaceful spirit forced Karen to think of the wall she'd put between herself and God. A wall that grew higher and deeper by the minute.

─┤ CHAPTER NINE ├─

"JACOB, LEAH, I NEED to talk to you upstairs," Karen said as soon as supper was finished. She didn't wait for either one to respond to her, but instead got up from the table and moved toward the back stairs just off the kitchen.

For a new building, the floors certainly creak a lot, she thought. With each step, the stairs seemed to groan, evidence of their shoddy carpentry. Karen didn't mind for once. She listened to the sound and heard her own heart in those wooden moans. She felt old and tired. How could it be that she had passed thirty years and had so very little to show for it? All of her girlhood friends were married with large families of their own. She was still single and cared for a dead man's children.

"This is about Pa, isn't it?" Jacob asked.

Karen waited until they were inside their room before she

spoke. "Mr. Ivankov brought back a letter."

"Then he's alive?" Leah asked with hope.

Karen met Jacob's fixed stare and knew she couldn't hold the truth from them any longer. "I don't know, quite honestly. Adrik found a man who resembled your father. He had this letter on him, but nothing else to identify him. The man had been battered by the avalanche, and Adrik had only seen your father on a couple of previous occasions."

Jacob said nothing, his face losing its color. His eyes refused to blink and he maintained his stoic gaze, while Leah cried out loud and threw herself onto the bed.

"No! He can't be dead!"

Karen handed the letter to Jacob and went to gather Leah in her arms. "I know this is hard. But, Leah, we don't know for sure that it was your father."

"I knew he was in trouble. I knew," Leah sobbed. "I told you, didn't I?"

"Yes, you did." Karen stroked the girl's hair as Leah buried her face against Karen's chest.

Karen watched Jacob as he read the letter. She knew the content, but she waited for him to say something about the message.

"Perhaps you could read the letter to Leah," Karen suggested.

Jacob looked up. "Let her read it herself." He threw the page at Karen. "Where's his body? I'll know if it's him. Even if nobody else can recognize him, I can."

Leah cried all the harder at this reminder, but Jacob refused to be moved. Karen could see the hardness in his eyes. He was walling himself in, just as she had.

"Why don't you talk to Mr. Ivankov about it?" Karen suggested. "I don't think this is the place or the time. I'll read the letter to Leah while you go find Adrik. He should be somewhere around the church. I heard him say he was helping to deliver supplies from the wharf."

Jacob, his blue eyes now damp with tears, licked his lips and pulled on his fur hat. Taking up his coat, he headed for the door.

"It won't be light for long," Karen called after him. "Don't be gone after dark. Things are getting more and more rowdy around here, and with the new load of stampeders, I wouldn't want you to get into any trouble."

"I'm not going to get into trouble," Jacob replied in a clipped tone.

He stalked from the room and slammed the door behind him. Karen felt as if her nerves had snapped with the crashing of the door. Tears came to her own eyes and without understanding why, she began to cry. It was as if all the pressures of the day began to overwhelm her all over again. Funny, she had never been given to tears prior to coming north. The long dark months of winter, the cold, the lawless greed, and the bad news that just seemed to keep coming ate away her final reserves of strength.

"Oh, Leah. I'm so sorry." Karen held the girl tight, needing comfort as much as the child did.

They cried for a time, then they just held each other as if the world had ended and they were the last ones to survive. Finally Karen spoke.

"I won't leave you," she whispered. "You don't have to be afraid of being alone. I won't let anything happen to you as long as I have breath in my body."

"But you might die, too," Leah said, straightening up to look Karen in the eye. "Everybody dies."

Karen couldn't argue that. "But while I'm here, I'll do

what I can to ensure you're fed and clothed and cared for. I just want you to know that."

Leah nodded. "Will you read the letter?"

Karen edged off the bed and picked the piece of paper up from the floor. The letter looked like it had been carried around for months, even though it was dated just yesterday. Why he had felt it necessary, Karen couldn't say. Perhaps he'd seen too much death along the trail. Hadn't Adrik told her of folks freezing to death within inches of the main path? Maybe Bill had seen this, as well.

Karen cleared her throat and took a seat on the corner of the bed. Leah wiped her eyes and moved close as Karen began to read.

"1898, 2nd of April.

Jacob and Leah Barringer, in care of Miss Karen Pierce, lately of Dyea.

Jacob and Leah,

I miss you more than I have words to say. You know I've never been a man for writing letters and such, but as time weighs heavy on my heart, I felt it necessary to send a post to you. The trail is hard and cold—there's never any real warmth. I'm glad you're safe back in Dyea. I seen a woman and child die yesterday from the cold. The woman's feet had froze 'cause she had no boots. Her man must have left her behind or got separated from her, but I kept thinking of you two and how even though I missed you, I'd done the right thing in leaving you behind. You might both hate me by now. I hope not. You might not understand, even with me telling you about the bad times on the trail, but I love you more than life. I'll come back for you, I promise.

Your father,
William Barringer"

Karen folded the letter and handed it to Leah. She waited for the girl to say something, anything. Leah took the letter and reread it to herself, then tucked it inside her blouse. She looked at Karen, her broken heart so clearly reflected in her eyes.

"If Pa is dead, they won't just leave him up there, will they, Karen?"

"No, honey, Adrik said they took the body to the morgue."

"Can we take some of the money and bury him all proper like? Can we order a stone with his name so folks won't forget who he was?"

Karen thought of her own father buried somewhere out in the middle of the wilderness. How comforting it might be to have him close by, to know she could go visit the grave as she did her mother's.

"Of course. We'll use all the money, if need be."

Leah nodded and lay back on the pillows. "Thank you. I knew you'd understand."

———

Jacob had no words for the way he was feeling. Responsibilities had come to him at a young age, and if his father were truly dead, the burden would be even greater.

"Mr. Ivankov!" Jacob called out as he climbed the church steps two at a time. "Are you in here?"

There was no answer. Jacob looked down the aisle to the podium where he'd heard the pastor preach on many a Sunday. He looked beyond the pulpit to where a cross had been nailed to the otherwise unadorned wall.

"I don't understand this at all," he said, knowing that somehow God would understand he was speaking to Him. "I don't see the sense in it. I don't know how this can be fixed."

"Some things can't be fixed," Adrik said as he came up from behind Jacob.

The boy turned to rest his eyes on the big man's sympathetic expression. He didn't feel like being strong and brave. He didn't feel like fighting or arguing. He simply wanted to be comforted. Falling to his knees, Jacob cried bitter tears.

"He shouldn't have gone. We needed him here. He shouldn't have gone."

Adrik knelt beside him. "I know, son. I know."

"I don't know why God is doing this to us."

"Why do you suppose it to be the way God wanted it?"

Jacob shook his head and wiped his nose with the back of his hand. "God is in charge of everything."

"Well, I do believe God is in charge. I believe He has power and authority over the universe," Adrik said. "But I also know God has given us free will to make choices and decisions for ourselves. He gave it to Adam and Eve in the Garden. Told them what they could do and what they shouldn't. Then He let them decide for themselves whether or not they'd obey. They chose to listen to other voices. Your pa did the same."

"My pa was a good man!" Jacob declared, glaring in anger at Adrik. "If you say he wasn't, I'll—"

"Whoa now, son, don't go getting riled. Everybody makes poor choices from time to time, and whether you like it or not, everybody sins against God. You know that as well as anybody."

Jacob continued to glare for a moment, then looked away and nodded. "But my pa was a good man. He was a Christian man, too."

"I'm glad he was. But Jacob, being a Christian doesn't mean you aren't going to make mistakes. It doesn't mean that bad things will never happen to you, even when you're doing the right and good thing. Why, I once saw a man go after another man who'd fallen off a ship. He knew the other man couldn't swim, so he went to help him. The other man was scared and desperate, and when his would-be rescuer came, he latched on to him and drowned them both. It wasn't fair or right—after all, the first man hadn't fallen in on purpose and the second man was going to help—putting his own life in danger to help his friend."

"So what's that got to do with my pa?"

Adrik leaned back and pushed his fur hat up away from his face. "Neither man would have died if they'd done what they were told to. They didn't listen to the advice of others. The first man wasn't supposed to be playing around at the rail. He was supposed to be loading salmon into the hold of the ship. They knew he couldn't swim and had given him a job in a place where he would have been safe. The second man knew better than to jump in after his friend, but his emotions got the better of him, and reasoning and logic went out the door. He should have thrown his friend a line or a life ring. If either man would have done what he was supposed to do instead of doing what he thought best, then both would be alive today."

Jacob's eyes narrowed. "My pa was doing what he thought was right. I'm going to do what I think is right. I have to find out if that man was my pa."

"You'd be hard pressed to learn that for sure, unless you found your pa face-to-face."

"Why do you say that?"

Adrik frowned. "Most of the dead will be buried together. You're not going to find him, and even if you do, well, you can't be sure of recognizing him."

"I'd know my own pa," Jacob declared. "I have to try, Mr.

Ivankov. I have to go and at least try to find him. If he's dead, then I'll take up where he left off. He had a dream of finding gold and making a better life for us. I won't let that dream die."

"It was a mighty selfish dream, if you ask me. He was a grown man with two children, and he knew you needed him here. He probably should have loaded you both up and headed back to the States, where you'd all be safe. Instead, he let himself buy into the stories of gold and put himself in danger and left you and Leah behind."

"Don't say that." Jacob's temper flared. He wasn't about to sit and listen to this man mean-mouth his father. How dare he say that his father had done the wrong thing. He got to his feet and stared down at the larger man. "I'll fight you for saying that." He balled his fists and held them up as if to prove his point.

Adrik pulled off his gloves and slapped them against his thigh as he got to his feet. "Jacob, I'm telling you this because I don't want to see you make a mistake. I know you're hurting and I know you're angry, but going north is foolish. Plain and simple. Greed is what's driving men north. Greed and wild stories about things that don't even exist."

"The gold is real," Jacob said. "My pa said it was real. Other people are coming back rich. You know it's real!" His voice was steadily rising.

"The gold might well be real, but so's the cost. Are you ready to pay that price? Folks on the trail were warned about the dangers. Avalanches were predicted for several hours ahead of when they actually started happening. The Tlingits stopped packing and went down the mountain. They told people why, but no one wanted to listen. They had to get just one more pack over the mountain. They had to press just that much closer to the goal of finding gold. Had they listened, they wouldn't be dead now. Your pa might very well be among those gone—if so, then he didn't listen, either."

Jacob felt a strange aching in his throat. He wanted to speak, but words wouldn't come. He wanted to hit Adrik Ivankov, but he knew nothing would come of it, either.

"I'm going. I have to find my pa. I was always going to leave, I was just waiting for warmer weather. But now I'm going on my own. Pa has a cache and money. If he is dead, then I'm going to see to it that his dream comes true."

"What about Leah?"

Jacob hadn't really thought of his sister. He had forced her from his thoughts because he knew he couldn't take her along. She'd be heartbroken at his departure. It would make her misery complete. After he left, she would truly have no one but Karen.

"I'll send for her. When I have enough money, I'll send some so that she can come by boat. Or if the railroad is built through by then, I'll have her come by train. Pa said the trail is too hard for someone like her. I won't have her freezing to death like that woman in his letter."

"Jacob, I wish you'd reconsider. You're going to tear that little girl completely apart if you leave her now—what with not knowing about your father."

"She'll understand," Jacob said, not at all convinced of his words. "She'll need to know the truth, same as me."

"And how do you think you're going to discover the truth? They were already lighting fires to thaw the ground for digging when I left. They aren't going to leave folks unburied so that you can get up there and figure out who's who. That man was tagged as Bill Barringer, and they won't wait on his kin to show up. Most of those fellows didn't have kin anywhere nearby. They'll bury them all quickly and probably en masse. You can't very well dig them all up to see if one of them is your father. If they can bring him back to bury in Dyea, they will. After all, I told them you and Leah were here. But chances are they'll bury him with the others. Even then we can't be sure it was really your pa."

Jacob held his ground. "I'll head north, then. I'll go to Dawson and check with the claims office and see if he has files. If he's alive, that's exactly what he'd do. If he's not alive, then there are supplies and money somewhere that belong to Leah and me."

"You don't know that, Jacob. If your father is dead, no one's going to worry about getting that stuff back to you and your sister."

"I don't care. I'm going. You'll let Leah and Karen know, won't you?" Jacob asked.

"You don't plan to go back and get your things?"

"I have some things hidden in the woodshed. Like I said, I've been planning to go all along."

Adrik nodded. "I suppose you have to do what you think is right, but just remember one thing. When you take off from here without the permission or advice of your authority figures, you are setting yourself up for trouble. When we walk away from God's authority, we are also walking away from His perfect protection. Do you really want that?"

"I'm not leaving God. I know He's got a reason for everything, and while I don't understand it, I'm not going to curse Him and die like Job's friends suggested." Jacob remembered the sermon preached on the Sunday before the avalanche. The words had impacted him. Job had lost everything and all that was left to him was to curse God and die. But still he hung on, and Jacob would, too.

"Jacob, why don't you just think about this overnight? Pray on it first and then make your decision. You don't know what awaits you out there. One trip up the summit and you'll see for yourself what a mistake this is."

"I don't care what you say," Jacob said, pushing his way past the big man. "I'm going and don't you try to stop me."

———————

Leah had known about Jacob's dream to join their father from nearly the moment he'd planned it. That's why she waited for him in the darkness of the woodshed. She knew he was going to leave her, and she knew he wouldn't come to say good-bye. Clutching the satchel he'd left there in hiding, she tried to think of what she'd say to him.

When the shed door opened and Jacob entered carrying a small lantern, Leah waited until he tried to retrieve his things from their hiding place before speaking.

"You're going away without saying good-bye. Just like Pa," she murmured, stepping out of the shadows.

"Leah!" He said the word almost accusingly.

"Why are you leaving like this? How could you do this to me?" She fought back tears and shivered in the cold. She threw the satchel at him. "There. Is that what you came for?"

She heard her brother's sigh. "I don't want to hurt you, but I have to go. We have to know if that man was Pa. Mr. Ivankov can't tell me for sure that Pa was the man he saw. We have to know."

"When will you come back?"

"I don't know. I'll probably have to go all the way to Dawson before I know for sure whether the man carrying Pa's letter was him or not. You'll be safe with Karen."

"But you're all the family I have left." Leah couldn't believe he was just going off like this. She'd known of his plans but had always figured on changing his mind. After all, they were close. They'd been each other's confidants for years.

Jacob moved to close the distance and put his hands on her shoulders. "Look, I'm going to send for you. I promise. I'll get enough money so you won't have to go up the Chilkoot Trail. I'll send you enough money so you can take a steamer all the way to St. Michael and then down the river to Dawson City. You'll ride like a queen!" He tried to make it sound wonderful, but Leah wasn't convinced.

"Take me now. Take me with you."

He shook his head. "You know I can't. The way is too rough. You read Pa's letter, didn't you? The way is just too dangerous for someone like you."

"It's dangerous for you, too. Grown men died in that avalanche—one of them might have been Pa. What makes you think it'll be any better for you?"

Jacob's jaw fixed in that determined way she'd come to recognize. It was a characteristic he'd inherited from their father. "All I know is that I have to try."

Wrapping her arms around him, Leah hugged him tight. "Please don't go, Jacob. I'm scared for you. I don't want you to die."

Jacob held her for several minutes, then gently pushed her away. "I'm not going to die. You just wait and see. I'll send for you before you know it, and who knows, maybe I'll find Pa and everything will be all right again." He turned from her but not before Leah saw the tears on his cheeks. Seeing him in such pain, she decided to say nothing more.

He pulled on his pack and reached into his pocket to hand her something. "I bought this and planned to give it to you for your birthday next month."

Leah opened her hand to find a delicate gold chain. At the end of the necklace was an equally delicate gold cross. "It's beautiful. I've never had anything like it."

"I know," Jacob replied. "I wanted you to have some gold from the north. I wanted you to believe in the dream."

She looked up and saw the hope he held for his future. "I believe in *you*, Jacob—but not gold or land or anything else but God."

He kissed her on the forehead. "I love you, Leah. Stay with Karen and I'll find you again."

Then he was gone. Leah stared after him, watching the amber glow of the lantern bob and swing as he walked away. "I love you, too," she whispered. Numb from the truth of the moment, Leah made her way inside and up to the room that she now shared with Karen alone.

She opened the door cautiously. The night was still young enough that Karen might well be reading or writing letters, and Leah didn't want to make too much noise. But the room was empty.

Sitting down on the bed, Leah unfastened the clasp on the necklace. Putting the necklace on, Leah felt the cold metal against her skin. It did little to reassure her.

"Nothing has gone right today," Karen declared as she came into the room and slammed the door. Seeing Leah, she halted a moment, then went on raving. "I'm so tired of bad news. Everybody is talking about one horrible thing after another downstairs. I came up here because I just can't stand to hear another word! I'm going to go wash up for bed."

Leah nodded and slipped the necklace beneath her blouse. Giving no further thought to telling Karen about Jacob, she curled up on the bed and cried softly into the pillow. She thought for a moment of a verse her mother had once read to her about how God collected your tears in a bottle and saved them. *He's sure going to have a lot of bottles from me,* she thought as sleep overcame her.

─┤CHAPTER TEN├─

WHEN KAREN AWOKE the next morning, she found Leah sitting cross-legged in the corner of the room. The child, rapidly turning into a beautiful young woman, had been crying. It broke Karen's heart to see the girl so grieved. Karen saw herself in Leah, recognizing the raw misery and open wounds of her father's death. She longed to say something comforting, but words eluded her. How could she comfort Leah when Karen could find no comfort for herself?

Yawning, Karen stretched, then pushed back the covers. The room felt like ice. She was surprised that Jacob hadn't started a fire in the small stove. Pushing back long strawberry-blond waves of hair, she looked to Leah.

"Where's Jacob? Why didn't he get a fire going?"

"He's gone." Leah's flat words registered no emotion.

Karen got up and pulled on her warm robe. "It's not like him to go off to work and leave the stove cold."

"He didn't go to work. Like I said, he's gone."

Karen looked down at Leah. "Gone? You mean gone from Dyea?"

Leah looked up mournfully. "He left last night."

"Why didn't you say so? Why didn't you wake me up so I could stop him?"

Leah picked up her skirts and stood. "You couldn't have stopped him. He didn't want to be stopped. I tried."

"You should have at least told me about this last night. I could have sent for Adrik to stop him."

Leah looked almost accusingly at Karen as if she were responsible for Jacob's disappearance. "You didn't want to hear about anything else that was bad. Remember?"

Karen could hardly comprehend Leah's words. Jacob was just a boy. Where had he gone? And for what reason? She tried to remain as calm as possible. After all, the boy had probably just taken off to mourn. Maybe even find out where they'd taken his father's body.

"I'm sure he won't be gone for long. It's still winter out there and too cold for pretty much anyone, let alone an unseasoned child." Karen picked up several pieces of wood and put them into the stove atop the cold, lifeless ashes.

"He's not coming back."

Karen straightened at this and looked at Leah. "Of course he will. You're here."

Leah shook her head. "He said he'd send for me."

"Send for you from where?"

"From the goldfields. From Dawson City."

A tremor ran through Karen. It started somewhere in her heart and radiated out from there until her entire body felt like it was shaking. "He wouldn't really have gone—would he?" She darted to the window and pulled back the drapes. The frost kept her from seeing beyond the room. She turned back to Leah. "He wouldn't just go like that, leaving you here. Not when he knew what it felt like to be left behind."

Leah nodded, and her tears began to fall. "He said he had to know if that dead man was our pa. If it was Pa, then Jacob wants to take up his dream. Either way, he's gone."

Karen paced the small room for several moments. The floorboards creaked in protest as she picked up her steps. She forgot about the fire and finally plopped down on the corner of the unmade bed. Angry, she reached out and threw one of the pillows. "That's just great. Things just seem to go from bad to worse."

Leah went to where Karen sat and took hold of her hand. "I know things have been hard, Karen. I've been praying for you. For us. My ma used to say that it seemed like it didn't rain but it poured. I guess that's the way it's been with us."

Karen softened as she met the child's red-rimmed eyes. "I'm sorry. I know you're hurting." She reached out and pulled Leah into her embrace. "I'm so sorry, Leah. I know you're feeling bad and that I'm not helping it."

"You can't help it."

The truth of Leah's words seemed to hold a double meaning. There was nothing Karen could do to change the events of their lives, and she seemed powerless to even say the right thing—to point Leah back to her faith and hope in God—to bring herself along as well.

"I'm sorry," Karen murmured. "Sometimes I just feel like . . . well . . ." She wanted to say that she felt deserted by God. That He no longer cared. She wanted to say that her anger was making her forget her upbringing. Then a picture came to mind—the angry face of Peter Colton. She had stirred his anger. She had caused his rage by promoting her own hatred of Martin Paxton. She saw herself in that angry face, knowing the only difference between her and Peter was that he would actually pull the trigger and kill Paxton. Karen could only dream of his reckoning.

"I know I should have told you last night," Leah said softly. "I shouldn't have just let you go to bed without knowing about Jacob. I'm sorry."

Karen shook her head. "Don't be. I deserved it. I pushed you away, along with everyone and everything else."

"Even God?"

Leah's softly spoken question seemed to rip apart Karen's stoic facade. "Yes. I suppose I must confess that, as well." She tried to smile at Leah, hoping the action would reassure her without words. It didn't.

"It's easy to trust God when things are going well," Karen began. "There's no real effort in that. But when things go wrong and then keep going wrong until you feel like nothing good is ever going to happen again . . . well, then it gets harder."

"It has to get better." It was Leah who offered the encouragement.

Karen nodded. "I want to believe that, but right now I feel as though my life is as cold and lifeless as those ashes in the stove. Nothing makes sense anymore. Everyone has either died or gone away."

"Everyone, 'cept you and me." Leah paused and put her hand atop Karen's. "I need you, Karen."

Karen saw the fear and questioning in Leah's eyes. She reached up and touched Leah's tear-stained face. "I need you, too. I know exactly what it is to lose the people you love. It makes you feel all alone—like nobody in the world even knows you're alive."

Leah nodded. "Like God's too busy."

Karen knew God was working on her spirit through the words of her young friend. She hated feeling the way she did, all bottled up and walled in, while at the same time so very resentful. "God's never too busy," she finally responded. She knew the words were true, and by speaking them she thought maybe she'd broken a little chink of the mortar in her walls.

Smiling, she took Leah's face in both hands. "Leah, I won't leave you. You needn't fear that. I made your father a promise to look after you, and I will do just that. This country is no place to be alone."

"Jacob's alone," Leah whispered.

"For now," Karen agreed. "But once we talk to Mr. Ivankov, I know Jacob won't be alone any longer. Adrik will go after him. You'll see." She tried again to smile for Leah's sake, but a weariness settled upon her. What were they going to do after they found Jacob? Should they board the next ship south? Should they return to Seattle and take up a home near Karen's sister? There were just too many questions and not enough answers.

"We should pray for Jacob," Leah said.

God still seemed so distant. So very far away. Could she possibly find her way back to His comfort? She knew He forgave sin—welcomed back prodigals. The only real question was how could she go back to God and carry with her the hatred she felt for Martin Paxton?

She looked to Leah's wide-eyed expression. The child had lost so much, but her face looked ever hopeful as she spoke of prayer. Karen nodded, knowing that she would never be able to lead such a prayer.

Leah seemed to understand Karen's reluctance. She took hold of Karen's hands. "Don't worry, Karen. I can pray for both of us."

"What do you mean you knew he was heading north? Why didn't you come to tell me?" Karen questioned in disbelief. "I thought you were my friend."

Adrik looked apologetic, but it wasn't an apology that came out of his mouth. "Look, I figure sometimes a man has to do what he feels he must."

"For a man that might well be expected, but we're talking about a fifteen-year-old boy."

"Fifteen is hardly a boy in these parts. There's more than a few fellows Jacob's age who are here on their own. They're out working to make their keep, to see themselves north in search of gold."

"I don't care about the gold, I care about Jacob. Adrik, it was very irresponsible of you to let him just head off like that. You should have at least convinced him to come back to the Gold Nugget and talk this through with me."

Adrik shook his head. "If you'll recall, I'm not responsible for Jacob. Bill Barringer gave that job to you, but even so, I did talk to him and I tried to encourage him to stay. He was bent on knowing the truth about his father. I remember someone else who was just as eager to know her father's whereabouts. Jacob wants to keep his father alive, and if not his father, then his father's dream. Before the fire left you so bitter, I'd heard similar things from you."

Karen hadn't expected Adrik to call attention to her bitter heart. It stung to hear the words, and she thought momentarily of some sort of defense. But there was none. She was bitter and angry, and those two qualities were slowly draining her of her strength.

Karen got up from the overturned crate Adrik had offered her as a seat. In his overwhelming presence, the tent seemed to have shrunk since she'd shared it with Leah and Jacob. "I suppose I should just go. I thought you might understand."

"I do understand," he said softly, the tone of his voice sending a small shiver through her. "I understand better than you give me credit for."

She turned her eyes upward and studied the ruggedly handsome face. The nose was a little too large, the mustache too thick. The jaw was too square and the eyes too . . . She lost herself for a moment. There was nothing wrong with Adrik's looks. He was perfect. Her feelings startled her back into reality.

Taking a deep breath, Karen barely managed to speak. "If you understand, then why . . . why won't you help me get Jacob back?"

"Karen, the boy will most likely come back on his own. And even if he doesn't, do you really want me to go out there and haul him back, only to have him run off again? And he will. He won't stand by and let some woman who's not even kin tell him what he can and can't do regarding his father. Do you honestly want that ugliness between the two of you?"

"But I can't just stand by and do nothing," Karen protested. "There's Leah to consider. Not to mention that there's hardly any reason to stay here. Everything has changed now. Nothing's the same. I came here with one thought—one hope and dream, and that's gone now. I have no reason to stay, but without Jacob I can hardly leave."

Adrik didn't reply but moved with a quickness that took Karen's breath as he pulled her into his arms and kissed her soundly on the mouth. Too stunned to even react for a moment, Karen relished the ticklish way his mustache moved against her face. She felt a warmth spread to her cheeks as she allowed herself to realize what was really taking place.

He ended the kiss as quickly as he'd begun it, but still he held her tightly. "I can give you a reason to stay, if you want to hear it."

Karen tried not to show her surprise, but in all honesty her feelings were so confusing that she feared what she might do or say. Pushing away, she shook her head. "You had no right to do that." She broke his hold but knew that had he any intentions of forcing her to remain in his embrace, he would have little difficulty in keeping her there.

"I apologize," he said. Then grinning, he added, "Not for kissing you, but for not asking first."

The boyish amusement in his expression irritated Karen and pressed her into action. "That was uncalled-for, Mr. Ivankov. I came here to discuss Jacob, not issues between us."

"I think the issues between us need to be discussed," Adrik replied. "Seems to me you're wrestling with an awful lot these days. You worry about the future, but it's the present that's killing you."

"You're wrong," Karen said, shaking so much from the encounter that she was certain he could see her tremble. "I'm merely trying to keep things under control. I can understand that you would be less than supportive of seeing Martin Paxton pay for his deeds. After all, you don't really know him and what he's capable of. But I felt certain you would care enough about Jacob to help me keep him from further harm."

"I do care, Karen. I care about a great many things, including you."

"I don't want to hear that. I haven't any interest in hearing it. I need to think of Jacob and Leah. I need to figure out what's best for their future, as well as my own."

"What's best for your future is exactly what you're running from," Adrik said matter-of-factly.

"What's that supposed to mean?"

Adrik refused to back down. "You know what it means."

Karen fought the attraction she had for Adrik and instead put her hands on her hips and shook her head very slowly. "No . . . I don't think I do."

"Have it your way," Adrik said with a shrug. "I'm not going to play games with you. I haven't got the time for it. Look, if it makes you feel any better, I'll go look for Jacob. But I'm not going to force him to come back."

Confused by her emotions and Adrik's unwillingness to continue their conversation, Karen picked up her gloves and hat. "Don't bother. I'll go for him myself before I ask you to do me any favors."

She headed for the Gold Nugget awash in a sensation of defeat and discouragement. What was she supposed to do now? She could hardly pack up Leah and head north, yet she couldn't leave Jacob to fend for himself.

"Why are you doing this to me?" She gazed upward to the snow-covered mountains as if she might very well see God seated on a throne atop the crest. The swirling snow arched upward against a sky so blue it almost hurt her eyes to look upon it.

"Winter's not long for us now," an old man commented as he passed by her, dragging a sled full of gear. "The thaw will be here afore ya know it."

She lowered her gaze and nodded. "I'll be glad for it."

The man smiled, revealing a mouth full of decaying teeth. "The thaw will melt the ice and snow. Everyone will be glad for it."

He went on his way, and Karen watched after him. His sled made two deep indentations in the icy mud as he pulled the heavy load forward. Karen thought on his words, knowing them to be true. How many times had she heard someone praying for an early spring—an end to the relentless darkness, warming winds to melt the ice?

"I'm glad you didn't get too far."

Karen whirled around to find Adrik holding up her handbag. "You left this in my tent. I thought you might need it."

Her temper had cooled and she nodded. "Thank you. It was kind of you to bring it to me."

"Look," Adrik began hesitantly, "I didn't mean to anger you."

"I'm the one who needs to apologize. I've been so short with you—with everyone," Karen said, sighing heavily. "I just have no answers. I'm tired. And it seems that everyone wants to hurt me. Even God seems to be taking part."

Adrik smiled. "Well, I for one have no desire to hurt you. Facts being what they are, I have something much more pleasurable in mind."

Karen's cheeks grew hot, and she quickly lowered her gaze to the ground. "You shouldn't talk like that."

"Why not? It's the truth."

"Be that as it may," Karen said, trying to maintain her control, "I don't think it very appropriate. I have more than enough to concern myself with, and pleasure isn't on the agenda."

"First you complain because there's nothing but misery in your life, but when someone offers you something else, you refuse it." Karen looked up, noting his amused expression. "I think you need to decide exactly what it is you want out of life, and go after it." He smiled in his good-natured way and tipped his hat. "When you figure it all out, let me know. Especially if there's a spot for me."

-| C H A P T E R   E L E V E N |-

GRACE SAT BESIDE the cabin window. She had returned to *Summer Song* to nurse her bruised feelings. Her heart was nearly broken by memories of Peter's rage and Karen's desire for revenge. Her dear friend had changed so much. How could she even be the same gentle woman who had so often admonished Grace to let bygones be bygones?

"I'm sure Peter will turn up soon," Amelia Colton said in motherly assurance. "He's never been one to admit to being wrong." The three Colton women had gathered in the small living space to still one another's worries.

"You don't have to take my side," Grace said softly. "You are his mother. I don't expect you to choose between us."

"But there is no us," Amelia stated. Miranda looked up from her knitting and nodded.

"The two shall be one," Peter's sister murmured.

"That's right. It's what I've often counseled Miranda about. That's why it is so difficult to be married to one who has no interest in what's most precious to you. What possible hope can you have of peace in such a household?"

Grace knew only too well of what Amelia Colton spoke. "We are, as the Bible says, unequally yoked. Like light and darkness. I have chosen to walk God's narrow path, and Peter, well, he's a good man, but being good doesn't save you for eternity."

Amelia nodded. "I blame myself, Grace. Ephraim and I . . . well . . . we got away from fellowship and worship. We got busy with life, and so often Sundays were the best days to take care of other needs. I spent many a Sunday, along with my children, on board one ship or another cleaning and scrubbing."

The expression on Amelia's face tore at Grace's heart. Her regret was so evident. "You mustn't be too hard on yourself, Mother Colton."

"Oh, but I was wrong, Grace. Miranda, I wronged you and Peter. I should have showed you a better way—a more faithful way to honor God. I never saw that it might cause you to turn away or find worship unimportant. I only desired to help Ephraim."

"I heard my name being bandied about," Ephraim Colton said, coming from the adjoining cabin.

Amelia smiled. "I assure you it was all for good. I was actually apologizing to Grace and Miranda for not having been more faithful in raising my children to fear God first and attend to duty second."

Ephraim nodded, and the same sadness that had tinged Amelia's eyes now touched his. "We've no one but ourselves to blame for taking such a lazy view of our faith and commitment to God."

"But you were and are good parents," Miranda said, putting aside her knitting. She went to her father and hugged him close. "God can restore our family and the wasted years. He's already doing quite a good job of it with us. Peter will come around."

A knock on the cabin door caught their attention.

"Peter!" Grace gasped, her hand going to her throat. She could only pray he had returned.

Ephraim went to the door, but instead of finding his son, he found his first mate accompanied by the local law officials. "Welcome aboard, gentlemen. To what do I owe this pleasure?"

"Ain't hardly pleasure," the taller of the two replied. "I have papers here from a Martin Paxton. He says he owns this ship and can take possession of it at any time. He wants you and your folks off the ship immediately."

Grace was on her feet. "*Summer Song* belongs to the Coltons. Martin Paxton has no say whatsoever."

Ephraim took the papers but continued to stare in disbelief at the lawman. "That's right. *Summer Song* is a part of Colton Shipping."

"I can't help that, mister. Read these papers, and you'll see they've been executed all legal-like back in San Francisco. We're here to uphold the law."

Grace went to Ephraim's side. "Father Colton, don't worry about this. There must be some mistake. We must go see Mr. Paxton and set things right."

It took further convincing on Grace's part, but finally Ephraim agreed. The sheriff's deputy, however, was of no mind to leave Amelia and Miranda on board while Ephraim and Grace went off to settle the affair. The two deputies ordered the party to gather their things and deboard the ship immediately.

Grace could hardly believe the order. She threw her things haphazardly into her trunks and watched helplessly as *Summer Song*'s crew went to work loading them off onto the dock. He was doing this to hurt her. Martin Paxton was doing this to punish the Coltons for helping her defy his plans. Perhaps Peter was right—perhaps Martin Paxton did not deserve forgiveness.

Mindless of the beautiful skies overhead, Grace allowed herself to be helped from the ship. The rush of activities along the harbor walk did nothing to take her mind from the moment. Peter would be furious. No doubt if Paxton thought he had rights to *Summer Song*, he would also take *Merry Maid*. *Dear Lord,* she prayed, *you must help us. Peter will kill Mr. Paxton if he hasn't already done the deed.*

They hurried along with the confusion and bustle of new arrivals and old-timers. Supplies were stacked everywhere, and the noise was enough that a deaf man might well seek solace elsewhere. Grace hardly noticed the new buildings and busy freighters. Skagway nearly doubled its size by the week, but it was so completely unimportant at this moment.

"Miranda and I will try to arrange rooms," Amelia said, putting her hand on her husband's coat sleeve. "I'm sure we'll find something nearby."

"But what if this is all a misunderstanding?" Miranda questioned. "Would we not be better waiting?"

"No, your mother is right. I can hardly have you standing here unprotected on the streets while I go find Mr. Paxton."

The deputy who had accompanied them this far spoke up. "Mr. Paxton is residing in the rooms above his store. I have to report to him, and you might as well come with me."

"I'm coming, too," Grace said firmly. "After all, he's doing this because of me."

Ephraim looked for a moment as if he might refuse her, then nodded slowly. "Get us rooms, Amelia. We can all meet for lunch at that little place on Third. Go there after you have secured us a place to stay, but be watchful and speak to no one. The town is full of ne'er-do-wells."

Amelia nodded and clung to Miranda's arm. "We'll be just fine. I'll keep two of the crew with me until you join us."

Ephraim looked past his wife to the men who had accompanied them. Laden with bags and trunks, the men's attention remained fully on their captain. "Watch over them."

The two men closest to them gave Ephraim their pledge. Grace looked to her father-in-law and saw the sorrow in his expression. Was he seeing his lifelong dream pass before his eyes? Had he come to the harsh north only to lose his fortune like so many others? She'd not stand for it! She would fight Martin Paxton with every ounce of her strength. She had to make him see that this feud was an exercise in futility. She was a married woman, and whether her husband desired her company or not, their commitment was still binding.

The deputy led them past the Pillbox Drug Company, the Yukon Outfitters, and Burkhard House. She knew well the location of Paxton's store, for it had been in place when she'd left the previous December.

Following the deputy into the store and past the curious stares of the onlookers, Grace tried to pray. She wanted to remain calm and rational. She wanted God to do her talking, rather than her own emotions. But it was hard. All she could think about was the harm Paxton had once again caused her. She thought of how Karen presumed that because Grace wanted to extend forgiveness to the man, she couldn't possibly understand the extent of his cruelty.

But I understand it only too well, Grace thought. It seemed like only yesterday that he had slapped her at their engagement party. She could almost feel his breath upon her neck, his hands upon her body. The thought made her feel physically ill.

They passed from the main floor and climbed up a dark passage of stairs. The deputy knocked at the door, and Martin Paxton himself opened it. He stared down at the man, seeing beyond him to Ephraim and then Grace. He rested his gaze upon Grace, then smiled with an expression that suggested he'd known she would come.

"Thank you, Deputy," he said and tossed the man a coin. "I can take care of the situation from here. Please make sure you have men standing guard at the dock. I don't want anyone getting the idea they can sneak back on board." The man nodded, then turned to push past Grace and Ephraim.

"Come in," Paxton said, walking away from Ephraim and Grace. "I have been expecting you both."

"Do you care to tell me what this is all about?" Ephraim questioned without waiting to so much as take a seat. "This man shows up on board my ship and demands we leave. He hands me these papers and tells me you have commanded my removal."

Paxton poured himself a glass of brandy, then took a seat behind a massive desk. He pulled a gold watch chain from his red print silk vest and popped open the cover on the piece. "I have exactly fifteen minutes. No more. If you care to sit down, I will do my best to explain. However," he paused and looked hard at Grace, "I am only doing this out of respect for my mother. I know she held you in highest regard, Ephraim. Otherwise, I'd have not let you cross the threshold."

Ephraim guided Grace to the leather upholstered chair opposite Paxton and sat down on its matching twin only after she had taken a seat. She smoothed out the soft lavender wool of her skirt and unbuttoned her jacket. She tried hard not to look at Paxton, but he seemed to pull her attention against her will.

His eyes were dark with hatred, and his hair seemed to have grayed a bit around the temples. Grace knew his severe looks were considered handsome by many women, but the coldness in his eyes only left her wanting to run from the room.

"To get right to business, you will find those papers are the ones you signed some time ago in San Francisco. Our agreement spoke of my investment and of the fact that should I feel that investment was threatened, I would have the right to withhold further support and stop any other action until I was confident that my investment was no longer threatened. It allowed me a great deal of interpretation when it came to defining 'threat to my investment.' "

"I still don't understand what that has to do with anything. We've been doing a tidy business. You've been paid back regularly," Ephraim replied. "How could you possibly see your business investment as being threatened?"

"Because there is bad blood now running between your son and me. I could only conclude that you were supportive of his decisions when you arrived here in Skagway with Miss—excuse me—*Mrs.* Grace Colton in your company." He scowled at Grace. "She was, in fact, to have married me. She broke her father's written and verbal agreement and fled to Alaska from Chicago. I took this in stride as her youth no doubt gave her over to a bad case of wedding jitters, but I had no tolerance for her deception in arranging her marriage to your son. Furthermore, Peter knew of my arrangement with Grace and chose to ignore it. Thus, I suffered great financial setback."

"I had no such arrangement with you," Grace countered before Ephraim could speak. "You are doing this only to punish me for thwarting your plans. You are throwing away a lifetime of friendship with a man who was good to you when no one else was there, all because I refused to be your wife. That hardly seems a sensible choice, Mr. Paxton."

"I've no doubt that to your simple mind, Mrs. Colton, the issues at hand seem to be less than sensible. But I assure you, they are. How much longer would it have been before your husband would have come blaming me for the destruction of his store in Dyea? Furthermore, how much longer would it have been before he and his father might have decided their arrangement with me was less than pleasant, and because many new businesses would happily purchase their goods, I might well find myself paying exorbitant prices for items of lesser quality? You do not truly believe that I would stand by and await those conclusions, do you?"

"You know very well that my father-in-law would never have done such a thing. I cannot believe you would perform such a childish deed, throwing the man and his family off his own ship, leaving us to seek refuge without warning."

Paxton swirled his brandy for a moment, then downed it quickly. He slammed the snifter to the desk, breaking its delicate stem and leaving it jagged and useless atop the now scarred wood.

He got up just as quickly from his seat and pulled on his outer coat. "Your time is nearly up. I want to add that *Merry Maid* is even now docked near Dyea. I have arranged for her to be brought here and for your son to be escorted from her as you have been escorted from *Summer Song*. I will expect your cooperation, and I will accept no further trouble in this matter."

"You ... you ... can't be serious," Ephraim gasped the words and clutched at his chest. "Colton Shipping is my life. It is my son's inheritance. I would never have signed it away to you. You have duped me. The business belongs to Peter."

"And Grace belonged to me," Paxton said without concern for the man's obvious distress.

Grace saw her father-in-law turn ashen. His eyes met hers, and she could see they were wild with pain. "He's sick! Can't you see that!" She reached out to touch the older man, desperate that she might keep him from further discomfort.

Paxton walked away from them and went to the door. He called out two names, and in a moment the same thugs who had tried to escort Grace to a wedding with Paxton appeared.

"Take Mr. Colton to the doctor two doors down. He appears to be suffering from some sort of heart attack."

The men moved quickly and hoisted Ephraim from his seat. The thick, stocky, bulldog-faced man was none too careful as he lead the way out of the room, knocking Ephraim clumsily against the doorjamb before heading down the steps.

Grace hurried after them, but Paxton stopped her. He closed the door and shook his head. "Sit."

"I thought you only had fifteen minutes to spare," she said with a tinge of sarcasm.

"I had only fifteen minutes for explanations to stupid men. You, however, are another matter."

"Indeed," Grace said, her anger besting her. "I am a married woman."

"I can easily remedy that. You have only to cooperate with

me, Grace, and I'll see that Colton's mediocre shipping line is returned to him. Divorce Peter Colton and marry me. Do this and they will have not only their business restored, but the contract between us will be dissolved and the bill paid in full."

Grace felt her mouth go dry. "I cannot divorce. It's a sin."

"Is it not also a sin to kill a man?" Paxton asked casually. He leaned against the door and looked at her in a way that suggested less than pure thoughts.

"I've killed no one," she barely whispered.

"That man is sure to die unless he finds his company securely back in place. He's heartbroken—literally," Paxton said, laughing.

Grace hated his snide remarks at the expense of her father-in-law. She reached out to pound her fists against his chest, but he easily caught her arms and held her tight.

"You can't fight me, Grace. I have more power than you could imagine."

"God's power is greater."

Paxton laughed heartily. "Then let God get you out of this one." He released her and walked back to his desk. "You know the price and the terms, so you're free to leave. I will expect your answer before the week is out."

"You may have my answer now. I will not divorce my husband. I made a covenant before God, and whether or not such things matter to you," Grace said, her voice betraying her fear, "they matter to me."

Paxton shrugged. "It's just a matter of time, my dear. Do you really imagine that when faced with losing the family business and the livelihood he's always known, your husband will desire to remain married? Especially when I explain to him how you could have saved his father all of this grief— how you could have kept his mother and sister off the streets.

No, I don't think your husband will worry half so much about keeping this covenant as the one I hold against his father."

"You're evil," Grace breathed, moving with shaky steps toward the door. "You're as evil and wicked a man as I have ever known."

Paxton leaned back against his desk and crossed his arms against his chest. His hard face tensed, and the thin scar that lined his right jaw seemed to become more prominent. His green eyes narrowed as he spoke. "Be that as it may, you have until the end of the week to reconsider this matter. Perhaps Ephraim will be dead by then—perhaps not. But no doubt your husband will be alive, and he'll want answers and he'll want his ships."

"What makes you think even if I were forced to divorce Peter that I would marry you?" Grace couldn't help but ask.

"That's simple. The deal wouldn't be concluded until my ring was upon your finger."

A coldness crept over Grace, and she feared momentarily that she might very well pass out. "Why are you doing this? You've already robbed my family of their fortune. I have nothing you could possibly want." She opened the door, feeling only slightly better for being able to see her way to freedom. She looked back to Paxton. "Why?"

"That's completely unimportant," he said, his voice low and menacing. "You have no understanding of my business, and neither will I afford you one. I want you, and that is all you need to understand. I will expect to see you again by Friday."

⊣ CHAPTER TWELVE ⊢

PETER COLTON STARED back from shore at the *Merry Maid*. Not but an hour ago he had labored over the log, tallying expenses to be offset by profits. In spite of the fire and the loss of his trading post, he was doing well enough. He had sold the extra supplies to half a dozen businesses and had made a considerable profit. But then his entire world had changed in a matter of minutes. Before he realized what had even happened, a group of men, armed with guns and badges, pressed into his cabin. Papers were served, and while Peter quietly considered their content, the men began ordering his men to ready *Merry Maid* for the trip into Skagway.

Now as he stood on the docks of Skagway, *Summer Song* resting easy in the waters not far from *Merry Maid*, he felt nothing but a numb sensation of disbelief. How could it be that his ship was gone—taken from him in a heartbeat? He hadn't even known his father was in dock. He had to find him and try to figure out what had just happened.

A million thoughts rushed through Peter's mind as he made his way along the wharf. Was his father angry with him for rejecting Grace? An anger strong enough that he signed *Merry Maid* over to Martin Paxton? Surely not. The thought was incomprehensible.

He spotted one of his father's crew and motioned the man to his side. "Are you going aboard *Summer Song*? Is my father to be found there?"

The man shook his head. "Haven't ya heard? Them lawmen came and took him and the missus and your missus and sister, as well, and sent them off the ship, they did."

"What?" Now Peter was truly confused. "Grace is here— Miranda? What has happened?"

"Don't know," the man said with a shrug. "I heard the captain sold off everything to pay a debt."

"That's impossible. My father owed no man that kind of money. My papers said the *Merry Maid* had become the property of Martin Paxton. Do you know anything about that?"

"No, Captain. But I did hear that your father took an attack of the heart and is lying sick in town."

"Where is he?"

"He's been moved a couple of times. Last I knew he was at the Hotel Alaska."

"Thank you," Peter said, pushing back his billed cap. "I'll get to the bottom of this. Don't let the men lose hope. Tell them we'll fight this."

"Yes, Captain. I'll tell 'em."

Peter hurried in the direction of the Hotel Alaska. The unpainted clapboard building did nothing to raise his spirits. He bounded through the front doors like he owned the place, determined that nothing would keep him from his father and the truth.

"We're full up," a grizzled old man told him from behind the counter. The man's face was hideously disfigured, having encountered a bear or some other equally harmful beast. One eye had been lost altogether, and thick white scars intertwined grotesquely around the empty socket.

Peter thought the man should have covered his misfortune with a patch, but the man seemed not to care. "I'm not here for a room. I'm looking for my family."

"And who might they be?"

"Colton is the name." Peter knew patience had never been his strong suit, but waiting for the man to answer was severely testing his limits.

The man eyed him for a moment, then nodded. "They're up at the top of the stairs and two doors down on the right. If you're figurin' to stay with them, I'm going to have to up the rent."

"I'm not staying," Peter said. "And hopefully neither are they."

He took the stairs two at a time and pushed his way past three men who appeared to be not only drunk, but close to exhaustion as well. They were wandering back and forth as if trying to find their room or some person. Ordinarily, Peter might have attempted to help them, but with his father lying ill, he had no interest in their plight.

Pounding on the door loud and hard, Peter found himself welcomed quite happily by Miranda. "Oh, Peter, you've come. We prayed you would. We couldn't find you."

"What's happened here? How is Father?"

He looked past Miranda to where his father slept. "Is he . . . worse?"

"Oh no. No, he's much better. The doctor believes in time he will be completely healed. Mother and Grace, oh, you didn't know we brought Grace, did you?" She watched his face as if expecting some sort of response. Peter wasn't at all sure what she expected from him.

"One of father's crewmen told me she was here. What in the world is going on, Miranda? Why was my ship taken from me?"

"That question," Ephraim called weakly from the bed, "would be better answered by me."

Peter rushed past his sister, not even pausing to consider where Grace and his mother might be. "Father, are you all right? What does the doctor say?" He stared down at the ashen-faced man and shook his head. "What has happened?"

Ephraim struggled to sit up, bringing Miranda quickly to his side. "Let us help you, Father. You know the doctor said you must rest and take care not to overwork yourself."

Ephraim relaxed and let Peter and Miranda help him. Plumping pillows around her father to assist his upright position, Miranda turned to Peter. "Mother and Grace have gone to buy food. They should be back anytime now."

"Why don't you go see to finding them?" Peter suggested.

Miranda seemed to understand that Peter wanted to speak privately with their father. She took up her coat and headed for the door. "You mustn't leave Father alone. You will stay with him, won't you?"

"I promise not to leave until you return," Peter assured her.

Once she had gone, he pulled off his heavy wool coat and tossed it to one side. "Now, let us get down to business. The sheriff showed up on board *Merry Maid*. He said the ship had been confiscated as a part of an agreement with Martin Paxton."

His father nodded sadly, affirming Peter's worst fears. "The papers I signed when Paxton advanced us the money for repairs—they held a clause that said should Paxton find his investment . . . compromised or threatened . . . he would have the right to take over possession of the company until such time as he felt the property was once again on sound footing."

"But he has no grounds," Peter stated. "Even if the contract holds such a clause—and mind you, I do not remember reading such a thing when I looked the papers over—he would have to have reasonable grounds for such an action."

"He feels his actions are reasonable," Ephraim said wearily. He closed his eyes, and Peter thought for a moment that he'd never seen his father look so old and tired. The dark circles under his eyes, the sagging of his jaw—it all made him look so very fragile. It wasn't something Peter dealt with easily.

"Father, I should let you rest." Peter said the words, but at the same time, allowing his father to rest was the last thing he wanted to do.

"No," his father said, waving his hand weakly. "Don't go. We must discuss this."

Peter sat down on the edge of the bed. The mattress sagged under his weight, leaving him little doubt its support was nothing more than ropes. "Why does Paxton feel he has a right to do this?"

Ephraim slowly opened his eyes. "He feels his investment is threatened because of your marriage."

A burning sensation arose in Peter's chest. How dare Paxton take this to such lengths, and over a woman! He would strip a man of his business, leave him on his sickbed from the shock, burn down his assets, and for what? To exact revenge over a missed opportunity for marriage?

"Paxton has done this because I married Grace?"

Ephraim nodded. "Apparently because of the bad blood between them, Paxton felt you might threaten his investment by siding against him."

"But Grace has nothing to do with the business. Nothing to say. Are you certain you understood him?"

"Ask Grace. She was there with me."

"Grace went to Paxton? After I told her to never be in his company?"

"She was only trying to help. The men had come to take us from *Summer Song*. I knew I had to straighten this matter out, and Grace offered to go with me. She already felt confident that Paxton had done this as a deliberate act against her."

Peter rose from the bed and began pacing in the small room. His father once again closed his eyes, as if telling such a woeful tale had taken his last reserves of strength. And perhaps it had. Peter immediately felt guilty for not concerning himself with his father's condition.

"What are the doctors telling you?"

Without opening his eyes, Ephraim drew a deep breath. "They tell me I've suffered a heart attack. With rest they believe I will recover. They are suggesting I go home as soon as possible, where better medical facilities and doctors are available to aid me in recovery."

"Then we'll see to it that you leave immediately. I'm surprised you brought Mother and Miranda here. Whatever brought that about?" He tried to make the question sound curious rather than disapproving.

Ephraim looked at his son quite seriously. "You left in a bad way. You hurt Grace deeply."

"Yes . . . well, she hurt me, if that's any consolation."

"It's no consolation," Ephraim replied. "Such matters are never easily consoled. Peter, she is your wife. You must find a way to deal gently with her. Your temper is easily provoked these days, and I fear this news will not bode well for your marriage. You must determine to put your differences aside and let the past go."

"I would love nothing more, but apparently Grace and Mr. Paxton have other plans."

Just then Miranda opened the door. Their mother, dressed somberly in a dove gray coat, came next, and Grace entered behind her. A delivery boy stood at the door, a box of goods in his arms. With the stranger there, Peter held his tongue and said nothing. While his mother paid the boy, Peter had a chance to meet his wife's eyes.

She looked at him as though she'd not seen him in years. Her expression was one of hope. It even suggested pleasure in seeing him. Peter softened momentarily. She was beautiful. Her dark eyes drew him like a moth to a flame, and just like the moth, Peter knew he could very well be wounded to the point of death if he got too close to Grace.

Grace ignored the distance and Peter's lack of movement. She went quickly to his side. "I'm so glad you're safe. We were terribly worried about you."

Peter had no words. He wanted to jump right to the heart of the matter regarding Paxton, yet he didn't want to further upset his father by creating a scene. What he needed to do was take Grace somewhere away from his family. Once he had her alone, he could question her and learn the truth.

The delivery boy placed the contents of the crate inside the room and turned to go. Amelia stopped him and handed him a coin, then closed the door behind him as he whistled off happily down the hall. She turned and met her son with an expression that suggested veiled displeasure. Peter hadn't seen this from her since he'd been a young man. She had always hated to take him to task as a child, and her reluctance and obvious distaste for such matters kept him in line more often than the threat of punishment.

"Peter." She said nothing more, but her expression said it all.

"I've been speaking to Father," Peter began. "I'm sorry I wasn't here to help you ashore. I'm sorry you were displaced."

"We've had quite the adventure," his mother admitted and crossed the room to gently kiss her son's cheek. "But we are all well and fine. Your father is recovering his health and soon will be back on his feet."

"I think Father should go home. You all should. There are better doctors and hospitals, and who knows if he's had the proper treatment here in the wilds of the north?"

"Passage home can still be rough at this time of year," his father replied.

"Have you the money for tickets?" Peter asked, still not daring himself to speak what was really on his heart.

"Mr. Paxton has offered us free travel home," Amelia said as Miranda helped her from her coat. She pulled off her bonnet and handed it to Miranda as well. "We plan to leave soon, but not until your father has regained more of his strength."

Peter felt slightly upbraided by her response. She wasn't asking his opinion or his advice. She was simply stating how it was to be. He nodded, then looked to Grace. "I need to speak with my wife."

"I should say so," his mother replied half under her breath. She turned to tend to the groceries, then turned back abruptly. "Do so in gentleness, son. I will not brook any nonsense of ill will between the two of you. Not now—not after all we've been through."

Now Peter felt his anger stirred. His mother was treating him as if he were a young boy again, chiding him to mind his manners and play nicely with the other children.

"The matter is between Grace and me. We will speak in private." He took hold of Grace's arm and tightened his fingers around her wrist. "Come, Grace."

He led her past his mother and sister, opened the door, and fairly pushed her into the hall. "Is there somewhere we can speak privately?" he questioned in a barely audible voice.

"Not really," Grace replied. "Why don't we go for a walk? The day has turned out quite nice, and we can walk away from the town and have a moment or two to ourselves."

Peter nodded and turned back inside to grab his coat. He allowed Grace to walk ahead of him as they went down the stairs and out the door. Freighters with teams of less than co-operative horses added to throngs of people, dogs, and mules, all obstacles of living flesh for anyone brave enough, or foolish enough, to join their numbers. Peter tired of the noise and the ordeal before they'd even walked two blocks.

The buildings thinned out quickly, however, as did the crowds. The town proper was all that really held the interest of these gold rushers. That and the trails to White Pass and the Yukon.

Grace clung to Peter's arm, more for support than intimacy. The muddy streets were difficult to maneuver, and even when they were treated to a few plank boards to negotiate the muck, the walk was still quite uneven.

Peter tried not to be physically drawn to Grace's presence. She seemed so small and helpless sometimes, yet he knew she was quite capable. Her hand holding his arm was less than half the size of his, yet he knew this woman could cause him more pain than men with fists double the width.

"I'm sorry you had to find your father in such a state," Grace finally said after they'd walked a good distance from the planned tracts of Skagway.

Peter stopped and turned to her. Calmly, he asked, "What happened? Tell me everything."

Grace licked her lips and looked quickly away. "The men came to *Summer Song* and escorted us off. When your father learned that this was Mr. Paxton's doing, he decided to go see what he could do to change his mind. I accompanied him, not to defy you or your wishes, but because I didn't want him to face Mr. Paxton alone. I knew his action was most likely on account of me." She looked up as if awaiting his approval or rejection.

"Go on," he said, trying hard to keep all emotion from his voice.

Grace seemed to consider the matter a moment. "Mr. Paxton stated that there was bad blood between our families. That his friendship with your father was completely threatened by my marriage to you. He said that you had taken what was rightfully his, and in turn he would take what belonged to you."

"Why, that—"

Grace held up her hand. "Your father told him that Colton Shipping was his life—your inheritance. Mr. Paxton didn't care. He felt it was only a matter of time before you blamed him for the destruction of the store in Dyea and that soon you and your father would conspire against him."

"Is that all?"

"No," Grace said.

The wind blew loose a strand of chocolate brown hair and

draped it across her face. Peter thought to reach out and push it back, but he held himself in check. If he touched her, even for a moment, he might well forget why he'd brought her here in the first place.

Grace's gloved fingers quickly tucked the hair back into place. She said nothing, but looked up at Peter as if awaiting instructions.

"What else?" he finally asked.

"When your father fell ill, Mr. Paxton called for his men to take him to the doctor. I wanted to accompany your father, but Mr. Paxton would not allow me to follow."

Peter could no longer hold back his rage. "Did he touch you? Did he?"

"He did not hurt me, except with his words," Grace replied. "He made it clear that my marrying you had caused this ordeal. I am sorry, Peter. I don't know why he insists on having me for his wife. The matter is settled, yet he acts as though it's only begun. His demands suggest he could change everything with our cooperation."

"What do you mean by that? What are his demands?"

Grace turned away. "I intend to send a telegram to my mother. I am hoping she might have some idea of what Mr. Paxton had said to my father. I am hopeful that she will have some idea of why he continues to pursue me even after he has destroyed my family and our fortune."

Peter gripped her shoulders much too tightly. He knew he was hurting her, but nevertheless, he yanked her back around to face him. "What does he want?"

Grace shook her head. "He wants me."

Peter looked at her and saw the fear in her eyes. He could feel her trembling beneath his hold and knew it was from fear of him. Ashamed, he dropped his hold and stepped back.

"You're married. How can he hope to resolve that?"

"He wants me to divorce you. He's already arranged for it and wants only my cooperation. He's probably bought himself a judge and court somewhere," Grace said, her words cold but honest. "Peter, he says he'll return everything to you and your father if I leave you."

"I'll kill him!" Peter said, no longer caring. Doubling his fists, he closed his eyes. He saw hot white stars against a field of blackened emptiness. He had never wanted to kill a man before now. His earlier anger and irritation with Paxton were mere annoyance compared to the feelings coursing through his body—feelings that were quickly fueling his rage and pushing him toward action.

Opening his eyes, he saw the tears streaming down Grace's face. "I suppose you want me to forgive him, madam? Maybe pray for him? Well, there will be none of that. Any prayers said will have to originate with you. I'll kill him before I'll allow him to hurt my father any further. I'll kill him before I'll see him in charge of Colton Shipping. And I'll surely kill him before I see him lay a finger on you."

⊣ CHAPTER THIRTEEN ⊢

KAREN SAT DOWN on the edge of the bed and brushed out her long, damp hair. She'd hated to give up her time in the bath, but others were waiting and there was no chance of keeping the place to herself.

With each stroke of the brush, Karen couldn't help but remember Adrik's touch. She shivered, even though the room was quite toasty and warm. What had he done to her? How could she be so easily moved by this man?

She thought of her father and Adrik's loyalty to Wilmont Pierce's memory. She had at first believed Adrik's interest in her was nothing more than an expression of that loyalty. But now . . . now that he'd kissed her, she realized it was something entirely different.

Licking her rather chapped lips, she felt her cheeks flush at the memory of his touch. He sparked a fire inside her. He left her weak-kneed and full of romantic thoughts. No one else had ever done that. Was this truly what it was to fall in love? Could she give her heart to this man? Love him? Marry him? Could she develop any relationship before she'd first dealt with the past?

Karen knew she must deal with her anger toward Martin Paxton. It was affecting everything else in her life. Leah knew it. Adrik and Grace had both endured the effects of it.

Poor Grace. Karen hadn't seen her young friend since their encounter. The thought of Grace being so near yet so far away—just a few miles away in Skagway—was frustrating. Karen longed to make things right between them again. She longed to sit down and put aside talk of Paxton and even of Peter. She longed for things to go back to the way they had been before they'd come to Alaska.

How many times had Karen faced a new day only to wish—even pray—that the reality of her life was nothing more than the remnants of a bad dream? But as bad as her own nightmarish existence was, there was Leah to contend with. Leah's grief had changed the girl. She added her brother's disappearance to her list of losses, tallying them like an account she could never hope to reconcile. Karen saw the child slip further away almost daily. Gone were the vibrant smile and childlike faith. In their place had come a touch of cynicism and defeat, emotions much too adult for a girl not yet thirteen.

It could still be worse, Karen reminded herself as she began braiding her hair into a single plait. She felt her stomach churn at the mental image of women young and old working in the cribs down by the harbor. Leah would most likely be there herself if not for Karen's protection. It was only—yes, she had to admit it—the grace of God that had kept them from harm's way this far.

"I know I'm acting the fool," she said softly to the God she'd resolved to turn from. She bowed her head and tied a ribbon around her braid. "It's just so hard to be here—to endure this life. You have no idea."

But of course, she knew that was wrong. Jesus had come to earth to know every part of being human. The insults, the sorrows, the loneliness. And oh, the loneliness was so overwhelming. Karen brushed a tear away and closed her eyes. Her soul cried out for real communion with God, but even as she contemplated surrendering her will, Martin Paxton's face came to mind once again.

He had no remorse for the things he'd done. He wanted only to have his own way and to hurt those people who stood against him. Karen balled her hands into fists, fists that she'd love nothing more than to use against Paxton. Her breathing quickened, and she jumped to her feet.

"How long must I suffer like this? I'm like two different women. Just when I think I can lay this aside and make peace with God, I see that man and know that I cannot leave the matter alone and walk away."

She began to pace. "I can't allow him to ruin my life."

She heard the words echoed back to her and stopped short. "But he is ruining my life. My hatred of him is destroying everything. My friendship with Grace . . . my love of God. It's even wreaking havoc with the potential love of a good man. And for what?"

She caught her reflection in a small mirror that hung near the door. Her expression reminded her of another person. The anger and bitterness was the same. That expression had belonged to Peter Colton.

"I have become what I thought impossible to be." The sorrow of it broke her spirit and left her devoid of hope.

———————

Grace had heard of the newly installed telegraph system and had hoped to get a message off to her mother. She had to know what it was that kept Martin Paxton so interested in her. She had to know why he refused to leave her in peace and let her life find some normalcy.

If it could find normalcy.

Grace wasn't at all convinced that anything could ever be right again, much less good. She had come to Alaska to flee one monster, only to find herself married to another. But she loved this beast. He had taken her heart as surely as she had taken his name.

Walking unescorted to the telegraph office, Grace found the strength to continue only by trusting in the knowledge that God would never leave her nor forsake her. Should everyone else desert her—leave her to die alone, she knew God would be there. Her faith had been strengthened by the adversity she'd endured. Peter's anger only served to drive her to prayer, where her heavenly Father sent comfort through His Holy Spirit.

Martin Paxton was a thorn in the flesh, to be sure, but he didn't frighten Grace half as much as Peter did, perhaps because she loved Peter and cared nothing for Paxton. Perhaps because she knew Martin Paxton could only take her life, but Peter would have her soul if he thought it possible.

Ignoring the men who eyed her and called to her, Grace quickly sent her telegram, paying the exorbitant sum of five dollars. She hurried back to the hotel, hoping that Peter hadn't returned and found her missing. He had warned her to stay off the streets of Skagway. Apparently, rumor had it that most of the passes were in perfect condition for pressing north. People were creating a new, smaller stampede from the one they'd left in the lower states. This stampede was leaving the comforts of Skagway to head into the vast unknown territories. Gold lured them forward—called to them. Gold beckoned them to forget their loved ones and face the risk of death.

But in spite of Peter's concerns, the town had emptied out onto the trails rather quickly. The stampede was gone, leaving behind those souls who had taken up residence in Skagway, along with stragglers who had lost their caches in games gone bad. Every day, however, new arrivals poured in, the fever glazing over their eyes, keeping them from seeing the truth of the disease that had come to grip them.

By night, Grace knew the rowdies would be out and about. Skagway's lawlessness rivaled nothing she had ever known, and Peter's concerns were well justified. Jefferson "Soapy" Smith and his men were notorious for the trouble they caused. They weren't alone, however. Scallywags and hoodlums of every sort were to be found in the town. Everyone wanted something from someone, and gold was almost always at the bottom of it.

In the exodus of gold seekers, Peter had managed to secure a private room next to his parents' for himself and Grace, and it was in this room that Grace sought her solace. The four bare walls offered no comfort. Gone was the beauty of the rooms she'd known growing up. Even the simplistic charm of the little room she'd once shared with Karen was preferable to these stark confines.

But as much as she desired the beauty and warmth of her childhood, she needed answers more. Answers to questions that seemed so illogical to even ask. Why did Martin Paxton desire to marry a woman who clearly held him in contempt? Why did he pursue her to the point of ruining lifelong friendships and giving old men heart attacks? Why, when she had nothing left to offer him but her body, did Martin Paxton find the price worth paying?

Then there were questions about Peter. Why did he so fervently refuse to see God's part in his life? How could he have no desire for spiritual truth? How had he lost his desire for her?

He'd not even come back to their room the night before until well into the morning hours. Grace had pretended to be asleep as he fell into the bed beside her. She had thought to herself, *If he reaches for me, I will willingly go into his arms.*

But he never reached for her.

"I love him so much, Father," she prayed. Picking up her Bible, she held it close for comfort. She didn't have the energy to read the Scriptures between the covers, but just holding it gave her a sense of peace. Settling into a chair, Grace lost track of the time. She dozed off, weary from the battle she'd been fighting, only to awaken disoriented.

She wondered at the time, then startled when a loud, insistent knock came at the door. Apparently it had been this that had brought her from her sleep in the first place.

Peter had already left by the time she'd awakened that morning and she'd not seen him since, so she hoped that it might be him. She put the Bible aside and hurried to the door. Throwing it back, she was surprised to find a boy, no more than twelve or thirteen years old, standing there holding out a telegram.

"Are you Mrs. Colton?"

"I'm Mrs. Grace Colton," she replied.

"Then this here telegram is for you." He thrust the paper

toward Grace and hurried back down the hall almost before she could take hold of the missive. Apparently he wasn't concerned with getting a tip.

Opening the telegram, Grace couldn't contain her surprise. It was a response from her mother. She scanned the lines quickly and felt all hope drain away. Her mother simply advised her that she should do whatever Mr. Paxton told her. That he could still hurt them both.

Grace didn't even remember to close the door. She walked back to her chair and sat down hard. How could this be? Why would her mother direct her to do such a thing when she'd previously been so supportive of Grace remaining free of Martin Paxton?

"May I come in?" Peter questioned from the door.

Grace looked up and found him staring at her as if seeing her for the first time. "Of course you may come in. It's your room as well as mine."

Peter crossed the threshold and quietly closed the door. Grace watched him, confused by his gentle nature and uncertainty. "Is something wrong?" she questioned.

"Yes." He came to where she sat. "I've been unreasonable and owe you a great many apologies." He knelt beside her. "I never meant to let things get so muddled. I don't even know who I am anymore or why I act as I do."

Grace felt her heart nearly break. He looked so lost. She reached out and took hold of his hand and brought it to her lips. "Oh, Peter, I'm so very sorry for all that you've had to endure. Especially for those things you've endured on my behalf."

"No, it's not your fault. You have no reason to apologize. Even your faith is not an issue that should divide us. I know that now, but I cannot pretend to believe as you do. I'm sorry

I've failed you as a husband. I'm a poor leader, both spiritually and physically. I'm responsible for losing my family's business, and I've nearly lost you. Please tell me I'm not too late."

Grace got to her feet, the telegram now forgotten. "You could never be too late. Oh, Peter, I love you. I'm sorry I'm not the wife you had hoped me to be. There is still so much we do not know about each other. So much that is yet to be overcome."

He held her close and buried his face in her hair. "I know I'm difficult at times. I know I've said things that hurt you." He pulled away and shook his head. "I know, too, that I can never take back those words."

He walked away from her and seemed to struggle with his thoughts. Grace stood still, afraid that she might break the fragile peace should she do anything but await his words. Turning to face her again, Peter frowned.

"I cannot make this right. I cannot hope to see Paxton pay for the harm he's caused, yet everything in me rises up to demand it. As a woman, you have no idea what it is for a man to face this humiliation. My father lies ill in the next room. My mother and sister have no hope of returning home except at the mercy of the very man who has caused their misery. The man openly covets my wife and sees nothing wrong in tempting her to divorce me and marry him."

"He has not tempted me," Grace said softly.

Peter stared at her for a moment as if trying to convince himself of her words. It was then he spied the telegram on the floor. "What's that?"

Grace looked quickly to where the paper lay. "It's nothing." She bent to retrieve the telegram and folded it to put it in her pocket. If she shared the news with Peter, he would know that she'd disobeyed him and had gone alone to the telegraph office. Furthermore, he would not be pleased by the message.

"That's a telegram. I didn't even realize they'd put a line through. Who is it from?"

"It's not important," Grace replied. "I'd rather hear what you have to say." Nervously, she warred within her mind. *If I tell him he'll be angry, and if I don't tell him he'll feel betrayed. Oh, God, what am I to do?*

"What are you hiding?" Immediately he sounded suspicious. "I demand that you allow me to see that message."

He took several steps toward her, and Grace knew she had once again managed to rile the beast. "Peter, it is to our benefit that you forget about this telegram. Please. I want only to sow peace between us." She looked up to him, hoping he could read the pleading in her eyes.

"So now you're making a habit of keeping secrets from me?" he questioned, but his tone made it clear that he'd already determined the answer.

"Peter, I do not desire to keep things from you. The telegram is unimportant. What is important is that you know you can trust me. I'm not the enemy here."

"For all I know you're in this with him."

"You don't really believe that. You can't believe that."

"Why not?" He shook his head as if he couldn't quite put the pieces together. "How am I to know what the truth is when you insist on keeping it from me? It seems quite reasonable that you could have formed some sort of alliance with Paxton."

"You aren't speaking rationally," Grace said. Fear flooded her heart, giving a trembling to her voice. "You . . . can't . . . say these things." How could this continue? She was only trying to protect him from her mother's suggestion that Grace cooperate with Paxton. He would hate her mother for saying such a thing, even as Grace suspected he now hated her for her secrecy.

"So now you think me mad? You think me incapable of seeing this situation for what it is—a betrayal of our marriage vows? Do you tell Paxton your secrets? Does he know your heart? And here I came to apologize—thinking I was the problem."

Grace drew her hand to her mouth to keep from crying aloud, but her muffled sobs were no less evident. He truly believed the worst of her. He thought her a traitor. She struggled to compose herself while Peter watched, eyes raging silent accusations at her.

"Peter," she finally managed to speak, "do you love me? Do you trust me at all?"

"Why do you ask me that now? You speak of words and their importance, yet you bandy them about as though they were halfpenny candy. I had a business and a good life before you came into my world. I should have known the worst would be upon me for disregarding my own misgivings."

Grace fought to keep her voice even. The pain was tearing her heart in two. "Then you truly wish we'd never married?"

"I wish I'd done whatever it would have taken to keep this regretful existence from happening. I wish I had a wife who trusted me enough to share her secrets and respected me enough to keep her faith to herself." He calmed considerably as he studied her. This calm was even more unnerving than his anger.

"I can't live up to your expectations, Grace. I cannot believe as you believe. I cannot provide as a husband should provide. Until I met you, I had thought my life well ordered.

Now ... well, now there's little hope that we can put this right."

Grace felt the tears stream down her cheeks but refused to wipe them away. She thought only of her mother's words to do as Martin Paxton had asked. She thought she ought to simply show Peter the telegram, but she realized the time for that had passed.

Peter went to the far end of the small room and took up his trunk. "I'll leave you to your telegrams and secrets. Perhaps you will find solace in them."

She felt ill. Would he really leave her? Divorce her? "Where are you going?"

"It doesn't matter. I know I'm not wanted here, and I don't intend to stick around and watch what I once thought of as love further crumble and die."

Grace watched him walk from the room. She crossed to the door and thought to call after him as he made his way down the stairs, but something held her back. Her hand went to the telegram in her pocket, and she knew it would have done little good to call after him.

"What are you doing out here, Grace?" Miranda questioned as she came from the room next door.

"Saying good-bye to my heart," she murmured.

Miranda came to stand directly in front of her. She took hold of Grace's arms, forcing her attention. "What are you saying?"

"Peter's left me. He's just now gone away ... and," she looked beyond her sister-in-law to the now empty stairs, "I don't think he's ever coming back."

Part Two

MAY 1898

He discovereth deep things out of
darkness, and bringeth out to light
the shadow of death.

JOB 12:22

—{ CHAPTER FOURTEEN }—

KAREN CALLED IT a meeting of grave importance. She had sent a note to Adrik and now sat across the small table from both him and Leah Barringer.

"It's been weeks since Jacob left, with no word from him. The town's abuzz with newcomers and would-be miners in every shape and size. Every day," Karen continued, "more and more people pour over Chilkoot Pass on their journey north to gold and fame. I can't sit here and wait and wonder what has happened to Jacob in the midst of that onslaught."

Adrik seemed to consider her words as he thoughtfully rubbed his chin. "Well, what do you have in mind?"

Karen looked at Leah. Only that morning she'd tried to encourage Leah by suggesting they go look for Jacob. It was the first spark of life she'd seen in the child since he'd disappeared. "I think we should go after him."

"To Dawson?" Adrik questioned in disbelief.

"Yes," Karen replied. "If that's what it takes."

"And what if we did that? What if we went all that way and still didn't find him? Then what?"

Karen hadn't considered the scenario any further than the idea of going along the same path Jacob would surely have taken. "I don't honestly know. I suppose we could settle in and put out word that we were there. We could put up posters asking for information. If they have a newspaper, we might even place an advertisement."

Adrik nodded. "You've thought this all out, I take it."

Karen shook her head and looked to the table. "Actually, no. I mentioned the idea to Leah this morning, and she liked it. Other than telling Mrs. Neal that we needed a quiet place to meet this evening, I hadn't considered anything else."

"Well, there's a great deal more to do with heading to Dawson than deciding it should be so. You have no idea what the trail is like and how demanding the ordeal will be," Adrik told her. "Not only is this a wilderness with pathways barely mucked out by those who've passed before you, but there are very real dangers."

Karen felt she had to persuade Adrik. Perhaps in doing so, she might also persuade herself. "I know that, but other women and children have made the trip and lived to tell about it."

"And others have died and lay buried alongside the trail in unmarked graves. I'd hate to see that for you or Leah."

"I want to find Jacob," Leah said, speaking for the first time in days without having a direct question posed to her. "I want to know if Pa is really dead. I know it won't be easy to hike the trail. My pa told us all about it. He'd read up on it. But I still want to go. I want to try."

Adrik smiled at her, and Karen saw the sympathy and kindness in his expression as he reached out to touch Leah's shoulder. "I know you love your brother and want to know the truth about your father, and no man could ask for a better sister or daughter. But, Leah, you have no idea what you'd be up against. The nights are bitter cold, even now with the spring coming. There will be floods with the thaw and wild animals. There are miles to go between here and Dawson City, miles that you will have to walk. Are you really up to that?"

Leah lifted her chin ever so slightly. "I'll do what I have to. Ma said that was the way it was with life. You face each day as it comes. And the way I see it, every day spent on the trail would put me that much closer to Jacob and maybe even Pa."

"She's got a point, Adrik," Karen said softly. "The reason I've asked you here is to find out if you'd be our guide. I could pay you."

Adrik frowned. "I'd hoped maybe I was something more than a guide."

"You're our friend," Leah responded before Karen could speak. "You're the only one we trust."

Adrik met Karen's eyes. He seemed to demand answers from her that she wasn't yet ready to give him. Understanding this, he drew a deep breath and put both his palms down on the table. It looked as though he might push himself up and leave, but instead he blew out his breath loudly and patted the tabletop. "I suppose we need to figure out what our assets are. The supplies needed to go north are extensive, as you well know. A ton of goods per person won't be cheap. Then there are tariffs to pay to the Canadians, and we can't hope to pack this stuff all on our own. I can hire a couple of natives to help, but they probably won't want to go any farther than Lake Bennett."

Karen smiled. He was going to help them. The thought sent a wave of relief washing over her. She flashed him a look of gratitude—at least she hoped he'd see it for that. "I have the list that appeared in the paper," she said, pulling the notice from her pocket. "Does this appear to suggest all of the necessary supplies?"

Adrik took the paper and scanned it. "I have tools—we needn't have those things for each person. I also have a large tent we can share and a cookstove, so we needn't buy those things, either."

"I don't know that it would be such a good idea for us to share a tent," Karen replied. "We aren't . . . well . . . that is to say . . ." She felt her cheeks grow hot. "We aren't family."

"We could remedy that," Adrik said with a laugh. "Wouldn't hurt my feelings none." He leaned over and playfully nudged Leah. "How about you? Would you be against Karen marrying someone like me?"

Karen felt mortified. He'd never talked of marriage—not outright like this. Leah giggled. Karen hadn't heard that girlish sound in weeks. Leah had been so lost in her sorrows that laughter had been buried along with the news of her father and her brother's disappearance.

"Enough!" Karen declared. "Just buy another tent. We have the money."

Adrik turned to study her for a moment. He raised a brow as if to question her certainty on the matter, then shrugged. Karen couldn't help but see something akin to regret, maybe even hurt, in his expression.

"You talk as though money is no object," Adrik said, looking back at the list. "I think we'd better figure out how much we have for this. I have nearly eight hundred dollars from my packing experiences. I want to leave some of it for Joe and his family. Packers aren't making much money these days, what with the tramway taking their business."

"That's perfectly fine," Karen replied. "We did very well with the store, and Mr. Colton was quite generous with our profits. I have my aunt's share as well as my own. There's probably twelve hundred dollars in my account."

"Well, coming from a camp where they charged twenty-five dollars for a dozen eggs, you're going to need every cent you can put your hands on," Adrik replied. "We've also got to remember the duty taxes. I've heard it said you'll pay a pretty penny to get the Canadians to let you cross their borders."

"I'm sure the stores here will give us a good deal. I was always generous with them when they needed something from me," Karen said. "Do you think we can get everything we need here in Dyea?"

Adrik continued to look at the list and nodded. "I feel confident we can, but you'll pay dearly whether they owe you favors or not. Can you maybe get Mrs. Neal to let you have some of her kitchenware rather than buying it all brand-new?"

"It's possible. What will we need?"

"Well, I have a coffeepot and a skillet, so we don't need to worry about that," he replied. "See if she can spare a couple of pie tins. You can use those over the fire if need be or just heat things up on the camp stove with them. You can eat out of them, wash out of them, and even dig with them if you have to. They make a very useful tool. If she doesn't have any, we'll buy rather than settle for plates."

Karen nodded. "I'm sure we can get them. What else?"

"You and Leah will each need your own tin cup and knife. I can find you a couple of good pocketknives. These are vital. You need them to stay alive. Never underestimate the useful-ness of anything. Why, I once saw a man pull his bootlaces out and make a fishing line with them and a safety pin. You just never know."

"Sounds like we'll have ample chance to use our imaginations," Karen said with a grin.

He laughed and looked at her in such a way as to warm her blood. "You don't know the half of it."

They pored over the supply list for another half hour before they all felt they knew exactly what their responsibilities were to be. Leah began to yawn, and Karen finally sent her upstairs, leaving only Adrik to sit with her in the dim lamplight of Mrs. Neal's empty dining room.

"So what do we do when we find him?" Adrik asked, his voice low and appealing.

They were so very alone, Karen realized, and for a moment the idea rather excited her. She wondered if he might attempt to kiss her again. And if he did, she wondered if she would try to stop him. "Find whom?" she asked, rousing herself from such thoughts.

Adrik looked at her, rather puzzled. "Whom do you suppose? Jacob."

Karen shrugged. "I hadn't thought past the search. And I really don't have any hope of finding Bill. Even if the man you found wasn't Bill, he could be so far away by now we might never find him. He may not even have survived another leg of his journey."

"Have you ever considered settling up north? Whitehorse or Dawson?"

Such thoughts had once accompanied Karen to Alaska, but they'd died out with her father's passing. "I don't know what I want to do. Things are so very confusing right now. I had thought about teaching the native children—you know that, of course, from our previous talks. Now I just don't know."

"You don't seem quite as angry as the last time I saw you," Adrik braved.

"No, I suppose not." She brought her elbows to the table and leaned her chin against her folded hands.

"Wanna talk about it?"

She heard the desire in his voice. Not a passionate desire, but rather one of hope that she would not shut him out. "I suppose there's really very little that you aren't already aware of. I miss my father. I'm confused about God and what He wants from me. I'm angry for being angry, and torn apart for hurting the people I care about most."

"Nothing's been said or done that can't be fixed," Adrik suggested.

"I can't bring the dead back to life, and that's what I really need. I need my father to tell me it's all right—that I can stay on with him and that he'll teach me how to minister to the people he so loved. I need Aunt Doris and my mother to encourage me and love me until I'm strong enough to stand on my own again. I need Bill Barringer to come back to his children—to father them and care for them as only a parent can.

"I need things I can't even identify," she said in complete exasperation.

"Well, I can't bring the dead back to life, either," Adrik said softly, "but I can tell you that it's all right—that you can stay on with me, and that I'll teach you how to minister to the people your father loved—the people I love."

Karen closed her eyes and buried her face in her hands. Why did she have to be so moved by his words? Why did she have to feel all weak and shaken? "I don't know what's right.

I don't know what God wants because I haven't bothered to ask Him."

Adrik took hold of her wrists and pulled her hands away from her face. When Karen still refused to look at him, he let go of her arms and put two fingers to her chin. "Look at me," he commanded.

She opened her eyes, but her vision blurred from her tears. She'd been so cruel to him. Why did he go on enduring her?

"God wants you to talk to Him. He wants you to put aside childish ways and trust Him. You've been fighting Him, wrestling Him for a blessing, and He's already provided."

"But He's taken away so much that I loved."

Adrik rubbed his thumb against her cheek. "But maybe He's given you new things to love."

She trembled under his touch. She wanted Adrik to hold her, to kiss her, to promise her that nothing would ever hurt her again. If only he would make that pledge, she could tell him that she loved him—would love him forever. But she wanted the same of God, and if God wouldn't give her that promise, how could this mere mortal?

Breaking the spell, Karen jumped up from the table, sending her chair flying backward to crash against the floor. For a moment she shook off the spell Adrik had woven over her, and by the time he got to his feet, Karen felt a firm resolve to send him on his way.

"I have to go," she said in a curt manner. "Leah will be wondering where I am."

She headed for the door, but Adrik caught hold of her before she could get that far. Swinging her around, he pulled her against his chest and held her fast.

"What are you afraid of?"

She swallowed hard. "Everything," she whispered.

"Don't be." He put his hand to the back of her head and buried his fingers in her coiled braid. His mouth came against hers in a kiss so sweet and passionate that Karen momentarily took leave of her senses.

She lost herself in his embrace, allowing her hands to travel up to the back of his neck. She memorized the feel of the scar that edged along the right side, leaving a deep furrow where his collar reached. She let her fingers toy with the thickness of his hair, all while being very much aware of his hands. One pressed against the small of her back keeping her snug against the warmth of his body, while he'd brought the other around to the side of her face.

He was all she wanted. Nothing else mattered. Not the trip north nor her damaged friendship. Nothing else even came to mind. She wanted nothing more than to stay forever in his arms.

Returning his kiss with a zeal she'd not known herself capable of, Karen all at once realized she was gasping for air. The smell and taste of this powerful, wonderful man had completely stolen her senses. Forcing herself to regain control, Karen brought her hand between them and pushed at Adrik's chest. She had to stop this now or she might forget herself all together.

"Adrik!" She staggered back and looked at him, embarrassment replacing the passion.

He grinned at her in an irritating manner that furthered Karen's journey back to reality. "What? Am I doing it wrong?" he asked, as if he had no idea what the problem might be.

Karen bit her lip for a moment, then shook her head. "Buy another tent. That's final."

She heard him laugh as she hurried from the room. No doubt he had no idea what he'd done to her. No doubt he had no idea how hard it had been for her to walk away.

―{ C H A P T E R   F I F T E E N }―

ADRIK GOT LITTLE SLEEP that night. And the next. Consumed with his feelings for Karen, he could only remember the way she'd felt in his arms—the way she had yielded to his kiss.

"She loves me," he said aloud as he pulled on his boots. "I'm certain of it, but how do I make her certain of it, as well?" He got up from his cot and went to the makeshift table he used for his tent. Picking up his Bible, he pored over the Scriptures between sips of steaming coffee. The book of First John spoke to him of God's love and the need to show love in return to God's children.

"I love her," he said prayerfully. "I know she loves me. I know she loves you, too. Oh, Father, she's just afraid. She's terrified that you have somehow forgotten her. She's worried that the love she's given has somehow been misplaced. Help her, Father. Help her to see that just because bad things have happened, it doesn't mean you haven't been there all along, grieving with her, sharing her sorrow."

Adrik closed the Bible and buried his face in his hands. He continued to pray in silence, losing track of the noises around him and the time.

Help me not to make a mess of things by pushing her for answers before she's ready to give them. Help me to take her and Leah north, to do it safely. And please, Lord, let us find Jacob. I probably shouldn't have let him go off like I did, but I know how it feels to mourn a father's death. I needed time to myself, and I was certain he did, too. I didn't mean to be neglectful of my duties as a Christian man. If I failed to respond in the right way, please forgive me.

He prayed for some time, and only when he felt he'd exhausted himself before God's throne did Adrik put away his Bible and head out to tend to business.

"Where are you headed?" Dyea Joe asked. His dirty white bowler was pulled down tight over oily black hair. Added to this, his heavy pants, coat, and best boots told Adrik that Joe was ready to head back up to pack goods on the trail.

"I have to buy supplies. Are you game for a bit of a trip?"

Joe shrugged. "I was going up with the others. Why?"

"I've agreed to pack north with Karen Pierce and Leah Barringer. They're desperate to find Jacob Barringer and to know the truth about whether the man I found in the avalanche was really Bill. I'm not sure what we'll do once we're up there, but we'll go until we find the boy and then decide. I just wondered if you and your family wanted the job packing."

"Sure," Joe said, nodding. He followed Adrik to the Yukon outfitters and stopped short of going inside. "How soon you want to leave?"

Adrik realized they'd not settled on a day or time. "I'm not sure. It'll take me a day or two to put everything together. Why don't you round up some reliable men and meet me tonight at my tent? We'll discuss the time and place then."

"I'll be there."

"Good. Now I have to buy a tent," Adrik said, pulling open the door to the shop.

"Buy a tent? You have a tent," Joe declared.

Adrik turned and smiled. "I don't have a big enough tent."

Joe shrugged in confusion, tapped down his bowler as if it had come loose, then sauntered off down the street. Adrik laughed, knowing the man couldn't hope to understand the situation. Then again, Adrik wasn't exactly sure he understood it all himself.

Four hours later, Adrik shook hands on the last deal. Eight hundred pounds of flour, three hundred pounds of split peas, and three hundred pounds of sugar were to be delivered by morning. This, added to the condensed milk, coffee, dried potatoes, fruit, rice, and beans that he'd already purchased earlier in the morning would round out their supplies rather nicely. He knew they could pick up other things once they got to Sheep Camp or the Scales. Discouraged men would be turning back by that point, and there was always a supply of goods to be bought.

Stopping by the Gold Nugget for lunch, Adrik figured to satisfy his appetite and talk to Karen at the same time. He walked into the dining room and spied her working at one of the far tables. A rowdy group of men seemed to be overstepping their bounds as she worked to maneuver out of their reach. Adrik frowned. It seemed the men had escaped manners and common decency when they came north. He crossed the room just as one man put his hand out to give Karen's backside a friendly pat.

Adrik plowed his fist into the man's jaw, leaving everyone at the table to stare up in stunned silence. Except, of course, the injured man. He howled like Adrik had mortally wounded him. Even Karen turned rather abruptly, startled by her customers' expressions and the man's obvious pain. Adrik noted her face had reddened considerably.

"What'd ya do that for, mister? I didn't mean any harm." The wounded man rubbed his jaw and winced.

"I didn't mean any harm, either," Adrik replied. "Just figured if we were putting our hands where they had no business bein', then I'd get in on the fun, as well. Now, if you apologize to the lady, I might be inclined to put an end to our game."

"Sorry, miss," the man said, sounding profoundly sincere.

Karen said nothing but seemed pleased that Adrik had come to her rescue. He winked at her and asked, "Do you have a table for me?"

She looked over her shoulder and motioned with her head. "You can sit over there."

Adrik spied the small corner table. "Can you join me?"

"In about ten minutes," she replied. "Mrs. Neal has a couple of girls coming in to spell us. We've been at this pretty much since breakfast. I think this must be a new group headed north."

Adrik nodded. "I'll wait over here. Whatever you're dishing up today is just fine by me." He grinned, then leaned close enough that only Karen could hear him add, "As long as you come with the meal."

She elbowed him away. "I'll bring you fish heads and seaweed if you don't mind your manners."

He laughed all the way to the table, knowing that if Karen

Pierce served them up, he'd find a way to digest them. He watched her work, admiring her stamina and grace. She conducted herself like a lady but wasn't averse to getting her hands dirty. Maybe it was because she came from a family of good hardworking folk who'd brought her up to appreciate manual labor as well as an education. And in truth, Adrik admired her mind, as well. She was smart—smarter than most women. Smart and pretty. Now, there was a combination.

Adrik continued watching her, needing to assure himself that she was safe. He caught the veiled glance of the man he'd punched and noted the fellow's nose was already turning purple. *Well, he had it coming,* Adrik thought. Then he rationalized that he probably shouldn't have hit him. He knew he could have handled it in a different manner, but up here folks seemed to better understand a physical deterrent. They weren't all coming for a summer social, after all. They were greedy and hungry for gold, and that tended to sever a man's brain from his actions.

True to her word, Karen joined him a short time later. She brought with her two steaming bowls of bean stew. One of the new serving girls followed behind with a tray of coffee and warm biscuits.

After the girl had gone, Adrik suggested they bless the food. He took hold of Karen's hand before she could protest and held it fast in his own. He prayed a simple prayer of thanks, painfully aware of Karen's presence. The softness of her hand was enough to distract the most pious of men. After he said amen, he continued to hold on.

"It's going to be difficult to eat if you insist on holding my hand," Karen finally said.

Adrik grinned wickedly. "I could feed you."

"I could toss this coffee over your head," she said, smiling sweetly. "What happened to us all keeping our hands where they belong?"

"But this *is* where my hands belong."

"Ah . . . yes . . . well, we can discuss that later. I'm hungry and would like to eat my lunch."

Adrik gave her fingers a squeeze, then let go. "I suppose you're right." He picked up one of the biscuits and downed it nearly whole. He was starved, and the sight of Karen only made him more hungry. Hopefully the food would take the edge off his appetite.

"So were you successful in getting supplies?"

"Yup. I have a vast warehouse of goods, and Dyea Joe's getting some men together to help pack. He might even consider bringing his wife, since this will be a long trip."

"Wonderful. Another woman would be very welcomed. Leah and I discussed our needs this morning, and she's going to take in some trousers for us to wear under our skirts. I figured it would be far to our benefit to wear something substantial."

"No doubt you're right. I've seen all manner of things on the trail. Some women have just taken to wearing men's clothes. Others make themselves split skirts and such. I think the long dresses are a definite danger when climbing steep grades. You might well want to shorten your skirts."

"That sounds like a good idea," Karen said, nodding. "I'll do that before we go."

"Speaking of which, when did you have in mind to leave?"

"Soon," Karen replied. "But first I have to see to something else. I wonder if you might have time to take me to Skagway."

Adrik frowned. "Why?"

"I have to find Grace. I have to apologize for the way I

treated her." Karen looked down at the table. "I've let weeks pass by and I don't even know if she's still in Skagway, but I have to try to find her. I hurt her, and I can't just leave without making it right between us."

Adrik smiled, knowing she couldn't see him. God was working on softening her heart, and while he knew it was probably painful for Karen, he rejoiced to see the change. "Sure, I'll take you. We'll borrow one of Joe's canoes. When do you want to leave?"

———

Grace finished penning her note to Peter and sat back to wipe the tears from her eyes. She'd not seen him since he'd stormed out of their room. Nor did she expect to see him. She had no idea where she would go or what she would do, but she wouldn't be forced into a divorce. If Peter wanted to end their marriage, that was up to him. She would leave the decision in his hands, but she wouldn't allow Martin Paxton to dictate her future.

"Grace, are you in there?" Miranda called from the other side of the door.

"Come in."

Miranda opened the door hesitantly and stepped inside. "Have you heard anything?"

"No. Have you?"

Miranda shook her head. "Not a word."

She crossed the room and sat down on the edge of the bed. Her dark green skirt swirled out around her feet, revealing dainty black leather shoes. Hardly suitable for dealing with the knee-deep mud of an Alaskan thaw.

"So what are you going to do? Mr. Paxton has arranged passage for us at the end of the week. Father is supposed to be strong enough to travel by then."

"I don't plan to stay here, but I'm not sure where I'll go. I had thought I might make my way back to my mother, but she's confusing me just now and I'm not sure that would be wise. I have some jewelry from when we first came here. I never needed to use it because the store Peter set up did so well. But I have it with me and figure to sell it. I'll give you some money so that you can see to Mother and Father Colton's needs, as well as your own. Then I'll take the rest and go wherever I feel is best."

"You can't leave us. You must come home to San Francisco," Miranda declared.

Grace shook her head. "It's not my home. It's Peter's home, and he's made it clear he doesn't want me there."

"Mother is heartbroken. Father said he would go after Peter himself if only his health would permit."

Miranda and her family's loyalty did Grace much good. It helped to know that they didn't blame her or hold her in contempt for the troubles between her and Peter.

"It's nearly suppertime," Miranda added. "I thought you might join us."

"I'm not hungry," Grace replied. "I'd just as soon—"

A knock sounded at the door and both women jumped to their feet. They shared a glance that assured Grace they were both thinking it might be Peter. Grace hurried to the door and threw it open. It was not Peter, but it was nearly as good.

"Karen!"

"Oh, Grace," she cried before entering. "I've been such a fool. Can you ever forgive me?"

Grace opened her arms to her former governess and hugged her tight. "I'm so happy to see you. I'm so sorry for upsetting you in Dyea."

"I'm the one who needs to apologize," Karen said, pulling away. "I was horrible and my anger caused me to take out all my disappointments on you. I had to come and tell you so before I left."

"Left? Where are you going?"

Miranda joined the women. "We're leaving, as well."

Karen eyed Grace. "Where are you going?"

Grace shrugged. "I don't know. I don't really have any place that calls to me."

"I'm heading north to the goldfields. Jacob Barringer has fled Dyea for Dawson. He hopes to find his father alive or at least keep his father's dream alive. He's taken off alone, and I mean to find him."

"How terrible. You must be so worried. But honestly, are you up for a trip as they describe? The journey sounds so perilous."

"Life is perilous. I can't just wait around for something to happen. I've asked Adrik Ivankov to take us. Leah and I plan to head out tomorrow."

"How exciting. I envy you," Miranda said, surprising both women.

"Why do you say that?" Grace asked.

"The adventure sounds marvelous. Besides, if I had money, I'd go north myself."

"You would?" Karen questioned. "But whatever for?"

"My family has been stripped of its fortune, so I would go north to find gold. Other women are doing it. Why, I heard one woman tell the clerk next door that she was heading up there for her second trip. She'd gone up by way of St. Michael the first time and now she was heading up over the pass."

"You could both come," Karen said, suddenly realizing the potential of such an idea. "We'd help each other. We'd be together. Grace, you said you had no other place to go, and Miranda wants to come north anyway."

Miranda frowned and shook her head. "There are no funds for such a trip. Mr. Paxton is allowing my family passage back to San Francisco, but he has ownership of everything else. Besides, I know my mother needs me especially now."

"What is this all about?" Karen asked. "What has Mr. Paxton to do with any of this?"

"It's a very long story," Grace replied.

"And Peter?"

"An even longer story."

"Well," Karen said, taking off her gloves, "I suppose you had better start talking, then. I intend to hear it all so we can make an educated decision about what is to be done."

In the quiet of Grace's hotel room, Miranda and Amelia Colton listened to Karen's plans for the trip. Amelia nodded and asked questions from time to time, then finally grew very quiet.

"I cannot say that I don't have misgivings," she said softly. Looking to Miranda, she reached out to touch her daughter's cheek. "Your father is much stronger. I'll be able to take care of him without your help. However, I do worry about allowing you to go off without telling Ephraim exactly what you're about. I fear if I tell him the absolute truth, it could bode ill for him. I wouldn't want to risk that."

"Neither would I," Miranda replied. "Why not simply tell him that Grace needs me? That I might yet act as a negotiator between Grace and Peter."

Amelia looked at her daughter-in-law and nodded. "That would be my prayer."

Mine too, Grace thought, but said nothing.

"Oh, Mother, I just know this is right. I feel so wonderful inside—so excited." Miranda fairly beamed from the joy of her mother's approval.

"We truly are left without hope of finances. I don't know what is to be done, but God will provide. I do believe that much. Perhaps it's best this way."

"I have enough money to buy additional supplies for them," Karen assured, "and we have plenty of protection. Adrik Ivankov and some of his friends and family are going along to guide and help pack the goods. I trust him with my life."

"I, too, trust him, Mother Colton. Because I trust Karen's judgment." Grace hoped her words would further heal the relationship between her and her mentor.

Amelia smiled. "Then that will be good enough for me. Miranda may go."

—[C H A P T E R   S I X T E E N]—

FOR MIRANDA AND GRACE, their last order of business in Skagway was to bid farewell to Ephraim and Amelia Colton. Miranda and Amelia cried, as did Grace, but the Coltons were not in the leastwise worried about their daughter and daughter-in-law. Their renewed faith in God had given them hope for Miranda and Grace and for Peter's repentance and return.

Miranda left her mother with the promise that she would write often and bring home a fortune. Grace kissed her mother-in-law and pressed half the money she'd managed to secure from the sale of her jewelry into her hand.

"Tell no one," she whispered. "God has provided it, and I must share it with you. But I wouldn't want Mr. Paxton to get wind of this."

Amelia said nothing. She didn't even look at the money in

her hand. She simply pressed a kiss upon her daughter-in-law's cheek and smiled.

With Amelia and Ephraim steaming off for San Francisco, Miranda and Grace took their things and, with Adrik's help, moved into Karen's hotel room at the Gold Nugget. The plans were set to leave early the following morning. Grace felt a certain amount of relief in the rapid pacing Karen encouraged. She in no way wanted Martin Paxton to catch wind of what they were about. She would much rather he assume she was hiding out or sulking somewhere than to imagine her daring to head north with the stampede to the Klondike.

Karen's pacing would also help her to conceal another situation. Grace was now certain that she was with child. Any extra time spent in Dyea or Skagway might well reveal this secret, and Grace did not wish to be left behind. She knew the trek north would be a risk to her unborn baby, but she felt confident that God had directed her this way for a reason.

She had labored long and hard with her decision of where she might go. She didn't feel right going back to San Francisco, and at the same time her mother's attitude concerned her and left Grace with little desire to join her in Wyoming. Then there was the whole idea of leaving the northern territories and Peter. She had no idea where he was or what he was doing. She longed to tell him about the baby and felt confident that it would impact his feelings toward her. But on the other hand, did she want his heart changed only because of the child she would bear?

After the Gold Nugget supper crowd had cleared out, Karen and Adrik gathered everyone for a flurry of planning for the next day's departure. Grace got a chance to better know Adrik Ivankov and thought it rather amusing to see how much he and Karen doted upon each other. Funnier still was the way they refused to give in to their feelings and made pretenses at just being friends.

"The first part of the journey isn't the hardest," Adrik told them, stretching out a handmade map. "The trail has been forged—at least better than it used to be. They've even laid corduroy roads here and there."

"Corduroy?" Miranda questioned.

Adrik smiled and explained. "The ground up here is a bit of a problem. Winter is actually the best time to pass through a great deal of it. Come thaw, the ground in a lot of places turns all boggy and wet. It makes the simplest of travel a real nightmare. So some have taken to putting down tree trunks—side by side. They cut logs or take up fallen branches, so long as they're thick enough, then strip them and cut them down to size. Some have tried to charge a toll for passing on these roads, but the gold rushers got impatient with that idea and pretty much just pushed their way on through."

"I see," Miranda replied. Then, leaning toward Grace, she added, "I sure have a great deal to learn."

"Well, Mr. Ivankov is the man to learn it from," Leah Barringer threw in. "He's taught us a whole lot, and he saved our lives."

Grace easily recognized the younger girl's glowing admiration for Adrik. If Karen wasn't careful, Leah would make herself competition for the man's affections. Although Grace doubted Adrik would consider anyone but Karen. It was nice to see that her mentor had found true love, even if she did deny it to herself and everyone around her.

"The important thing is that we pack only the essentials and outfit ourselves appropriately. None of those flimsy satin dancing slippers for this hike," he said good-naturedly. "Only sturdy boots, and pack an extra pair. This won't be easy.

Spirits and soles will wear out before you know it."

Grace tried not to worry about the journey ahead, refusing to be left behind. When they were well away from any chance of sending her back to Skagway, she would tell them about the baby.

A baby! Just the thought completely consumed Grace's senses. How could this be? How, in the midst of such anger and confrontation, had a baby been conceived? God's plan for her life certainly seemed to differ from the plan Grace had thought up for herself.

She was happy about the baby, though, despite her sorrow over her current marital situation. She was glad to have some small reminder of her love for Peter. It was so hard to think of him hating her. Hating God. She mourned that thought more than his absence. If he didn't want her for a wife, she could deal with that. Her heart felt completely broken, but it was her own fault. She should never have married him—not with him so adamantly against having faith in Jesus. No, what truly pained her was that Peter should so completely alienate himself from God. God would not be mocked. Grace knew this full well, and she did not want to see Peter suffer because of his decision.

Please be merciful with him, she prayed. *Please guard Peter, Lord, and help him to see the truth about you.*

Grace scarcely heard the discussion around the table. She was lost in thoughts of Peter and the baby and had very nearly decided to go upstairs to rest when Martin Paxton came through the doors of the otherwise silent dining room.

"I've been looking for you, Mrs. Colton. I want to speak to you . . . now."

Everyone at the table looked up in unison. Grace stood, but Karen reached out to touch her arm. "You don't have to give him the time of day, Grace."

"What do you want?" she asked softly. She hoped he didn't find their little gathering too suspicious and quickly added, "We were just about to retire for the evening. Perhaps we could speak another time—say, next week."

Martin Paxton leered and folded his arms casually against his chest. "Next week won't work. I think it's time we discussed your answer."

A wave of nausea threatened Grace's resolve. "My answer?"

"Leave her alone," Karen demanded. "She wants nothing to do with you."

Adrik stood as if to challenge Paxton's claim. He said nothing, but Grace could see the protective nature of his stance. The last thing she wanted was a showdown in front of Leah and Adrik, not to mention Miranda.

"I'll talk with you," she finally said, getting to her feet. "But only if Karen is with me."

"I want to see you privately."

"I think you heard the lady's conditions on the matter," Adrik said, stepping next to Grace.

Paxton seemed to size up the situation before relenting. "Very well. Let's find a quiet corner."

Grace nodded. "Karen, where is that little office where I first met you upon my return to Dyea?"

"Right this way," Karen said, leading them across the room. "It's well within earshot of Adrik should the need arise." She looked at Paxton with great defiance—challenging him to comment on her words. He did not.

Karen and Grace went into the office first, with Paxton close on their heels. Karen protectively put her arm around Grace's shoulders for support. Grace felt blessed to have her friend so close at hand. If Paxton should have demanded she speak to him alone, she would have had little choice but to refuse him. Perhaps this way, she could resolve the past and put an end to his demands.

"Have you determined to divorce your husband and marry me?" Paxton asked without delay. He eyed Grace in the same cold, calculated manner as before.

She could very nearly feel his hot breath upon her neck— his hands upon her body. Shuddering, she shook her head. Very softly, almost inaudibly, she replied, "If my husband wishes to put an end to our marriage, he will have to do so on his own. I will not divorce him. It is against my beliefs."

"I see." Paxton reached into his pocket and produced a cigar. He toyed with it a moment, then pinched off the end and procured a match from his vest pocket. Striking the match, he lit the cigar, his gaze never leaving Grace. He puffed silently, staring at her as if deciding what to say next.

Praying silently, Grace knew she had to stand up to Paxton. She wouldn't tell him of her plans, but neither would she cower. God was on her side. There was nothing Paxton could do to further harm her.

"I don't believe you do see," Grace said, straightening her shoulders a bit. "I am a married woman. I am very much in love with my husband, and in spite of your actions to harm him and his family, I will support him and help them through."

"I saw for myself that the youngest of the Colton clan stayed behind at your side. She's a pretty woman."

"Leave Miranda out of this," Grace said firmly. "If you have some sort of vendetta against me, then hear me now. I am not afraid of you. I have a source of strength and power that you cannot even begin to understand. You are lost and alone inside the pits of evil that you've dug for yourself." Her chin raised ever so slightly, her confidence in God fueling her bravery. "You are not a threat to me, and I would thank you to give up this nonsense."

Paxton moved toward her. "Let me show you just how evil I can be." He grinned at Karen and tossed the cigar onto the paper-strewn desk. "Funny how easily things catch fire up here."

Grace saw Karen's face flush as she rushed to the desk to make certain the cigar caused no damage. Meanwhile, Paxton pressed toward Grace.

"You belong to me, Grace. Your father gave you to me, and I intend to have you."

Karen looked up and opened her mouth. Grace could only presume she meant to call for Adrik Ivankov, but Grace decided on another course of action.

"In the name of Jesus, I command you to leave me."

Paxton stopped and looked at her as if in disbelief. "I beg your pardon?"

Karen moved toward the door shaking her head. "I'll get Adrik."

Grace never faltered. She stood her ground, feeling a legion of angels as her protectors. "In the name of Jesus, I command you to leave me."

"Do you really expect that nonsense to mean anything to me?" Paxton questioned.

Karen stopped, seeming to forget about Adrik. She watched Grace with as much intensity as Paxton, but Grace could not give her attention to her friend.

"Jesus gave His children authority over the devil. And while you may not exactly be the devil himself, you are about his work. Therefore, I command you, out in the name of Jesus."

Paxton's expression changed to one Grace had never witnessed. Confusion. He looked at her and seemed to lean forward as though he might still advance, but his feet seemed nailed to the floor.

"Your faith and your God mean nothing to me," he said. He growled as if fighting some unseen assailant. His hands were raised as if to take hold of her or at least strike her, but he made no move to complete such tasks.

Grace felt awash with peace. There was no fear. It was as if all of heaven battled for her and she had only to stand and await the outcome. The faithfulness of God had been proven over and over to her, but never so dearly as in that moment.

"You're going to regret this," Paxton said. "You think you've already paid for trying to dupe me, but I've got news for you. This isn't over. It's just begun. You haven't yet tasted my wrath."

"Nor will I," Grace said, putting her hands to her hips. "I am no threat to you, Mr. Paxton. I have no interest in you and no desire for anything you might offer. I ran from you twice, taking matters into my own hands. I'm not running anymore. I'm standing here face-to-face with you. I'm here to tell you that my God is more powerful than you could ever imagine. I'm here to tell you that you have no power over me—no rights whatsoever to me. You have only accomplished what you have thus far because God has allowed it and my own hand has often even encouraged it. Well, that is done."

"None of this is done," Paxton said, his eyes narrowing. "It isn't done until I say it is done."

Grace said nothing more. There was no need. She could see that she'd shaken the man. He didn't understand this new manner of business, but Grace did. Grace remembered a sermon she'd heard not but a month ago. A sermon that talked of how God's children need not live in fear. That Satan was the one responsible for stirring fear and worry through his lies and doubts, and that God's children had power they'd never even begun to tap into. Well, she was staking her claim on that power here and now. She had to. For her sake and for Peter's, not to mention their unborn child.

Walking past Paxton without fear, Grace turned at the door. "Mr. Paxton, if you would spend half as much time in pursuing God as you have pursuing me, you would understand where my strength comes from."

She left him standing there, eyes burning and jaw fixed. His surprise was no less evident, however, than Karen's. Her friend stood with mouth agape, eyes wide and full of wonder. Grace knew Karen had been struggling with God's sovereignty and love. She could only hope that this demonstration of God's power to keep evil at bay would help to strengthen Karen's walk of faith.

Karen watched in disbelief as Martin Paxton stormed from the hotel. She followed him in silence to the open front door and watched as he joined in with the throngs of lost souls who headed to the gambling halls and saloons.

Quietly she closed the door and looked up the steps as if expecting Grace to still be standing there. She'd never witnessed anything such as what Grace had just done. The confidence and power that seemed to exude from her friend were impressive, to say the least. Where had she acquired such faith? To face evil, not but a few feet away, and refuse to back down because of the power of God—it was inspiring.

Shaking, Karen hugged her arms to her body and shook her head. It was nothing short of miraculous. Miraculous . . . and perhaps even terrifying.

—|CHAPTER SEVENTEEN|—

THROUGHOUT THE WINTER of 1897–98, Karen had understood why Skagway and the surrounding area was called what it was. Coming from a Tlingit word that meant "people of the north wind," Skagway bore the brunt of the chilled arctic air that bore down on the coast from the northern mountains. Dyea was no different. Now, however, with summer upon them, the reverse was true. Winds coursed in from the coast and rushed through the valleys and canyons toward the mountains.

This often made travel up the Chilkoot Trail very difficult. Karen tried not to think about the trials and tribulations and focused instead on Jacob and the land itself. Adrik gave her botany lessons, increasing her understanding of the land and the people who dwelt there.

Determined to carry her share, Karen had allowed Adrik

to decide how much she should carry. He had fixed her with a twenty-pound pack, advising her that once she grew used to this, they could increase the weight. She adjusted well at first. She even thought him silly to have given her so little. But by the end of the first day, Karen was grateful for Adrik's wisdom. After a long day twenty pounds felt more like two hundred pounds.

Casting her load aside, Karen dropped wearily to the ground and sought the support of a nearby spruce. With its heavy branches towering above her, Karen leaned back to look toward the sky. How long had they been at this? How long would they journey until they found Jacob, Bill, or the promised land of the Yukon?

Day after day it was the same. They trudged through muck and mud, forded streams and rivers, and bedded down at night to the restless sounds of the coastal rain forest.

"When do you think we might find Jacob?" Leah asked after they'd been on the trail for nearly a week.

Karen shrugged. "With your brother's determination, that would be hard to say. He was bound and determined to get north before too much time passed. He has a two-month lead on us, and up here timing is everything."

"She's right, you know," Adrik told Leah. He threw more wood on the fire, then sat down on the ground beside them. "Jacob's probably already in Whitehorse, knowing him."

"Where is that?" Leah asked, her face lit up in eager anticipation. She had talked of little but Jacob since they'd begun the trip.

"Whitehorse is over the mountains and farther north. Remember the map?" Leah nodded. "It's north past Lakes Lindeman and Bennett, Taggish and Marsh," Adrik said, stretching his hands out to the fire. "You'll get your fill of it all traveling by boat, that's for sure."

Yawning, Leah stated she was on her way to her tent, where Grace and Miranda were already bedding down for the night. She first turned and looked to Adrik and Karen for hope. "You do think we'll find him, don't you?"

"You mean Jacob?" Karen asked. She couldn't really say why, but she felt that Leah had begun to give up thoughts of finding her father. Maybe it was easier for the child to think of him as gone and deal with the loss, just in case it was true. Karen smiled at Leah's hesitant nod.

"I wouldn't be here if I didn't believe we could find him," Karen replied. She sincerely hoped she wasn't giving the child false encouragement.

The chill of the evening made Karen forget that it was already the first week in June. She shivered and decided it might be just as well to turn in with the rest. Even the packers were bedding down for the night. In fact, Dyea Joe and his sturdy little wife, Merry, had long since made their way to bed.

She thought it even more sensible to leave when Adrik scooted closer and put his arm around her. Her instincts suggested she flee, but her heart bade her stay.

"The nights are unpredictable," he murmured.

She turned, her face only inches from his. More than a little aware of the intense way in which he regarded her, Karen nodded. "I'm sure they aren't the only unpredictable thing up here."

Adrik smiled in that roguish way she'd come to love. He raised his brows and leaned closer. "Being unpredictable only adds to the adventure. But, on the other hand, if you learn to watch for the signs, you'll come out just fine."

"The signs, eh?" Karen said, unable to look away. She wasn't sure at this point if she could have willed herself to look elsewhere under any circumstances.

Adrik ran his hand up her arm before giving her shoulder a squeeze. "I've lived up here all my life, you know. Maybe not right here, but close enough. You'd do well to stick close to me. I can teach you things."

"What kind of things?"

His smile broadened. "All sorts of things."

Karen lost herself momentarily in eyes dark as the coffee they'd shared at supper. She trembled, but this time it wasn't from the cold. She jumped to her feet, uncertain as to whether she'd imagined his mouth moving closer to hers.

"I think I should join Leah and the others."

He looked up at her and shrugged. "Guess you have to do what you have to do."

Karen had half expected him to try to convince her to stay a while longer. When he didn't, she couldn't help but be disappointed. "All right, then," she said, still not entirely convinced of her mission. "I'll see you in the morning."

"All right," he murmured and stretched out on his side before the fire.

She looked down at him and saw the amusement in his expression. He knew how she felt. He knew she wanted to stay, but he wasn't going to ask her. Frustrated, Karen turned sharply on her heel, causing her shortened skirt to flair.

"Nice ankles," Adrik called. "Been meanin' to tell you that all day."

Karen felt her face grow hot. If she turned around now, she knew she'd find some excuse to stay. *Stay true to the mission*, she told herself. *Go to bed with the others and sleep off this silly infatuation. Tomorrow things will seem a whole lot different.*

She reached for the tent flap just as she heard Grace pose a question to Miranda.

"Will you do that with me? We could get up before the others and pray for Peter and even Mr. Paxton. We could pray for your folks and my mother. Not to mention the trip and our safety."

"I think that would be wonderful," Miranda replied. "Of course I'll pray with you."

"I thought you would. I know Karen isn't feeling too interested in such things. We should also pray for her. She's been deeply wounded. I know exactly how she feels. Sometimes it's hard to accept that God's ways are not always our own. I haven't always liked how things turn out, believe me. Mr. Paxton has been nothing but a thorn in my side, but I am willing to trust that God's Word is true. I will pray for my enemy, and I will pray for my husband."

"I'm glad you haven't lumped them together," Miranda replied.

A deep sensation of loneliness flooded Karen. She had been replaced by Miranda in Grace's life. Grace had demonstrated such strength of character in dealing with Mr. Paxton and others around her that Karen felt almost like a student— she was no longer the teacher and mentor.

She couldn't help but remember the stand Grace had taken with Paxton back in Dyea. She wasn't afraid of the man in any way. She had simply taken a stand on her faith in God.

Have I only been playing a role? Karen wondered silently. She had been raised in a loving Christian home and had never known a day when God wasn't revered and honored. She had prayed almost before she'd learned any other form of communication. Had it all been for naught?

Grace has something I want, she thought. *She has a grasp of God that I cannot seem to take hold of. Yet I'm the one who taught her. I'm the one who brought her into an understanding of faith in Jesus. How can it be that she has grown so far beyond me?*

Miranda and Grace's words had ceased, and Karen could only suppose they'd concluded their discussion. She entered the tent, grateful for the dim lantern light. It had been very thoughtful of them to leave it turned up so that she could see.

Karen prepared for bed quickly. The choices were limited and desiring to stay as warm as possible, she wasn't about to worry about bathing or other notions. She turned down the lamp until the flame went out, then made her way to her pallet. Slipping into her sleeping bag, compliments of the latest shipment from Sears Roebuck, Karen snuggled down, relishing the feel of the sheep's wool against her cold cheeks. The contraption had cost her thirteen dollars, an outrageous sum, but Adrik had thought it a worthwhile purchase. He'd reminded her that the product would eliminate the need to bring so many separate pieces of bedding. With that in mind, she'd purchased a bag for both herself and Leah. By the time Grace and Miranda had decided to join them, however, the bags were completely sold out.

But Adrik was ever to the rescue. He had procured heavy wool blankets and promised they'd work just as well. Karen prayed it was so. The nights could still be quite cold, as tonight was.

"Karen?" Grace's whisper came through the silence of the night.

Surprised, but pleasantly so, Karen turned onto her side so that she might not disturb Leah, who slept behind her. "Yes?"

"Thank you for inviting me to come along. I don't know what I would have done without you. The months away from you were . . . well . . . I missed you greatly. Miranda is a dear sister to me, but you were like a mother. I needed you then, just as I need you now. I just wanted you to know how very much I love you and thank God for you."

Karen felt engulfed in her friend's love. She felt a lump in her throat constrict her words. "That means so much," she barely whispered.

Karen reached across the distance between them in the darkness. She touched Grace's shoulder and followed the contour of her arm down to her hand. There, Karen clasped their hands together.

"Grace, I want to pray with you and Miranda. I know I haven't worked through all my feelings yet, but I know that prayer is where I must begin. I need help, however. Would you and Miranda stand by me?"

"But of course," Grace whispered as if there had never been any doubt of Karen's decision.

Karen felt Grace tighten her hold. Without meaning to bring up the past, Karen said, "I see he never bought you a ring."

"No, he never did," Grace replied.

"I'm sorry, Grace. I'm sorry things have been so bad. I'm sorry Peter is so angry, and I'm sorry I helped to fuel that anger."

"Mr. Paxton has a way of bringing out the worst in all of us," Grace murmured. "It should be no different for you or Peter."

"He brought out the best in you," Karen replied. "I still have the vision of you standing up to him in defiance. It reminded me of David and Goliath."

"Me too. I kept thinking of David's declaration. 'Thou comest to me with a sword, and with a spear, and with a shield: but I come to thee in the name of the Lord of hosts. . . .' I felt the strength soar through me and imagined what David must have felt being in the presence of God's mighty protection and power."

Karen breathed a sigh and knew that God had given *her* that display of power as much as he had Mr. Paxton. He wanted her to know He was still God and He understood her pain and suffering. He wanted her to know that He had not forsaken them nor handed them over to the wicked—to Paxton.

"Good night, Grace," Karen said, giving her friend's hand another squeeze before pulling back to snuggle back down into her bag. "You are truly the image of your name, and I thank God for the honor of calling you friend."

The next morning Adrik was surprised to find Joe hunched over the campfire, talking to a long forgotten friend.

"Crispin Thibault!" Adrik called out as he bounded from the tent. "In all the world I never thought I'd find you here." He laughed heartily and waited as the man stood in greeting before wrapping him in a big bear hug.

"Adrik Ivankov, still the bear of the north, I see," Crispin said with a laugh that betrayed his absolute delight. "I saw Joe and figured you had to be close by. Then I spied your red-and-white flag and knew it had to be you." Crispin pointed to the strip of material Adrik kept tied to his tent flap. This same type of material was tied to the caches that represented the group's supplies.

Adrik had used the red-and-white material to mark his tent since he'd been a boy. His father had taught him this simple method for identification. It was almost as good as painting numbers on the doorpost of a house, and in some ways it was even better. Friends knew each others' markings, while strangers had no idea of the significance.

"What brings you back to Alaska?" Adrik questioned.

Crispin shrugged. "Gold—what else? I was residing very comfortably in the house of one of my French cousins when all this gold rush news came to entice us. I thought, why not travel north and see my old friend Adrik? I figured I'd find you in Sitka but heard tell you'd taken to living on the coast at Dyea."

Adrik nodded. "Been there a little over six years, off and on. I still travel more than I stay in one place. That's why I live in a tent instead of a house."

"You should come to stay with my French cousins," Crispin teased. "You'd not willingly go back to tenting."

"Maybe you have a point at that. So what news have you brought us? The communications are poor up here. We're lucky if we get a newspaper from Seattle now and then. What of the problems with Spain?"

"Well, let me think," Crispin said, looking rather thoughtful. "President McKinley has called for seventy-five thousand more volunteers to help out with this misunderstanding."

"It's a bit more than a misunderstanding. They blew up the *Maine*," Adrik replied. "We can't be havin' that."

"The rest of the world, including your Russia, has asked President McKinley for a peaceful end to this matter."

"It's not my Russia. I'm an American. I was born in this territory and plan to remain here," Adrik said, adding, "This land has been pretty good to the both of us, and it didn't happen by letting other folks push us around."

"Be that as it may, America may well fight this war alone."

"I'm sure we won't fight alone," Adrik replied with great

confidence. "We'll fight with God on our side."

Crispin laughed. "You Americans are always believing such nonsense. I think winning your revolution went to your heads."

"You sound like an Englishman."

"Forbid that!" Crispin declared rather dramatically. "My dear departed mother would swoon if she heard it said that I remotely resembled those tyrants. She'd rather I be called an American!"

"Now, that's a thought," Adrik said, slapping Crispin on the back with a hearty laugh.

"What's all the commotion?" Karen asked as she emerged from her tent. Miranda Colton was on her heels, tucking her long braided hair into the confines of a warm wool bonnet.

"Come meet my good friend Crispin Thibault," Adrik called. He motioned to Karen and Miranda. "I've not seen him in, what? Seven years?"

"To be sure," Crispin replied, his gaze fixed on the ladies. "My, but you travel in much prettier company than when I left you."

Adrik laughed. "There's two more just as pretty inside the tent, but these will do for starts. This is Karen Pierce and Miranda Colton."

Crispin drew his six-foot-three-inch frame to full attention, then gave a deep bow. "Ladies, I am charmed." He straightened and grinned at Adrik. "You are a man of many surprises."

"Not half as many as you, my old friend," Adrik leaned closer to Karen and added, "It is rumored that our Mr. Thibault is in line for the throne of some small European principality."

"How very interesting," Karen said, nudging Miranda.

"We're in the presence of royalty."

"Nonsense!" Crispin declared rather theatrically. He waved his arm and lifted his face to the cloudy skies. "It is a very minor principality, indeed, and my place in line is a dozen or more cousins away from ever being crowned." He lowered his face and leaned toward Karen as though he would tell her a great secret. "Perhaps if I strike it rich, however, I may yet buy myself a throne."

Miranda giggled and even Karen smiled.

"So who are you traveling with?" Adrik asked, not entirely happy to find Crispin's attention so strongly focused on Karen.

"I came up with a rather disgruntled group who call themselves by the family name of Meyer. I dare say, I've little desire to go the course with these very unpleasant folk and thought I'd appeal to you, Adrik. Might I join you and your . . ." his voice fell away as Grace and Leah pushed back the flaps of the tent and joined Miranda and Karen. They looked to Adrik as if questioning him about Crispin's identity. Crispin leaned closer to Adrik and added, "Gentle women?"

Karen turned to Grace and Leah. "This is Adrik's friend Mr. Thibault. He is of some European aristocracy, and we must be very nice to him, as he plans to buy himself a throne."

"Oh!" Leah said, her mouth round in surprise. "Are you a king?"

Crispin laughed and bowed low before Leah. "Not at all, but I dare say, you are surely a princess."

Leah's expression fell and her frown surprised them all. She turned rather abruptly and ran off toward the river, leaving them all in stunned surprise.

"What was that all about?" Adrik questioned, looking to Karen for answers.

"Her father is believed dead," Karen said, looking to Crispin. "He used to call her that. I'll go talk to her."

"No, please, allow me," Crispin begged. "For I am the offending person."

"You are also a stranger," Karen replied.

Crispin smiled and pulled the woolen cap from atop his head. "I do not wish to be a stranger to either of you. I would be most stricken, however, if you refused me this. I feel quite bad for having hurt the young lady."

Karen looked to the tent and then to Adrik. Adrik nodded, knowing she was looking for his approval of the situation. "Her name is Leah Barringer and she's just turned thirteen. I do not believe she's very well acquainted with the . . . shall we say . . . charms of aristocracy." She eyed the taller man with great intensity, and Adrik might have laughed out loud had the matter not involved the child's feelings. Crispin was no threat to anyone; he knew that as well as he knew his own name. The man was one of the most sensitive and caring fellows Adrik had ever known, in fact, and should Karen deny his request, Adrik knew it would have cast a cloud of despair over his friend.

"I shall endeavor to prove myself worthy of your trust, my dear lady." He lifted her hand and placed a kiss atop her fingers.

Karen, still very serious about the entire matter, nodded as Crispin lifted his gaze. "Very well."

Crispin pulled his cap back on and headed after Leah. Adrik followed the gaze of the three women as they watched him disappear into the woods. He then observed as each woman looked to the others with grins that suggested they knew a secret he had not been privy to.

"My, my," Grace spoke first. "I don't believe I've ever met anyone quite like him."

"Me neither," Miranda replied. "Did you see his hair? All those lovely black curls."

"And his eyes," Karen added. "Such a dark blue, yet so bright and full of laughter."

"And such a regal bearing. Why, I've no doubt he must be from the lineage of kings," Miranda said, straining to catch another glimpse of the man.

Adrik rolled his eyes. Women! What a lot of nonsense. He could personally run circles around Crispin Thibault. The man possessed great endurance and courage, there was no doubt about that. And he was charming and quite the orator when necessary, but he wasn't anything that special. Scratching his chin, Adrik listened to the three women chatter on and on. At first he'd been happy to see Crispin, but maybe his initial joy would be short-lived. After all, he had no intention of fighting his friend for Karen's affection, yet she seemed just as enthralled as Miranda and Grace Colton.

"We're going to be striking camp in thirty minutes," he said after hearing his fill. "I'm not waitin' on anyone."

He doubted they'd even heard him, for not one of the women acknowledged him. Walking away, he met Joe's stoic expression and shook his head. "You've got black hair, and I never saw them get all swoony over you."

Joe pulled off the white bowler and rubbed his head. "Got no curls."

Adrik grinned. "Me neither. But I've got my sights fixed on having a bunch of redheaded children someday, so I guess me and Mr. Curlylocks better have us a talk."

—| C H A P T E R   E I G H T E E N |—

DAY AFTER DAY the little band of travelers pushed forward along with hundreds of other weary souls. Karen, Grace, and Miranda rose early every morning to pray, and it wasn't long before Leah was joining them, as well. Whatever Crispin had said to her had remained between her and the aristocratic traveler. But her spirits were much improved, and she shared Crispin's company very easily.

Morning prayers and Scripture reading were helping them all to keep their perspective. Even Karen, who was still confused about her feelings toward God, seemed to thrive. And she wanted very much to thrive—to put aside her anger. The labor of each day allowed little time for such grudges. Still, there was a hesitancy in her soul, the fear of one who felt betrayed. Could she trust God again? Did she have a choice?

Grace never tried to push her beyond her ability, and for

that Karen knew a gratitude that went far beyond their years of friendship. It was as if Grace understood the pain and anger and was determined to love Karen right through it.

Pulling on her pack, which now weighed almost thirty-five pounds, Karen squared the load and secured the belt Adrik had fashioned to keep the pack snuggly in place. Her spirit soared on the hope of a new day. With each group of stampeders they passed, Karen searched for Jacob. Sometimes she even looked for Bill, though she felt almost certain that it must have been his body Adrik had found. Leah said nothing, but Karen was certain she was beginning to accept this as truth, as well. Perhaps the young girl rationalized that it would be easier to believe him dead and accept the loss than to have hope in his existence only to lose him again. Whatever the reason, Leah said very little about her father and only mentioned Jacob.

"You're awfully quiet," Adrik said, coming up behind Karen to double-check her load. He adjusted the straps, then nodded. "You thinking about anything you want to share?"

Karen licked her chapped lips and smiled. She felt her heart give a jump at the nearness of the broad-shouldered man. "I'm just contemplating the day ahead of us. Wondering if we'll find Jacob—or Bill."

"I wouldn't get your hopes up. This is almost the end of June. Jacob's been on the road for over two months. He didn't come up here with the tons of supplies we're packing, so he could move a lot quicker. He probably spent time here earning some money so he could buy supplies from someone who'd made it this far but was giving up. My guess is, he's found some group to hitch up with, and in trade for work, they'll help him move his supplies along with their own."

"Well, I intend to ask around when we get to Sheep Camp.

You said we'd make it today, right?"

"We ought to, barring any unforeseen problems."

Karen had already begun to look forward to the little town, where Adrik promised her she could pay for a hot bath. "Your friend seems most intent on entertaining Leah and Miranda," she finally said, motioning to where Crispin carried on with sleight-of-hand tricks.

"They seem pretty intent on being entertained," Adrik replied.

"I don't think your Mr. Thibault likes me very much," Karen said, looking to Adrik. "I don't suppose you know anything about that, do you?"

Adrik's mustache twitched at the corner as he appeared to be fighting a smile. He glanced sidelong and then toward the skies overhead. "Maybe he doesn't like redheads."

Karen believed Crispin's lack of attention had far more to do with Adrik than with her honey-red hair. "Perhaps he doesn't."

Adrik leaned close and whispered in her ear. "Well, I like redheads just fine. So don't you go worryin' about gettin' lonely." He paused and dared to place a kiss upon her cheek. "I know a few tricks I can do with my hands, too."

Karen felt her face grow hot. "Mr. Ivankov!" She tried to sound indignant rather than impassioned, but her attempt sounded feeble even to her own ears. His name came out more closely resembling a term of endearment.

"It's a nice name—Ivankov. Don't you think?" His grin broadened to a full-blown smile, amusement dancing in his dark eyes.

"I think we'd better get on the trail," Karen said, grabbing her bonnet. She headed for the path only to hear Adrik chuckling behind her.

"I don't know when I'll see you again," Adrik called.

Karen turned around as she tied her bonnet snug. "What are you saying?" Surely the man wasn't going to leave her simply because she refused to play his games. She eyed him quite seriously. "You aren't leaving us, are you?"

"Nope, but you are if you keep heading in that direction," Adrik replied. "Sheep Camp is that way."

He pointed in the opposite direction, leaving Karen little choice but to retrace her steps and walk past him once again. "You're a scoundrel, Mr. Ivankov."

Adrik laughed and tipped his hat. "Yes, ma'am, I am."

"Rockslide!"

The desperate call split the afternoon air, sending a cold sensation of dread into Miranda Colton's heart. She had heard the rumbles of rock off and on all day as they tumbled down the canyon walls, and each time she had feared for her life. This time, however, she had good reason to fear.

As rock and dirt began to rain down around her, Miranda froze in place, unable to remember Adrik's instructions. Was she to try and outrun the slide? Should she back up and retrace her steps?

Without warning, Miranda felt strong hands upon her waist. Then, as if she weighed nothing more than the pack on her back, Crispin Thibault lifted her and swung her around to flee the dangerous area.

They crashed to the ground as Crispin lost his footing, but he rolled in such a way that he took the full impact of the fall. Miranda, although shaken, was cushioned against the man as rock and debris continued to rain down upon the path where they had stood.

When the noise died down to little slips of pelting gravel, Miranda seemed to regain rational thinking. She stared down into the face of the most beautiful man she'd ever seen. His dark eyes were edged with ebony lashes, so thick and long it seemed almost unreasonable that they should belong to a man. Especially the man who'd just saved her life.

"I—I—I couldn't move," she stammered.

He gave her a lopsided smile. "Just as I cannot move now."

Miranda realized all at once that she was stretched out full atop the poor man. Without giving it another thought, she rolled to the left and found herself in peril once again. She'd managed to roll right off the side of the trail and now clung precariously to Crispin's arm while her feet dangled in the air beneath her. With her free hand, Miranda fought to take hold of the rock and dirt on the edge of the ravine. All she managed to do, however, was pelt herself with a mouthful of earth.

"Be still," Crispin commanded. "I'll pull you back up, but you must stop flailing."

He held her tight and again, with surprising ease, pulled her back to safety. Together they sat, side by side, panting from the momentary exertion and panic.

"I wasn't really complaining," he said, catching his breath. "You needn't have run off like that."

Miranda swallowed dust and grit. "I'm so sorry. I just thought . . . well . . . it seemed highly inappropriate."

"So does throwing yourself off the side of a mountain," he said, grinning. He reached out with a handkerchief and wiped the dirt from her face. "Are you hurt?"

Miranda shook her head tentatively. "I don't think so."

"Crispin! Miranda! Are you two all right?" Adrik called as he climbed over the gravel and debris to reach them.

Getting to her feet, Miranda watched as Crispin surveyed

the massive pile of rock and debris. He met his friend's worried expression with one of calm confidence. "We're quite all right."

Adrik looked to Miranda and back to Crispin. "You're neither one hurt?"

"Not that we have ascertained," Crispin replied. He reached down to help Miranda to her feet.

Miranda looked to Adrik and smiled. "I'm fine. I don't think anything is broken, unless it's poor Mr. Thibault. I'm afraid I used him rather abusively and allowed him to break my fall."

Crispin exchanged a glance with Adrik. " 'Twas my pleasure."

With a raised brow, Adrik began to laugh. "Yes, I'll just bet it was." He glanced back to the slide. "It's not too bad, at least. Could have been much worse. I heard them say this road was blocked for two days last week when a slide worse than this one sent boulders big as houses down the mountain."

"Now if only the gold would come in boulders that size, every man would be content."

"Every woman, too," Miranda added.

"Well, let's move out. I know the others will worry if we don't catch up to them soon." Adrik made his way up and over the debris and picked up his pack on the other side. "I'll go on ahead and let them know you're coming."

Miranda squared her shoulders and hiked up her skirt. What a nuisance, she thought. Men walked about in trousers and boots and no one thought twice about it. But let a woman wear trousers and the entire world considered her mad. Madness to Miranda's way of thinking was trying to hoist heavy lengths of corduroy and wool with one hand while steadying yourself with the other.

Crispin helped her navigate the slide, and before she knew it, Miranda was once again on the path. Contemplating the vast wilderness around her, she thought it most magnificent. Deadly, but nevertheless marvelous. Crispin Thibault was marvelous, as well. *How wonderful that he would risk his life to save mine. What more could any woman hope of a man?* Thinking such thoughts, Miranda began to see Crispin in a new light. Perhaps Peter would approve of such a man for her. That was, if they ever saw Peter again.

Her brother's disappearance had gravely worried her. Not so much for herself or even her parents, but mostly for Grace. She knew Grace was strong and full of faith in God, but the poor woman was battling her worry within herself daily and had grown quite distant. Aside from their morning ritual of praying for the men in their lives, Grace had withdrawn and kept to herself more and more.

Or perhaps I have drawn myself away to spend more time near Mr. Thibault, Miranda thought guiltily. But when Crispin turned on the trail and smiled warmly at her, Miranda lost all thoughts of guilt.

By nightfall they were settled in Sheep Camp. Grace had gone to bed very early, only minutes after a supper of rice, dried ham, and a yellow cake that Leah proudly announced as her own creation.

Adrik had walked Karen and Miranda to a place where he knew they could get hot baths for fifty cents. The Hotel Woodlawn stood just a few feet from the River Taiya, and because of this, they had set up a bathhouse behind their establishment. They'd even found a Tlingit woman who could cut hair in a decent fashion. Adrik had used her on many occasions to keep his hair from growing past his collar. Tonight, he allowed her to shave the stubble of beard from his face and trim his hair, as well. He was just splashing on tonic water when he heard Karen and Miranda approaching.

He tossed the woman four bits and jumped up from the chair to join his party. He wasn't prepared for the sight that met his eyes. Neither woman had bothered to bind up her hair, and, with the hotel's towels in hand, they were still blotting the water from their heads while carrying on an animated conversation in the cool night air.

"You'll catch your death like that," Adrik teased, but inside his heart was racing like a sled dog on the homeward stretch.

Karen looked up, and in the glow of firelight and lanterns, her eyes seemed to twinkle with amusement. Adrik figured she knew the effect she had on him. He also suspected she was rather pleased with the power she held. But when she handed him her brush, he concluded that she was meanspirited and cruel.

"Here, you brush my hair out while I brush Miranda's."

He took the brush and his hand trembled. Miranda turned obediently as Karen took the younger woman's brush and began the process of untangling the lengths.

For a moment, all Adrik could do was stare at the wavy mass. He'd wondered—in fact, he'd wondered quite a bit of late—how she might look with her hair down and all soft around her shoulders. This wasn't quite the picture he had in mind, but it would do. He brought the brush to her hair and gently, almost fearfully, began to brush it.

He could smell the sweetness of lavender soap, something Karen had no doubt brought for herself. His hand shook as though the temperature had dropped below freezing. He reached to touch Karen's shoulder to steady himself and felt her trembling, as well.

"It's cold out here," he said abruptly. "Let's get back to camp."

Karen turned to face him, and he could see that the moment had affected her as much as it had him. "I think that would be wise," she murmured.

The next few days were devoted to moving their provisions up to the Scales. Adrik felt it unnecessary to move the women away from the safety and provision of town, so he and the other men headed out before dawn every morning and moved the tons of provisions at a steady pace that left them exhausted by nightfall. To their credit they were making remarkable time.

Karen spent her days searching through the small town, desperate to find any news of Jacob and Bill Barringer. Leah went with her faithfully, refusing to be left behind, determined to be with Karen when she learned the truth.

They finally got word on the third day. Having searched through all the hotels and stores, Karen finally broke down and began asking in the saloons. It was at the Big Tent Saloon that a burly man, who acted as both owner and bartender, remembered having given Jacob a job cleaning.

"He was here for about three weeks," the man said. Standing behind a makeshift bar that consisted of a plank board set atop two whiskey barrels, the man seemed less than inclined to offer more.

"Do you know if he continued north?"

The man wiped out a glass, spit in it, and wiped it again. "Don't guess he'd go south. He was workin' to buy provisions.

Worked here cleaning every morning." The man set aside the glass and picked up another. His idea of hygiene left Karen less than eager to visit any of the area establishments.

"Do you know if he teamed up with someone? Do you know when he left Sheep Camp?"

The man shook his head. "Don't keep track of everybody that goes through. He came to me for a job and I gave him one. He worked over at the drugstore during the day—you could ask there. They might be inclined to tell you more."

Karen nodded and thanked the man before pulling Leah with her to the muddy street. "Did you hear that? He's actually seen Jacob!"

Leah nodded. "Can we go to the drugstore and ask them, too?"

Karen felt a ray of hope for the first time in weeks. "Yes. Let's hurry. Maybe they know more."

But the drugstore proved to be no help at all. The ownership had changed, and the man knew nothing of Jacob or his whereabouts. Dejected by this, the two tried to take heart that at least they'd heard something about Jacob.

"Well, we know he's alive and headed north," Karen said, trying to encourage Leah.

"Yeah, but nobody remembers Pa." She looked beyond Karen to the mountains that rose up to the north. "I don't think he's alive, Karen." She shook her head and met the older woman's eyes. "I think my pa is dead, and the sooner we accept that, the better off we'll be."

"You can't be sure," Karen said, not wanting the girl to feel too hopeless or depressed.

As if understanding, Leah pushed back her braids and pulled her bonnet into place. "I talked to God about it, Karen. I'm going to be all right, even if Pa and Jacob are both gone.

God's given me a special promise."

Karen looked at the girl, who suddenly seemed years beyond thirteen. "And what promise was that, Leah?"

The girl lifted her face with an expression of peace and contentment. "God promised He was all the Father I'd ever need and that He'd see me through this."

Karen thought about Leah's words all the way back to camp. The child radiated contentment, and Karen knew that it was this very substance that she herself so desperately sought.

God, she prayed in the silence of her heart, *out of the mouths of babes come your wisdom and words. May I know the contentment she knows. May I trust the way she trusts.*

"There you are!" Adrik called out as he strode out to meet Karen and Leah. "We're packing it up and moving up to the Scales."

"Already?" Karen said, looking to where the men were already tearing down the tents. Grace and Miranda were working silently to ready their packs.

"We've made good time," Adrik said enthusiastically. "We're making good time still. We've got extra help at the Scales—more men. Our things are already being packed up the mountain."

Karen thrilled to the news and yet dreaded it. The summit seemed like the first hurdle in their path of obstacles, a monster that would stand in their way to deny them their dream.

She had heard many men say that this climb was by far the worst. In winter they climbed the ice staircase, man after man, one after the other. The row of men and women that moved up and over the pass could be seen from far below as a black, inching line that never ended. But in summer, things were done much differently. The path lost its staircase, and a treacherous mountainside of boulders and shifting rock became their adversary. There was nothing easy about climbing the Chilkoot Pass.

"We found someone in town who knew Jacob. He said Jacob moved on after working here for several weeks. Perhaps he isn't so very far ahead of us after all," Karen said, looking to Adrik for encouragement. "Maybe he even got held up at the Scales or at the summit. If he didn't have the tariff money, they surely wouldn't let him pass, would they?"

Adrik shook his head. "I don't think they would, but you need to remember, he may have teamed up with a group. It's always best that way. Someone else might well have been able to foot the expenses for tariffs and such but lacked Jacob's muscle to move their goods."

Karen nodded, feeling rather discouraged. She looked at Leah as she helped Grace pack up the kitchen equipment. "Oh, Adrik, I just want to find him. I want to be up and over the mountain and safely on our way with the worst of it behind us."

"Well, the summit is a bad climb, that's for sure, but this won't be the last of our woes by a long shot." He looked to her with such a serious expression that Karen couldn't help but grow worried.

"You don't think we'll make it, do you?"

"I wouldn't have brought you this far if I didn't believe you could make it," he replied softly. "It won't be easy, though. You have to understand that much. You have to be realistic about it."

Karen laughed almost bitterly. "Was it realistic to make this trip to begin with?"

"You've got a point. You givin' up?"

Karen looked at everyone working so willingly and quickly

to break camp. They were in this together, each one with their reasons and needs.

"No, I'm not giving up," she finally murmured. "That mountain isn't going to best me." She looked up to see Adrik's expression of approval. "I'll give the mountain a run for its money, just see if I don't."

Adrik guffawed loudly, causing everyone to stop and look. Calming, he turned to go, then looked back at Karen. "I believe you will, Miss Pierce. I believe you will."

⫟CHAPTER NINETEEN⫠

KAREN STARED in disbelief at the climb to be made. The mountain rose up at a forty-five-degree angle to a summit that was lost in the clouds. It looked as though they very well might be climbing all the way to heaven. Thankful she'd only have to climb it once, instead of the multiple times the men had endured over the past weeks, Karen steadied her nerves.

"It's only about two and half miles from this point," Adrik told them in his authoritative way. "But it's gonna feel like it's at least two hundred miles once you're climbing.

"I don't want any of the women wearing packs. We'll get your things added to our own or send them up with the packers. In the meanwhile, we're going to pair up. Joe will take Grace, Sakatook will see to Leah, Crispin to Miranda, and I'll lead Karen."

Karen knew exactly who'd been in charge of figuring out

the pairing. Miranda seemed content enough and nodded enthusiastically. Only Grace and Leah remained perfectly silent. They continued to cast skeptical looks up the mountainside.

"This isn't going to be easy," Adrik continued. "In fact, I think it's a whole lot easier in winter with the packed down snow making a pretty smooth trail. But we don't have that now. Wear your heaviest boots, as the rocks are sharp enough to cut right into them, and don't forget to take your canteens. Water is mighty important up here, and in spite of there being plenty of rivers and lakes, you'll do well to keep a canteen close at hand."

"How long will it take to climb up there?" Leah questioned.

"That depends on several things," Adrik answered. "The weather, the land, the folks around us, and each of you. We'll stop to rest from time to time—there's no sense havin' anyone collapse on the trail. If you need to stop sooner, just give a holler."

The sun warmed them generously despite growing cloud coverage to the south. After an hour on the trail, Karen paused to ease out of her jacket. The well-worn white shirtwaist that she wore underneath had seen better days. Nevertheless, it was no different than everyone else around her. She had no reason to worry or fret over her wardrobe. The Chilkoot Trail was a far cry from the ballrooms of Chicago's finer homes. Not that she'd ever spent much time upon those dance floors herself, but she'd certainly dressed Grace for enough parties.

Glancing down the mountain to where Joe carefully assisted Grace, Karen couldn't help but wonder about her friend. She spoke very little about Peter and their separation, though they prayed faithfully every morning for him, along with their party of travelers, the packers, the stampeders, and even Mr. Paxton. Karen, however, seldom allowed herself to truly pray for the latter.

Otherwise, Grace had become progressively more silent. She helped with the camp and almost immediately after every evening meal, would make her way off to where she could clean up in private, then took herself to bed.

"You coming?" Adrik asked, breaking through her worried thoughts.

Karen nodded. "Can't stop now, I guess." She wrapped her jacket around the top of the walking stick Adrik had made for her before continuing up the rocky slope.

She'd scarcely taken three steps, however, when her foot hit a shelf of loose gravel. Instantly she started to slide backward. Her balance was hopelessly lost, and for a moment, Karen envisioned herself falling all the way down the mountain. But before that could happen, Adrik's powerful grip held her fast. He looked at her as if her slip hadn't surprised him in the least.

"You've got to keep your eyes on the trail," he admonished. "Otherwise, you'll end up buried alongside it."

"Sorry," Karen muttered, embarrassed by the entire matter. She had just boasted to Adrik that very morning that she could manage no matter the route. Pride had nearly taken its toll.

An hour later, Karen was hurriedly pulling her jacket back on and wishing fervently that she'd not wrapped her coat up with her sleeping bag. The day had been so fair at the Scales, but now heavy clouds moved in, and based on her experience with her first winter, Karen felt almost certain they would see snow.

"Um ... Adrik," she began hesitantly, "does it snow in July?"

"It can snow up here any time of the year. See those white patches up the way?" he questioned. "That's winter left over."

The wind whipped at her skirts, making Karen glad for the woolen trousers she'd fashioned to wear beneath. "Is it going to snow today?" She looked to Adrik's eyes for the truth of the matter.

He reached out a hand and pulled her up to the rock on which he stood. "It just might. But I hope we'll be to the top by then. Worried?"

Karen couldn't help but nod. "I can't lie and say I'm not. I've never known two miles to take such a long time. Then again, I've never had such obstacles to endure."

"If we keep pressing forward," Adrik said in an assuring tone, "we'll be there before suppertime."

Karen allowed him to keep hold of her hand as they maneuvered over the rocks. "What was it like here in the winter?" Her breath came in quick pants as she fought against the altitude and the angle of the mountain.

She tried to imagine the stairs cut out of ice. It was called the Golden Stairway by some of the locals. The name had spread, she'd heard from Grace, all the way to California.

"Cold," Adrik said, grinning. "They sometimes get as much as thirty feet of snow up here."

"Thirty feet? Surely you jest."

"Not at all. It's a severe land with a temperament like a feisty woman."

"My mother wrote once saying it played the part of inhospitable neighbor. Cold and difficult."

"I can imagine her saying that," Adrik answered, resting for a moment against a rock.

Karen knew he was stopping to allow her to catch her breath again. It seemed she could only take ten or twelve steps without becoming completely winded. Settling on the rock beside him, she noticed the lichen and moss that clung to the crevices of the great boulder. How could anything survive being buried under thirty feet of snow?

"It can drop to fifty below in a matter of hours," Adrik said, gazing off across the valley. "But it's really not a bad land. You simply have to respect the dangers that surround you. Just like handling feisty women." He grinned at her and winked.

Karen knew the reference was intended for her. She ignored his teasing. "Would it have been this bad in April?" She was thinking of Jacob again.

"It was bad enough," Adrik answered, reaching out to steady her as they began to climb again, this time over a rather precarious place in the trail where the rock was loose and offered no secure hold on the trail. He swung her up and over some particularly jagged rocks, bringing her back to the ground directly in front of him.

She faced him momentarily, her face lifted to his. My, but he was handsome with the wind reddening his cheeks and his dark eyes glowing. He searched her face as if seeking an answer to an unspoken question. Karen knew she might have told him most anything had he asked, for her mind and heart were so completely swept up in the moment. She thought he might have kissed her, thought she might have liked it, but Leah's laughter rang out and Karen looked away.

Crispin and Miranda walked along behind Leah and Sakatook. Crispin was regaling them with some tale or another, and Leah thought it all good fun. "Sounds like they're out for an afternoon picnic instead of the climb of their life," Karen said, smiling. It was good to hear Leah so happy. She was glad

Crispin had joined them, if only because he made Leah laugh.

"Come on," Adrik said, letting go of her. "We're going to be there before you know it. Then we'll all sit and laugh and share a meal."

"And pitch tents and wash dishes and freeze in the wind," Karen said, hiking up her skirts in one hand and planting the walking stick ahead of her with the other.

"You make it all sound like such fun," Adrik said, giving her a wink. "Then again, I know I didn't have this much fun on any of my other hikes up this mountain. Must be the company."

Karen warmed under his attention. She had fallen in love with Adrik Ivankov sometime between Grace's marriage and her own departure from Dyea. Her emotions and disappointment at the sad turn of events in her life had kept her from enjoying this new discovery, but she couldn't avoid the truth forever.

―――――

It had started to rain as the party finally made their way to the summit. Exhausted and discouraged by the weather, the travelers wanted only a shelter from the impending storm.

They located their caches by Adrik's red-and-white flags. Two men, along with Joe's wife, had been left to guard the materials and set up camp, and Adrik knew the women were more than a little happy to see they wouldn't have to set up camp.

"You ladies go ahead and get inside the tent out of the weather. Joe and I will get dinner together and bring it to you."

Karen was too tired to argue, much to Adrik's surprise. She nodded and followed Grace inside the tent. Crispin relinquished his hold on Miranda and waited until she'd followed suit with Leah close behind before turning to Adrik.

"How can I be of assistance?" He followed Adrik and Joe into the largest of three tents.

"Help me dish up this stew. Joe's wife put it together, and she's one of the best cooks I know." Adrik directed Crispin to a stack of pie pans and spoons. Then turning to the small camp stove, he lifted the lid atop the cast-iron pot and breathed in deeply. "Oh, this is going to hit the spot."

"I heartily agree," Crispin replied.

Joe pulled out his knife and began slicing a loaf of bread. The women had made several loaves while awaiting their departure in Sheep Camp, and this was the last of them.

As the rain began to fall more steadily, Adrik hurried to dish up the stew. No sense in letting a downpour spoil the meal. Crispin transported the stew two plates at a time back to the women's tent. Miranda met him at the door and without a word took the pans inside. They exchanged food in a like manner two more times as Crispin finished by bringing them bread.

Adrik followed up with four cups of a special tea Joe's wife had brewed. The aroma made him all the more glad for having sent the woman ahead. This was going to be a nice surprise for the weary travelers. He hadn't told any of them how proud he was, but the fact was, he'd had some doubts about whether or not they could make it. He knew Karen would climb the mountain energized by sheer willpower if nothing else. But Grace Colton was such a delicate little thing, and so, too, was Leah Barringer. Miranda Colton seemed spirited enough, but he knew from what she'd said that outdoor activities had not been her focus of attention back in San Francisco.

"I have tea for you," Adrik announced as he followed Miranda into the tent. "It's pretty good and will help you regain your energy." He had wrapped his fingers through the metal rings of the cups and now tried to disengage his hand without spilling the contents.

Karen looked into the cups and then back to Adrik. "What is it? It smells wonderful."

"Joe's wife put it together. It's a concoction of rose hips and wild blackberry leaves. It's the best drink for travel and living up here. Full of good things that revive the soul."

"Sounds perfect," Karen said, pushing a cup toward Grace. "Sounds like just the thing for you."

Grace took the drink and thanked Adrik. "You've been very good to us. I can't thank you enough for agreeing to bring me along."

Adrik looked around him at the four exhausted women. "I never thought I would take a group of women on such a perilous journey, but I must say, it's a whole lot more fun traveling with you than with Joe and his sons."

Karen seemed to instantly sober at this. "They aren't really heading back tomorrow, are they?"

Adrik nodded. "But don't go frettin'. We'll pay the Canadian tax and then hire a mule team to cart our goods down to Lake Lindeman. With Crispin and me you'll be just fine. And who knows, maybe we'll pick up Jacob on the way."

Leah perked up at this. "He could be up here right now. I wanted to go look for him, but the weather got bad."

"We can look for him tomorrow. I think we should rest up a bit before pressing on anyway," Adrik said. "Now, you ladies have a nice supper. I'm going to go eat with the boys. If you get too cold, come on over to the big tent. There's still a bit of warmth in the stove, and we might even be able to build the fire back up for a short time. There's not much in the way of fuel up here, however, and you'll pay dearly for it if you have to buy it off someone else."

He paused at the tent flap and smiled. "I just want you all to know I'm proud to have been leading you. You were all real troopers, and I shouldn't wonder but that we'll make it to Dawson without any of you being any worse for the wear."

With that he left them, smiling to himself and contemplating how in the world he was going to convince Karen Pierce to marry him by the time they reached Dawson City, or maybe even Whitehorse.

After supper, Adrik decided to make his way over to the customs tent. He wanted very much to see what they might expect when they moved on in the days to come. He hadn't gone ten steps, however, when he found Karen at his side. The rain apparently was not a deterrent to her.

"What are you doing out here?" he asked.

"I want to look for Jacob."

"I thought I told you to rest. You'll have time to look for him tomorrow."

"But there's still plenty of light, in spite of the overcast."

"And there will be even more light tomorrow after the rain has passed."

Karen stopped and put her hands on her hips. "You have no way of knowing that it won't be raining tomorrow. I won't perish in the rain, you know. I just want to come along and see if anyone remembers Jacob. Surely the Canadians keep a list of people passing through."

Adrik frowned and decided to come clean with her. "They do. They also keep a list of the dead. Word is sent down from the other posts to the north. Eventually the list will make it all the way back to Skagway. I thought maybe I'd spare you from having to . . . well . . ."

"Find Jacob listed with the dead?" Karen asked softly.

Adrik nodded and wiped rain from his face. "Look, let's get out of the rain. We're going to have a hard enough time staying warm tonight, so there's no sense in being soaked to the bone."

He led the way to where the British flag hung limp and drenched. Ushering Karen inside, he introduced himself and asked first about Jacob. The Northwest Police officer appeared skeptical but nevertheless pulled a book from his desk. Adrik prayed in silence as the man thumbed through the register.

"I show a Jacob Barringer passing through on the twenty-eighth of May," the man told them, glancing up to see if they would make further comment.

"What of William Barringer?" Karen asked. "He might well have come through last winter—even as long ago as December."

The man returned his attention to the ledger but shook his head. "This register only goes back to April. We've had thousands come through," the official told them. "The other records have been passed on to our headquarters."

Adrik saw Karen's expression of hope pass to one of worry. He took hold of her hand and shook his head. "No news is good news. Bill could have passed through here months ahead of the avalanche and given that letter to someone who was headed back to Dyea. People post letters and packages like that all the time. I can't tell you how much mail I've carried down the trail."

"I wish we knew for certain one way or the other. The waiting is taking its toll on us. Leah is certain she must give him up for dead, and I can't offer her much hope to do otherwise."

Adrik understood. He felt more than a little frustration that he'd played such an inadequate role in all of this. He'd brought them the letter and word of the dead man, but he couldn't be sure it was Bill Barringer who lay in that grave and not some other poor fool.

———

Karen awoke quite early the next morning. The skies had cleared and the sun had come up somewhere in the middle of what would normally be night. She had trouble adjusting to the long days. The sun would stay up so long, not setting until around ten o'clock, only to rise again at four in the morning. Adrik had told her it would only get worse as they journeyed north. He had told her of a time when he'd ventured far to the north. The sun had set at midnight only to lighten the skies again two hours later. Karen didn't think she would like that very much, but it seemed to be the way of this strange new land.

Of course, winter had been even more difficult. The reverse had been true, with the sun long absent from the sky. And even when the sun made its debut, it seemed many days were overcast and gray. The darkness had nearly driven her mad. She'd had no one to talk to save Leah and Jacob, and while they were dear children, they couldn't begin to understand her feelings and needs.

True to his word, Adrik arranged for their things to be freighted down to Lake Lindeman. The Northwest Police checked through their supplies, took their money, and issued them receipts to show they had cleared the checkpoint. After this, the goods were loaded onto mule trains and transported down the rocky decline.

The weary band of travelers followed, depressed at the lack of civilization. Leah was glad to hear news of her brother, but the understanding that their journey had just begun weighed heavy on their hearts.

Adrik moved out ahead to converse with the freighters and pick up any news or information that might make their passage north a bit easier. Karen felt both a loss and a relief in his absence. Her growing feelings for Adrik were so overpowering that they terrified her at times. She found herself daydreaming constantly about what it might be like to share this man's life.

Her father had trusted Adrik, and to hear Adrik tell it, they had enjoyed a strong friendship and camaraderie. Karen had no reason to doubt the truth of his words. In fact, she worried that her attraction to Adrik had been based upon that relationship with her father. Now, however, thoughts of her father were only distant memories when she was with Adrik Ivankov.

Desperate to think on something else, Karen caught sight of Grace as she lagged behind Miranda and Leah. Crispin seemed to be once again caught up in some animated tale of his adventures. But Grace held an almost visible wall around her—a wall that seemed to keep her safe inside herself. Or maybe it just kept others out.

Karen pondered her friend for a moment. Dressed in a dark green skirt and jacket, Grace walked the trail with a refined elegance that reflected her background. She had spent a lifetime being trained for high society. Karen shook her head. Some society!

"Going down is almost harder than going up," Miranda called as she passed with Crispin and Leah.

"I was thinking the same not but a minute ago," Karen replied.

"Mr. Thibault is telling us about his adventures in Africa," Leah threw in with wide-eyed wonder. "He's actually seen an elephant!"

Karen laughed at the young girl's excitement. Here she was risking her life in the northern wilderness, her brother missing, her father possibly dead, and it was the musings of a roaming aristocrat that allowed Leah to forget it all. *Good for her!* Karen thought. And good for God, too, for having sent Mr. Thibault their way.

Grace came walking down the same trail, her walking stick clacking along the rocks as she passed by. Karen watched for Grace to lift her face and acknowledge Karen's presence, but she never did.

Preoccupied and silent, Grace had no idea that Karen even stood by watching. "I thought," Karen began, "that we might chat while we walked."

At this Grace looked up. "I'm sorry. Were you talking to me?"

Karen joined her on the trail and linked her arm with Grace's. "Yes, I was talking to you. You've been far too distant to suit me. I want you to tell me what's locked up in those thoughts of yours."

Grace looked at the ground but allowed Karen to pull her forward. They walked a few minutes in silence before Grace spoke. Her voice barely audible, she said, "I miss him so much."

The sorrow in her words was intense, and Karen was struck by the depth of her emotion. Poor Grace. Just looking at her expression caused Karen to feel like the most neglectful of friends.

"I'm sure he'll read the note you left him at the hotel and come join us. It isn't like he couldn't find us if he wanted to."

"But he may not have the funds. He might not be able to get supplies," Grace argued. "Oh, I should never have come."

"Nonsense. Peter Colton is a strong, determined man. I'm certain he probably has set aside money for just such occasions and concerns. He'll read your note and wire his bank— you did say the telegraph to Seattle was in place in Skagway now, right?"

Grace nodded. "But he may not have returned to the hotel. I only left the note on the hope that he might. I have no reason to believe he will."

"You're the biggest reason I can think of for his return." Karen squeezed Grace's arm. "He's hotheaded and worked up about all that has transpired. But give him time."

"I'm afraid of time," Grace replied, looking up to meet Karen's eyes.

"But why? Time can heal all wounds, or so they say," Karen replied, trying her best to sound lighthearted. "You'll see. Peter will think things over, and he'll go back to the hotel in search of you."

"And I won't be there, and he'll be hurt and angry with me."

Karen shook her head. "He has to make a choice, Grace. He has to put aside the past and deal with the future. There's too much at stake for him to do otherwise."

Grace nodded and returned her gaze to the ground. "Far more than anyone realizes."

Karen wondered what her friend meant by such words, but she let it go and decided against probing for more information. Grace's sorrow over her husband's absence was nothing that Karen could resolve for her friend. She would simply have to bide her time and trust that Grace would open up to her as she always had in the past.

─┤ C H A P T E R   T W E N T Y ┠─

LINDEMAN TOOK THE ENTIRE PARTY by surprise. Adrik hadn't seen the city in over three years, and he was rather dumbfounded to find it so well established and planned out. The rest of the party took absolute delight in the lakeside town. Despite being comprised mostly of tents, there were hotels, bakeries, restaurants, and stores to lure weary travelers. Promises of hot meals and soft beds were tempting, but other than stopping long enough to stock up on supplies, the plan was to move the party forward.

Adrik had planned to have them rest in Bennett, a town north of Lake Lindeman, but seeing his companions so completely worn out, he changed his mind.

"There's plenty of materials and such that we'll need for building a boat," he told the group the afternoon of their arrival. "I believe instead of building a boat in Bennett, we'll go

ahead and do the deed here. Perhaps even find additional supplies and such—if they're not too expensive."

"Sounds like a capital idea to me," Crispin said, wiping his
hand against his perspiring forehead.

"Where will we stay?" Karen questioned.

"Well, we can pitch our tents and make things as comfortable as possible. If the weather stays nice and the materials
aren't too expensive, we won't need to be here all that long.
I've built many a boat in my time, and with Crispin's help, we
ought to have something decent put together in a couple of
weeks. We don't want to rush and make something that will
just break apart when it hits the rocks."

"It looks as if much of the good timber is gone," Karen
said, looking around at the hillsides.

Adrik noted the stumps where hundreds of hemlock,
spruce, and fir had grown years earlier. "It's a sorry state to
see the land so stripped, but I'm sure we'll find the necessary
goods. First, however, we need to make camp. I don't want
you ladies worrying about anything for a few days. We can all
wear dirty clothes and eat canned food. We can buy our bread
at the bakery or do without if it's too expensive."

"We won't wilt, Mr. Ivankov," Grace threw out.

But Adrik wasn't convinced. The poor woman looked almost green from her travels. She'd been so tired coming
through from Crater Lake that Adrik had thought it impossible for her to take one more step, much less travel for miles.

They settled the matter of their camp by following the example of others before them. Setting up with the lake a short
walking distance away, Adrik was almost sorry he'd allowed
Joe to head back to Dyea. He missed his companionable silence, along with that of his sons, and Adrik also felt safer
having more men in their party. There were no doubt plenty

of scallywags and no-goods who would be tempted to trouble the women when Crispin and Adrik were off gathering supplies. It was a grave concern, but no more so than the idea of getting the small troop north.

Two days later, with Karen looking quite rested, Adrik permitted her to accompany him while he looked for lumber. She was eager, almost restless to be doing something more than sitting in camp, while the others were still bemoaning their sore feet and weary bones.

"Are you certain you're up to this?" Adrik questioned as they hiked away from the lake and up the rising slope.

Karen kept even with his every step. "I'm doing quite well. I think this country agrees with me after all. It's difficult to get used to the long hours of light in the summer and the equally long hours of dark in the winter, but I must say, the lack of formality agrees with me." She laughed softly. "I never thought I would be saying that. I was such a stickler for keeping rules when I first arrived."

"So you think you might stay?" Adrik dared the question he'd been longing to ask. If he couldn't convince her to marry him just yet, he had to at least persuade her to stay in the north.

Karen paused and turned to look down on the lake and tent city. "I believe I could be tempted." She lifted her face to him and smiled. "It is a lovely country. I can see why my mother and father loved it. Then again, they had a purpose for being here."

Adrik sat down on a stump and eyed her quite seriously for a moment. "You could have a purpose, too."

Her expression grew quite thoughtful. Her delicate brows arched ever so slightly as her blue eyes bore holes in his heart. He felt his breath catch. He'd already teased her about marriage and about giving her a reason to remain in Alaska. What he needed to know was where her interest pointed. Could she really give up the lively civilization of the larger American cities? Could she spend her life living in the wilderness? Raise a family here?

Finally she spoke. "I have struggled—wrestled, really— with God." She looked away from him and this time cast her gaze to the mountains. "I have tried to put my anger aside. I've tried to let go of all that has caused me to question God, but I find some things are most difficult to bid farewell."

"Such as?"

She continued to look toward the peaks. "I cannot understand His ways. I try. I really do. I know that faith is required and that in faith comes the ability to trust, even when the way seems unclear."

"But?"

She looked at him now, and Adrik had never thought her more beautiful. Her hair, void of its typical bonnet, glinted gold and red in the summer sun. He longed to reach up and pull loose the ribbon that held her braid. He thought back on the night she'd asked him to brush her hair. He could almost feel himself trembling again. He was grateful she'd not asked that favor of him since, but then again, he almost wished she would.

"I suppose forgiving Mr. Paxton will have to be a daily event for me," she said in a most resigned manner. "I don't feel like forgiving him. However, neither do I desire to grant him more effort or time than is absolutely necessary."

"So wouldn't giving him to God be the wiser choice?" Adrik asked softly.

He heard her sigh, and he longed to hold her in his arms.

Instead, he remained seated, hoping she would continue to open up to him.

Changing the subject, Karen returned her gaze to the lake below them. "So many people will pass through here. They'll come and go, and I can't help but wonder if many will stay."

"Will you?"

She said nothing for what seemed an eternity. Adrik could hardly bear it and stood to suggest they continue their exploration. But when he got to his feet, she turned, and he saw the tears that were running down her cheeks. What had he said to cause this? His expression must have betrayed him, for she smiled and wiped at her eyes.

"You might think me very silly," she said in a barely audible voice, "but I feel that I belong here. I feel I must stay, but I have no idea of how to do that or where to go. I can't even tell you what I would do once I figured those other things out."

He reached out to put his hands on her shoulders. "I don't think it's silly at all. I think God has a purpose in your being here. Selfishly, I want you to stay, but you know that. I think you understand a great deal more about it than you've been willing to let yourself see. You're a fine woman and a good teacher. I've seen you teach Leah, and you have a gift. Why not put that to good use up here?"

"With the stampeders' children? With the natives?" she asked.

"Why not? Either one would be a fine choice. Just look at the children here in Lindeman. There are a lot more running around than I would have ever believed. There are only going to be more in the years to come. Then with the natives . . . well, trust takes time."

"Would they ever accept me? I mean, just because they

accepted my father doesn't mean they would like me, as well."

Adrik grinned and inside, his heart soared. He would find a way to convince her. "They'd like you well enough. I'd see to that."

Karen looked intently into eyes, then suddenly pulled away. "I'm heading back to camp. I need to check on Grace and Leah."

Stunned, he watched her go, not at all sure what had just taken place. Women were queer creatures, with strange ideas and ways about them. How could he ever hope for her to understand that he loved her more than life, when she wouldn't stand still long enough for him to tell her?

———————

Working for the railroad proved to be a form of salvation for Peter Colton. With Skagway's city fathers seeing the benefit of such transportation, it wasn't long before they found the money and men to back up their dream, and Peter now played a part in it. In some ways, Peter Colton found his job with the railroad to be less taxing than his duties had been aboard *Merry Maid*. Here he was in charge of no one but himself. And in some ways not even that, for he took his orders just like the others.

He worked six days a week, helping to blast out a road from the rock and gravel. The railroad was rapidly taking shape, in spite of the difficulties. So many people were certain the plan would fail, that no one could put a railroad in the midst of such a chaotic land—but they were succeeding.

The railroad company had a bigger problem than the land, however. Keeping workers on the lines was taxing the patience of even the most saintly supervisors. The company paid the workers high wages to keep them from running off prematurely to the goldfields, and still they suffered losses. Peter had no illusions of gold, except for getting together enough to buy back his father's company—*his* company. Of course, there was still the matter of his wife to deal with. He did his best not to think of her sitting in Skagway alone and frightened.

"So you heading down to Skagway?"

Peter looked up to find Jonas Campbell studying him with an intent look on his face. "I was thinking about it."

The man nodded and pulled a pipe from his pocket. "Do you suppose you could bring me back some tobacco? I'm packing my last bowl."

Jonas had been a good friend to Peter. At least a dozen years his senior, Jonas had taken on a brotherly role when Peter had come to work for the railroad, anger and sorrow his companions. Without Peter even realizing what was happening, Jonas had managed to befriend him.

"I'll be glad to get it for you," Peter said, washing his face with cold water from a bucket. He took the scarf from around his neck and dried his face, then rinsed the scarf out, as well.

"Will you be visiting your little family?" Jonas asked, appearing not the least bit concerned about intruding on Peter's privacy.

"I suppose it's time," Peter replied rather sheepishly. "But to tell the truth, I don't even know if they'll still be there. I left without word, and it's been months. They may well have gone south, back to San Francisco."

"They might have at that, but weren't you just telling me last night that you had no notion of your wife doing that— that she'd probably stay behind?"

Peter tied the wet scarf back around his neck. "I just don't know." And that was the truth of it. Disgusted by the way he'd treated Grace and his family, he had no way of knowing how they might have responded to his actions. Surely there was a breaking point for everyone, and with the way he'd behaved, Peter feared he'd reached that point with each one of them.

"Don't give up hope," Jonas said softly.

Peter looked at the man for a moment, a question on his heart that begged to be asked. "Jonas, you've been a good friend to me these last few weeks. You've fed me when I was without food. You've talked to me when I didn't have another friend in the world. You've gotten me to talk, as well—to share things with you that I wouldn't have shared with another human soul, much less a stranger."

The older man nodded thoughtfully and dragged slowly on the pipe. Peter could read a quiet contentment in the man's brown eyes. He always seemed at peace. Jonas often spoke of longing for the company of his wife and son who'd stayed behind in Kansas. He'd not seen them in over six months, and yet he remained in good spirits.

"I envy the peace you have," Peter said, turning his gaze to the ground. "I know that I have to find a way to make things right. I have to know that peace."

"Friend, I know you're weary. I know that even though we've shared a meal and some passing conversation, you've kept yourself closed off from the rest of the world. But I know that your wife deserves to see you and to hear you ask for forgiveness."

"There's that word again," Peter said, looking up with a smile. "I used to hate that word. I thought it was nothing more than a sign of weakness."

Jonas guffawed loudly, causing several of their retiring co-workers to look their way. Jonas paid no attention to the others, however. He pulled out his pipe with one hand and slapped Peter on the back with the other. "Ain't a man alive who is strong enough to deal out forgiveness on his own. Takes a higher power than what's here on earth."

"I'm beginning to see that, but I'm not entirely sure I understand it. Grace believes in it—she believes in God and that God desires a relationship with each of us."

"And that bothers you a mite, doesn't it?"

Peter looked at Jonas and raised a brow. "It bothers me more than a mite."

Jonas nodded and said, "Well, at least you're being honest, which is more than I can say for you a month ago. Go to town. Go see your wife and have yourself a talk. Nothing says you can't come back here after it's done. If she's not there, then you take the next step."

Peter could feel all the longing and desire for Grace's company rise up in him as he asked, "Which is?"

"You go find her."

———

Making his way into Skagway from up the rail line, Peter thought of Jonas's words and of the need to forgive. He knew Jonas was a godly man, but he was different somehow from the pious preachers and churchgoers of his home port. Jonas had never once tried to beat Peter over the head with his faith. Instead, he'd offered friendship and kindness, a listening ear, and occasional advice. And in that advice Peter heard the same truths that had come from Grace.

Just thinking about his wife tore Peter up inside. Was this what it was to be broken in spirit? And, if not this devastating void in his heart, then what? He felt as though he had irreparably damaged his wife, and even though Grace had always offered him forgiveness, how could he possibly expect such a gift now?

Still, what would she say when he suddenly appeared after so many months of separation? She might not ever want to see him again. She might have even . . . No, he wouldn't let himself think that she had sought out Martin Paxton for help.

Martin Paxton and the harm he'd caused was the reason for all of this. Peter had been so humiliated by the situation and his wife's obvious mistrust that he'd taken himself away from the town and family he loved. Now, months later, he could only hope they were still in port and that they might speak to him and listen to what he had to say.

He had enough money to take them all home to San Francisco. He knew Paxton had offered them passage, and even if his parents and Miranda had gone, surely Grace would have remained behind in hopes of his return.

But I gave her no reason to believe that I might return, Peter thought solemnly.

With determined steps, Peter walked with a single purpose. He would go back to the Hotel Alaska, and if Grace should be there, he would beg her forgiveness and offer her his plan. If his family were there, so much the better.

───────

But the proprietor of the hotel hadn't seen Grace or Peter's family in months. He had no idea of their whereabouts, leaving Peter quite troubled. Stepping out onto the busy street, Peter scanned the crowd for some sign of a familiar face. There was no one. He thought for a moment about telephoning Karen in Dyea. A new line had been put between the two sister towns, but Peter had no idea of where he might find Karen. What was the name of that hotel she was staying at? He wracked his memory but could recall nothing.

In complete exasperation, Peter sighed and shoved his

hands deep into his coat pockets. He contemplated the people who crowded Broadway Street. There wasn't a friendly face among them. They were intent on their dreams of gold—of fame and fortune. Perhaps he should just give up and go back to camp. Perhaps this had been nothing but a hopeless cause.

For a moment he did nothing but watch the people. Fresh-faced boys mingled with grizzled old-timers, and all of them appeared to be carrying the weight of the world—or at least their homes—upon their backs. Dogs barked and strained against their owners' control, while horses laden with packs whinnied nervously when strangers drew too close. They all seemed drawn to the same purpose—gold. Picks and shovels, pans and sledges peeked out from packs along with tents and food supplies. This gathering of strangers knew what they wanted out of life. Would that Peter could say the same.

Then, against his will, Peter knew what he had to do.

Without thought, he pivoted and headed down the street to the one place he had never intended to go again. Paxton's store. If Paxton was still in town, then he would most likely know where the Coltons had gone. If not the whole family, Paxton would certainly know what had become of Grace.

Martin Paxton seemed almost to be expecting Peter when one of his thugs ushered him through the door. He smiled and casually took his seat behind a rather regal mahogany desk. It was new—something perhaps brought aboard *Merry Maid* or *Summer Song* while under Paxton's jurisdiction? Peter tried to quell such thoughts. They only served to stir his anger.

"I must say this is quite a surprise. I figured you went south with your family."

"I'm here to find out about my family," Peter replied. "Where are they? Where is Grace?"

Paxton shook his head. "What? No time for formalities?

No groveling for the answers you seek from me?"

Peter's temper threatened rational thought, but still he remained calm. "Where have they gone?"

"Home, I would imagine," Paxton replied. "I gave your father and mother passage to leave and they went."

"And my sister?"

"I have no idea."

"And Grace?"

"Your wife is still here in Alaska."

"How do you know that?"

Paxton's expression grew smug, further irritating Peter. He was toying with him, playing him like a poorly tuned instrument. "How do you suppose I know? Grace did not leave with your family."

"Then she is still in Skagway?" Peter questioned. "If that is the case, I wish to see her."

"Well, she doesn't wish to see you," Paxton replied, getting to his feet. "You left your wife, Mr. Colton. You tossed her aside and I picked her back up. Ironic, given that she was always mine to begin with."

Peter took a step forward, then stopped. He gripped the back of a leather chair in order to keep from plowing his fist into Paxton's face. "Where is she?" he growled between clenched teeth.

"I am not at liberty to tell you," Paxton said, coming around from behind his desk. Peter was certain the action was to show him he felt Peter was no threat to his well-being. "She doesn't wish for you to know. She is deeply wounded. She has agreed to end this farce of a marriage."

"I don't believe you," Peter replied, torn by a wave of emotions that threatened to destroy his composure. She wanted to be rid of him. She had put aside her fear of Paxton's abusive nature and had sought him out for help. How could that be? How could it be that she saw Peter as a worse threat than Paxton?

"You must believe me," Martin Paxton said, crossing his arms. He leaned back against his desk and looked for all the world as though he'd given information no more important than his shoe size.

"You see, Mr. Colton, your wife is perhaps wiser than you give her credit for being. She listened to me, and now she is ready to settle this matter. My advice to you is that you return to San Francisco and divorce your wife. Make it easy on all parties concerned. I will pay for your transportation, and I will even accommodate you in seeking legal counsel. Once you have accomplished this and the decree is finalized, I will return Colton Shipping to you."

"What?" Peter could hardly believe the man was suggesting such things. Worse still, he could scarcely imagine that the man was serious. Colton Shipping was worth hundreds of thousands of dollars.

"You heard me correctly. I will not only return your ships, I will sign over any further interest. I will consider our transaction, my loan to your father and all the investments, to be completed. Paid in full."

Peter shook his head. "A divorce would not be possible."

"Oh, but I think you might reconsider. You see, Grace told me all about your fight. How you wished that you'd never married her—how you never intended to return to her."

"That's not true!" Peter declared. "I was angry and I said . . ." His voice trailed away. He had said things he didn't mean. He had spoken out of anger and driven away the only person who really mattered to him.

"I know what you said. She told me everything." He

looked at Peter with a pitying glance. "I could have warned you that she wasn't for you. She is spoiled and willful. It was the reason her father thought best to agree to my plan. You see, in spite of my desire for revenge, Mr. Hawkins found his daughter's behavior to be a social disgrace."

"You lie, sir! You forced yourself upon that family for purposes of your own. Grace told me how you savagely attacked her."

"Much as you did, only with words. We are not so very different, Mr. Colton." His words hit like a blow to Peter's stomach. The truth of his statement was more than Peter could stand.

"Now, what of my deal? Will you return to California and do as I have asked? Better still, we could both make the journey. I could help you to find proper counsel, and you and your father could join me in arranging the transfer of the business."

Peter shook his head. "I'm not leaving Skagway until I see Grace. You'd better tell her." He forced himself to leave before he released his pent-up anger on Paxton. Opening the door, Peter dared to look up. Paxton was actually smiling. "I'll check back tomorrow. She'd better be here."

Paxton circled his desk and reseated himself as Peter Colton exited his office. "If I had the power to bring her here, she'd be here already," he muttered. He threw open his top desk drawer and pulled out two folded sheets of paper.

One was clearly addressed to Peter Colton. The other was a hastily scribbled request to send a telegram to Wyoming.

At first Paxton had found it amusing that Grace had fallen for the biggest scam in Skagway. There was no telegraph to the lower territories and states. Soapy Smith had made money hand over fist with that little gem. Too bad the man had gotten himself killed in a gunfight only days before. As irritating as Smith could be, Paxton had figured one day he would buy the man over to his side of the fence. Together they could have ruled Skagway and Dyea and controlled the commerce and people coming in and out of the north. But instead, Smith had been too threatening—too greedy. And the people had risen against him.

Paxton got up from his desk and headed over to the cast-iron stove. Poking up the fire, he took one last look at the words Grace had penned to her mother. Words that never reached the woman, but were instead answered at no small expense, with Paxton's own suggested content. He tossed the paper into the stove and smiled as the corners curled and caught fire.

Then he looked at the letter Grace had left at the Hotel Alaska for Peter. He hadn't known of the letter until just the week before. After Grace had disappeared from Dyea, Paxton had set out once again to find her. Quizzing the hotel manager at the Hotel Alaska had been difficult, for the man had taken ill and his nephew had been put in charge. Finally, however, the manager regained his health and had returned to take charge of his business. At that, Paxton's men had quizzed him about Grace. He admitted to knowing nothing of her whereabouts but added that he held a letter for her husband, Peter Colton.

Paxton had the letter in his possession before the end of the day, and with it he found all the answers he needed. She'd gone north. North to Dawson City. Once again she'd fled his hold. He'd thought to keep her in Skagway, or Dyea at least, and he'd paid a good sum of money to see that no captain would give her passage on any ship heading south. But Grace had outwitted him once again, and for that Martin burned in anger, just as the letter burned when he cast it inside the stove.

"Colton will never know the truth," Paxton said as he slammed the door shut on the stove. "But with a little incentive and a great deal of money, perhaps the man can be persuaded by a lie."

⊣ CHAPTER TWENTY-ONE ⊢

ADRIK WASN'T AT ALL SURE he should have given in to the idea of building a boat in Lindeman. He wasn't prepared for the high cost of materials and the shortage of good lumber. He also wasn't prepared to hear about the One Mile River and the rapids that connected Lake Lindeman to Lake Bennett.

Still, he had to face the truth of the situation. They needed transportation north, and they could either pay for freighting in someone else's boat or take a chance on their own. Coming from seafaring people, Adrik didn't question his ability to build a decent craft. He listened intently to the advice given him by other builders and added it to his own knowledge, designing a boat that would be ideally suited to the strenuous travel they would encounter. Still, he wished he might have considered other options.

Supplies were scarce, and the available lumber was green

and spongy. Not the kind of thing you wanted for building a ship. Green wood would shrink and lead to disaster on the trip. Many people were waiting to build boats in Bennett, and while that had been Adrik's original plan, he counted it as the divine providence of God that he'd changed his mind. Bennett was quite overcome with dysentery and typhoid fever. And while one police officer told him things were looking better, Adrik didn't want to take a chance. Those were two problems he didn't care to take on. Sickness and scarcity of goods were enough to discourage and send many a man packing. But apparently it wasn't as daunting to the women in Adrik's party.

The women wanted to press on and did everything within their means to see that it happened quickly. September would soon be upon them, and their options were quickly narrowing. With God smiling favorably upon them, it would take four weeks to reach Dawson by water. Yet in that time, the Yukon could freeze up solid and be hit with ten feet of snow. Adrik didn't like thinking about the odds.

These thoughts fouled his mood, causing even Crispin to avoid him. Karen generally eyed him from afar, saying nothing—for once. He knew she had troubles of her own. She continued to fret over Jacob's whereabouts. Leah had taken a cold, causing the child to be greatly discouraged and saddened. Between her mood and his, Adrik had no doubt Karen was feeling rather overwhelmed.

"So are you still planning for us to leave tomorrow?"

He hadn't heard Karen come up behind him. He turned and smiled, determined to prove to her that all was well. "That's the plan."

She studied him for a moment. Her red-gold hair, now lightened considerably by the long hours spent in the sun, blew wisps around her face. Her eyes, so intent on understanding his mood, were exceptionally blue. He wanted to reach out—to touch her. He wanted to beg her to marry him and put an end to his loneliness. But now wasn't the time.

"I thought we were friends," she said matter-of-factly.

Adrik hadn't expected this and was taken aback for a moment. "What?"

Karen crossed her arms. "You heard me. Furthermore, you know exactly what I'm talking about. You've been nothing but a bear all week. You've grunted around here, barely talking to anyone. Your mood has sent the entire camp into a spell of depression, and I want to know why."

"I have a lot on my mind. Getting this party north is a big enough task to weigh heavily on anyone. It's already the middle of August."

"So?" She refused to back down, and her expression caused Adrik to actually smile.

"So . . . winter isn't that far off. There are signs that it just may come early. And if you'll remember, it gets kind of cold up here. And when that happens, the water freezes and the snow falls and makes living a little more uncomfortable—and transportation a great deal more difficult."

"Is that all?"

"Isn't that enough? The odds are no longer with us."

Karen shook her head. "I've never known you to be overly worried about the odds. No, this is something more."

Adrik turned away from her and picked up his hammer. He wasn't ready to tell her how he felt. How loving her was tearing him apart inside because he didn't know if she could ever love him enough to share her life with him. He began to pound a nail into the piece he'd been working on all morning, but just as he raised his hammer, Karen took hold of his hand.

She didn't say a word, and finally he had to look at her.

Her expression softened as his eyes met hers. "Adrik, please don't be this way. Just tell me what's really troubling you. I promise to be understanding and to do my best to help you figure out what we should do."

"Will you, now?" he said softly. He jerked away from her and put the hammer back on the table. Then turning back around, he pulled Karen into his arms. Mindless of the crowds that worked around him and the throngs of strangers who coursed right through their camp, Adrik lowered his mouth to hers for a long and leisurely kiss. She didn't resist him. Adrik felt lost in the power of the moment. He wanted to forget that there were decisions to be made and trials to be faced. He wanted Karen, and nothing else mattered quite so much. Realizing that he had to put an end to their embrace, he abruptly ended the kiss and let her go.

"There," he said. "Figure out what's to be done about that."

She stared at him in wide-eyed surprise. Her cheeks were red and her mouth was slightly open, as if to speak. Adrik knew it would be better for both of them if he simply walked away. So that was what he did.

Miranda and Crispin had just returned from a foray into town when they came upon Adrik kissing Karen. The passion displayed in that kiss had caused Miranda no small amount of discomfort. How she had longed for someone to love her as dearly and completely as she knew Mr. Ivankov loved Karen Pierce.

"It seems we are interrupting," Crispin said good-naturedly. He leaned close to whisper, "I wonder how long it will take until they both realize they are in love?"

Miranda giggled, but Crispin's warm breath against her ear

caused a shiver of delight to run up her spine. "I'm sure I don't know," she replied without thinking, "but perhaps we should invest in another tent."

Crispin laughed out loud. "What a woman. Your thoughts could well be my own."

Miranda suddenly realized how inappropriate her remark sounded. "I only . . . well . . . I meant that should they marry. . . ." She gave up when she saw that her words only served to amuse Crispin all the more.

"I knew exactly what you meant, my dear. I was thinking much the same."

They watched Adrik march off as if to war, while Karen stood looking after him in dumbfounded silence.

"Ah, true love," Crispin said, nudging Miranda. "Theirs will be a match for all eternity."

Miranda nodded, but the statement made her feel suddenly very empty. "I think I'd better take these eggs and see about supper." She held up the small basket where only moments ago she had placed the two precious eggs. Paying a dollar for the two, Miranda thought they might as well have been golden eggs.

She left Crispin and hurried to where they had set up a makeshift kitchen under a canvas awning. The awning had been stretched out between the two tents and made a nice, almost cozy living area in the evening and a wonderful kitchen in the daytime. At night Adrik would lower additional pieces of canvas from the sides and create the effect of walls. Then, by tying the canvas strips to the tents, he closed them off from the rest of the world and allowed the heat of the stove to warm both tents. At least it warmed them marginally.

Miranda actually liked the cold weather and enjoyed the crisp feel to the air. She'd heard one man say that winter was due to come early this year, and she thought that was marvelous. She wanted to see the snow stacked ten and twenty feet deep, as Crispin had spoken of. He had traveled the world and had seen all manner of things, and it thrilled Miranda to the core of her being. How wonderful to simply travel at will and see the world and all that it had to offer.

"Were you able to get any eggs?" Leah asked as Miranda approached.

"I was able to buy two, and they were quite expensive," Miranda replied. "But for one of your cakes, Leah, I know it was worth the price."

Leah didn't respond with the excitement Miranda had anticipated. "They work a whole sight better than those powdered ones we brought along."

"You're a good cook, Leah. You'll have us all forgetting the cost before the end of the meal."

Leah merely nodded and went to work. Taking the eggs from Miranda's basket, she cracked them into a bowl. Miranda's heart ached for the young girl. Leah had prayed so passionately that morning, pleading with God for the safe return of her brother. Miranda couldn't help but speak a similar prayer. They were bound in a strange way by their wayward male siblings. And until that morning, Miranda had never truly realized the connection.

"Leah," she said, knowing that she had to share this thought with the girl, "you and I are very much alike."

Leah looked up from her work and coughed lightly. "What do you mean?"

"Our brothers," Miranda replied.

Leah shook her head. "I know Jacob and Peter knew each other, but I don't see how that makes us alike."

Miranda moved closer and smiled. "We are both longing

for our brothers to come back. Your brother has gone north, mine has gone away without any word of his whereabouts. You love your brother and I love mine. Both are important people in our lives, and both hold our hearts in a special way."

"I see," Leah replied, turning her attention back to the cake.

Miranda reached out to stop her for a moment. "I know how hard it is. I know you're worried and that you can scarcely think of anything else. I know you wonder about your father and long to know the truth.

"When I heard you pray this morning, I realized the words could have been from my own mouth. I long for Peter to return home, just as you need to find Jacob."

Leah's eyes filled with tears. Miranda reached up to wipe away the drops as they fell onto the girl's cheek. "My mother always said that a burden shared makes the load less heavy. I will share this burden with you if you will let me."

Leah wrapped her arms around Miranda's waist. "Thank you, Miranda. Sometimes it just scares me so much. Sometimes I'm afraid I'll never see him again."

Miranda stroked Leah's hair and sighed. "I know. I fear sometimes that I'll never see my brother again." Just then Miranda looked up and saw Grace standing not five feet away. Her expression made it clear that she'd overheard a good portion of their words.

Miranda decided to speak from her heart. "When I get very afraid, I pray that God will give me strength to endure and that He will take away my fear and help me to remember that He loves me."

She smiled at Grace and hoped that she would remember that long ago she had once spoken similar words to Miranda. The moment had been when Miranda had feared God might never send her a husband Peter would approve of. Her heart had been close to breaking at the thought of never knowing true love. Grace had comforted her with those very words.

Grace nodded, as if remembering the moment herself. She slipped off between neighboring camps and disappeared from sight while Leah raised her head and offered Miranda a weak smile. "My mama always said that I should come and tell her when I was afraid. She said that God was always with us and that when we're afraid, the Psalms said we could trust in Him."

"Your mother sounds like she was a very wise woman—and a very loving mother."

Leah drew a ragged breath and laid her head back against Miranda's shoulder. "She was a wonderful mother. My pa was a good father, too. Even though he left us, he still loved us."

"I'm sure that's true," Miranda replied, her heart filled with love for the girl. How very much she would have liked to have a little sister like Leah. Perhaps that was the reason God had allowed her to come on this journey. He knew Leah would need her. Even more, God knew Miranda would need Leah.

———

Adrik stood back with a great deal of pride and no small amount of reservation. The flat-bottomed scow he and Crispin had completed sat afloat in Lake Lindeman without the slightest hint of taking on water.

"It would appear, my friend, we have built a seaworthy craft," Crispin said joyfully.

"It would seem that way," Adrik replied, continuing to check every inch of the deck for some sign of a problem. Apparently the oakum and pitch caulking was holding well.

The flat-bottomed scow was exactly what they needed to take them north to the goldfields. Adrik knew the boat would easily accommodate their passengers and tons of goods within its forty-two-foot length. What he was less convinced of was whether or not the women would have the strength to help row and pole as they passed through the rapids.

Then, too, he'd already been warned that even with a sturdy square sail rigged to the bow mast, he'd be a fool to rely on the winds and currents alone. The doldrums, it seemed, were quite common on the still waters of the larger lakes. And when storms came up without warning, as they were wont to do, the oars would be necessary to make it to the safety of the shore. Could he and Crispin handle it alone?

"Face it, my friend," Crispin said, slapping Adrik's back, "you've built a masterpiece. Michelangelo couldn't have done better."

"Well, I don't know who he is," Adrik said, blowing out a breath of relief, "but I almost wish he were here to help us sail her."

Crispin laughed, then surprised Adrik by waving. Turning, he saw that Crispin was bidding welcome to the women, who stood watching from shore. "So what do you think?" Crispin called out.

"It looks awfully small," Karen called back. "Are you sure it's going to hold us all?"

"It's bigger than you think," Adrik answered. "Just wait until tomorrow. You'll see for yourself."

"It's nothing short of a floating palace," Crispin announced, and the ladies laughed.

Adrik gazed heavenward and shook his head. "I wouldn't exactly call it that, but it's floating and that's what counts."

"Well, it cost as much as a palace," Karen called out from

the shore. "Who would have ever thought pitch would cost seven dollars a pound?"

By now a crowd had gathered to see the finished master-piece by Adrik Ivankov. They laughed at Karen's statement and threw out comments of their own.

"No worse than paying a dollar a pound for nails!"

"If you can get them!"

"You can't even get lumber for building, and the trees to cut are five miles away."

"And it helps if you know how to build with them when you get them," another poor soul called out. At this everyone laughed, and even Adrik stopped fretting momentarily and joined the fun.

"Well, perhaps I would do better to open a boat-building school rather than to head north to the goldfields," he replied.

"No doubt the money would be better," Karen said, laughing.

"Well, be that as it may," Adrik said, putting his hands to his hips, "are you ladies ready to leave in the morning?"

"I was ready to leave a week ago," Karen answered. He watched her turn to the others. "Come on, we've got some packing to do. I know this captain of ours, and he's the pushy sort. If we aren't ready, he'll leave without us."

"That's exactly what I'll do," Adrik said, laughing, but he didn't mean a word of it.

The excitement of his accomplishment finally outweighed his worry. Looking to Crispin, he nodded. "We've got ourselves a boat, and she looks to be all that we could hope for."

Part Three

LATE AUGUST 1898

It was meet that we should make
merry, and be glad:
for this thy brother was dead, and
is alive again; and was lost,
and is found.

LUKE 15:32

—{ C H A P T E R   T W E N T Y - T W O }—

TRAVERSING LAKE LINDEMAN proved to be an easy, almost carefree trip. The biggest problem was avoiding the other twenty or more boats that were attempting to launch at the same time. There was nearly a carnival-type atmosphere as the various pilots steered in one direction and then another. It soon became quite clear who had prior experience in boating. Adrik, steeped in years of childhood sailing and fishing, took to the water with great ease. Even Crispin, for all his upper-society manners, was quite adept on the boat. The boat itself proved to be a seaworthy vessel. The shrinkage of the raw lumber remained minimal, and the rocky passageways caused little damage.

Karen thought Adrik's worry was all for naught as the One Mile Rapids and Lake Bennett soon became nothing more than exciting memories. After registering their boat in

Bennett, along with scores of other desperate souls, the party pushed on and made exceptional time. Even Adrik had to admit that God was smiling on them. They'd managed to keep the boat clear of most obstacles, and even when the waters had grown rough, it was almost as if an unseen hand had maneuvered them through the dangers.

The little scow proved to be much bigger than Karen had originally believed. Once they'd positioned the smaller of their two tents in the middle of the boat and set up their provisions around those canvas walls, Karen felt they were living rather well. It wasn't perfect and it wasn't anything luxurious, but it was better than most.

But perhaps most surprising of all, Karen enjoyed life upon the water. She enjoyed the passing scenery and the glorious colors of the changing seasons. There was something simply marvelous about moving to a new place every day. After living a life of rigid convention in Chicago for the ten years prior to coming north, the Yukon offered a sort of liberty that appealed to Karen. She didn't even mind the frost that touched most everything that morning.

Winter's clutches were approaching, yet Karen refused to let her spirits be defeated. She thought of her mother's letters describing Alaskan winters—bitterly cold and deep snows. Yukon winters were surely the same, and having survived the long dark season in Dyea only the year before, Karen was convinced she could manage the days to come.

That night Karen slipped away from her tent and found Adrik sitting near the small campfire they'd enjoyed earlier in the evening. She smiled at him and pulled her coat together to ward off the chill.

"I couldn't sleep," she said softly. "I'm much too excited."

"We're doing well," he admitted. "I had my concerns, but

I have to say things are going along better than I could have planned."

"Hand of God," she whispered.

He glanced up. "Is that a question?"

Karen folded her arms and looked to the skies. "You needn't worry about me. I'm all right." She stated the words, knowing he would understand, but was surprised when he questioned her further.

"What do you mean, you're all right?"

Karen wondered if he needed to hear her confess she had yielded her will. Why was it that God and Adrik Ivankov always demanded she completely surrender her innermost secrets?

"Why don't you sit down here beside me," Adrik suggested, "and tell me exactly what's on your mind?"

Karen hesitated for a moment. Could she trust herself with Adrik? She knew her heart in the matter. She wanted very much to declare her love for him, but she was so uncertain of how he might respond. He obviously found her desirable, but love—now, that was a different story. Could he really love her? And if he did, what would that love require of her?

She inched closer and knelt down beside the fire. "I just wanted you to know that I've yielded my anger to God." She stared into the fire rather than risk Adrik's eyes. "You've so often borne the brunt of that anger and had to keep me from making a fool of myself—"

"On more than one occasion," Adrik interjected with a laugh.

She turned to him and saw that he intended only to lighten her mood. "Yes, well, I thank you for that. I know I can be difficult at times."

Adrik nodded. "That's what your pa always said."

"He said that?" Her tone betrayed her surprise.

"He said that you were the one pea in the pod that just refused to be alike. Your sisters were calm, quiet children who settled down to marriage and family, but not you. You thirsted for knowledge and adventure and went after both with great enthusiasm."

Karen laughed softly. "Yes, I can imagine him saying just that."

"He loved you, you know."

Karen felt tears come to her eyes. "I loved him, too. I still can't believe he's gone. I was certain he was the treasure I was coming north to find. I was certain he would give me answers and purpose for my life."

"Only God can do that, Karen."

"I know that—at least now I do. I'd always espoused that belief in words, but I guess God had to bring me through fire to help me make it something more than words."

"He's making you grow. Making your faith grow. Your pa used to say that a man's faith was like building a house. You give it a good foundation, and then you have something to build on. Even then, you have to add to that basic structure. A house has to have walls and a roof."

"A floor's nice, too," Karen said with a smile. After living with the ground beneath for her tent floor, she was ready for real wood under her feet.

Adrik chuckled, "Floors are good, too." He reached out and touched her hand. "Faith has to be added in order to make it strong. It doesn't happen overnight."

"My mother used to say that God's love for us was instantaneous, but that human beings needed time to learn to love." Karen had spoken without thinking, and now the memory burned in her heart as she looked deep into Adrik's eyes.

She knew he cared—of that she was certain. But did he love her? Did he love her enough to want the rest of his life altered by a wife—children? He'd teased her in Dyea about getting married in order to share a tent. He'd kissed her until Karen had lost all reasonable thought. But did this constitute that kind of love that meant "forever"?

Adrik was a free spirit. She'd known that from the moment she'd first met him. He'd told her tales of wandering the land, of living among his grandmother's people, of learning what the land had to offer him. He'd shared sad tales of the battles fought over the land, of whites who destroyed the Tlingit commerce and livelihood, of sickness that had destroyed entire villages. He knew this land and people and loved them both. Karen knew that in order to have Adrik Ivankov, she'd have to accept his land and people as her own. Could she do that? Could she give herself over to this frozen north—this deadly but beautiful land?

She felt his fingers stroking her hand. The sensation caused her to tremble. He was the only man in the world who could make her feel all weak in the knees.

"You'd better get to bed," Adrik said abruptly. "We've got a full day ahead of us tomorrow." He fairly jumped up from his seat on the ground.

He helped Karen to her feet but didn't wait for her response. Confused by his actions, Karen shook her head. Who was this man, and what did he want from her?

———

"What do you mean we have to walk around the rapids?" Karen declared.

Adrik stood his ground. He'd known Karen was going to be a problem. "The Northwest Mounted Police have set the regulation for Miles Canyon. The rapids are too rough there, and people have drowned while trying to make it through."

"But we made it through other rapids just fine," Karen protested.

"Maybe there's something different about this particular area," Grace suggested.

Karen shook her head. "Even if that were true, why not merely tell us of the dangers and leave the decision up to us?"

"Karen," Adrik began in a firmer tone, "I have no say over what the officials of this country dictate. They have decided the rapids are too difficult for women."

"Just women? What about men? Why don't the men have to walk?"

Adrik clamped his mouth shut and looked heavenward. The woman could be so argumentative when she decided to be. Why couldn't she just accept the ruling and deal with it in the same calm manner as her traveling companions?

"I happen to enjoy the exhilaration of the rapids," Karen continued. "I want to ride them out with you and Crispin. If Grace and Miranda and Leah wish to walk, I have no objection."

"You aren't going, and that's final!" Adrik declared louder than he'd intended.

"You're just trying to control me!"

"Well, somebody has to."

Karen gave him a look that would have frozen a weaker man in his steps, but not Adrik. He knew only too well that this was for her own good, and he wasn't about to let her run roughshod over him. "You'll walk and that's final. If I die taking the scow to Whitehorse, then I die. I built the boat and I'll stand by it. But I won't risk the rest of you, and that's my final word." He turned to Crispin and added, "They have men to help pilot the boats through the rapids, so you don't have to come with me."

"Nonsense," Crispin said with a gleam in his eyes. "I wouldn't miss it for the world."

Karen looked at Adrik as if waiting for him to change his mind. When he didn't, she stormed off to the women's tent. When suppertime came, she was still there, and Adrik knew she'd be difficult to contend with. Why couldn't she see that he was only trying to keep her safe? Personally, he was glad for the rule. He'd heard many accounts of the dangers from passing travelers. In fact, that day in the small community that had formed at the head of Miles Canyon, he'd nearly called the trip off after hearing about all the problems with broken ships and lost souls.

"It's the reason we must insist that you portage your goods and passengers," one of the officials told him firmly. "There's a tramway, and your supplies may be loaded onto flat cars. The walk is a decent one except for the mosquitos. Your women will much prefer it to the ride down the canyon."

Adrik would have laughed had the situation not seemed so grim. Most women might have preferred it, but not his women. At least not one woman in particular.

By morning Karen was still not speaking to him, and Adrik had decided enough was enough. He wasn't going to sit around and wait for her to come to her senses. He marveled that she could be so level-headed one moment and so completely obstinate the next. Resolving to concentrate on the task at hand, however, Adrik put in his request for help with the rapids and waited his turn to battle Miles Canyon.

"You're being awfully hard on him, aren't you?" Grace questioned as they washed up the breakfast dishes.

Karen shrugged. "He's just doing this to control the situation." She scrubbed hard at a pie pan, almost imagining she was scrubbing out Adrik's image. Why did the man have to so completely infuriate her one moment and leave her breathless and trembling the next? What kind of madness had overtaken her?

"The authorities have set this rule, not Mr. Ivankov. He only means to see us safe, Karen. I think you're judging him too harshly."

Karen paused and eyed her friend. Grace's color was rather pale, and Karen had worried about her ever since leaving Lindeman. Perhaps Karen's anger was only adding to Grace's exhaustion. With a sigh she set the pan aside. "Grace, I don't know what to do with my feelings. One minute I think I'm in love with him, and the next minute I'd just as soon push him into the river."

Grace offered a bittersweet smile. "I'd like to tell you it gets easier, but I can't. I'm a poor example to follow. I have no idea where my husband has gone. He could very well be dead for all I know, and it breaks my heart to think that the last words we shared were such harsh ones."

Karen nodded. "I know and I'm sorry, Grace. I shouldn't be telling my woes to you. My problems pale compared to your heartbreak."

Miranda bounded into the tent announcing, "Crispin says we're to pack up and head out within the hour. They've made the final arrangements, and we're to meet them on the other side of the rapids. We'll actually be in Whitehorse tonight!"

"I've heard it's grown into quite a city," Grace said. Then she clutched at the edge of the tent, appearing as if she might collapse.

"What is it?" Karen exclaimed, going to her friend's side. "Are you all right?"

Grace nodded and steadied herself against Karen's arm. "I just got a little dizzy for a moment. I'm sure it's just the lack of sleep and decent meals. Oh, what I wouldn't give for a large bowl of fruit." She smiled reassuringly. "How about you?"

Karen wasn't at all convinced of her friend's health. "I think you'd better see a doctor once we get to Whitehorse. You haven't been well the entire trip, and frankly, I'm worried. It isn't like you to be so pale and weak."

"I'll be fine," Grace said, walking to where she'd left bread dough to rise. "I guess we'll have to figure a way to carry this with us or throw it out. I can't see wasting it."

"Let's put it in the big kettle," Miranda suggested. "We'll cover it and pack it with the other things and let them portage it for us. Maybe it will be ready to bake by the time we get to the other side."

The two women went to work on the bread dough while Karen considered the situation. Guilt set in, making her miserable. She couldn't let things go on between her and Adrik as they were. What if something happened to him on the trip through the rapids? Other people had died. Other boats had broken apart on the rocks. A cold shiver ran down her spine. She would rather die with Adrik than live without him. For the first time in her life, Karen was certain of what it meant to be in love with a man. She couldn't let him leave without her. She just couldn't stay behind.

"It's like nothin' ya've ever known," the boat pilot told Adrik as he moved them out into the water. "It's the most untamed stretch of water in the continent. We'll be through it right quick, but ya'll be wonderin' what happened to ya for weeks to come."

Adrik wanted to ask the man about his experience—his abilities—but instead he said nothing as they maneuvered away from shore. He had no idea whether the man knew what he was talking about or not, but he'd paid the exorbitant sum of twenty-five dollars to have the boat taken down the water, and Adrik would have to trust that the man knew his job. After all, his life was as much on the line as Adrik's or Crispin's. Still, he looked awfully young, and he was even shorter than Karen. He was just a kid, as far as Adrik was concerned— a kid who held their lives in his hands as he controlled the scow.

The man seemed unconcerned with what they were about to experience. He chattered incessantly as he worked the boat to the middle of the river. "Ya have to ride the midriver crest in order to survive the white water. Running the white ain't for the faint of heart. I'm glad they've taken to puttin' the ladies off the boats. Just ain't safe."

Adrik could agree with the man there, especially after conversing with one of the officials. The man seemed to positively delight in giving him the details of crafts that had crashed and broken apart on the rocks. It was as if the story were the man's own personal melodrama and Adrik was his only audience.

There was little time to worry any more about it, however. Adrik could feel their speed pick up as the current caught them and pulled them down into the canyon. The water was swift, but not unduly rough. At least not yet. Thick stretches of pines and spruce topped walls some one hundred feet high on either side. The walls seemed to narrow as the water picked up speed and roughness. As the scow lifted up and slammed down against the churning water, Adrik was glad the women had left by foot hours earlier. They'd be safe and sound once Adrik and the men got the scow safely through the canyon. *If* they got the scow through. Adrik had the distinct sensation they were being taken to their graves. Within a few minutes he knew he had good reason to feel that way.

"Hold on to yar hats," the pilot called, "there's rocks ahead. Ya'll want to keep yar poles ready."

The scow dipped and pitched, and Adrik steadied himself as best he could. He could have anticipated the rocks that sent the little boat into a bit of a spin. What he could not have anticipated was the crash of a human body landing at his feet.

Karen looked up from the deck with a lopsided smile. "Surprise," she said meekly as the boat pitched once again and water sprayed up around them.

———

"The man actually expects me to take this lying down," Peter told his friend. Jonas simply nodded and looked to Peter for further explanation. In the weeks since Paxton had first suggested Peter put a legal end to his marriage, Peter had received two letters from the man further outlining the procedure. "I won't divorce her. I won't give either one of them that kind of satisfaction."

"You're mighty quick to judge that she's agreeing to this matter," Jonas replied. "I would have thought if she were in such an all-fire hurry to get rid of you, she would have allowed that Paxton fellow to help *her* get the divorce rather than waitin' for you to see to it."

"Perhaps Paxton believes I would have an easier time of it," Peter said, pushing back his hair in exasperation. "But I won't do it!"

"Then don't," Jonas said, reaching across the table to help

himself to his pipe and tobacco.

"I wanted to kill him," Peter said, looking to his friend for some kind of comment. "I honestly wanted to see him die on the spot."

"Can't say as I blame you. If a man were keepin' my wife from me, I'd probably feel the same way. Especially if he'd caused as much trouble as this Paxton fellow has for you."

Peter finally stopped his pacing and sat down at the table. "What am I supposed to do? Grace is gone. I've no doubt lost her forever. My anger and stupidity have put up a permanent wall between us." He buried his face in his hands. "I miss her so much. I need her."

"Then what are you doing here?" Jonas asked.

Peter raised his gaze and saw that the man was staring at him as if awaiting an answer. What could he say? Why had he left Skagway and Paxton to return to the railway camp? Why had he gone without beating the truth out of Paxton and insisting on Grace's return?

Shrugging, Peter suddenly knew the answer. "Because I'm not man enough to do anything else. I'm less than a whole man without her."

Jonas smiled. "I can well understand how ya feel. A good woman completes a man—makes him see what's been missin' in his life. God said it wasn't good for man to be alone, and it sure as well ain't."

Peter looked at Jonas, and an aching filled his heart. "Jonas, tell me about your God. Tell me why He should care about someone like me—why He should forgive me or need my adoration. Religion makes no sense to me."

"Me neither," Jonas said with a laugh. "All that mumbo jumbo and risin' up and sittin' down. I could never carry a tune, so I didn't figure it made much sense to put myself in a place that made a point of havin' singin'." He put the pipe aside and shook his head. "Knowin' God has nothin' to do with religion."

Peter shook his head. "I don't understand. Grace went to church every Sunday and read her Bible all the time. She wanted the same for me, and I couldn't give it to her. She wanted me to forgive Martin Paxton. I couldn't see the sense in that, either."

"Your little wife went to church because it pleased her to do so. She no doubt had friends there and folks who were of a like mind. That's fellowshipin', and I don't mind that one bit. But you can't box God into a buildin'. He's everywhere, Peter. He most prefers to be here." He pounded his chest for a moment. "Right here, in your heart."

"I just don't know," Peter said, getting to his feet once again. "It doesn't make sense to me. All I can think about is my family. I need to know if my father is well, if my mother is safe. I need to know where my sister is and what she's doing. And I need Grace."

"In more ways than you realize," Jonas said with a grin. "My advice to you is to skedaddle out of this place and go home. Start with your folks. And maybe on the ship ride home, you could have a word or two with the Almighty. I'm thinkin' He'd be pleased to listen to the matter if you were of a mind to tell Him about it."

⊣ CHAPTER TWENTY-THREE ⊢

THE RIDE DOWN Miles Canyon was like nothing Karen Pierce had ever experienced. Thrown first one way and then the other, she had been as surprised as Adrik to fly out of the tent and land at his feet.

"Stay put!" Adrik yelled, his face contorting in anger.

Karen had no intention of going anywhere, but as the boat lurched and crashed upon a projection of rock, she rolled across the deck. No sooner had she reached the right side of the scow when the entire platform seemed to shift directions. Without a hope of stopping herself, Karen rolled across to the left side of the boat. Only this time, there was nothing to grab on to and she felt herself slipping over the side.

"Adrik!" she screamed, her fingers slipping on the watery deck.

She couldn't see him or even know if he'd heard her. She

felt the waves push them up into the air, and before she could so much as snap her fingers, the boat slammed back down in the water. For a long moment, she seemed to be suspended in the air, wondering if there would even be a deck to come back down to. But there was. Thrown against the hard wood, Karen again found herself hopelessly rolling to the right.

If ever there was a moment of reckoning, Karen Pierce found one in this moment. Catching sight of Adrik frantically working to keep the boat from the canyon walls, Karen knew he had no way to help her. The same was true of Crispin, as well as the young man who handled the sweep. There was no one to cry out to—no one but God.

"Oh, God, help me!" she cried out as the icy water poured over the side. She felt herself slipping, sliding ever closer to the edge. Why hadn't Adrik built a rail around this deck?

"Hold on!" she heard the stranger sound above the thundering rapids.

But there was nothing solid to hold on to. She couldn't quite reach the tent, and that would have offered her very little in the way of support anyway. Then Karen spied one of the benches Adrik had nailed to the deck to offer relief from the tent or standing about on deck. If she could make it to the bench, she might be able to wrap herself around it and hope for the best.

Please, God, help me. Don't let me die without telling him how much I love him, Karen thought. She continued her prayer as she fought to make her way across the deck. *Father, I know I've held a grudge, and I'm sorry. Please don't drown me here in the river just to punish my stupidity.*

Inching her way to the structure, Karen felt only a marginal amount of relief as her hands grasped the bench. "Thank you, God!" She sighed and clung to the bench as though it were the most precious gift in all the world. And for all the most important reasons, it was.

Glancing up, Karen saw that Adrik stood only a few feet away. His expression told Karen he was anything but happy to see her—either that or he was angry at the Whitehorse Rapids. *Never mind,* she thought as the boat rose up on a wave and crashed down again. Water seemed to explode around them, dousing them both. *He'll get over it. He'll see why I had to come when I explain the matter to him.*

Water poured across the deck, drenching Karen's heavy wool skirt. Earlier she'd slipped away from the other women, pretending to want to be alone, and so they'd believe her to be returning, she'd left her coat and taken only the knitted wool shawl Aunt Doris had given her last Christmas. Wrapped up in that and wearing a long-sleeved white blouse, Karen felt the icy water bite into her skin as if it had teeth.

The deck pitched back and forth while the bow forced its way through the water. As she managed to figure out the best way to secure herself, Karen realized she was having a wonderful time. The waves and water, the canyon walls—it was all rather like a carousel ride gone mad.

Laughing, she looked up to find Adrik fighting with a long thick pole. She had no idea what he was doing but surmised he was probably helping to keep the boat from crashing against the rocky cliffs.

Then, almost before the ride had begun, the waters calmed, and Karen found them heading to shore. She whispered a prayer of thanksgiving, seeing for herself that they were all still in one piece—as was the boat. The latter was a critical issue, almost on equal footing with their own safety. There was still a great distance to head via water, and they would need the scow to get them through. As they approached the land, Crispin caught sight of her and laughed.

"Where in the world did you come from? Drop down from the skies, did you?"

Karen nodded and pulled her wet body up to the top of the bench. "I felt as though I had."

"So we have a stowaway," the pilot said, taking note of Karen. "Women don't know what's good for them. They ain't gonna like it one bit that you broke the rules and rode down the rapids."

"Tell them to throw her into jail," Adrik said, turning away to help secure the scow at the makeshift dock.

Karen knew she'd have her work cut out with him. She stood and tried to wring out some of the water from her shawl. Crispin offered to help her, and while he took charge of her wrap, Karen worked on the bottom of her skirt.

She looked at Crispin rather conspiratorially and whispered, "That was the most fun I think I've ever had. Of course, I thought for a minute that I was going to go right over the side. God seemed to just pluck me right up. But as dangerous as it seemed, I'd do it again in a minute!"

He nodded toward Adrik. "Looks like there's going to be quite a price to pay."

She looked over to where Adrik stood scowling at them and said, "I suppose I should attempt to unruffle his feathers."

"I think it will take more than that," Crispin replied. "But a word of advice, my dear."

Karen leaned closer. "Yes?"

"Never underestimate your feminine charms."

Karen grinned. "Why, Crispin Thibault, what a splendid suggestion."

She forgot her shawl and sauntered rather boldly up to where Adrik stood. Her legs were a little wobbly after the ordeal, but she steadied herself and grinned. "Permission to go ashore, sir," she said in a teasing manner.

Adrik stepped from the scow and pulled her with him onto the deck. Then without warning he hoisted her unceremoniously over one shoulder and stalked off away from the river.

Karen tried to raise herself up, but Adrik's steps were bouncing her around something fierce. She caught sight of Grace and Miranda, who stood to one side with Leah. They looked at her as if to question this latest escapade, but Karen couldn't even so much as shrug.

"Adrik, put me down!" she protested as his long strides took them farther from the shore. He crossed the tramline and headed deeper into the forest, all while Karen pounded on his back to get his attention. "Adrik, I mean it. Put me down." This ride was almost as perilous as the course on the rapids.

They were well away from the crowd by now, and Karen couldn't see a single sign of civilization. All around her were spruce and pine trunks and vegetation that had begun its autumnal transformation. Then, as quickly as he had hoisted her to his shoulder, Adrik dumped her onto the ground. Her bottom smacked against the hard earth, causing the wind to go out of Karen in a great whoosh.

Gasping, she managed to sputter, "How . . . how . . . *dare* you!"

"How dare me? How dare *you*!" he countered. "You were told to stay off the boat. You were told to go with the other women. You were told a great many things, but you refused to listen."

He turned as if to go, then attacked again. "Do you realize you could have been killed?"

"Of course . . ."

"Do you give any consideration to those who travel with you?"

"Yes, you know I—"

"I can't believe," he said, stalking toward her, hands out-stretched, "that you would put your life in danger." He pulled her into the air and dropped her back on her feet.

"Adrik, I can explain!" she said, demanding to be heard.

"You can explain!" He turned away and paced. "You can explain that you gave little thought to the laws of the land—to your authority? You can explain that you took matters into your own hands and disregarded everything I said to you?"

Karen could see there would be no talking to him. He wasn't at all willing to listen. Shaking the dirt and debris from the back of her skirt, she let him rant and rave. His righteous indignation, however, did much to lighten her spirits. He loved her. He would never have reacted this way if he didn't. His anger was born of fear. Fear for her. Fear that she might have died or gotten injured. Smiling, she lifted her face and waited for him to conclude.

"You could have been killed. You could have easily been swept overboard, and you very nearly were. Do you know that my heart actually stopped beating when I saw you struggling at the side and knew I could do nothing to save you without jeopardizing everyone else? The rapids have claimed many a life. The Canadian authorities wouldn't have seen fit to make laws regarding that particular passage on the river if it hadn't been for their desire to keep folks alive. But you..." He turned to look at her and stopped. "What are you smiling about? Do you think this is funny?"

"You're funny," she replied. "You won't let me talk or even attempt to explain. All you want to do is yell."

"You bet I want to yell. There's absolutely nothing you can

say that will make one bit of difference to me." He shrugged out of his wet coat and tossed it aside. Rolling up his sleeves, Karen actually wondered for a moment what he had planned for her. His well-muscled arms strained against the drenched flannel of his shirt sleeves. It was little wonder, she thought, that he could throw her so easily over his shoulder.

Karen opened her mouth to speak, but again he silenced her.

He held up his hand. "There's nothing you can say. Nothing!"

"I beg to differ with you. I think there is something I can say. Something very important, and if you would settle down and stop being so pigheaded, I might get a chance to say it." She put her hands on her hips, not caring that she must look a sight.

Adrik waved his arm in front of him. "By all means, have your say. What in the world do you think could possibly explain what you just did?"

"I love you," Karen said matter-of-factly. She smiled and shrugged. "I love you. I think that says it all."

He looked at her as if dumbfounded. His dark eyes simply looked her up and down before he began shaking his head. "That's just great. That only makes matters worse."

"What?" Karen exclaimed. "How can you say my love makes matters worse? I know you love me, too. Tell me that you don't."

Adrik looked at her as if she'd suddenly gone daft. "Of course I love you!" he yelled. "That's what makes it so awful."

Karen laughed. "I must have hit my head on that boat ride, because you aren't making any sense to me at all."

He crossed the distance between them in two strides and took hold of her. Shaking her hard, he said, "This is nothing to laugh about. I love you so much that I would have spent the rest of my days with a broken heart had anything happened to you. Don't you understand? This is a deadly land, and you are playing at it like a child with a puppy. Instead of a puppy, you're dealing with a grizzly bear, and you don't even know the difference."

He let her go but didn't move away. Karen thought of what Crispin had said and reached up to touch the side of his cheek. The stubble of a two-day growth of beard scratched her hand as she ran her fingers along his jaw.

"I love you. You mean the world to me, as well," she said softly. She lifted her face and prayed he'd see the sincerity in her eyes. "I couldn't bear the thought of losing you. You must understand—I kept hearing all the stories of death and destruction. I couldn't bear for you to go without me."

"But if you knew the risk, why would you do that?" he asked, his voice low and guarded.

Karen wrapped her arms around his neck and laced her fingers together. "Because, my darling man, I would rather die at your side than live without you." She stretched up on her toes and placed a kiss upon his unresponsive lips. "Don't you see? I had to go with you. I couldn't bear to be left behind and know that I might never see you again."

She heard his breath catch in his throat as he grabbed her and buried his face against her neck. Sighing, Karen knew things would be all right. She clung to him as he wrapped her in a fierce embrace.

"You could have died. You will die if you aren't willing to do what you're told—if you won't learn to respect the land and the danger she hands out."

"Then I'll listen and learn," Karen promised. "Just please don't be angry with me for loving you."

He pulled back, still holding her fast. "I could never be angry at you for loving me, but I swear I'll be tempted to wallop the tar out of you if you ever pull another stupid stunt like that again."

She grinned. "You won't wallop me, Mr. Ivankov."

"Don't bet on it."

She ran her finger over his upper lip, playfully toying with his mustache. "If you wallop me, I won't marry you."

"What makes you think I want to marry you?" he asked, finally offering her a smile. The twinkle returned to his eyes.

"Hmm," she said, gazing sidelong, "maybe you should tell me. Unless, of course, you don't want to marry me. And if that's the case, then I think you should stop caressing my neck and step away."

"You are the most aggravating woman I've ever known," he said, bringing his mouth toward hers. But before he kissed her he added, "I'll have to marry you just to keep you from hurting yourself—or me."

Karen's heart soared on wings of delight as Adrik kissed her most passionately. She was in love, and though the future contained many unanswered questions, she knew the answer to the most important question. Did Adrik really love her? The answer was most assuredly yes! And that made all the other uncertainties in her life seem rather unimportant.

Adrik continued to hold her as he trailed kisses across her cheek to the lobe of her ear. "So will you?" he whispered.

Karen giggled, feeling a dozen years younger. "Will I what?" She wanted to hear him ask her properly.

"Will you marry me?" He straightened and let go of her. Stepping back, he locked his gaze with hers. "Will you?"

Karen nodded enthusiastically and threw herself back into his arms. "Yes! Yes! A million times yes!"

—{ C H A P T E R   T W E N T Y - F O U R }—

JACOB BARRINGER MOANED softly as he rolled to his side. Opening his eyes in the fading light, he watched the trees swirl in circles overhead. Whoever or whatever had hit him on the head had done a real good job. Struggling to keep his eyes open, Jacob thought he heard the muffled barking of dogs. Maybe someone could help him. Maybe there was a chance they'd hear his call for help.

Pushing up on his side, Jacob cried out in pain and collapsed against the bank of the river. An icy cold washed over him, and all at once Jacob realized he was partially submerged in water.

By nothing more than sheer will, Jacob struggled to inch himself out of the water. He would freeze to death if he stayed there, and only God knew how long he'd already been there. He touched his aching head and noted that his hand was sticky with blood. Jacob's stomach gave a lurch at the sight.

The sound of the dogs seemed to fade and grow muffled. Jacob strained again to take in his surroundings. Tall spruce stood guardian around him, and jagged rocks lined the river on the opposite shore.

"Where am I?" he wondered aloud. He couldn't remember a thing. He couldn't imagine why he was here at the edge of this river. What river was it?

He heard the dogs again and called out, "Help me!" His voice sounded weak and unnatural. Straining to sit up against the trunk of a nearby tree, Jacob tried again. "Help!" He closed his eyes and thought to pray, but blackness surrounded him and there was nothing more.

When Jacob opened his eyes again, he was surprised to find himself warm and comfortable and inside a room he didn't recognize. He tried to remember what had happened, but his memory failed him. Then after a moment he remembered traveling on the river with a group of companions. He had worked to earn his keep. *Yes!* He thought for a minute, closing his eyes. *I was headed to Dawson for gold. But what happened?*

"So you're awake."

Jacob looked up to find a grizzled old man staring at him from a doorway. "Where am I?"

"Back room of the Mud Dog Saloon," the man said, then spit on the dirt floor. "Found you on the side of the river."

Jacob nodded with a brief recollection of the icy water. "I don't know how I got there."

"Well, I figure you were either coming through the rapids and got thrown overboard, or someone jumped you and left you for dead. Either way, you weren't in good shape."

Jacob reached his hand up to his forehead and felt the

knot that seemed to throb with every beat of his heart. "I don't remember what happened, but I thank you for your help." He looked to the old man who seemed no bigger than his own five-foot-six-inch frame. Jacob's father might have called the man wiry. He was skinny but muscled in a way that left Jacob little doubt he could fend for himself.

"So what town is this?" Jacob asked.

"Whitehorse."

Jacob remembered the name. He had been headed to Whitehorse—that much he could remember. But why couldn't he remember what had happened?

"I know I was coming this way," he told the man, "but . . . well . . ." He shrugged. "Guess I'll never know."

The old man shook his head. "Don't see as it much matters. It's done happened, and you can't very well take it back."

Jacob nodded. "Did I have anything with me? My pack?"

"Nah, you barely had the clothes on your back."

Jacob eased back against the pillow. "Well, I thank you for what you did, mister. I'm beholden."

The man started to leave, then turned back around. "The name is Cec Blackabee. When you get to feeling better, we can talk about you working to pay me back."

Karen put aside her happiness over Adrik in order to concentrate on Leah and Grace. Neither one looked well. "Adrik says we're stopping in Whitehorse. He wants you both to see the doctor."

"Nonsense," Grace replied. "I'm fine. A decent meal or two and I'll be back on my feet."

Leah gave her a solemn nod. "Me too. I don't want to stop now. We'll never get to Dawson before the snow if we don't keep moving. I have to find Jacob." She fell into a fit of coughing that ended with the teen gasping for breath.

"Yes, I can see that you're just fine," Karen replied. "Nevertheless, I promised Adrik I'd heed his wishes."

"Well, that's a first," Grace said, moving to sit beside Miranda.

Karen thought her pallor rather green as they floated down the river on their way to Whitehorse. "Well, now that I've agreed to marry him, he thinks I owe it to him."

Miranda smiled. "I'm so happy that you've found each other. I sometimes despair of ever finding true love."

Grace patted her hand gently. "You will. Never fear. God has a special man out there for you—somewhere."

"That's right," Leah said softly. "Who knows, maybe he'll own a big old gold mine, too."

"It couldn't hurt," Miranda said with a laugh.

"Maybe he'll be European royalty," Grace said, nudging Miranda good-naturedly. The younger woman blushed but said nothing.

Karen smiled. "Well, either way, we're tying up in Whitehorse, and I'm to see you two to the doctor."

"It'll just cost more money," Grace protested. "We've already spent so much of what we started with. The taxes, extra supplies, the boat, and the tramline—it's all taken far more than we'd ever dreamed."

"I know exactly how much it's cost us," Karen answered, "but we're stopping and that's final."

Whitehorse was already a booming town with businesses and riverboats lining her shores. Ferry service was for hire to take you all the way up to Dawson, if you were of a mind to part with your cash. Tents were staked in every conceivable nook and cranny, and saloons and gambling halls abounded.

Karen was almost disappointed to be set again in such civilization. She'd rather come to enjoy the isolated ruggedness of the life they'd been leading.

"Miranda, if you don't mind staying here with Crispin," Adrik said as he came ashore with the others, "I'll escort these ladies to the doctor. We can all go exploring later, but I'd just as soon have someone keeping an eye on the boat. We don't really know much about this territory, and I wouldn't want to see us lose everything now."

"I'd be glad to stay," Miranda replied with a glance toward Crispin. "I'll have Mr. Thibault entertain me with stories of his youth."

Crispin bowed low. "Always a pleasure, ma'am."

Karen grinned and looked at Adrik. "I don't think either one will be too put out with the arrangement."

Grace turned to Adrik, as well. "I really don't need a doctor, but I do think we should have one look at Leah."

Adrik put his arm around Grace's shoulder. "There's no sense in taking any chances. You haven't been feeling well. You might as well see if there's something wrong."

Grace shook her head and looked from Adrik to Karen. "I know what's wrong, and the doctor can't help me. At least not for several months."

Karen eyed her friend curiously. "What are you saying?"

Grace's face reddened. "I'm going to have a baby."

"What!" Karen exclaimed. "Why didn't you say so sooner? How long have you known?"

Adrik looked positively stricken, but Grace reached out to touch his forearm. "I'm sorry for not telling you, but I knew you'd leave me in Dyea, and I couldn't let that happen."

"You mean to tell me you've known about this since

then?" Adrik questioned. "You climbed the Chilkoot carrying a child?"

Obviously uncomfortable with the personal nature of the conversation, she could only nod. Karen, scarcely able to comprehend this information, stepped forward to embrace her friend. The news left her completely speechless, as it did the others.

Karen looked past Grace to Adrik's accusing expression. Shaking her head, she whispered, "I swear I didn't know."

Grace pulled away. "Look, I know this is a shock, but there's only a couple of weeks left at most and then we'll be to Dawson City."

"But that's just the start of it," Adrik replied. He brushed back his dark hair and looked to the sky.

"I can't believe Peter just ran off and left you there, knowing you were going to have his child."

"He didn't know," Grace replied, tears coming to her eyes. "I barely knew the truth of it myself. I fully intended to tell him, but he never came back."

At this, Miranda rushed forward to take Grace in her arms. "Oh, poor dear. Never worry. We'll make a way. I'll be there to help you through this."

Karen felt a twinge of jealousy at the way Miranda seemed to cut in on her friendship. She had been like a mother to Grace for over ten years. If anyone would see Grace through this, Karen intended for it to be her own duty.

"We will all help you, Grace. But more importantly, we need to find Peter. He must be told about his coming child."

Leah began to cough. She'd said nothing up until that time, but the fitful spell brought all attention to her. Adrik put his hand on Karen's shoulder. "I'd suggest we get Leah to a doctor and discuss this matter with Grace upon our return."

Grace nodded. "Yes, please. Get Leah some medicine and then come back and we'll talk. I'll stay here with Miranda. You'll see, I'll be just fine."

Karen hesitated. She didn't like being dismissed from her friend's side. Nevertheless, as Leah's guardian, she had to see to her responsibilities. Looking to Adrik, she saw the deep concern in his expression.

"Come along, then." She reached out to pull Leah to her side. "We'll be back as soon as we can."

Adrik couldn't believe the turn his life had taken. He would never have seen himself playing escort to a boatload of women. Only Crispin's presence kept him from being completely befuddled. And now . . . now he had to face the responsibility of a pregnant woman being among their group. What more would he endure before the trip was finished?

God, he prayed as he wandered the street outside the doctor's tent, *I don't know what you have planned, but it sure looks like quite a confusing load. I find a woman to marry, even though I never figured to be marrying. I find myself taking on the care of not only a wife, but a young girl—and her brother—if we ever find him.*

He paused and looked back toward the river. *It wasn't what I planned on.* The turmoil settled sourly in his stomach. *And now this. Grace Colton is going to have a baby. What more can be heaped upon us?*

The real fear in his soul, however, had to do with their rapidly depleting finances. He was almost afraid to check the ledgers and see what exactly they had left. They'd all been good to pool their money and supplies, but there was only so much to go around. He'd hate to have to ask Crispin for help—or anyone else, for that matter.

"Oh, there you are!" Karen called as she came from the tent with Leah. "The doctor said her lungs sounded clear, so it isn't pneumonia." The petite girl's blue eyes were as big as saucers against her milk-white face.

"Well, that's good news," he said, forcing a smile for Leah's benefit. "I guess it's sheer orneriness that's making you cough."

Leah smiled, as he'd hoped she would. She leaned toward Adrik, rather embarrassed. "The doctor said I had to drink whiskey."

"What!" Adrik roared without thinking. "What in the world . . ." He saw Karen shaking her head as if to show her disapproval at his reaction. "What is she talking about?" he asked, calming considerably.

"He doesn't have any medicine. At least nothing that isn't laced with opium. I won't have her taking that. It's addictive," Karen answered. "The doctor suggested we give her whiskey instead. Just small amounts to help the cough dissipate."

Adrik calmed. *Of course,* he thought. That made sense. "I'll have to scout out some." He leaned toward Leah and nudged her gently. "You'll be the scandal of us all." She laughed, but this sent her into a fit of coughing once again.

Adrik straightened. "Look, I'll walk you two back to the boat and then go after a bottle."

"We could use some other things, as well."

"Make me a list, then. I'll get whatever I can find."

Adrik left the women safely in Crispin's care before heading back to the main part of town. Crispin and Miranda had already begun to set up camp not far from where the scow was docked. Adrik was glad they'd have a few days to rest and make repairs. The boat was holding up well, but there were places that had been damaged by the journey through Miles Canyon, and this would give him a chance to strengthen and improve their lot before heading back toward the Yukon.

Of course, there was still the matter of dealing with Grace's news, as well as seeing to his own change of matrimonial state. Karen wanted to marry as soon as possible, and it wouldn't surprise him at all if she suggested they wed right there in Whitehorse. Perhaps he should scout out a preacher as well as a bottle.

He tried not to have misgivings. It wasn't for a lack of loving Karen that he felt apprehensive. Facts being what they were, it was probably *because* of his love that he worried about rushing into marriage. After all, he was already facing the responsibility of one pregnant woman. What if he married Karen right away and she found herself in a similar fashion?

Listen to yourself, he chided. *You've lived in this wilderness all your life. You've gone from plenty to poverty and back again. This is a good land with a heap of opportunities. There's no reason to fear raising a family here any more than anywhere else.*

But in his heart, Adrik realized it wasn't his own inabilities, but rather Karen's that worried him. She was city born and raised. Sure, she'd endured an Alaskan winter, but there had always been a harbor and a ship that could take her back to Seattle. There wouldn't be a ship up here. At least not one that could escape the frozen north on a year-round basis. What if she found herself hopelessly unhappy? What if they married and after a time she couldn't bear living in the wilds? Adrik certainly couldn't envision living in a city down south. What would they do then?

There was no time to consider the matter further. The crooked sign of the Mud Dog Saloon caught Adrik's attention. This would be as good a place to start as any. He walked through the open door of the poorly built log cabin and waited a moment for his eyes to adjust to the dark.

"What can I do for you, stranger?"

Adrik looked in the direction of the voice and squinted at the old man. "I came for whiskey. I need a bottle."

"Well, it's not going to come cheap," the man said, reaching down behind the counter. "I only sell the best here." He slammed a small bottle up on the counter.

"It'd better be the best," Adrik said, stalking toward the bar. "I have a sick child who needs it."

The man shrugged. "Don't much matter to me one way or the other. It'll cost you ten dollars for a pint."

Adrik knew the man could probably name any price and get it. Without the promise of regular supplies, they were definitely at the mercy of whoever had the goods this far north. Still, there were other saloons in the town. Maybe he should check them out instead. He glanced at the door.

"Maybe I'll try elsewhere," Adrik said, looking back to see how his words had affected the clerk. Bartering was nothing new to the north, and Adrik was better at it than most. Problem was, he really had no desire to spend the rest of his day looking for a good deal.

The man spit again and scratched his chest. Adrik could see the ragged state of his long underwear beneath his thin flannel shirt. Apparently his profits didn't extend toward replenishing his wardrobe. Figuring the old man wouldn't budge on his price, Adrik started for the door.

The older man muttered under his breath, then said, "Well, seein's how this is for medicinal purposes and all, maybe I could give you my special rate. Eight dollars."

The negotiations were open. Adrik smiled. Perhaps they

could reach a compromise. Reluctantly he pulled out the money and put it on the bar.

"Six," Adrik said firmly. "I still have food to buy."

The old man looked at the money, then back to Adrik. "Well . . . I suppose . . ." He reached for the money and quickly shoved it in his pocket.

Adrik took the bottle and pocketed it in turn. He'd just tipped his hat when he heard a familiar voice ask, "Where you want these, Cec?"

Adrik turned on his heel, unable to believe his eyes. "Jacob?"

The boy's eyes positively lit up. He put the tray of glasses on the counter and ran to Adrik. "I can't believe it's you!"

The two men embraced and pounded each other's backs as though they'd been parted for years instead of months.

"You're as thin as a rail," Adrik said as Jacob stepped back.

"Oh, it's been bad. Had the typhoid in Bennett. Then I finally got started for Dawson again and met with a bad end. Cec here found me half dead."

"More like three-quarters dead," the old man said, spitting to one side.

"What happened?" Adrik asked.

"Well, as best as Cec can figure out, the men I was traveling with did me in. They took my gear and left me for dead. Either that or I fell out of the boat when we came through the rapids, but if that were the case, I would've had my watch and money in my pocket. It was all gone when Cec found me."

Adrik eyed the codger suspiciously. "I can well imagine."

"Weren't my doin', mister, so stop lookin' at me like I sunk the *Maine*."

Adrik nodded. "Well, I'm grateful you found him. His guardian is going to be mighty glad to know he's safe." He turned back to Jacob. "Get your gear—or whatever you have coming to you. We're docked on the north side."

"Whoa, now," Cec called out. "You can't just up and take the boy. He owes me."

Adrik forced his temper to remain under control. He nudged Jacob in the direction he'd just come. "Get your things." Jacob nodded and disappeared while Adrik walked back to the counter where Cec stood. "Just how much do you figure the boy owes you?"

"Well, I did save his life. And I've been feedin' him all this time. Oh, and I gave him a change of clothes."

"How much?"

He could see the old man nervously trying to figure out how much he could wheedle out of Adrik. Finally, Adrik had more than he was going to take. He reached into his pocket and pulled out several bills. "Here. I don't imagine it was more than this, and if it was, we can take it up with the law."

The old man shook his head and snatched the money. "No, this'll be just fine."

"I thought it might."

Jacob came back carrying a rolled-up knot of clothes. "I'm ready. Who'd you travel with, Adrik?"

Adrik waited until they were outside and headed back to the boat before answering. "You're going to find this hard to believe, son—after all, I find it hard to believe myself. I've come here with Karen and your sister, as well as Grace Colton and her sister-in-law. Oh, and my friend Crispin Thibault joined us along the way."

"Leah's here?" Jacob asked as if he'd not heard anything else. He stopped and turned in disbelief. Dark half-moons under his eyes were more apparent in the sunlight.

The wind picked at the boy's sandy brown hair, pushing it

around just enough to reveal a rather nasty cut at the hairline. Adrik reached out and pushed Jacob's hair back. "Yes, Leah's here, and I think that old man was right. You probably were three-quarters dead with a gash this size."

Jacob pulled away and kept walking. "Don't worry about me none, Adrik. I had a headache for a few days and I bled like all get-out, but I feel fine now. Is Leah all right?"

"She's a bit under the weather, but not too bad off. I came to the saloon for some whiskey. Doc figured it would do her good, help with her cough."

"But she's going to be all right?"

Adrik could read the worry in the boy's eyes. "Why don't you ask her yourself? We're setting up camp just over there. But, Jacob, there's just one thing."

The boy looked to him and stopped in his tracks. "What?"

"I think it might be best if we leave out the part about you being three-quarters dead when we tell Karen about this. She's been worried enough about losing you, and it was all I could do to keep her from coming for you the day after you disappeared. She's here because of you, and it wouldn't do her any good to add more guilt to how she's feeling."

"She's up here because of me?" Jacob asked in disbelief.

Adrik could see it impressed the younger man. So many folks he'd cared about had left him behind, he was probably amazed to learn that someone would actually chase him down. "Yes, she's here because of you. Leah too. There didn't seem to be any reason to stay in Dyea when they were worried over how you were doing."

Jacob bit his lip and looked away. "I won't say a word about the accident."

"Believe me, things will go better for both of us if you

don't." Adrik put his arm around the boy and laughed. "You know how Karen can be."

Jacob looked up, wiping a tear from his eye. "She's a real lady, Miss Karen. She's got a good heart."

"That she does, but I feel I should tell you," Adrik said, laughing, "we're going to get married. So don't be getting any ideas about her."

"Married! That's great!"

They were nearly back to the camp by now, and Adrik could see the women helping Crispin set up the second tent. Leah was nowhere in sight, and Adrik figured she was snuggly tucked inside the erected tent.

Karen was busy helping to secure the tent pegs. She worked silently with a small wooden mallet as Crispin adjusted the guy lines. Adrik marveled at her efficiency. She never complained, yet Adrik knew many a time she was spent of strength and hope. Now that she'd managed to regain her faith, Adrik saw her anger fading with each passing day. And as the bitterness left her, a new, stronger woman seemed to emerge. How could he not marry her? He couldn't imagine life without her. He'd become so attached to her these past few months that to let her get away was simply unthinkable.

"Karen," Adrik called. "I have what you've been looking for!"

Karen looked up, and for a moment her face registered nothing but a blank, rather stunned expression. Then realizing the identity of Adrik's traveling companion, she squealed with delight and came running across the short distance.

"Oh, Jacob!" She wrapped herself around the boy, who was nearly as tall as she was. "Oh, you're here. You're safe."

Adrik exchanged a smile with Jacob over Karen's shoulder. "I thought you might want me to bring him back rather than the other things you sent me for. Oh, but I did bring the whiskey."

"Oh, I'm so happy to see you!" Karen exclaimed. She stepped back and held him at arm's length. "Oh, you're so skinny. You must be starving."

"I'm doing all right, Miss Karen. How's Leah?" Jacob asked softly.

"Go see for yourself. She's in the big tent," Karen replied. "Oh, she'll be so happy to see you. This will do wonders for her—much better than any medicine or whiskey."

Jacob took off running, forgetting all about the pack of clothes he'd dropped on the ground.

"Come on," Karen said. She picked up the clothes, then pulled Adrik along. "I want to be there."

Adrik wrapped his arm around Karen's waist and together they walked past Grace, Miranda, and Crispin. Pausing at the open flap, Adrik could see Jacob kneeling beside his sister. He held Leah in his arms as she cried.

Adrik reached for Karen's hand. "Let's give them some time alone."

Karen seemed reluctant but finally picked up her steps. When they were back near the boat, she threw her arms around Adrik and hugged him tightly. "You are the most incredible man in the world," she declared. "I simply love you more and more every day."

Adrik held her tight. "There wasn't much to this one, Miss Pierce. The boy just sort of came to me. I think God had more to do with this one than I did."

Karen pulled back and frowned. "Well, if He sends Mr. Colton your way, let me know. We've got one problem solved, but there's that new one to deal with. Grace's baby is due shortly after the New Year, as best we can tell."

Remembering their situation, Adrik felt the weight of his responsibilities falling heavily on his shoulders. "We ought to find a way to get her back to Dyea or Skagway. She could take a boat out and at least return to San Francisco."

"By your own admission, it's too late to turn back. She'd not make it before the snows got heavy and the rivers froze over."

"I know. It was more wishful thinking than anything."

"We'll just figure this out as we go," Karen said softly. "You keep reminding me that God has a plan."

"Yeah, but He doesn't seem exactly eager to share it with me."

─┤CHAPTER TWENTY-FIVE├─

MARTIN PAXTON CRINGED at the sight of the four walls. His office and living quarters were the best money could buy in Skagway, but the walls were closing in on him. The weather had turned foul, and for three days it had rained and snowed off and on. There was little to entertain himself with, and now that he knew for sure Grace Colton had gone north to Dawson City, he was up against a major decision. Should he send someone to fetch her back? Should he go after her himself?

He thumbed through the latest packet of mail and shook his head. The game with Grace was growing rather dull. Still, he had his reasons. Money. At the bottom of everything that motivated Martin Paxton, money—and large sums of it—was generally the object that caught his attention. Grace Colton had the potential to be worth a fortune to him.

Of course, she didn't know that. No one did, short of her

father's lawyer in Chicago, and that man had been paid a tidy sum to keep his mouth shut. No, Paxton was the only one who knew Grace stood to inherit a good sum of money upon the day she legally wed. Not even Mrs. Hawkins knew of the arrangement.

Martin himself had only learned the truth of this after Frederick had passed away. And nothing had ever angered him quite so much. It seemed that while Martin was systematically relieving Frederick Hawkins of his fortune, the man had connived to transfer vast sums of money to his daughter. The trust was untouchable—irrevocable. Martin could only suppose that Hawkins had figured Grace to be rid of the marriage agreement between herself and Paxton when she'd fled to the north. He probably assumed he could give his daughter the money, and once Paxton was out of their lives, Hawkins could reclaim his fortune. But he died instead. He died without telling his beloved wife yet another very important fact of his life. The thought of duping the dead man kept Martin going—pressing him to search Grace out. That and his desire to get even with the brat for making him the laughingstock of Chicago.

Even now he could remember the way people had talked about him in the finer dining establishments. More than once he'd taken a table for dinner, only to watch as those around him caught sight of him and began to whisper among themselves. He heard their snickers and knew he was the object of their scorn. Just as he had been as a boy. But no more.

Still, there he stood at a crossroads. He had the ordeal of Colton Shipping to settle, as well as other enterprises that needed his attention. Several of his investments were doing quite poorly, and without his immediate attention, they were sure to go bust. He could chase after Grace or attend to his affairs, but he couldn't do both. Not with any real assurance of success.

Getting up from his desk, Paxton walked to the window and looked down on Broadway Street. Tracks for the train had been routed through the heart of town only months earlier. And thanks to his investment along with others, the Pacific and Arctic Railway and Navigation Company would soon be the only reasonable way to make passage north.

The country had made him a very wealthy man. It should have been enough. It should have been satisfactory knowing that he had ruined the man who had destroyed his mother—that he had left that man's family destitute and miserable. He could probably go on paying Hawkins' lawyer, and Grace would never know of her good fortune. Martin would continue his revenge without Hawkins' widow and daughter ever even knowing it. But the revenge was hollow. Martin knew his mother would have been disappointed, even ashamed of the way he'd conducted himself. She would never have understood—but Hawkins did, and that was what counted. Hawkins had used his mother as a mistress, and just when she needed him most, he had discarded her, never to return again.

Martin could still see his mother day after day looking out the door or window. Watching and waiting for Hawkins' return. After a year had passed, she had begun to fade. The life went out of her in the absence of his love.

Convinced the man had met with great distress or even death, Martin had gone in search of him. It hadn't been difficult to find Hawkins. Everyone in Chicago seemed to know the man—and his family. He could still remember learning the horrible truth. He remembered seeing the grand family all together in their polished surrey. They were traveling to church, as he recalled. All prim and proper—a family.

Hawkins hadn't met with death or illness; he had simply dismissed the Paxtons without so much as a good-bye. Martin's anger started to grow on that day, roaring to life like an unquenchable inferno. Turning from the window, Martin knew the fire had somewhat abated now. There came a time when a plan merited reconsideration. He figured that time had come in the situation with Grace Colton.

He regretted having hurt Ephraim Colton. Martin wasn't, after all, completely without feeling. Still, the man had to understand that what his son had done—what he himself had condoned—did not come without a price. Perhaps the best thing to do was to let things rest for the time and see where Ephraim Colton would take them. Better still, perhaps to avoid the onset of winter, Martin would make his way to San Francisco and offer magnanimously to affect a solution or agreement.

He smiled to himself. He had earned his weight in gold and then some. He could afford to be generous with his mother's only friend. And in doing so, maybe he could even drive the wedge a bit deeper between Colton and his wayward son. If Ephraim agreed to never allow Peter to return to the business, if he cut him completely from his life, then perhaps Martin could see his way clear to returning *Summer Song*. It bore some consideration.

———

Peter Colton considered Jonas's words on the journey to Skagway. He had thought to force Martin Paxton to deal with him, but Jonas's steady logic kept Peter in check.

"A grizzly bear doesn't much care how you go about reasonin' with him," Jonas had said. *"He only wants one thing, and that's to kill you."*

Paxton would seemingly love nothing more than if Peter would fall over dead. But truth be told, Peter desired the same for Martin Paxton. Funny how all of his worries and problems might simply disappear with the death of one man.

It could be self-defense, Peter reasoned. Then Jonas's words of warning would come back to haunt him.

"If you go gettin' yourself in trouble with the law, you'll never see that pretty wife of yours again."

No doubt the man was right. So instead of exacting revenge, Peter would simply mail the letter he'd labored over so diligently. He had written to his parents and Miranda and begged their forgiveness. He wanted—needed—them to understand that he'd never intended to let things get so carried away. He'd hurt them. He knew that much. He could only pray they might forgive him.

Forgiveness. It was a hard word for Peter. Grace had talked about it so often that the word left a bitter taste in his mouth. But that had been before. Before his father's heart attack and Grace's disappearance. And it had been before Peter had opened his mind and heart to hear what a godly man like Jonas had to say.

Peter posted the letter, hoping it might reach his folks with great speed. He needed to hear from them—to know that all was forgiven and that they were all right. Leaving the letter behind, Peter took himself to the Second Hand Store down the street. Something had been on his mind since Jonas had first started talking to him about letting go of the past.

"Do you have any wedding rings?" he asked the clerk behind the counter.

"We've got a couple," the man said with a grin. "Find yourself a little gal to marry, did you?"

"I'm already married," Peter replied. "Just never got around to finding the ring."

The man chuckled. "Well, here's what I've got." He plopped down two rings. "Don't know what you had in mind, but I got these rings off a wealthy woman who was bartering for gear."

Peter hadn't thought of the rings belonging to someone else. He really wanted Grace to have her own brand-new ring. "Don't you have something . . . well . . . something not used?"

The man frowned. "This is a used goods store."

Peter nodded. "Do you suppose anyone else in town has rings?"

The man shrugged. "I wouldn't doubt it. There are some jewelers working down on Fourth Street. Making all sorts of doodads and such out of gold nuggets. You might get them fellows to make you a ring."

Peter thought it just might be exactly what he needed. Thanking the man, he made his way to the jeweler and posed his question.

"I just need a simple wedding band," Peter told the man.

"Do you know the lady's ring size?"

Peter's heart sank. "No."

"She a big gal or little?"

"Oh, she's small. Very small. Why, her hand is quite tiny in mine." Peter held up his hand to demonstrate.

The jeweler slipped into the back and returned with a plain gold band. The small circle seemed to gleam with a life of its own. "That's perfect," Peter declared, hoping it would be the right size.

"It should fit, if she's as small as you say. That'll be a dollar and thirty cents."

Peter put the money on the counter and pocketed the ring. "Thanks."

He drew the ring out once he was headed back to camp. Holding it up to see it in the sun, Peter thought of Grace and how he should have given her a wedding band a long time ago. Why had he put it off? Maybe his actions had caused her to think he was less than serious about their marriage, but that was far from the truth.

Peter loved his wife. He loved her more than life, and it hurt to think she no longer cared for him. After all, if she loved him, why hadn't she waited for him? Or at least left him a note to let him know where she'd be?

He wondered if Grace was really with Paxton. It didn't make sense for her to seek his help, but she *had* accompanied Peter's father to see him. *Perhaps the real problem is that I don't know her very well*, he thought. She had the loveliest brown eyes in the country, and her voice was soft and gentle—warming his heart just with the memory. But those were outward qualities. Peter needed to know her heart.

Rubbing his finger over the ring, Peter's soul cried out within him. *Oh, please let me find her.*

Jonas had supper on the stove when Peter got back to their tent. They had thrown their lots together, and with the snow collecting in the passes, the railroad's progress was slowing down. There were rumors that the men would all be laid off and that progress wouldn't resume until spring. Peter had no idea of what he might do in the meantime.

"So'd you get that letter posted?" Jonas asked, wiping his hands against his pants.

"I did. I also did something else I should have done a long time ago."

"What's that?" the man eyed him as if trying to guess his answer.

"I bought Grace a wedding ring. Now if I can just find her."

"The good Lord is in the business of finding the lost. You might want to ask Him," Jonas stated. Then, without waiting for further comment, he turned back to the stove. "I've got beans and corn bread if you're of a mind to eat with me."

"I'm starved," Peter replied, taking off his coat. He slipped the ring from his coat pocket to his pants pocket and grabbed a tin plate. Peter dished up beans and threw a big hunk of corn bread into the tin as well. "You suppose they'll close down the line?"

Jonas joined him at the table with his own plate of food. "They just might. It wouldn't be that strange to have them wait until warmer weather."

Peter feared Jonas was probably right. He stared at his plate for a moment, then looked at Jonas. "Are you going to pray?"

The older man grinned. "I thought maybe it was about time you did."

"You may be right at that," Peter answered, his tone quite serious. "But I think I'll require a teacher to show me how."

"Don't know as I've ever taught anything of such value before," Jonas said. "But I'm game to try."

—| CHAPTER TWENTY-SIX |—

A CROWD OF WELL-WISHERS gathered along the banks of the Yukon River in Whitehorse the next morning. Anxious for any excuse to break the routine, those who had settled permanently in the town seemed game for a party. Hearing about Adrik and Karen's impromptu wedding gave them the perfect reason to celebrate. Even those who were making their way north to the goldfields paused long enough to make certain the gathering wasn't the call to another, closer, gold strike.

The day was cold, much colder than it had been, and the threat of snow was in the air. The crowd was tense in anticipation of the winter freeze to come. Most of the sourdoughs understood the severe contrasts of this land and took the changing weather seriously. The cheechakos, however, were less concerned. They had braved the cold in their hometowns. They knew what it was to shovel a bit of snow or hunker down through a blowing blizzard. The sourdoughs laughed as they listened to the newcomers' comments; even Karen had to chuckle at their preconceived notions.

But at this moment Karen's mind was far from the comments of her neighbors. She stood in a tight-knit group of three: herself, Adrik, and a preacher who seemed happy to marry someone instead of bury them.

Nervous at the very idea of what she was undertaking, Karen twisted a handkerchief in her hands during the entire ceremony. She loved Adrik. She knew that without any doubt, but there was that nagging feeling that perhaps they should have waited. They really didn't know each other all that well, and Karen was still trying hard to figure out what her future might hold. Of course, perhaps Adrik *was* her future. It was possible that God wanted nothing more of her than to keep company with this good man and be a friend—even a teacher—to the people he loved so much. The people her parents had loved, as well.

It wasn't until the preacher asked if Adrik had a ring that Karen stopped trying to second-guess her tomorrows. And then, it was only because Adrik took hold of her hand.

"With this ring, I thee wed," Adrik said in a low but firm voice.

Karen gazed up into his dark eyes and felt her breath catch in her throat. He was clean-shaven, with exception to his mustache, which had been neatly trimmed. The ragged edges of his brown-black hair had been cut to an orderly fashion that Karen longed to reach up and touch. His rugged outdoor looks appealed to her in a way that the Martin Paxtons and Crispin Thibaults of the world never would. He was a man of action. A man who knew what he wanted and knew how to go about getting it. She supposed it had been that way with his desire to marry her. He simply had decided on her heart and refused to stop until it belonged, in whole, to him.

He lifted her hand to his lips and kissed her finger where the gleaming gold band rested. "For now and all time, Mrs. Ivankov."

Karen swallowed hard and looked at the ring. The symbol of their never-ending love—the symbol of forever.

"You may now kiss your bride," the preacher said with great gusto and enthusiasm. The crowd cheered as Karen lifted her face to Adrik's gaze.

Tenderly, Adrik wrapped her in his embrace. Karen felt the warmth of his body against her own. She was married! She, who had thought herself to be a spinster, now kissed her husband.

Adrik seemed in no hurry to end the kiss. He pulled her tighter, closer, and Karen longed for the moment to go on and on. She didn't even mind that she was the focus of so much attention. Her joy overcame any concern of what others might think.

When they finally did pull away, ruddy in the face and well aware of their crowd of well-wishers, Karen managed to catch Grace's expression. She seemed sad, almost tearful. Karen wondered if she were contemplating her own rushed wedding. Grace had married in the fear and horror of Martin Paxton's threat. Did she regret it?

Someone began playing a fiddle, and it wasn't but a moment before half a dozen other instruments joined in. Impromptu dancing broke out even while one by one people came forward—most complete strangers—to wish Karen and Adrik well on their day. Many came with a gift, usually giving the couple a few bits or as much as a dollar to start them on their way. Karen thought their generosity very touching. Some of these people were struggling and suffering to make it north before winter. Others were fighting to prepare for a winter of isolation. Reckless charity was not a luxury these people could afford.

When Karen finally had a chance to slip away and find Grace, her young friend had already retired to their tent. She could see that Grace had been crying, and for once she was rather at a loss for words. Not so Grace.

"I married Peter for all the wrong reasons," Grace said softly. "I thought I needed to help God. I didn't realize what I was doing."

Karen overturned a packing crate and sat down on it. "You did what seemed best. What we all thought best."

"But it wasn't right. There were too many crucial differences between us, and I knew that. I knew Peter hated talk of the Bible and of my faith. I knew it was a source of contention between us." She looked up, her brown eyes red-rimmed from her tears. "I dishonored God by marrying a man who had no respect for Him. Now I'm bearing the punishment of that."

"No, Grace," Karen said, reaching out to take hold of her hand. "Maybe you are enduring the consequences, but I don't believe God is punishing you. We are only human. We are fearful and weak. We make choices that aren't always God directed, but we do what we can—what we must.

"God is a loving, merciful God. I know that, even though I wanted to forget it or, better still, deny it. When Aunt Doris died, after I'd already lost Father and Mother, I felt so deserted. You were gone and I was very much alone. You had been my sole companion for over ten years. You were like a daughter and sister and friend all wrapped up in one person. But when you went away, I found an emptiness bigger than any I had ever known—even with my parents."

Grace clung to her hand. "I missed you terribly after I'd gone. I loved Peter most dearly, but he was often too busy for me. Then there was the matter of our differences." She sighed. "Oh, Karen, every time the issue of God and His love for us and our need for Him came up, Peter simply could not bear my company. I became most undesirable to my own husband."

"Apparently you weren't too undesirable," Karen said, trying hard to make Grace's mood lighter. "You are carrying his child."

"Don't remind me," Grace replied. She looked away as if ashamed. "I know that only God says when a soul lives or dies, but I don't understand why He would give this union a child. How very disappointed He must be in me."

"Nonsense," Karen answered. "Where is that strength of character I saw when you faced Martin Paxton in Dyea? I could hardly believe it. The Spirit of the Lord simply seemed to overcome you and fill that entire room. I felt almost as if I were standing on holy ground."

"I try to not battle this on my own," Grace said. "I know from everything you've taught me and from all that God has shown me in Scripture that He has a plan in all of this. That He has never turned away from me or left me to fight this alone. I know that He will give me the strength to endure whatever I must, but . . . ."

"But what?" Karen asked, confused by Grace's words.

Grace looked up, her eyes flooding with tears once again. "I love my husband. I love Peter more than life, and if he has no desire to be my mate, then I might as well die. This child, too."

A shudder coursed through Karen. She had never heard her friend talk in such a way. It frightened her terribly. "Don't say that," she admonished. "I would be overwhelmed with grief if you were to die."

"I'm sorry I've ruined your wedding day," Grace murmured before breaking into sobs. She buried her face in her hands and cried softly.

Karen drew Grace into her arms. "You haven't ruined anything."

Holding Grace while she cried, Karen began to pray unselfishly for God to intercede. *I know I've been far too compelled to worry about myself and my feelings*, she told God. *I know that I've been a difficult and disobedient daughter, but, Father, this child needs your touch. She needs to feel that you have not forsaken her because of her decision to marry. Please, Father, please show her that you are with her.*

Grace rested her head against Karen's shoulder for a moment, her tears abating. "I feel so foolish."

"Why?"

She lifted her head and squared her shoulders. "I feel foolish because I know better than to give in to these feelings. You taught me that God is with me through the bad and the good. I know He is faithful."

"It doesn't mean that we won't have our moments of weakness. As I said before, we're only human. Look at how I acted. I knew it was wrong to blame God for the bad in my life. I knew it was wrong to bear Him, who loved me so much, a grudge." Karen felt her chest tighten. She hadn't really thought of her relationship with God as the same as that of her earthly father. Had she acted that way with her earthly father, it would have surely broken his heart and left him in utter despair. Was that how it was for God? Did He weep when His children called Him unjust?

"Look," Karen continued, "we'll pen a letter to Peter. We'll send it on the first available post. There won't be time for him to get north before the winter freeze, so that much can't be helped. I'll see you through this, however. Adrik and I will make a home for you as long as you need. When the baby comes, we'll help you through that, as well. Then in the spring, we'll get you home to Peter."

Grace shook her head. "But what if he doesn't want me home? And maybe worse yet, what if he does, but his heart is still bitter toward God? Maybe it's best that we remain separated."

Karen considered that thought for a moment. "Perhaps you married for the wrong reasons, Grace, but I believe God will use you and your marriage to reach Peter. I believe He already has. Let's not worry about the future. We have plenty to concern ourselves with in the here and now." She smiled and gently touched Grace's face. "You're going to be a mother. That is a precious and most wonderful thing. And it's a gift from God."

Those words suddenly shot arrows of hope through Karen's heart. Yes, a baby was a gift from God. The psalmist said as much. "Oh, Grace, I know God is with you."

Karen got up and went to where she had put her father's Bible. Turning to Psalm 127, she found the verse she was looking for. "Here, see for yourself." She handed the Bible to Grace. "Read verse three."

Grace did so. " 'Lo, children are an heritage of the Lord: and the fruit of the womb is his reward.' "

"God hasn't deserted you, Grace. He's rewarded you for your faithful love and desire to know Him better."

"But what of you?" Grace replied, looking up from the Bible. "You are a wonderful woman, and in spite of your difficult times, you have been faithful. Why did God not bless you years ago with a husband and children of your own? What of the barren woman? Does God not love her equally as much if she is seeking His heart, as well?"

"Of course God loves her, as well. Of course He loves me. It doesn't say that children are the only reward God gives. God is a god of infinite ability. His rewards are many, as are His mercies. Do not limit the Almighty God of the universe," Karen said, almost laughing. Her own heart was lighter than it had been since Doris had gone home to God. *I have limited you, Father. How like you to use my own student to reteach me a valuable lesson.*

"I know you're right," Grace replied. She reached up and dried her cheeks and eyes. "But, Karen, if Peter doesn't love God—if he still rejects the idea of accepting God into his life—I don't know what I will do. I cannot stand by and let him subject both the child and me to further tirades. I will raise this baby to love God first and foremost."

"Then we have only one choice," Karen replied with great confidence. "We must pray and ask God to bring Peter into His number." Karen got up and smoothed her blue wool skirt. "Adrik says we're to break camp and leave within the hour. I don't think they'll have much luck of it with us in here. What say I help you pack?"

"But this is your wedding day," Grace protested, getting to her feet. "You shouldn't have to work or travel. You should have a wonderful night alone with your husband."

Karen laughed. "And where would we have that? Out under the trees? We have two tents, one for the men and one for the women. There are now four women and three men since Jacob has come along."

"Then I think we should get another tent," Grace announced rather matter-of-factly.

"Well, they don't grow on trees around here. And even if they did, someone probably would have already cut down the tree to make a home or fuel a steamer."

Grace smiled and nodded. "Maybe I should ask around and see if there is anything to be done about it."

"Oh, don't bother. There's precious little time as it is. If we're not ready to go when Adrik gives the call, it won't matter that we've just wed. He'll leave me here just to teach me a lesson about heeding his directions."

Grace grew very serious. "He's a good man, Karen. I'm so pleased that God put you two together. And I know He'll give you children and great happiness."

"I know He will, too."

"I'm so glad you agreed to walk with me," Crispin told Miranda as they left the crowd and headed toward a nearby stand of spruce.

Miranda experienced both a sensation of danger and excitement as Crispin paused and looked with great longing into her eyes.

"You know that I've completely lost my heart to you, Miss Colton," Crispin said with great flair. "You are the most incredible woman."

Miranda, unfamiliar with flirtatious encounters, looked away quickly. "You shouldn't say such things. It isn't proper."

"And why not? It's true. This country throws off convention with great abandonment. Surely you won't allow yourself to be steeped in prim and proper Victorian rhetoric when my heart is overflowing with the need to tell you how I feel."

Miranda couldn't help but smile at his words. She looked up to find his dark eyes searching her own. He looked for all the world as if he might very well perish if she refused to give him the answer he desired.

"I am cautious," she replied. "Cautious because it bodes well to be so. Not because of any presupposed rules of society. Healthy fear keeps one from peril."

He grinned at her rather roguishly. "Do you fear me, Miranda?"

"I'm not certain that fear is the proper word," she answered, a charge of electricity stealing up her spine. He knew what she was feeling, of this Miranda was certain. Furthermore, he very much seemed to be enjoying her vulnerability.

When he stepped toward her, Miranda steadied her shaking knees and tried to appear as if clandestine moments in quiet woods were nothing out of the ordinary.

When he reached out and took her face in his hands, Miranda thought she might very well stop breathing. Forcing herself to maintain eye contact, she was unprepared for the kiss he pressed upon her lips. She realized all at once she was staring at his closed eyes, but soon she realized nothing at all. Nothing save the warm, delightful feel of his hands caressing her face and his mouth on hers.

"Say you love me," he whispered hoarsely. He pulled away only far enough to allow her a full view of his beautiful face.

"I scarcely know you," Miranda said, her breath ragged. Her pulse raced so wildly she thought she might actually faint.

"Then get to know me," he murmured and began planting gentle kisses upon her cheeks and forehead. "For I am in love with you, Miranda Colton. I have loved you from the first moment I laid eyes on you."

Miranda forced herself to back up, leaving the warmth of his touch. "Crispin, I'm not a fast woman. I do not play loose with any man. Perhaps I've given you the wrong idea by walking here with you today. Worse yet, by letting you kiss me."

He looked hurt, almost as if she'd slapped him. "So you are rejecting my love?"

Very slowly, Miranda shook her head. "Not at all. Merely suggesting we take it slowly. I would enjoy knowing you better, understanding your aspirations for the future. I would like to hear about your family and know what things you value most in life. I would like to know who you are. Most of the time on the trail you were busy packing goods or building the boat. I feel I know very little about you."

His expression softened, and she could see his delightful nature return. "I will spare no detail. I will keep nothing from your scrutiny. Ask me anything. Demand the moon—only promise me that you might one day love me."

Miranda smiled. "I will make no promises, but neither will I demand the moon. Let us keep company and see where our hearts lead us from there."

Adrik loaded the last of their supplies onto the scow while Jacob finished securing the tent on board. Adrik had built in special rings on the deck to which they could stretch out the base of the dwelling. This, along with the canvas ties he'd had the women sew to the tent, allowed for the structure to ride rather securely.

He worked up a sweat restacking their supplies. Jacob was a good extra hand to have on board, in spite of his thin, almost frail, appearance. Adrik knew Karen would have him fattened up in no time—at least if their food held out, she would. He had already decided they would need to start some serious fishing and hunting as they made their way to Dawson. Fish would certainly be plentiful, and Adrik was quite capable of putting together a smoker to preserve the fish for some time to come. The forests away from the rush of the gold stampede were no doubt full of wildlife. Stopping long enough to spend a day hunting might pay off in the long run. They could easily butcher the meat and use the river's steadily dropping temperature to keep it cold.

What he tried not to think about was how much he wanted to be alone with Karen. He ached to hold her—to share their wedding day isolated from the rest of the world. But it wasn't to be. They couldn't even have a decent wedding night alone together.

"We're all ready here," Jacob announced, coming up behind Adrik. "Shall I bring everyone aboard?"

Adrik glanced around to make certain everything was in its place. "Yeah, looks like we'd better get a move on. I figure we'll have at least ten good hours of light. I'd like to make it to the other side of Lake Laberge, but I'm not holding my breath. That's at least sixty miles. We'd have to have perfect winds and no obstacles to cross that distance."

Jacob looked upward. "It looks like a fair sky."

Adrik followed his gaze. "Let's just hope it stays that way."

—|·C H A P T E R TWENTY-SEVEN |—

"THERE'S A LETTER for you," Jonas said, coming into the small cabin. He plopped down a cloth bundle, then reached back to close the door.

Peter had been working to build up a fire in the stove, but this news left him far too excited to worry about the growing cold. "Is it from Grace?" He picked up the bundle and began to explore the contents.

"Can't say." Jonas pulled off his fur cap and hung it on a peg. "I will tell you this much." His voice came to an abrupt halt.

Peter paused and looked up at the older man. "What?"

Jonas shrugged out of his coat and tossed it over the cap. Turning, he eyed Peter quite seriously. "There's talk that Martin Paxton is leaving town."

"Who told you this?"

"When I was over to the railway office, I heard that he was planning to head south before winter got too hard. Ain't recollectin' who exactly told it, but he sounded like a knowledgeable fellow."

"If he's leaving, perhaps Grace is leaving with him," Peter said, leaning back in complete dejection. "Maybe I should just hide out and follow him around."

"Why don't you give a look-see and read that letter first? Maybe it's from Grace," Jonas suggested.

But the letter wasn't from Grace. It was nearly as good, however. Peter's mother had penned a lengthy note full of information and good news. Peter's father was on the mend, and Amelia Colton predicted it would only be a few days before he was out of bed. Even from his bed, Ephraim Colton had hired a good family friend to see to the legal matters of Paxton's illegal action. Amelia again optimistically predicted that God would intercede on their behalf and let justice be done.

Peter didn't resent his mother's comment about God. In fact, over the passing weeks with Jonas, he'd taken on a whole new attitude toward such matters. After all, he had sunk down as far as he cared to go. Oh, he knew others had sunk further—sometimes giving themselves over to drinking and even crime. But for Peter, this lack of self-confidence and feeling that nothing was within his control was close to the lowest rung on his ladder. The last rung he reserved for the effects of Grace's absence.

"So who's it from?" Jonas questioned. He stood over the stove with the ingredients for their supper of oatmeal.

"It's from my mother. She says my father is much improved." Peter read on before speaking again. "She talks of being anxious to hear from Grace and Miranda." He looked up. "That must mean they are together. But Paxton said he knew nothing of my sister."

Jonas shrugged. "Don't 'spect you can trust that critter to tell the truth."

Peter nodded. Perhaps he had given Paxton's words too much credence. "She goes on to say that she prays I will restore my marriage. She wants me to stop being willful and prideful and seek Grace out for forgiveness. Then her heart's desire is that I would bring Grace home and settle down in San Francisco with them—to build a new future."

"Sounds like a good idea."

Peter put the letter down. "It sounds like a wonderful idea, but Grace is nowhere to be found. Even if she were, she'd have nothing to do with me. I hurt her more deeply than even Paxton did."

"Son, you keep comin' up with excuses as to why you can't fix this problem. Truth is, you can't fix it no matter the excuse or the solution. Some things are only resolved through prayer and the good Lord's divine meddling." Jonas grinned.

"But I don't know what to do," Peter admitted. He looked at the letter, then folded it up. "I don't know how to find her, when I can't even find the right road for myself. I'm lost."

Jonas stirred the pot of boiling oats and nodded. "At least you can see that much. Some folks take forever to see that. They just sort of wander in circles most all their life."

Peter knew he had nothing left to lose. The most important elements of his life were gone: his family, his business . . . Grace. He'd let pride and arrogance dictate his path, and both had served him poorly.

"What do I have to do, Jonas?"

The older man pulled the oats from the stove and plopped the pan down on the table in front of Peter. "You have to repent of doing things your way instead of God's way."

Peter met his friend's serious gaze. "Is that all?"

"Nope. You have to be willin' to accept that you're lost without Jesus. You have to accept that He died to save you."

"Save me from what?" Peter questioned.

Jonas laughed. "From sin. From the devil. From yourself."

Peter wanted to believe it was true. After all, he needed saving. If he let things go along as they had been, he might very well lose hope and give up. Then he'd never see Grace again—or his family.

"I'm as lost as a man can be," Peter finally said. His voice was low, almost a whisper. "I can believe that Jesus died, although that He would die for me is a hard stretch."

"More important, Peter, He lives for you. Jesus rose from the grave, and that's the part that makes His gift special. Ain't no simple matter of going to the death. Folks have done that for folks as far back as there have been friends. What makes Jesus' love for us different is that He not only died in our place, He rose again to show us that with Him we don't need to fear death. Death ain't the end of things."

Peter struggled against his old way of thought. To believe in the need for a savior—to believe and accept Jesus for himself—went against all the things he'd steeped his life in. He had built his world on a foundation that suggested he, Peter Colton, could accomplish anything. And now that foundation was crumbling around him.

"I want to believe, Jonas. I really do," Peter said, tears coming to his eyes. "Do you suppose God knows how hard this is for me?"

Jonas put his hand on Peter's shoulder. "He knows, son. He knows your heart, and He'll give you the strength to see this through. If your heart is willing, then all you need to do is pray and ask Him to forgive and save you."

Peter drew a deep breath and wiped his tears with the back of his hand. "I'll do it. I can't bear the mess I've made of things. His way would have to be better than my own."

Jonas smiled. "Then let's pray."

"Grace, how are you feeling?" Miranda questioned. Having seen that everyone else was busy at various tasks on the boat, she had crept into the tent to find her sister-in-law alone.

Grace sat up on the cot Adrik had fashioned for her and smiled. "I'm fine. Truly. I'm just a little spent."

Miranda pulled a crate over and sat down by Grace. "Why didn't you tell me about the baby?"

Grace smiled sadly. "I didn't want anyone to know. Not you or even Peter. I think at first I didn't even want to admit it to myself."

"But why? I know you love my brother. Don't you want children?"

Grace bowed her head and looked at her hands. "I would love nothing more than a house filled with the laughter and joy of children. But, Miranda, I can't offer this child a happy home—much less a dwelling to live in. Your brother made it clear that I wasn't welcome in his life."

"But that was before. Once he knows about the baby, he'll forget about the past and change his ways. He'll want you back."

"That's what I'm afraid of," Grace said, lifting her head.

Miranda could read the pain in her sister-in-law's eyes. "I don't understand."

Grace reached out and took hold of Miranda's hand. "I

don't want Peter coming back out of obligation. I want him to come back because he loves me."

"Sometimes," Miranda began, "obligation is also important. Maybe Peter needs a dose of obligation."

"And maybe I should be less romantic in my notions," Grace replied.

"Perhaps. And that brings me to the other reason I've sought you out."

"Pray tell?"

Miranda felt her cheeks grow hot as she remembered Crispin's kiss. "I wanted to talk to you about Crispin Thibault." She lowered her voice. "He has shown, with great dramatic flair, that he's taken a liking to me. In fact, he calls it love, but I fail to see how that can possibly be the truth of it."

"Why?"

"Because we've only known each other a few short months."

"Yes," Grace agreed, "but our adversity has certainly made it seem longer."

Miranda shook her head. "He tells me he has loved me since the first moment. He kissed me," she said rather abruptly. "He kissed me, and it warmed me through and through. Still, I cannot say that I love him."

"Perhaps you should give it time," Grace replied. "I'm a poor teacher in such matters, but I know that had Peter and I more time, we might have given more consideration to our like interests. If Crispin has no interest in what you hold dear—God and the Bible—then you should definitely beware of losing your heart. After all, look what that has done to me."

"I've never heard him voice beliefs of one kind or another," Miranda said thoughtfully. "Perhaps that's where I should start. I'll ask him when the opportunity arises."

"Unless he shares your heart for God, Miranda, I fear you will never know a moment's true joy or peace."

Grace's words stuck in Miranda's heart long after their conversation. The winds had failed, and the party was forced to make for the shore of Lake Laberge before nightfall. Miranda helped to gather firewood and thought on her sister-in-law's counsel. Crispin's love of life had drawn her to him, there was no doubt of that. As had his splendid appearance and attentive nature. Still, Miranda knew very little about the man. He spoke of family and of childhood memories. He spoke of travels around the world and of the people he'd met. Miranda couldn't recall any stories related to past love affairs. If he'd shared his heart with any woman prior to Miranda, he gave no inkling of it.

When Miranda dumped a small armload of branches and kindling beside the fire, Jacob Barringer looked up at her with a smile. "I think we have enough for a while."

He was already busy preparing their food, and Miranda thought it rather odd that he should be about the chores of supper. "I can help if you like," she offered.

"That's okay. I'm pretty good at this. My pa thought it was important for me to learn, and it's served me well." He went back to preparing the fish Adrik had managed to catch. Miranda didn't recognize the type of fish, but there were two rather large ones—surely enough to feed them all. She could hear her stomach growling in anticipation.

Seeing that Leah and Karen were putting the finishing touches on the land tent, Miranda thought to offer her help. Then Crispin came into view. He carried a makeshift fishing pole and was headed down the rocky bank. Drawing a deep breath, Miranda decided to follow behind. *Perhaps I can engage him in conversation,* she thought. *I need to know more about him before I let myself get carried away.* Whispering a prayer, she slipped past Karen and Leah without a word and made her way in the direction Crispin had taken.

He walked a considerable distance from their camp, and when he seemed satisfied with the setting, he paused only long enough to bait the hook. Miranda had no idea what he was using for bait, but she took the moment as an opportunity to call to him.

"Mind if I join you?"

He looked up with an expression of pure delight. "I could never mind finding myself in the company of the most beautiful woman in the world."

Miranda shook her head. "I do not know this woman, but perhaps you will accept my company instead."

He smiled and gave her a sweeping bow. "You are most welcome here, m'lady."

"Do you mind conversation while you fish? Or are you like my brother, who prefers absolute silence?"

He finished with the hook and cast out the line. "I must say I prefer the conversation and company of a lovely woman. I have never made a good fisherman, and I'm only here because Adrik bid me do so."

Miranda considered his comment and opened her line of inquiry. "Have there been many women in your life?"

"Oh, positively hundreds," he replied, seemingly unconcerned about such a declaration. "There are over ninety cousins in my lineage. Both my mother and father were from families of a dozen or more children, and all of them were wonderful in reproducing heirs."

"What about women who were not cousins or aunts or sisters?"

He gazed heavenward as the wind blew off the lake and

ruffled his black curls. "Are you asking if there has been another lady of love in my life?"

There was a part of Miranda that didn't want to know the
answer, but at the same time she knew she needed to know
the truth to better understand who he was. "Yes," she finally
whispered.

"There were several times when I thought I was madly in
love. But they proved false." He looked back to her and
smiled.

"How can you be so certain they were false?"

"Why, that, my dear, is quite easy. I recognize them as false
in light of the truth. Comparing those ladies and those feelings
up against what I have come to feel for you . . . why, they are
only pale reminders of days gone by." He stuck the end of his
pole in mud and walked to where Miranda stood.

As he drew near, Miranda felt her heart begin to race. She
could feel the blood pounding in her ears. There was no denying the feelings he stirred, but Miranda knew she could not
rely on feelings alone.

"I know why you're here," he said in a husky tone. "You
want the same things I do, only you are young and inexperi-
enced and do not know how to ask."

"That's not true. I'm asking you questions," Miranda
countered, suddenly feeling very shy and nervous.

He stopped only inches from her. The heavy coat he wore
made his shoulders seem much broader. The dusky twilight
shadowed his face, but Miranda could still read the passion in
his eyes.

As if frozen in place, she did nothing when he reached out
to touch her face. His caress felt warm and soothing. He
touched her neck and gently rubbed the knotted muscles that
betrayed her weariness.

"You must love me," he said softly, almost hypnotically. "You simply must."

Miranda felt the worries and concerns she'd spoken of earlier with Grace disappear as he continued to rub her neck. When he slipped his hand behind her neck and pulled her forward to meet his lips, Miranda felt helpless to refuse.

He slanted her head ever so slightly and deepened his kiss. Miranda tried hard to remain calm and in control of her senses, while at the same time her body seemed to have a mind of its own. Crispin continued to kiss her while toying with her waist and gently massaging the small of her back. The rhythm was alluring—hypnotic. Miranda might very well have found herself swept completely under his spell, but he made the mistake of trying to pull her with him to the ground.

"Stop!" she said, pulling back in shock. She didn't know with whom she was more surprised—herself or him. Panting, she looked at him and questioned, "What are you doing?"

"I thought you were showing me how much you cared," he said without alarm. "I thought we were taking advantage of a quiet moment of privacy."

"I came to talk."

"Did you?" he questioned, his voice so smooth and low that it gave Miranda a shiver.

"Yes," she replied. "At least that's what I had thought. I cannot deny the physical attraction, Mr. Thibault, but I hardly think our behavior appropriate. I know very little of you, as I said before. I came here seeking to know more."

He shrugged and walked leisurely back to his fishing pole. "Ah, 'tis my bad fortune. The woman I love has no interest in me."

Miranda took several uncertain steps. "That's not . . . what I said." She stammered over her words, fighting the sudden urge to apologize. But for what? For defending her honor? For keeping an unseemly situation from becoming even more dangerous? Her emotions and logic were completely jumbled.

"So what would you like to know of me?" he questioned, pulling up the line. There was no fish on the end, so he cast it out again and this time bobbed the pole up and down.

"Everything," Miranda said without hesitation.

"Everything?" he asked, looking to her with a grin. "Would you leave me no secrets? No dark shady past to remain forever hidden from view?"

"No, I'd rather know everything up front."

"Starting with what?" He looked back to the lake and seemed completely at ease.

His lackadaisical spirit bolstered Miranda's courage. She studied his profile for a moment, greatly admiring the aristocratic line. Somehow his pose seemed quite regal, as if he were surveying his kingdom from some lofty perch. Thinking of him as a king reminded Miranda of why she'd come here in the first place.

"Mr. Thibault . . . Crispin . . . what are your thoughts . . . your heart toward God?"

He laughed. "Oh, that's easy enough. I have no thoughts or heart toward God. I don't believe in any god. Life is complicated enough by all manner of superstitious nonsense. I know you have your beliefs," he said, turning with a shrug. "It doesn't bother me in the least. Just as Adrik's devotion to such nonsense has never affected our friendship. Let each man be his own dictator."

Miranda was speechless. She could scarcely believe what she was saying. Here was the man she had only moments ago allowed such an intimate moment with denying the very God she served.

"I . . . don't . . . I never . . ." She halted, having no idea how to reply.

Crispin seemed to understand and turned back to the lake. "Give it no thought, my dear. It needn't come between us. I'm perfectly content to allow you to go on with your practices. It doesn't change my regard for you."

Miranda could stand it no longer. "Well, it changes mine for you," she replied and started to go.

"Wait, don't leave. I know you're confused," he called. Once again he abandoned his fishing pole and came to her. He reached out to touch her, but Miranda pulled away. "Don't let this come between us. Why should it bother you that I see no need for such matters? My educational training and life travels have proven to me over and over that there is no such thing as a divine being. And even if, on some remotely distant chance there is, I know He has no interest whatsoever in the daily lives of human beings. I mean, how very audacious of us to presume upon something like that."

"How can you say that?"

He shrugged. "How can I not? I've traveled the world over and experienced many different religions and cultures. Everyone has some notion of spiritual matters. Americans certainly haven't captured the market on it, if that's what you think. Why, I have sat in the presence of many great men who expounded on issues of faith. I believe that such matters are better left to those who need them."

"But we all need Jesus," Miranda said, unfaltering.

He smiled. "My dearest, don't you see? Everyone needs something. You won't hear me say otherwise. Please don't let it come between us that I have different ideas. Perhaps in time you will come to better understand my beliefs, but in the meanwhile you'll get no umbrage nor disdain from me in regard to what you desire to believe."

"I'm sorry," Miranda said, shaking her head. "I have to go. I don't understand you, and I don't wish to continue this conversation."

"Give it some thought, my dear," Crispin replied. "You'll see. Life is much too short and sweet to worry over such conventions."

———

It was nearly midnight before the camp grew quiet and the obvious sounds of sleep could be heard. Occasionally Leah coughed and Crispin snored, but otherwise gentle rhythmic breathing filled the air.

Karen, however, couldn't sleep. Nestled there between Grace and Leah, she longed for her husband's arms. *This is my wedding night. I should be with Adrik.*

They had already agreed to delay their consummation, given their travel situation. Had they managed to obtain a separate tent or had the nights been less cold, they might well have chosen otherwise. And Adrik had promised her they'd rent a room in Hootalinqua, but that was a whole day away.

Knowing trying to sleep was an exercise in futility, Karen slipped out of her bag and pulled on her boots. Without bothering to lace them, she pulled on her coat and unfastened the tent flap.

The crisp night air hit her face, but in the moon's brilliant light, Karen could see Adrik standing a little ways from the fire, as if waiting for her to come to him. Eager to be in his arms, she hurried to cross the distance and tripped on her laces.

Adrik caught hold of her before she fell, but it threw him off balance and sent him onto his backside with a dull *thump.*

He took Karen with him, pulling her protectively across his lap. Surprised, Karen looked up and smiled.

"You do have a way of getting right to the heart of things, don't you, Mr. Ivankov?"

Adrik chuckled softly. "I wasn't the one throwing myself at folks." He pushed back her loose hair. "You don't know how many times I've dreamed of this."

"What? Having me trip over my own feet?"

"Nah, I saw plenty of that on the trail. No, holding you like this is what I dreamed of."

She sighed and nuzzled her lips against his neck. "Me too." Wrapping her arms around his neck, she added, "I couldn't begin to sleep. It just didn't seem right that I couldn't be with you."

"I know. I felt the same way."

Karen lifted her face to his and leaned forward to kiss him. She had very little experience in such matters, but prayed that she might please him. *Oh, God*, she thought, *I only want to make him a good wife.*

She needn't have worried, however, for Adrik's low moan of satisfaction told her he was quite content with her forward action. She touched his chest, feeling his heart racing—the beat clearly matching her own wild pattern. How marvelous to know this feeling. How wondrous to share this kind of love.

"I don't want to leave you," Karen whispered against his lips.

"I don't want you to go," he murmured as his kisses trailed up to her ear. "But I think you must."

She nodded even as he kissed the lobe of her ear. "I'll leave in a few minutes." Reaching up, she lightly massaged the skin at the base of his neck. His skin felt so warm and inviting. She blushed at the thoughts that ran through her mind.

In the distance a wolf cried out in lone adoration of the night. Soon other cries followed, and Karen startled. "They won't bother us, will they?"

Adrik shook his head and smiled. "You have nothing to fear. I'll never let harm come to you so long as there is breath in my body."

She forgot about the wolves' serenade and looked deep into her husband's dark eyes. "I love you so much, Adrik. I didn't know it was possible to love another human being this much."

"I know," he said nodding, "I feel the same way. I can't imagine my life without you in it."

"I want to be a good wife to you," she said, toying with the hair around his ear. "I will try very hard to be obedient." She kissed him again, slow and lingering. It was a habit she could very easily get into.

Abruptly, Adrik ended the kiss and surprised her by getting them both to their feet. "I really want you to stay," he said, his breath coming quickly, "but I need for you to go back to your tent. We'll both be better off for it in the long run."

"I know," Karen replied rather breathlessly. She turned to go, then paused and smiled. "Hootalinqua?"

He grinned. "Hootalinqua."

-|CHAPTER TWENTY-EIGHT|-

LAKE LABERGE ONCE AGAIN became an obstacle for the boating party. Positioning themselves among one of a dozen or more crafts, Adrik found himself confronted more than once by strangers in search of answers.

"How much farther to Hootalinqua?"

"We need fresh meat, do you have any to spare?"

"Our boat's breakin' apart, do you have any extra nails? Any rope?"

The list went on and on, but once in a while a scow would draw up close simply to exchange pleasantries. People were starved for conversation and news of the outside. But Adrik had little to offer on either account.

Concern for his own party was growing, making him less than pleasant company for his companions. Crispin had been unusually quiet, almost sullen, since the night before. Miranda and Grace were huddled in conversation, and if the expressions on their faces suggested anything, it was a sign of additional trouble. Karen concerned herself with improving Leah's health, but from time to time Adrik could see the longing in her eyes for time alone with him.

The frustration of not being allowed enough privacy to have a decent wedding night was enough to cause Adrik to consider a cold swim. Especially after last night. Oh, but the woman could make his blood run hot. He knew a good deal of his agitation was steeped in his desire to spend a good long time alone with his new wife. Still, he'd brought this on himself. He should have insisted they wait to marry until they'd reached Dawson City.

Have I been a fool, Lord? Adrik began to pray. *Tempers are running high, and patience is nearly gone.* Adrik missed his regular times of devotion and quiet moments of prayer. Perhaps that was what was eating at him. Since they'd left Lake Lindeman he'd had little time for either prayer or Scripture. He felt as if he were starving to death. Maybe he should join the women for morning devotions.

Of course Crispin wouldn't be interested, but it surely wouldn't hurt for him to listen in. Adrik thought of his friend. Crispin believed in his own power. To Crispin, the only one worth serving was himself. "Why bother with anything or anyone else?" was Crispin's declaration.

Lost in thought, Adrik wasn't even mildly concerned when the wind picked up. But soon the choppiness of the water drew his attention. Steering the boat became increasingly more difficult, and before he could make a reasonable decision, a light rain began to fall.

"Looks like we're in for it!" Crispin called, pointing behind Adrik.

Adrik turned to look to the southwest. Heavy gray-black clouds were fairly boiling on the horizon. Overhead, the brooding rain clouds were unleashing an increasing flow from their reservoirs. "We'll need to head to shore!" Adrik yelled above the winds. "Get that sail down."

But there was little time. As was often the case in the north, the storm came tearing across the sky in a matter of minutes. Roaring out across the area, it seemed to devour everything in its path.

Karen came from inside the tent and looked to Adrik. She could barely stand steady. "What's happening?"

"Storm," he said, knowing that no other explanation was necessary. "Better make sure everything's tied down tight. Get Miranda to help you, and send Grace into the tent with Leah. Jacob!" The boy turned from where he'd been working with Crispin to bring down the sail.

"We'll put her downwind and try to make our way to shore. Grab the oars! I doubt we'll have much luck in rowing, but maybe we can keep her from going broadside to the wind."

Jacob and Crispin finished securing the sail and went immediately to where the long-handled oars waited in reserve. As the wind rocked the craft, Adrik began to fear that reaching the distant shore would be more of a trial for the group than he'd originally figured. He'd have to work hard if they were going to bring the boat to land in one piece.

"Jacob, you come take the sweep. Guide her toward the shore as best you can," Adrik ordered. "I'll row." He knew his strength was greater than the boy's.

Miranda and Karen worked diligently to check the supplies. They covered the flour and sugar sacks with a canvas tarp and fought against the wind to tie it down. The storm was shaking loose everything that wasn't actually nailed to the deck, and Adrik began to worry that they'd lose their goods. Handing over the sweep handle to Jacob, Adrik went to help the women only long enough to settle the canvas in place before taking his place with the oars.

"Karen," he called over his shoulder, "keep close to Jacob, and give him any help he needs."

The skies blackened overhead, stealing the light. The storm was unlike any Adrik had ever seen. "God help us," he prayed. For surely only God could deliver them from the moment.

The boat pitched wildly, nearly sending Adrik off his feet. Water rushed over the sides and drenched his boots. He'd been a fool for his daydreaming. He knew how dangerous the Yukon could be. Why had he allowed himself to be caught unaware?

Another wave came crashing, and with it the wind seemed to change direction. The scow rode the crest and slammed hard against the lake's surface. A woman's scream pierced the air, and Adrik felt his blood run cold. Fighting for all he was worth to keep them from capsizing in the storm, he had precious little time for additional problems.

Glancing over his shoulder, he saw Karen lying in a heap on the deck. He breathed a sigh of relief. At least she was safe. He would worry about whether she was hurt after they reached dry land.

Rain pelted hard against his face as the storm intensified. The wind howled at them in protest, and the lake did its best to expel the boat from her unsettled body. Adrik's arms burned from the intensity of fighting the water and the wind. They were making precious little progress, but at least there was some.

He looked to Crispin, who fought the same battle from the

port side. Adrik couldn't help but wonder what Crispin did for comfort in times like these. Adrik prayed and prayed hard. But Crispin had his own notions, and Adrik couldn't imagine how they could ever sustain a man through trying times.

Another scream rent the air, and this time Adrik knew instinctively that something horrible had happened. He turned, pulling the oar from the water lest it be ripped from his grasp.

"What's wrong?" The sound of his voice was swallowed up in the storm.

Karen and Jacob were pointing wildly at the stern. Karen shook her head and began to make her way to Adrik. At the same time, Crispin seemed to come out of his stupor and with great strides leaped over several of the crates to make his way to the back of the boat.

Karen fell against Adrik, her red hair plastered to her face, her lips blue from the cold. "Miranda!" she cried against the wind. "Miranda has fallen overboard!"

Adrik felt a sickening sensation settle in the pit of his stomach. There was no hope of finding the woman in this raging gale. But already Crispin had tied a rope around his waist, and before Adrik could stop him, he dove into the water.

"Stay here!" Adrik commanded Karen. He thrust the handle against her. "You'll have to help me! Just help Jacob keep her headed to shore."

Karen nodded, but Adrik could see the fear in her eyes. He positioned her where he'd stood, then lashed a rope around her waist. Fighting the pitching waves, he tied the other end to one of the tent rings secured in the deck.

"Don't let her go broadside to the wind, or we'll all be in the water!" he told her.

Then crossing the deck, he picked up the lifeline that

· connected Crispin to the scow. Pulling, Adrik fought to bring Crispin back to safety. He could barely see beyond the rope to the water. There was no sign of Crispin, but the weight at the end of the rope told Adrik the man was still fastened.

With superhuman strength, Adrik pulled on the line, all the while fighting to maintain his balance. Gradually the line yielded, and in a matter of moments, Adrik was pulling Crispin's icy frame back onto the deck.

"I couldn't find her!" Crispin called out.

Adrik shook his head. "We won't find her in this. We have to get to shore. It's our only hope to save the rest."

Reluctantly, Crispin nodded. He struggled to his feet with Adrik's help, then shielded his eyes from the rain trying to see where Miranda had gone.

"Come on," Adrik commanded. "We're nearly there."

The men finished maneuvering the scow to shore just as the worst of the storm came upon them. They secured the boat as best they could, then began unloading the supplies just in case the lines didn't hold. They could build another boat if necessary, Adrik reasoned. It would be difficult, but not impossible. But food, weapons, clothing ... those things were much harder to come by.

The wind fairly howled around them as a deluge of icy rain tormented everything in its path. Everyone worked. Even Leah and Grace. The entire party seemed to understand Adrik's insistence at completing the task at hand. There would be time for warming up and drying off after the storm had passed. For now, the best they could hope for was to secure the supplies, then seek shelter with their things.

Grace sat huddled under the canvas tarp in a state of complete shock. She'd become so numb from the cold she could barely feel her feet or hands. The baby moved within her. The movement comforted her.

As the worst of the storm passed, leaving only a light rain falling, the men left the women and went in search of firewood. Adrik promised a large bonfire, big enough to warm them all to the bone. Grace doubted she would ever feel warm again. The worst of it was the cold that washed over her in the knowledge that Miranda was gone.

Grace hadn't even realized it until just moments after they'd pulled the tarp around them to hide from the storm. "Where's Miranda?" she had asked, only to receive the pain-filled expression of her companions.

"She just can't be gone," Grace murmured.

Karen patted her hand, and even Leah reached out to touch Grace reassuringly. "Maybe someone in one of the other boats will find her. We weren't the only ones caught unaware," Karen stated evenly.

"That's right, Grace," Leah added, "Miranda told me she was a strong swimmer. Maybe she even made it to shore."

"The storm was too bad," Grace replied. She looked to her longtime friend. "No one could swim in that weather. And the cold . . . oh, Karen . . . the temperature of the water was surely enough to . . ." She couldn't say the words.

"Adrik said they'd go down the shore tomorrow and look for any signs of Miranda. There are Indian villages in the area, and she could very easily have been swept ashore."

Grace buried her face in her hands. "Oh, what am I going to tell Mother Colton?"

The thought of having to break such news to her in-laws left Grace overwhelmed to the point of complete despair. *Oh, God,* she prayed, *please let me wake up and find this nothing more than a horrible dream. Please let Miranda come back to us now, safe and unharmed.*

"Let's wait until we know for sure that there's something we need to tell her," Karen suggested.

Grace looked up, tears blurring her vision. "It should have been me. It would have solved everything."

"No!" Karen declared, reaching out to shake Grace's shoulders. "You must not talk that way. You're just feeling the effects of the shock and the cold. You must be strong, Grace. You must be strong for your baby."

Grace felt the fluttering movement again. It seemed the child wanted to show his or her agreement with Karen's statement. She wanted to take hope in the child—wanted to have a reason to live in the midst of this awful, suffocating despair. But she felt so weak. So inadequate to deal with something so monumental. Martin Paxton's threats were nothing compared to the loss of her sister-in-law.

The men had a fire going in a short time, thanks to Adrik's knowledge of the outdoors. The rain eventually abated, leaving everything damp and cold. Grace huddled with Leah at the edge of the flames. The warmth felt good but did little to relieve her sorrow. Crispin, too, looked completely devastated. He sat opposite Grace, and from time to time their gaze met across the flames.

He must have loved her, Grace surmised. *His expression speaks it.* The pain she saw there so clearly reflected her own heart. She tried not to think of Miranda as dead, but there was nothing else to consider. The weather had been too foul, the waves too high, the water too cold. No one could have survived such an accident.

The next day, after Adrik and Jacob made repairs to the scow, they floated the remaining distance to Hootalinqua.

Grace faced their arrival at the little community with mixed emotions. The Northwest Mounted Police had a station here, and she would have to go and make a report on Miranda's accident. It would be important to let the officials know what had happened in case her body washed ashore. Adrik had offered to do the deed, but Grace had insisted she be the one to take care of the matter. After all, she had stated, Miranda was family.

Adrik walked with her to the log building headquarters of the Canadian officials. "Are you sure you don't want me to take care of this?" he asked.

Grace shook her head and looked up to see his compassionate expression. He was such a kind man. So gentle and caring. "I will be fine. You need to take care of the others."

She turned away without another word and made her way inside the station. A young man in a red coat that seemed much too small for his broad-shouldered frame looked up in greeting.

"Good morning, ma'am. I'm Sergeant Cooper. What can I do for you?"

"My name is Mrs. Grace Colton. I have come north with a party of my friends." Her hands began to tremble, and for a moment she felt light-headed.

The officer seemed to understand and quickly came to her side. "You should sit," he commanded and led her to a chair.

"Thank you. I've had quite a shock." She tried to steady her nerves, but visions of Peter and Amelia and Ephraim kept coming to mind. She saw them in their sorrow and knew the pain they would feel.

"Would you care for a cup of tea?"

She looked up at the man and shook her head. "I must be about my business. My party is anxious to move on."

"Very well. Why don't you begin?"

"We were on Lake Laberge yesterday when the storm came up. It was fierce, and our boat was barely able to handle such a storm. We made for shore, but before we arrived, my sister-in-law, Miranda Colton, fell overboard. We tried in vain to rescue her."

The man took the news in a stoic fashion. "Were you able to recover her . . . well, that is to say . . . did you find her?"

Grace bit her lip to keep from crying. She forced herself to draw a deep breath. "No. We did not find her body."

"I see. Let me take this down on paper." He went to his desk and took up his pen. "The name is Colton, correct?"

Grace continued to answer his questions and waited for him to complete his task. When at last he finished writing, he put down the pen and looked up at Grace. "We've had some trouble with the telegraph, but as soon as the lines are repaired, I'll get word of this down to Whitehorse. Should anyone find her, it would be on record for the purpose of identification."

Grace knew it made sense, but her fear was that Miranda's parents might learn the truth before she had a chance to write to them herself. "I would like to send a letter to her parents," she finally said. "It would be unfair for them to receive word of this from strangers."

"If you care to leave a letter with me, I'll see to it that it goes out with the next post."

"Thank you. I'd like that very much."

The sergeant's heart went out to the young woman. There were so many tales of loss among these stampeders. They came seeking their fortune and often lost their lives. He looked down at the report he'd just written. Such a waste.

Why, the woman was no older than he, and now, by all reasonable accounts, she was probably dead.

"Sergeant Cooper," the voice of his superior called from outside the door.

Leaving his desk, Cooper made his way outside. "Sir?"

"I saw a young woman leave the office just now. What was her business?"

Cooper looked down the path to where the woman was making her way back to her party. "That was Mrs. Colton. She came to report the drowning death of her sister-in-law. Seems they were on Lake Laberge when they were caught in yesterday's storm, and the young woman, a Miss Grace Colton, fell overboard. They were unable to recover her body."

—[CHAPTER TWENTY-NINE]—

WITH A COLD OCTOBER WIND howling at his back, Peter Colton made his way to Martin Paxton's store. He had to meet with the man, though it was the last thing in the world he wanted to do. Since deciding to follow Christ as his Savior, Peter had known he would have to make this trip. Nevertheless, it was hard. He needed Paxton to tell him where Grace had gone. He needed his adversary to be gracious—merciful.

"What can I do for you?" the clerk asked from behind the counter as Peter came through the door.

Struggling to close the door against the wind, Peter barely heard the question. With the door secured, Peter turned and pulled his scarf from around his face. "I need to see Mr. Paxton. I have business of a personal nature."

The clerk recognized Peter and shook his head. "I doubt the boss wants to meet with you."

"I don't care what he wants," Peter stated, working hard to keep his anger under control, "I need to see him nevertheless."

The man stood his ground, staring hard at Peter. "And if I'm not of a mind to disturb him?"

"Then I'll start tearing this store apart until you are of a mind," Peter replied calmly.

The man weighed Peter's words for a moment, then shrugged. "I'll tell him you're here, but that don't mean he'll see you."

Peter waited until the man had moved from the front of the store to follow after him. He knew the way without an escort. He waited at the bottom of the stairs while the clerk announced him in the room above.

"Send him up," Peter heard Paxton say.

The clerk turned and saw Peter standing at the bottom of the stairs. "The boss says he'll see you."

Peter took the stairs two at a time and had reached the top before the clerk had so much as attempted to descend. Bounding into the room, he was unprepared for the sight of the once fashionable room. The furniture stood as ghostly images, covered in white sheets. Paxton's desk and chair were the only pieces not yet hidden away. To one side of the desk sat an open trunk. Paxton apparently had been packing even as Peter had come to call.

"Where are you going?" Peter asked.

"Not that it is any of your business, but I'm headed south. The winter promises to be severe, and I have little desire to find myself here when the snows grow heavy. One winter in Alaska was enough for me."

"What of Grace?"

"What of her?"

"I want to know where she is," Peter said firmly. "I don't intend to leave until you tell me the truth."

Paxton shook his head. "I have no reason to tell you anything."

Just then a big burly man stormed into the room. Peter turned, certain the man had come to take him from the premises.

"Boss, I got something you need to see. Just came in on the train about an hour ago. Mayor thought you'd want to see it right away."

Paxton slammed down the book he'd been holding. "Can't you see I'm busy?"

"Yeah, but this is important."

Paxton eyed the larger man for a moment, then held out his hand. "What is it?"

Peter watched in irritation as the man passed a folded piece of paper to Paxton. Paxton read the missive, then looked up in stunned silence. Peter thought perhaps the man might have been having some sort of spell as he moved around behind the desk and fell into his chair.

Paxton looked up at his man. "Are they certain about this?"

"Yeah, boss. Mayor said to tell you it came direct from the police headquarters in Whitehorse."

"Leave us," Paxton told the man. The man did as he was told, but not without some hesitation. He paused at the door and looked as if he might question Paxton, but he had no chance. "Go!" Paxton demanded.

Peter stood, uncertain. Would Paxton demand his exit, as well? And if he did, how would Peter ever find out about Grace?

"It would seem I was in error," Paxton began, his gaze

rather glassy and distant. "I told you that I had no reason to tell you anything. It would appear that has now changed."

"I don't understand," Peter said, stepping toward the desk.

Paxton extended the paper. "Your wife, Mr. Colton."

Peter snatched the letter with great speed. Opening it, he scanned the few lines and let the paper drop to the desk. "No. Grace isn't dead."

"The Northwest Mounted Police are, I'm afraid, quite thorough and reasonably qualified at their job. If they've declared her dead, she's dead."

Peter felt the room spin. His breath refused to come, and he pulled at the scarf around his neck as though it had somehow tightened. "She can't be dead. She can't be!"

"It would seem she has eluded us both," Paxton replied.

"But you told me she was here. You said she was with you."

"I only let you believe that. I haven't seen her since she went north to Dawson with your sister and that Pierce woman."

"No!"

Peter crossed the distance between them and, without warning, reached across the desk and pulled Paxton up by his lapel. Shaking the man hard enough to rattle his teeth, Peter demanded the truth. "You're only doing this to throw me off track. You're trying to make me believe she's dead so you can have her."

Paxton shook his head. "I'm just as surprised at this news as you are and just as devastated for my own reasons. This is no game, Colton. She's dead."

"Stop saying that!" Peter declared, sending his fist into Paxton's face.

Without realizing what he was doing, Peter hit the man

again and again. "She isn't dead! You're lying to me!" He felt the aching in his own hand as his knuckles made contact with the unyielding bone of Paxton's jaw.

"I don't care what you believe," Paxton said as he started to fight back. "Now leave me before I call my men." He slammed his fist into Peter's nose, causing blood to spurt out across the desk.

Peter, stunned at the blow, let go of Paxton and backed up a pace. "I'll go to the mayor. I'll go to the police. I'll learn the truth."

"You already know the truth," Paxton said, nursing his bleeding lip.

Hours later, after getting the same reassurance from the mayor, Peter let the realization sink in that what Paxton had said was true. It was no sham. No game to take him away from Grace. Devastated and stunned, Peter collapsed near the docks and gave himself over to his grief.

She can't be gone, he told himself. *She just can't be gone. We left on such bad terms, and there was so much that I needed to apologize for. Words I can never take back. She must have died hating me—hating me enough to go north into the wilds of the Yukon.* He thought of Jonas and of what insight or comfort the man might offer. Then just as quickly, Peter dismissed the idea. He couldn't bear to see the man and explain that his pride had caused him to be too late to reconcile with Grace. Jonas expected Peter to find his wife and head south to San Francisco and a new life in the Lord. Now that could never be.

Uncertain of how to pray for himself, Peter moaned as he

buried his face against his knees. "Oh, God, what am I to do? How am I to face this alone?"

"Peter Colton?"

The voice seemed to call from somewhere out of Peter's memory. Looking up, he found a childhood friend, a rival in the shipping industry from San Francisco. "Wesley Oakes?"

"Good grief, man, what's happened to you?" the man reached out to help Peter up from the ground.

"I just got word my wife is dead," Peter said in an almost mechanical tone. "I didn't know where else to go."

The man's face contorted. "I'm sorry, Peter. I had no idea you were even married."

"We've not even been married a year," Peter replied, his brain taking on a fogginess that seemed to mute the pain momentarily.

"Where are you headed?" Oakes questioned.

"I don't know." Peter looked to the steamers in the harbor. "I should go home. There's nothing to keep me here now."

"I leave in two hours. You can have a place on my ship," Oakes offered. "Get your gear and be back before we leave."

Peter looked at the man and shook his head. "Everything of value is with me already. I signed off my job with the railroad and bid my friends good-bye this morning."

"Then come with me now. We'll find you some private quarters, and I'll send someone to tend to your nose. It looks as though it might be broken." Oakes reached out and pulled Peter to his side.

"It doesn't matter," Peter said without the will to protest the man's decision.

True to his word, Wesley Oakes had Peter put in one of the better cabins aboard the steamer *Ellsbeth Marie*. The ship's cook, who also doubled as the ship's doctor, examined Peter's nose and declared that it was not broken, then cleaned Peter up and left him in the silence of the room. Without the will to go on, Peter crawled into the berth and closed his eyes.

"Let me die, as well, Lord," he begged. "If she's dead, I can't go on." He felt hot tears on his face. "Just let me die."

―――――――

Peter slept through the night and might well have slept through the entire following day, but for Wesley Oakes. The captain of the *Ellsbeth Marie* wasn't about to leave Peter to his own sorrows.

Bringing a hearty supper of dried beef stew and biscuits, Oakes acted as if nothing was out of the ordinary. "You've got to eat," he announced. "It's acceptable to miss the morning and noon meal, but I draw the line at missing your supper."

"I'm not hungry," Peter said, easing his legs over the side of the bed. He'd never known such exhaustion. His limbs felt like lead.

"I've no doubt that's true," Wesley said with a compassionate smile, "but nevertheless, you need to keep your strength up."

Peter realized the man would no doubt stay there to harass him until he yielded. "Very well. I will eat."

"That's a good man. Now I need to slip down below and check on my men. You eat up, and we'll have us a talk tomorrow."

Peter nodded and sat down at the table where Oakes had placed the tray of food. Picking up a biscuit, he put it to his mouth and bit into it. It tasted like sawdust. Peter said nothing, however, as Wesley took his leave.

Letting the biscuit drop to the plate, Peter stared at the food in disinterest. If a man could will himself to die, then

Peter was eager to learn the secret.

He thought of Grace and of the letter reporting her death. It said she drowned in Lake Laberge. He couldn't help but wonder what had happened. What had been the circumstances? Why her and not Karen Pierce? Not that he would have wished either one dead, but why Grace?

Peter lost track of the time, feeling no interest in his surroundings. He had lost the love of his life. The only woman he would ever love—ever want to spend his days with.

"Why, God?" He shook his head and let out a deep sigh that went all the way to his soul. "Why?"

Boom! Suddenly the entire room rocked with the impact of the explosion. Peter looked up, uncertain of what had just happened. Another explosion followed close behind the first one, and this time Peter got to his feet and went to the door of his cabin. Flames shot up from the deck below as people screamed and ran for safety.

The black water below was illuminated by the fire on the *Ellsbeth Marie*. Peter tried to make sense of the disaster, but could not.

"Abandon ship!" the call went out. "Abandon ship!"

But to where? Peter wondered, moving stiffly toward the stairs.

It seemed that only moments passed before the entire ship was engulfed in flames. People fought each other for the few lifeboats that were on board. Peter inched down the stairs amidst the panicked passengers. He caught a glimpse of Wesley Oakes. Charred from smoke, Wesley stood as a pillar of stability in the madness.

"Peter!" he called out, "Get off, man! There's no time to lose. The *Seamist* is just behind us. She'll pick up the passengers."

Peter's senses seemed to return all at once. He knew he had to get off the ship, but a greater part of his captaining instincts told him to help the other passengers first. He made his way to the flaming deck and, dodging the fire, managed to make his way to where an older woman struggled.

"Here, let me help you," he said, taking hold of her. He maneuvered the woman to the only lifeboat nearby. Helping her gently, Peter saw her safe, then turned to help the others.

The screams and sounds of panic were terrifying. His own pain seemed insignificant compared to that of a mother who stood screaming for her baby.

"Where is he?" Peter questioned.

The woman pointed down the long deck of flames. "Our cabin—the last one on the right!"

Peter nodded, then darted through the flames and headed in the direction she pointed. He thought only of the child—praying he might not be too late. Thick black smoke bellowed up from the fire, blinding him and stinging his lungs. He coughed and pulled his handkerchief from his pocket. He had to hurry.

The door was locked tight, but Peter would not be stopped. Throwing himself against the door over and over again, he finally felt the wood give way. Gaining entrance to the smoke-filled cabin, Peter tried to see through the illuminated haze. Cautiously feeling his way about the room, he found the cradle. The baby didn't so much as cry as Peter lifted him from the bed. He tucked the baby into his coat, hoping to shield him from the heat and smoke.

Making his way back down the deck, Peter heard a man pleading for help. "I'll be right back," Peter called, seeing that the man's door was somehow jammed. The man waved his hand from the few inches of space.

"No! Don't leave me!"

Peter had no choice but to leave the man. He had to return the baby to his mother, otherwise they might both be lost. He accomplished his goal quickly, meeting the teary-eyed woman with a smile. "He seems just fine," Peter announced, then pulled the still-sleeping baby from beneath his coat.

"Oh, my baby. My sweet baby," the woman said, pouring kisses over the child's head. "Oh, thank you. Thank you so much!"

Peter didn't wait to hear more. Amidst the cacophony of certain death, he made his way back to the man in the cabin.

"I'm here!" Peter called.

"Get me out! The door won't budge. The blast sent a beam across it."

Peter pushed at the door even as the dull roar of the fire climbed the wall behind him. The heat burned the back of Peter's neck, but still he worked to free the stranger.

The door moved ever so slightly, and Peter felt encouraged. The man pressed his bruised face to the door, causing Peter to step back in shock. "You!"

Martin Paxton was unconcerned. "Get me out of here, Colton."

Peter thought of all that the man had done to harm him. Leaving him to die on the burning ship would be sweet revenge. Frozen in place, Peter contemplated what he should do. Paxton deserved to die.

"*Peter, it will serve no purpose but that of darker forces if you continue this hateful battle,*" Grace had once told him. He could almost hear her sweet voice pleading, "*Please listen to me. Forgiving Mr. Paxton is the only way to put the past to rest.*"

"Colton, I'll give you whatever you want. Just get me out of here."

"I want Grace back," Peter said, shaking his head. "But you can't give her back to me."

"Just get me out of here, and I promise to return your father's business. I never meant to hurt him anyway."

Peter recognized the pleadings of a desperate man and could only think of Grace's gentle nature and loving heart. He couldn't leave Paxton to die. It would negate everything Grace had stood for. Everything Peter now believed in.

Giving it all he had, Peter pressed his body to the wood.

"Just a little more!"

Peter felt his heart pounding against his chest as he pushed with his full weight against the door. Without warning, it gave way, and Peter fell into the room, landing soundly on his back. Looking up, he found Martin Paxton staring down at him, a smirk lining his lips.

"You fool."

Paxton kicked Peter square in the jaw, then pressed through the opening, pulling the door closed behind him. Peter barely registered what had happened. Dull-headed and struggling to see, Peter got to his feet and reached for the handle of the door just as a third explosion tore through the night and into the room.

Peter felt himself hurled through the air, the walls around him seeming to splinter into a thousand pieces as the blast carried him into the night skies. Something hit Peter hard against the head, and as he began to lose consciousness, he felt the icy waters of the canal engulf his body and pull him down.

It's only fitting, he thought as he slipped into oblivion. *Grace drowned. It's only fitting that I should drown, as well.*

–{ C H A P T E R   T H I R T Y }–

PETER'S FIRST SENSATION of consciousness was the rocking of his bed. He thought for a moment he must be dreaming. Beds didn't rock. He heard voices around him, but he felt too weary to open his eyes. He heard someone call his name.

Grace! He knew it must be her.

Struggling, he tried to say her name. Nothing—not a single sound would come from his lips.

Grace, don't leave me! he silently pleaded.

The next time he awoke, Peter found himself in a hospital bed. The nurse who hovered over him was an unappealing woman whose pinched expression gave him little hope for his recovery.

"I'll tell the doctor you're awake," she said curtly before turning to leave.

Peter thought to say something, but his throat pained him.

The smoke had nearly choked out his voice.

The doctor, a thin man with a compassionate look to him, came to Peter's bed. "My boy, welcome back to the living. You're at a hospital in Seattle."

Peter tried to speak, but again the words were hoarse and inaudible.

"Don't try to talk, son. The smoke has damaged your vocal cords. Just give it few days of rest and fluids, and you'll be fine."

Peter nodded. It felt as though his head were three times the normal size. Every movement hurt, and Peter couldn't help but wince.

"You took a blow to the head. You were fortunate that you weren't in the water too long. The captain saw you floating and managed to keep you that way until help arrived."

Wes had saved his life. Pity he didn't realize Peter didn't want to be saved. Peter thought of Grace and of how close he had been to joining her.

The doctor gave Peter a cursory examination, then discussed his orders with the nurse before turning to go. "We don't expect you to be here long. You're a strong young man. You'll heal fast."

The doctor's conclusion proved correct. Within a week, Peter found himself nearly as good as new and ready to leave. He'd asked the nurse to write a letter to his mother only the day before. He hoped and prayed she hadn't heard about the catastrophe on the ship. Or that if she had, she wouldn't have any reason to believe that Peter was aboard the steamer.

Now that he was out of danger, however, he wanted his parents to know where he was and to tell them about Grace. He wouldn't do that via letter, he'd decided, but he would explain his journey home and let them know he'd be back in

San Francisco within the month.

"You have visitors," the pinch-faced nurse announced. Then turning to Ephraim and Amelia Colton, she announced, "You may see him for ten minutes. No more."

"Mother!" Peter said, his voice finally regaining strength and clarity.

"Oh, Peter!" Amelia opened her arms and crossed the room to embrace her bedfast son. "We were so worried. Wesley Oakes telegraphed us and had one of his ships bring us up."

Peter hugged her close, then pulled away to greet his father. "You look like a new man."

"I feel fit as a fiddle," his father announced. "But you look a little worn."

"I've had better days, that's for sure."

"Oh, we're so grateful to Wes," Amelia continued. "We had no idea you were heading home. What of Grace and Miranda? Did you see them?"

Peter didn't know what to say. He had hoped to avoid the subject of Grace until later. His mother's imploring expression, however, made it clear she had come for answers.

"Grace is the reason I was headed back to San Francisco."

"How so, son?" his father asked.

Peter eased up in bed a bit and folded his hands. Drawing a deep breath, he tried to figure out the easiest way to break the news. "Grace wasn't with me in Skagway."

"No, we realize that. She and Miranda were to travel north to Dawson City with Grace's friend Karen Pierce."

"You already knew?" Peter questioned. "Why would she do that?"

Amelia became quite grave. "She felt you had abandoned her. And after hearing what had occurred between you two, we had no reason to believe it to be other than true. Then later your letter arrived, but of course Grace and Miranda were long gone."

"Yes," Peter murmured. "Gone."

"Well, I'm certain that if you want to restore your marriage, son," his father began, "you can make your way north, as well."

"I can't restore my marriage," Peter said flatly. He knew of no other way to tell them the truth of the matter than to simply say it. "I've had word regarding Grace. It was the reason I was headed home. You see, I didn't realize she had gone north until a report came to Skagway that she had met with an accident."

"What kind of accident?" Amelia questioned, her hand going to her throat.

"Grace apparently fell overboard while their boat fought a storm on Lake Laberge. She was lost."

"No!" Amelia and Ephraim cried in unison.

"What of Miranda?" his mother quickly added.

"I don't know. Remember, I didn't even know they were together until receiving your letter. And you never said in that letter where they'd gone. The Northwest Mounted Police were merely sending down a report of United States citizens whose lives were lost in the territory. They would have no reason to speak of Miranda unless she also had been lost."

"Oh, son, we're so sorry. How very hard this must be on you," Ephraim said solemnly.

"I was coming home to tell you and decide what I should do."

"Poor little Grace. Such a sweet, sweet girl," Amelia said, shaking her head. "How very sad this news is."

"It seems unreal," Peter replied. He looked to his parents,

then past them to the door. "I keep thinking that if I concentrate hard enough, she'll come walking through that door. We first met here in Seattle, you know. It would be rather seemly that she return to me here." He shook his head and sighed. "But I know she's not coming back." How very empty his life would be without Grace.

"This will not be an easy burden to bear," Ephraim declared. "But we must help one another through the pain."

"Oh, my poor sweet Miranda. She must be devastated with the death of Grace," Amelia said, looking to Ephraim. "Oh, what should we do?"

"It's too late to get north now," Peter replied. "The snow is blocking the progress of the train. The routes are often impassable from day to day and the rivers up north are freezing up. We'll have to wait until spring."

"But that's over six months away," Amelia replied. "What will Miranda do in the meanwhile?"

"She's with Karen Pierce," Peter said thoughtfully. "Karen is a good woman, and she'll be just as devastated as Miranda. They'll comfort each other. There is another matter, however, on which I wish to speak to you both."

"What is it, son?" Ephraim asked.

"I want to apologize for my behavior. My actions and opinions reflected a poor character, and I now see myself for the man I was and regret it greatly."

His mother reached out to touch his hand. "We all make mistakes."

"Yes, but mine has caused the death of someone I loved very dearly. If I hadn't acted in the manner I did, Grace would be safely beside me instead of lost in the Yukon."

"You don't know that."

His father's words did little to offer comfort. "The truth of the matter is, while in Alaska I met a man who helped me to see what Grace had tried to make me see all along. The need for God." Peter looked to his mother and squeezed her hand. "It seems too late, but I have made my peace with God."

"Oh, Peter, it could never be too late." Amelia hugged him close. "With God as your comfort, you will know joy once again. Let Him help you through this."

"I am," Peter admitted. Amelia released him and smiled. Peter thought of Martin Paxton for some reason. Perhaps it was because Paxton had become Peter's greatest challenge to his new faith.

"There's something else," Peter said. "Martin Paxton was on the *Ellsbeth Marie* when she blew up."

"Yes, we know," Ephraim replied. "He's dead."

"Dead?" Peter hadn't heard this news.

"He was killed in an explosion," his father answered.

Peter suddenly felt a chill. "I had gone to help a man who was trapped in his room. The door was blocked, and as I pushed it back, I found myself face-to-face with Martin Paxton. I wanted to leave him there." Peter looked up. "Does that shock you?"

Ephraim shook his head. "I probably would have felt the same."

"I thought of what Grace had said about forgiveness—about letting the past go so that real healing could begin. I knew if I left Paxton there, I would never be able to heal. I would never be able to face God."

"What did you do?" Amelia asked.

"I decided to help him. I pushed the door open and fell into the room as it gave way. Paxton called me a fool, kicked me in the face, and fled, pulling the door closed behind him. I was stunned for a moment and struggled to my feet. I'd barely stood when the explosion cut through the room and blasted me out into the water."

"Paxton's evil intent kept you alive," Ephraim replied. "He thought to leave you to die, but it was his own death he met. While you were protected by the walls of the room, albeit only marginally, Paxton was torn apart by the intensity of the blast."

Peter found the news disconcerting. "What he'd intended for evil, God used for good. My friend Jonas told me that's often the way it is with God."

His mother nodded and reached out to touch her son's face. "Oh, my dearest, I'm so very grateful that God spared you. I could not bear to lose you."

"I wanted to be lost," Peter admitted. "I felt no will to live without Grace."

"But we need you, son." His father's words were firm, not sympathetic or even filled with pity. They were merely stated as fact.

"But without her, my life feels useless. There's nothing to look forward to. My heart feels cold and lifeless." Peter closed his eyes and laid his head back on the pillow. "I never had a chance to tell her how sorry I was for my actions. I never had a chance to hold her again—to kiss her. She died thinking me a hateful and mean-spirited man."

"No," Amelia interjected. "That's not true. The last words she spoke to us were of her love for you. She was filled with love for you."

Peter opened his eyes. His vision blurred from the tears. "She was filled with love, period. She knew the love of God, and it permeated everything about her, including me. I wish she could know how she changed my heart."

"I'm sure she does," his mother said, her own tears falling freely. "I'm sure she does."

————

The taste of muddy water and grit in her mouth did little to rouse the half-conscious Miranda Colton. She had no idea where she was or what had happened. She only knew that the icy cold of the water left her numb and leaden.

Oh, God, she prayed, *I'm dying. Perhaps I'm already dead. Oh, God, help me.*

She heard voices, in a dialect she found unintelligible and senseless.

She felt herself being rolled over and then lifted from the watery grave of the lakeshore. She lay as dead weight, unable to move or even open her eyes.

Is that you, God? Have you come to take me home?

Her thoughts began to fade. Her time was drawing nigh. She smiled at the thought of heaven.

—| C H A P T E R   T H I R T Y - O N E |—

"THAT'S DAWSON!" Adrik called to his weary and sorrowed travelers.

Karen came immediately to his side and stared across the water to the buildings and tents assembled at the water's edge. Warehouses and sawmills stood near the docks, while an idle steamer and a dozen or more boats of various build floated casually in the river nearby. Chunks of ice were even now forming as a light snow began to fall.

"It's a lot bigger than I'd figured," Adrik said, embracing Karen with his right arm.

"It looks marvelous. I don't know when I've ever wanted something half as much as I've wanted to reach this town."

"Well," Adrik said, pulling her close for a kiss, "I can think of something I've wanted more than Dawson."

"Silly man," Karen replied, kissing him quickly. "You've already got me."

"Now, how did you know I was thinking of you?"

She jabbed him in the ribs, then stepped away. "You're impossible."

"Yes, ma'am."

"Is that it?" Grace asked, her voice hopeful.

Karen nodded. "Dawson City." She looked to her friend. Grace had blossomed overnight, and her rounded belly gave little doubt of her condition. "We'd better sit down. Adrik's about to dock. I don't want you to lose your footing."

They went to one of the two benches Adrik had secured and took their place. Karen reached out to hold Grace's hand as Adrik called out orders to Crispin and Jacob.

"Just look at it!" Leah Barringer called from where she stood leaning over a crate of goods. "It's like nothing I've seen since we left Seattle."

"Well, it's not quite that settled," Karen said, laughing.

"It wasn't more than a trading post last time I was up this far north," Adrik said. "It came up out of nothing."

They docked uneventfully, and when Adrik gave the word, Karen made her way to the shore. She waited for Adrik to help Grace from the boat, wondering if her friend would ever get over the losses in her life. So much had been taken from her. Karen thought how very similar their lives had been. They both had lost people so very dear to them.

"Oh, aren't you excited, Karen?" Leah called, coming up beside her to take hold of her arm. "We're finally here." Then remembering their recent loss, Leah bowed her head and added, "I wish Miranda could be here."

"It's awful cold," Jacob said, glancing around. "Where we gonna live?"

"That's a very good question," Adrik replied. "We're going to have to check things out quickly and figure where we can best hold up through the winter."

"What about a claim? Aren't we here for gold?" Jacob questioned.

"Nothing says we can't look for it," Adrik said. "But we're also going to need some regular money coming in. We'll have to get jobs as soon as possible. That might mean working for somebody else's claim."

"No, sir!" Jacob declared. "I came here for my own claim. My pa said . . ."

Leah left Karen and reached out to Jacob. "Our pa is dead. We need to make our own dreams now."

He looked down at her with such love and compassion that Karen was nearly moved to tears. What a marvelous bond they shared. Jacob slowly nodded and gave Leah a hug. With that simple gesture, Karen knew things would be all right. Jacob had learned much about foolish choices. Perhaps it would be enough to take him into adulthood without too many additional scars.

Crispin came up from behind, his face blank of expression. He hadn't been the same since Miranda had fallen overboard. Karen felt sorry for him. Adrik had said that Crispin was an atheist—that he didn't believe in the existence of God. She wondered how he could bear the thought of a tomorrow without the certainty that God had already seen the day—had planned it through.

"Well, what now?" he asked Adrik.

"Now we start over," Adrik replied. "This is a new adventure. The old is passed away. We find a home or make one. We find a claim and work it. We settle ourselves in for the winter and do the best we can with what the good Lord has given us."

Crispin looked back to the boat. "Someone should stay here. No sense in having our things taken." He began to walk back to the boat.

"Doesn't Crispin want to see the town?" Leah asked.

Adrik shook his head. "I think he needs some time to himself. But what say we all head up that way? Might as well begin checking things out."

Leah rallied from her thoughts of Miranda and pulled on her brother's arm. "Come on. There's so much to see."

"Oh my," Grace said as it began to snow in earnest, "I forgot my bonnet." She turned to go back to the scow, but Adrik stopped her.

"I'll get it. You stay here."

"Thank you," she said, looking to Karen. "He's a good man. He'll be a wonderful husband."

Karen nodded. "I know he will. But I know something else, as well." She looped her arm through Grace's. "You make me proud to call you friend. I so admire your strength and courage. You have been put through trials of fire and still your faith has grown."

"I'm only putting into practice the things you taught me," Grace said, her brown eyes meeting Karen's gaze. "You planted the seeds within my heart, and God grew them. You should be proud of your job as a teacher, for you taught me much about life and about love."

Karen felt tears sting her eyes. "Things will be better, you'll see. God is not finished with this matter. He has a plan."

"But there's nothing left."

"Then just as the stampeders did with Dawson City, God will create something out of nothing. He can do that, you know. He thawed my icy heart after I turned away from Him. He shattered my illusions of self-sufficiency and proved to me that He alone could see me through. He'll do the same for you, Grace, because you're His and He cares for His own."

"Like He cared for Miranda?"

Karen saw the sorrow wash over Grace as she looked past Karen to the river. "He was with Miranda even when she fell. The Bible says that even the falling sparrow doesn't escape His notice. I don't know why God allows these things to happen, Grace. I don't know why bad should plague the lives of people who desire only to do good, but my faith is restored, and I know that God in His infinite wisdom will have things as He wills."

"Then there's nothing we can do?"

Karen smiled. "We can trust Him. Trust Him to know the path and the way to go. Trust Him to raise us up from our worldly, daily deaths."

Grace put her hand on her rounded abdomen. "I know He will keep us—I trust Him to deliver us."

"Here's your bonnet, Mrs. Colton," Adrik said, coming back up the walk.

Grace looked to Karen for the briefest moment and smiled. Karen knew in her heart that God would make a way for all of them, but especially for Grace, who had tried so very hard to honor Him.

"Thank you, Adrik," Grace murmured. She took the hat and started up the road toward the congestion of town.

Karen looked to her husband and saw the hope gleaming in his eyes. "Are you ready?" she asked.

He nodded. "Are you?"

"I'd follow you to the ends of the earth," she said, embracing him with great pride. "And I think I've proven that by coming here."

He chuckled. "It's not the end of the earth, but you can see it from here."

Karen smiled and leaned up on her tiptoes to kiss her husband's lips. "It's not an ending at all," she murmured. "It's a beginning."